FAITH AND FAT CHANCES

Faith and Fat Chances

A Novel

Carla Trujillo

CURBSTONE BOOKS

NORTHWESTERN UNIVERSITY PRESS

EVANSTON, ILLINOIS

Curbstone Books
Northwestern University Press
www.nupress.northwestern.edu

Printed in the United States of America

10 9 8 7 6 5 4 3 2 1

This is a work of fiction. Characters, places, and events are the product of the author's imagination or are used fictitiously and do not represent actual people, places, or events.

Library of Congress Cataloging-in-Publication Data

Trujillo, Carla, author.
  Faith and fat chances : a novel / Carla Trujillo.
    pages cm
  ISBN 978-0-8101-3164-4 (pbk. : alk. paper) — ISBN 978-0-8101-3165-1 (ebook)
  1. Santa Fe (N.M.)—Fiction. I. Title.
  PS3620.R855F35 2015
  813'.6—dc23
                                                              2015017331

For Leslie

The biggest sin is sitting on your ass.
—FLORYNCE KENNEDY

FAITH AND FAT CHANCES

1

PEPA ROMERO SPLASHED LEMON OIL into her hands, massaged it through her fingers, and rinsed everything off in a basin of Pecos River water. She grabbed a clean towel, spotted her first patient of the morning, and beckoned him in. Looking no more than twenty and sporting the heft of a few too many beers, the young cowboy gazed at the paintings lining the waiting-room walls—all of them bartered to Pepa as payments. He turned from the artwork, took off his hat, and stepped into the clinic. Like most New Mexican men, he stood no taller than a prickly pear cactus, but he'd been blessed with such luscious eyes and full lips that Pepa figured any girl, big or small, would think twice when she looked at that man. What he lacked in height he covered with swagger and a new pair of Tony Lamas. Pepa gave him a fat eyeball as she started taking his vitals. Hijo, this guy's got a hell of a gift in that face, yet all he's done since he stepped through the door is talk about how much money he's making. Still, he came to her clinic "a little worried" about his health. This surprised her, since men like him rarely showed weakness. Yet people weak and strong came to Pepa, especially with problems no one else would tackle.

"Bueno, Emilio, you want to make a million dollars by the time you're thirty, no?" Pepa felt his pulse and checked under his eyelids.

"I do, Señora."

Emilio's twang gave off the sheen of too much time in Dallas. She sighed as she eyed the lizard boots and guayabera shirt—pushing the rich cowboy act a little too far. He even carried a cigar in his pocket.

"Ven acá. Stand over here." Pepa instructed him to take off his boots and step into a low, wooden box lined with clear plastic. She took a blue speckled egg and began rolling it over his body. The egg nearly leapt out of her hands when she got to his heart. She finished rolling, cracked the egg, and dropped it into a jar of purified water.

"Siéntate, por favor." Pepa pointed to a worn leather chair. "We have to sit and wait just a little bit."

Emilio studied the egg, and slowly sat down. He spotted an ashtray next to the chair, and pulled out his cigar. "Mind if I smoke?"

"Hell yes, I mind," said Pepa, surprised he even asked. "You're having a limpia, hombre. You can't be smoking."

He shrugged and shoved the cigar back in his pocket.

Pepa lit a cigarette and sat down across from him.

"Wait, didn't you just say no smoking?"

"Sí," she said, exhaling. "No smoking for *you*." She crossed her legs and alternated her gaze between his hands and eyes, each revealing the scars of the past, or the pain of the future.

She finished her cigarette then studied the egg's shape in the water. "Come close," she said, motioning Emilio over. "This part," she said, noting the buoyant shape of the egg, "says you have strong spirit—un ánima muy fuerte."

Emilio nodded and grinned. Pepa always started the readings with Baby Jesus cocktails, the words patients wanted to hear. "So if you're going to make a million dollars, hombre, you probably can."

"That's good, no?" Emilio replied, still grinning.

"Yes, pero I see a little problem." Pepa pulled the jar closer.

"Where?" he asked, eyes crinkling with worry as they darted between Pepa and the egg.

"There." She pointed to a dark spot on the yolk. "That spot says you're going to get a heart attack if you do. And not one when you're sixty either. Think whether you want to work so hard to make your million dollars, because I guarantee, you're going to get one and a heck of a lot sooner than most hombres, too."

Emilio coughed then cleared his throat. "Do you mean one of those mild ones, Señora, kinda like Dick Cheney? Or one just a little bigger, kinda like John Belushi?"

Pepa knew John Belushi's heart attack was drug induced, but in this case it didn't matter. "Mijo," she said, patting his hand, "I wish I could say Dick Cheney."

Emilio's neck splotched heatstroke red. Pepa noticed, but didn't let up. "And this heart attack . . . will kill you. So think very seriously about your life. I can see you with a beautiful woman, three kids, and muy contento, pero no millionaire. Or a millionaire who works too damn hard, then keels over at thirty-six. Qué quieres, my friend, money or life?"

The handsome cowboy dropped his head, his life's dream shattered. Pepa felt bad for the guy, but knew without a doubt her diagnosis was solid.

"Bueno, Señora . . . I'm going to think real hard about this."

Pepa could tell he wasn't buying it. So she prepared a solution of frankincense and lavender. "I want you to take this—" She grabbed a ceramic diffuser. "And put a little of the oil inside. Then hang it in your office. This stuff will calm you, pero it won't stop a heart attack. Only you," she said, tapping his chest, "can do that."

Pepa's clinic occupied a former beauty parlor attached to an old adobe on the outskirts of Santa Fe—Dogtown, the locals called it. A large, fenced yard, a thriving garden, and a fifty-foot cottonwood surrounded the house Pepa called home for forty years. The tree, planted on the day her daughter Luz had been born, had grown from a sapling the size of a finger to a towering giant shading most of her clinic.

Worn, chipped statues of San Martín de Porres and la Virgen de Guadalupe governed Pepa's altar inside. Metal plates for burning incense, white votive candles, and a tarnished copper urn surrounded each saint. Above the altar hung her mother's picture, taken several months before she died, her eyes still soft, yet solemn. Dried herbs: ruda, malva, oshá, trementina, and altamisa, tied together with purple string, dangled below an old roof beam. Pepa also kept eggs, lemons, oils, and piedra de alumbre next to the altar inside a wormwood cabinet.

People far and wide believed Pepa possessed a gift, creating a high demand for her services. Despite the long days, she woke early to walk, taking her dog Joaquín out past city limits to the mesa over the ridge. Seeing the mountains at daybreak inspired her, reminding her of life's enduring beauty. On the way, she stopped to pick up her neighbor Irma's little pit bull, since a midlife crisis had propelled the lady to take up in-line skating. The resultant broken leg kept walking the dog out of the question for a good six weeks.

"Ay Pepa, thank you for taking my perrito, pero can't you do something about the leg?" Irma pointed to a cast covered in a collage of pit bull heads done by her artist boyfriend.

"Pues, no, broken legs take time. Pero I can give you something for your nerves." And something for your cabeza también, she said to herself. I don't know how that old goat thought she could skate como un teenager.

"No gracias, I think I just need a cure for my bone."

"The one in your head or the one in your leg?"

"Very funny."

Pepa scratched the pit bull's back as her neighbor hobbled around searching for the leash.

"I don't know where the heck Frankie put it when he took her out last night." Irma sifted through several drawers and rummaged around the closet. "Oye, speaking of Frankie, he took his mother out the other day to pick up her government commodities and saw a couple surveyors out here."

"Surveyors? Where?"

"Over by Mrs. Gallegos's store and the Chula Cafe. Then on the way back—aquí 'stán." She handed Pepa the leash. "He saw them right down at the corner."

"Here?"

"Right here."

"What the heck were they doing?"

"I don't know, but Frankie went up to them and asked. They didn't want to say anything at first, but he wouldn't leave till they told him."

"Y qué dicen?"

"They said some guy wants to buy out a bunch of people here, but wouldn't tell him what for."

"Hmm." Pepa hooked the leash to the smaller dog's collar.

"Give or take a few garbage bins, I don't think anyone's paid much attention to our little patch of dust in ten or twenty years, que no?"

Pepa stared at her friend, hoping what Frankie heard wasn't true.

"Bueno, go walk the dogs," said Irma, waving Pepa out of the room. "No use worrying about it till something happens. Frankie says they can't take our land anyway without us saying so. Go on," she continued, waving. "We'll see what tomorrow brings."

Pepa's walk usually revived her, especially after long sessions of stubborn patients. Today it only softened the dull thud of anxiety creeping through her heart. Buyout or not, she couldn't afford to move, nor did she want to.

As she marched across the packed clay of her street, the scent of burning piñón from Mrs. Madrid's horno permeated the air as a raucous gang of crows cawed their daily greeting. Pepa continued walking, wading through a sea of dogs, offering hellos, especially to Lucky, the three-legged Lab who limped over for a stroke behind the ears. She clucked her own dogs forward, passing rusty cars and an occasional adobe flourishing under a new coat of stucco. She hit the well-worn trail that wormed its way up to the mesa as the dogs romped playfully through the scrub. A drought had persisted through-out the spring, yet the yucca flowers managed to bloom, their white torches framed against the red, dusty dirt. Pepa felt the day's heat rise as she crested the mesa. She took off her shirt, lit a cigarette, and sat on a rock to smoke. The Sangre de Cristo Mountains shed their violet hue as she received their daily blessing. Smoking her cigarette down to the nub, Pepa watched the sun blink over the hills and rounded up the dogs to head back home. Turning the corner onto her street, she spotted a line of patients waiting at the door.

"Hijo 'la madre," she said, looking at her watch. "It's gonna be a hell of a day."

2

TALA CÓRDOVA LOCKED UP the "Feed Your Steed" store and headed out to her parents' house. They were getting up in age, so she stopped by each week to check on things and to make sure all was well. She spotted an unfamiliar car in the driveway and was surprised to find her brother, Gilbert, sitting in the living room.

"Hey guy, good to see you." Tala gave him a hug, noting the fancy suit and flashy silk tie. "When did you get into town?"

"Yesterday," he said, with a quick glance at their father. "Popped in for some business. How are things?"

"Not bad. The drought's been tough, but spring's bringing in ranchers and gardeners, so I can't complain."

"And Nina? Still working at the doughnut shop?" Gilbert's eyes strayed to the notepad in front of him.

"Yep, still dealing doughnuts and still doing art."

Their father at the moment had eyes only for her brother. "So how'd it go with the mayor, mijo? And did you get any time with council members?"

"The mayor's definitely interested," Gilbert said, grinning. "Says he wants to touch base in a couple weeks." He studied his notes. "As for the council, I spoke with most of them, and I'd say the majority support it, especially with the new life it'll bring to the area. Of course a couple dinosaurs gave it a thumbs down, but that's to be expected. So I'd say the plan's a go."

Tala listened for another minute, then wandered into the kitchen. "Hi, Mom," she said, giving her a hug.

"Hi, mija. How was work today?" Her mother opened the fridge and slid in leftovers.

Tala grabbed a beer. "Sold three tons of alfalfa to the Larson ranch."

"Oh yeah? That's pretty good." Her mother pulled out a bowl of panocha from the fridge. "Glad to see sales are picking up. There's beans and chile if you're hungry."

"No, thanks." Tala eyed the panocha. "Think I'll just stick to beer and dessert . . . So, uh, what are Dad and Gilbert up to?"

"Bueno, I think you should ask them." Her mother grabbed cups, plates, and spoons, set them on a tray, and shoved it toward Tala.

Tala took a long pull from the bottle, hoisted the tray, and rejoined her father and brother in the living room.

"Mijo, do you really think you can grow grapes in the sagebrush? Summers out here can singe the hair off a Chihuahua."

Tala watched her brother, waiting for his response.

"You're definitely right about that, so I talked to three growers who said I can do it. They even told me with the experience I have that I should be able to crank out a whole new level of quality."

Gilbert beamed with excitement. Tala had never seen their old man give her brother this kind of attention. "Sounds like you're planning to make wine in the Land of Enchantment," she said.

"Hopefully," he said. "I've always wanted to come home and run my own place."

"But I thought you loved California. And what about Claire and the kids?"

"Claire's game, and she's on board for the viticulture. The girls are young, and the schools where we want to live are really good. It's all a win-win. Mom, Dad, and Claire are partnering financially. Couple more investors and we're set to go. Even our big brothers Junior and Marty might pony up."

Tala found it odd Gilbert hadn't asked her. He probably figured she didn't have that kind of cash, which happened to be true. Still, he could have asked.

Their mother walked in with the coffee and panocha. Gilbert's face lit up when he saw the treat. "Hey . . . all right! Thank you, Mom." He served himself a large portion, loosened his tie, and started eating.

"You're welcome, mijo." She spooned a bit for herself and poured them all coffee. "Vicente, you having dessert?"

"In a little bit."

"Natalia?"

"You bet," she said, piling up her bowl.

Satisfied, their mother sat on the sofa and relaxed.

"So whereabouts you planning this winery? Belen? Farther south?" Tala grinned at the thought of her brother coming back to help keep an eye on their parents.

Gilbert shot a glance at their father. "Dad didn't tell you?"

"I didn't tell her nothing," Vicente said, pouring cream in his coffee. "Only because the deal wasn't in the bag yet." He added Sweet'N Low to the cup, stirred, and licked the spoon. "I've been waiting to hear about the mayor's blessing, especially since you got zoning changes and other red tape. So, no, mijo, I didn't say anything. Maybe *you* should."

Gilbert closed his eyes and sighed, then focused back on Tala. "Well, I ran a bunch of assessments and talked to a couple planners, and the cost benefits all pointed to keeping it in town, specifically Dogtown."

Tala sat up straight. "What?"

"Yeah, well they did all kinds of analyses on building it there versus open land. And they said keeping it in city limits gets me a new business loan, primo tax reductions, water access—which is harder than hell to get, and—"

"Tourists," added their mother.

Gilbert nodded and smiled. "The architect's already drawn up plans for tanks, a cellar, and a nice tasting room. We figure the whole thing will start making money in five or six years. But the good thing is that it'll start bringing in jobs right away. Once everything's going, I'll pick up a few acres down south to expand."

Tala set her half-eaten dessert on the coffee table. "But you know me, Nina, and a truckload of people live exactly where you're planning to build. And I'd say most of the folks there can't afford to move anywhere else."

"Yeah, well, we pretty much know that, but we're getting enough financing so you can all get nice relocation packages." He glanced at their father again.

"But Gilbert, look at me." Tala pointed to herself. "Do I look like an old horse you can just round up and truck away? This is a completely assholian plan, and I got to say it's pissing me off." Tala felt her face redden with anger.

"Hey, hey, hey, watch your language there," said their father. "So what your brother hasn't said is that everyone knows Dogtown is a dump and it's gotten worse through the years, making it cheap to buy, relatively speaking. Gilbert's got a good business plan and the financing's coming together. And now that the mayor's on board . . . hell, I gotta say, I'm feeling damn proud of our little businessman." He slapped him playfully on the shoulder.

"So the backroom dealers have been working on this for a while and no one bothered to tell me," said Tala. "You could have called, Gilbert. I mean, how hard is that?"

"I'm sorry this is the first you've heard of it," said her brother, looking a little sheepish.

"Don't worry, mija. We're gonna make sure Gilbert gives you a good price for your house," said their mother, patting Tala's hand and casting a stern look toward Gilbert.

"But Mom, I don't want to sell my house. I got a big yard for my pets, nice neighbors, and I remodeled the kitchen last year. So the place has even appreciated."

"Except your house is probably the only one that *has*." Gilbert shot another glance at their father.

Tala was starting to hate their newfound father-son bonding crap. She took a long pull from her beer and finished it off. "I think you've been out of town too long, little brother, since you have no idea how much houses cost now."

Gilbert's eyes hardened. "My head hasn't exactly been in the sand. Plus, I have friends out here who do real estate, you know."

"Oh yeah? Well let me refresh your memory anyway. Condos," said Tala, pointing with her beer bottle. "Are going for a half mil! You know any gardeners, maids, or teachers who can afford that?"

"Hey, hey, come on! Come on! Tranquilos, you two. Knock it off!" Their old man waved his hands in the air like a weary referee.

"Pero, Vicente, Natalia has a point," added their mother.

"Damn right I do!" Tala said, pounding the table. "That's why Gilbert's got to take this project of his someplace else."

Her brother scraped the last of the panocha from his bowl, tossed in the spoon, and refused to look at her.

Their father pulled a small box of cigars from under the table and offered one to Gilbert. "Quieres?"

"Nah, I don't smoke . . . Hell, on second thought," he said, casting a sullen eye toward his sister. "Why not?"

Tala watched him light the cigar and suck on it like a damn rookie. Their mother opened a window and left.

"Bueno . . . I gotta say there's only one problem you got here, mija." Their father crossed his legs and relaxed into his cigar.

Tala forced herself to answer. "And that's what?"

"And that's that this thing's already rolling. And it's going full steam ahead. So if you aren't on board, it's gonna run you right over."

3

Tala lit out of her parents' house, hopped into her truck, and raced down Agua Fria to the doughnut shop where Nina was doing a double shift. She needed to talk to her girl and get her take on Gilbert's plan. Tala didn't think her brother had the money to pull off this kind of caper. But he'd lived in California, and if there's anything Californians know how to do, it's make money. Besides, he already had that pot-o-gold he married and her other brothers didn't live here. So, why would they care? Tala roared into the parking lot, glanced at the *Mingo's* delivery van, and bee-lined straight for Nina.

Sleek as an ocelot, with a temper to match, Nina slapped open a bag as she waited on a customer. "This one?" she asked, pointing to a gooey jelly roll.

"Nina—"

"Hey, Baby. What's going on?" Her face brightened at the sight of Tala. She ran her hand through her spiky hair, shaking out a thin dusting of sugar.

"Sorry to bother you." Tala stood next to the customer, counting the seconds as she stared at Nina's art on the walls. She held her tongue as her girl waited on the customer and focused on the portraits of Nina's Tecolote series—a town everyone swore time had forgotten. Finally, Tala couldn't hold back any longer and blurted out what she'd been dying to reveal. "I just came from my parents' house. Gilbert's moving here and wants to buy out Dogtown to build a winery."

"A what?"

"A winery."

"Out here? What's wrong with California?" Nina grabbed the roll and shoved it in a bag stamped with a roadrunner tucking a doughnut under his wing.

"He wants to follow his dream," Tala replied, rolling her eyes.

"He richer now?"

The customer handed Nina a five-dollar bill. She double-counted his change. "There you go. Thanks."

"Not as rich as his in-laws, but close. And he's got everyone pulling strings, including my parents, who are totally jazzed about it, especially Señor High-spanic."

Nina laughed as she waited on the next customer, revealing a gap-toothed grin and a pierced tongue. "You better stop calling him that. One of these days he's gonna hear you." She rang up the order.

"Who cares? It's the truth. Plus my brothers are kicking in money to help their her-ma-no with his little project—never mind where his sister and her girlfriend happen to live."

"So now what?" Nina handed the customer her change.

"So we have to do something."

"And stop the Rico Latino? Forget it." She took a rag and wiped off the counter. "It's a lost cause. Plus, I got better things to do."

Tala reached over the counter and grabbed Nina's hands. "Yeah, and one of them will be looking for a new place and studio with cheap rent."

"Uh, well that's kind of an important detail."

"Gilbert doesn't sound like he's playing either. He wants to plant grapes, make wine, have a tasting room. The whole bit."

"OK, OK, I hear you." Nina rubbed tired-looking eyes.

Tala noticed Nina's fatigue, but felt too upset to care. "I hope so. It's only the whole neighborhood we're talking about."

Nina checked the clock. "I get off at nine."

"So you'll stop by?"

"Yeah."

"Good." Tala leaned over and kissed her. "See you soon."

※

"No, I can't do that." Pepa crossed her arms, making sure Nina and Tala could see she meant business.

"Would you at least consider it?" asked Tala.

"No."

Pepa liked the girls. Knew them both as babies. Saw them grow up into little chingonas. But just because she liked them didn't mean she'd do what they asked.

"But Pepa, we need you," Tala persisted. The two had stopped by to explain the Gilbert problem, bringing a bottle of Presidente brandy, and planting themselves in Pepa's kitchen.

"The mayor's involved, no? And every time I speak up against that pinche culero, I get screwed. When he gets mad, he makes it hard for me to make money."

Nina opened the brandy. "It's gonna be a lot harder when they kick you outta your house." She retrieved three glasses and filled them to the top.

"How can they do that?" Pepa asked. "How can they kick me out of my home? Your brother doesn't own it. I own it." She tapped her chest for emphasis.

"Yes, you do." Tala spoke softly. "But it doesn't matter. People find a way to get what they want."

Pepa smacked the table with the palm of her hand. "The hell they do! Y también it's the stupidest thing I ever heard of. Nobody's gonna let Gilbert knock down our houses to build a winery. They only do that for freeways—" she paused to think—"and subways." She lit a cigarette, exhaling smoke like she was spitting.

Nina sipped her brandy. "Drink, Pepa." She pushed the glass closer. "Look, I didn't believe it either till I saw what he's got planned. Plus he's got the cash and the city council helping him."

"Nina's right," Tala added. "My brother wants this damn thing so he can come home. And that cabrón mayor thinks it's a good idea."

Pepa listened, her drink still untouched. She studied the girls as they talked, their bodies tense with worry. Pepa realized they wouldn't have come to her if they weren't truly frightened. "Bueno," she said with a sigh. "I guess I'll try to do something."

Tala's shoulders relaxed. "Good, because we really need you."

"Pero, what can I do?"

"Well," Tala said with a shrug. "We haven't worked out the details. But we need my brother and the mayor to—well, to change their minds."

"That's right," added Nina.

Pepa snorted, then laughed. "I'm not a bruja. I can't just cast a spell. If I could I'd be on Wall Street, or at least the Wheel of Fortune."

"We're not asking for a spell," Tala persisted. "Just your help."

"But like I said, how?"

Tala paused, then looked over at Nina.

"OK." Pepa put out her cigarette. "I'll think about it. Pero I need more information. I can't just jump into something without knowing all the mierdita going on. You go out and get me todo, and I mean *todo* about who's behind this, and why. Then I'll see what I can do." She picked up the brandy, stared at the glass, then belted it back.

"Pepa, you're the best." Tala wrapped her arms around her. "Thank you for saying you'll help."

Pepa stared at the wall wondering what else the mayor had up his sleeve. "Bueno, I have to get ready for work. You girls get me what I told you. And figure out how to get updates on what your brother's up to."

"Gracias, Pepa." Tala grabbed her hand and squeezed it.

"Don't forget." Pepa said, holding on to Tala's hand. "I said I was only going to think about it."

Nina's eyes flickered with delight. "We like it when you think."

4

Lupita "Pepa" Romero, though almost sixty, possessed the stamina of a prizefighter. Her deceased mother, a healer once well known throughout northern New Mexico, had died young of leukemia. Pepa was certain it was due to the tests done by the Los Alamos Lab in their quest for the bomb. Stunned by the inability to save her mother, Pepa realized she still had much to learn. So she packed a suitcase and left town to study with Don Gabriel, an old curandero who lived in San Geronimo, hidden deep in the Mineral Hills. Don Gabriel, also a gifted healer, was rumored to be Pepa's father, and nearly a century old.

Pepa spent a year with the old man and then moved back to Santa Fe, casting off her wreck of a husband after raising two children. Her son Martín left home early to join the Merchant Marine. Pepa missed her boy, yet understood that his restless spirit compelled him to travel far. Her daughter Luz sold handmade jerky from a shop near the Plaza. Thinking she was clever, Luz named the place "What A Jerkee," though those who knew her felt the name far more perfectly described Luz. Yet everyone agreed the delicious, grass-fed jerky more than made up for her sour disposition. Pepa felt certain Luz got the worst parts of both her parents' personalities. And though she tried everything she could to soften Luz's heart, nothing seemed to work.

Despite this failing, Pepa had a dedicated following from greater New Mexico. She preferred working with believers—which made her clientele largely "Hispanic," a term Pepa thought many misconstrued. Pepa had read plenty of history and claimed the only place real Hispanics lived was Spain.

"All of us got a little Indian in us. That makes us a lot more than just Spanish," Pepa lectured her daughter, who stopped by on a lunch break from the jerky shop.

"Well, we mostly are," said Luz, serving herself a heaping bowl of beans. "Everyone knows we're direct descendants of the conquistadores. Can't get more Spanish than that."

"Maybe that's where you got the nice part of your personality, eh? Pero, me and your father both know we got Indian in us." Pepa tore off a piece of tortilla and shoved it in her mouth.

"Oh, no," Luz replied with a flick of her wrist. "You're what the Native people call a faux Indian. Haven't you seen enough blond braids and turquoise around here to know better?"

"Since when did you get yourself an anthropology degree?" asked Pepa, frowning. "Besides, no soy como esos."

"Sorry, Mom, but you're not really that different than those faux Indians. You and Dad got told what they call a cultural myth. You're not part Indian. Just like everyone else here isn't either—except the real Indians."

Pepa flattened her hand on the table. "You're just saying that because you have shame."

"Shame for what? I love brown men and my brown skin."

Pepa rolled her eyes. "Bueno, Miss Anthropology, where do you think you got your brown skin, eh?"

"OK, then what do I have shame about?" She pushed away the bag of tortillas.

"For being Indian," Pepa said, pounding her finger on the table. "I know for a fact, everyone here is part Indian—except los gabachos," she continued, glaring at Luz. "But these people like to pretend they're not. They think they're better than the Indians, and you're just like them, always saying you're *Spanish*." Pepa scooped the last of the beans from her bowl and held everything momentarily in front of her. "Qué Spanish ni Spanish!"

Luz's comments always seemed to gouge little cuts into Pepa's heart. Lamenting this, she opened a bottle of wine at the end of the day and called her neighbor over to share it. In less than three minutes, Irma stood at the door with a bag of García's bizcochitos.

"You know Luz came over today. And I have to say that whenever she stops by I always want to drink." Pepa dipped her cookie into the wine and took a big bite.

Irma's leg lay carefully propped on an old milking stool. "Híjole, that girl can talk, too," she added. "She's got something to say about everything!"

"Como un expert, no?" Pepa munched another bite of the cookie.

"Sí, de todo. I almost hate saying anything to her because she always acts like she knows more than you. She's un M. K. I. A. de la chingada."

Pepa stopped chewing. "Qué es un M. K. I. A?"

"Miss-Know-It-All."

Pepa laughed because Irma was right. "Eee, and she's so tight. The other day I went to buy some jerky from her 'cause I'm thinking I should support my daughter's business—you know, give a little treat to my dog. So I went down to the store and bought a quarter-pound, pero she charged me full price! Not even un nickel or dime discount for her mama." Pepa grabbed another cookie from the bag. "I told Lico it was his fault for being in the army when she was little. I had to make ends meet, so Luz spent a lot of time sitting in the waiting room."

"Probably read too many magazines," Irma said.

Pepa finished her glass and poured herself another. "I think so, either that or she was just born that way."

"Mm-hmm," said Irma, sipping her wine. "Oye, I heard you were helping those girls with that winery chingadera; you know, the one Gilbert Córdova's planning."

"Yes, I am," said Pepa, hoping she wasn't making a mistake.

"What made you want to get involved?"

Pepa eyed her friend, suddenly serious. "Because I don't want to lose my house and business. Simple as that."

※

Several days later, Tacho Montoya, a patrolman for the Santa Fe police, dropped by to treat his male energy problem. Pepa knew Tacho was a closet case, yet he still sought a magical cure for his longings. Pepa did her best to keep his energy pure, because she knew as well as anyone that there was never a cure for desire.

"Pepa, you think this stuff you're doing is ever gonna work?" Tacho stood in his underwear, hands resting on hips. Pepa didn't like guns or uniforms, but she could appreciate a good-looking man. So she used the guns and uniform thing to get Tacho to strip down every time he saw her.

"Quién sabe?" she said, feeling his pulse. "I don't have guarantees."

"Pero, I've been coming to you for two months now and I don't think anything's changed."

"Depends on what we're changing." Pepa answered, concentrating as she prepared a mixture of strong-smelling oils. She poured them into a bottle and waved it under Tacho's nose. Fit and virile in his calzones, he jolted at the smell.

"Hijo, what is that?"

Pepa smiled since she'd given him a dose of ylang-ylang flower—a powerful aphrodisiac. "I want you to take great big whiffs of this way up into your nose ten times a day." She took a big sniff to demonstrate. "Then come back in a week and tell me if you notice anything."

Tacho grimaced, then went to the bathroom to change.

Pepa took his money and wrote his name down in her appointment book for the same time next week. She also made a notation in her chart of today's treatment. "Mira, don't forget what I told you."

"Sí, Señora." He took another sniff of the potion as he walked toward his patrol car.

Pepa followed him outside into the hot New Mexican sun. "You drive that thing a lot, don't you?" she asked, pointing to his car.

"Well, yeah," he replied.

"Wait, then." She walked back to her clinic and returned with a cerámica. "Put some of that oil inside this and hang it on your mirror. This way you can smell it when you're driving in your police car all day."

Tacho scratched his handsome head and tried to hand it back. "Pero, I'm a cop. I can't drive around with a posy smell dangling from my mirror."

"Y por qúe no?" Pepa replied, squinting in the sun at the troubled man. "Aren't you the guys who make the rules?"

"Yeah, but well, *we* have regulations about what goes in the cars."

"So you can have guns, and bullets, and handcuffs," she said, gesturing toward the car. "But you can't have one little thing that might cure your huevos?" She held two fingers an inch apart to illustrate her point.

Tacho looked at the cerámica, then over at the patrol car, then back at the cerámica. "Bueno, I guess it won't matter too much."

"I don't see why it would, que no? The only other people who are gonna be riding in your car are criminals, no?"

Tacho nodded uncertainly.

"Try it, Tacho. It's gonna do something good for you. If it doesn't work, I'll give you your money back."

"OK. So how much does this cost?" he said, peering at the cerámica.

"I'm gonna give you a deal. They're expensive, because they're from San Francisco, but I'll let you have it for twelve—make it ten. Ten for you. Pero, for everyone else I charge fifteen."

"Bueno, Señora, I'll give it a try." He got in his car and hung the cerámica on his mirror. He poured in a couple drops, twisted the cap, and put the vial in his pocket. "Gracias Señora. See you later."

"Que te vaya bien."

5

TALA GOT TO WORK. She'd just met with a clerk in City Hall, wanting to understand how new projects and developments get approved. Grabbing a seat in the lobby, she dialed Gilbert's number in California. "Yes, I'd like to speak to the Vino Latino please."

"Very funny," Gilbert replied. "Let me call you back, OK? I'm just finishing a meeting with my accountant."

"Well, it's kind of important and I promise it'll take just a couple minutes."

Tala heard a sigh.

"Hang on."

She heard talking, then a door close.

"OK, what is it?"

"I was calling to see if you got Junior and Marty on board and if you pulled in any new partners?"

"That's private information, Tala, and not really appropriate for us to discuss."

"And I don't think it's cool to keep what you got planned from me anymore either."

He paused. "I guess that's fair."

"So are you still raising capital?" Tala saw a rubber band on the floor and bent over to pick it up.

"Just a little more."

"And are you thinking you'll need help getting that land?" She slid the rubber band on her wrist and studied her nails under the lights.

"Probably not. I got people coming through for me. Like I said, the mayor's interested and most of city council. Should be a slam dunk I'd say, in six or seven months. Just gotta get zoning done and an impact report."

"Everything's getting all squared away, then, huh?" Tala started popping the rubber band against her wrist.

"Almost . . . look Tala, before you get too bent out of shape, I'm planning to give everyone decent prices—not market rate—mind you, since the neighborhood's wrecked. But totally fair deals."

"Except you keep forgetting one thing."

"Which is what?"

"I live there."

"Yeah, but you'll be able to move and get something better. Use the money I'm giving you to buy an acre in Española or maybe Pecos. You act like I'm telling you to move to hell. Most people would welcome this offer. Probably be better than that old house you're living in."

Tala took the rubber band off her wrist and fired it at the portrait of the mayor. "You know, Dogtown has a lot more going for it than what you or City Hall sees. Plus, I happen to like my *old* house and my *wrecked* neighborhood. In fact, I like them so much I don't want to leave."

"Well, sorry, Sis. This is the price of progress, and people have to make sacrifices."

"Except you want to raze my neighborhood—so you can build a winery. Sounds like we sacrifice for your progress."

"Uh, we've already talked about this, so I'm not going to sit here and argue with you. Is there anything else?" Gilbert's voice cut through the phone.

"Actually, there is," Tala said, pausing to gather herself. "I'd like to have my old brother back please, the one I used to have."

He didn't reply.

Tala gritted through her feelings, willing herself not to cry. "I know I've asked already, but is there any way possible you can find another piece of land?"

"I'm sorry, I can't. I already got this baby rolling."

"In case you might have forgotten, I'm still your sister."

"Of course I haven't forgotten, so what's your point?"

Tala swallowed, eyes tearing up. "My point is that I'm still part of this family. Not just something attached to an old house that happens to be in your way. I don't know who or what got to you, but you're different now. We always had each other's backs. Now you're someone I don't even know."

There was a long pause. "Look, we're not kids anymore. I've got a family and now a business to think about."

"Yeah, OK, I see." Tala wiped her eyes. "Bueno, if that's how you feel, then I would at least like the respect of being kept updated about your plans. In exchange I'll let you know as best I can what Dogtown is doing."

"I got Bill Takash helping me with that, so I don't think—"

"Bill Takash?" Tala started pacing around the lobby. "That guy's only a partial-brain thinker. I had geometry with him in high school and always had to help him with his homework. He's smart, don't get me wrong, but you need someone with teeth in their brain."

"I'm still retaining him. He's a good lawyer and has been there for me from the get-go."

"All right, but I still need to know what you got planned."

"I'll think about it."

Tala walked out of City Hall taking deep breaths of the warm spring air. "Don't forget you want to kick me out of my house. And since our relationship seems to be only about business now, I insist on market value—that is, if you succeed. Hey, did I tell you I have the perfect name for your winery? Sangre de la Tierra. Sound good?"

"Very funny, Tala. I'll think about what you asked."

"Please do, little brother. But do let me know soon."

6

PEPA FINISHED A CIGARETTE and smashed the butt into her frog-mouth ashtray. She spotted Father Miguel outside and welcomed him into the clinic. The St. Francis priest stopped by from time to time for a quick fix, claiming no one else could help his gastritis.

After Pepa brewed him a cup of yerba buena tea, the priest began to talk. Pepa thought he looked a little roñoso—like he'd been doing yard work and hadn't washed. He hadn't shaved either, and his eyes looked saggy and red. He began speaking about the church, how great it was to be a priest there, but the pressure was tough since his liberal politics ran amiss of the bishop's.

"Bueno Padre, where are you from?" Pepa brought a bunch of dried altamisa to the table, and sat down to de-stem the leaves.

"Española. My dad came out here on leave from the army and met my mom at a restaurant where she was working. They claim it was love at first sight. She came from a traditional New Mexican family, though, and they didn't approve of my father."

"Por qué?" Pepa pulled the leaves from the stems into a tidy little pile.

"Well, because he was white, first of all. You know how things are out here. And he had a little too much trailer in him," he said, half smiling. "Plus being a private in the army didn't help. Anyway—they got married and had me and my brother in a two-year period. My dad took a liking to the military and went career. We moved a few times following him, but he was gone a lot. We were still little when he went off on a long assignment to Nicaragua and fell in love with a local girl."

"Oh . . ." Pepa studied the priest as she continued plucking the herb.

He ran his hands over his chin. "Worse, we found out what he'd been doing while he was down there—"

Pepa paused to give him her full attention. "Contra?"

"Yeah. Made his living training soldiers to kill. When my mother found out about *that* and the other woman, she divorced him. But she was too proud to move back in with her parents. She didn't do college, so money stayed tight. Mr. Military gave her the bare minimum in child support, and she didn't remarry. She died, I think, of a broken heart."

"Lo siento, Padre . . . Pero, is that why you wanted to be a priest?"

"No," he said, staring at his tea. "Well, maybe. Something about being in the church—the ritual of Mass—calmed me. Some of the homilies the priests gave made me think about what I was doing with myself in the world."

"Really?" Pepa lit a cigarette, eyeing him through the cloud of smoke.

"Yeah, can you believe it? So I became an altar boy, went to catechism, Catholic high school on scholarship, the whole nine yards." He sniffed and rubbed his nose. "To get as far as I could from my dad, I legally took my mom's last name and started calling myself Miguel instead of Michael—even learned Spanish. I finally decided it was my true calling to become a priest."

Pepa studied the man, who with his light skin and reddish-brown hair hardly appeared Chicano. He'd been talking nonstop for a good twenty minutes. The evening sun softened the light around the two of them and the waiting room stood empty, so she let him continue. He spoke of life as a priest, growing increasingly agitated until one thing led to another, and he blurted out that he didn't know if he truly believed in God. Pepa knew it wasn't common for a priest to say this, and more than likely it was something he probably didn't want repeated. But he confessed it to her as she sat listening, smoking silently until he finished.

"Padre," Pepa asked, taking a deep breath. "Would you like a little whiskey?"

Sweating from his confession, he nodded, grateful when Pepa slid through the Virgen de Guadalupe beads separating her clinic from the kitchen to retrieve a bottle of Wild Turkey. She poured two glasses and the padre downed his in one gulp. Pepa sipped hers slowly, averting her gaze again to the waiting room to see if she had any other patients. Seeing only the sun's waning light, she turned her attention back to the priest.

"Mire, Padre . . ." Pepa felt at a loss for words. "I—" she paused again.

"Bueno, you need something I don't think I can give you. I have faith in what I do, and it works for me. Pero, I don't know if there is a God, and I don't know if he, or she, or even I can help you."

"Ya sé, but that's not why I came today." The padre poured another glass.

"No?" Pepa sat back, surprised.

"No. I came to see if you can help me—" he paused, looking away—"be a better man."

Pobrecito, thought Pepa. "But why?" she asked. "You are a good man with a good heart . . . que no?"

"Yeah, I'd like to think so, but it's not enough." He sniffed again, then reached into his pocket, pulled out a handkerchief and blew his nose. "I thought there might be more I could do with my life. Something fulfilling, inspirational. That's why I became a priest."

Pepa lit another cigarette. "Then how come you didn't be a doctor?"

"Funny you should ask, because I tried. Went to college, studied biology, but it was the hearts of people I was interested in. I wanted to do more, like you." The padre poured himself another glass. "It wasn't like I could stitch up a wound or set a bone and feel fulfilled."

"Pero, you could've done it in a jungle or a barrio—someplace where people don't have doctors; you know where los pobres have to run around with cleft palates and crossed eyes."

The padre let out a big sigh. He hunched forward, looking dejected. "Pepa, I'm not a young man anymore. I can't go back to school at forty-four."

She could almost kick herself. Her listening skills were way out of whack ever since she treated her last patient. The woman had come in desperate—complaining to her doctors about a swinging in her side. Those doctors X-rayed, CAT-scanned, probed, prodded, and poked, and still couldn't find anything wrong. Thinking she was going crazy, she came for a limpia. Pepa luckily figured out the problem, but it took nine limpias on nine consecutive days to cure her. As Pepa listened to the priest, she admitted being a little fatigued. I think I need to knock off early tonight, she thought. Maybe I'll take myself out to dinner. The priest droned on for a while, drinking most of her whiskey. Pepa glanced at her watch.

"Mire, Padre. You need una causa. A reason to live. I have no treatment to give you, because there really isn't anything I *can* give you. But keep your eyes and ears open, and I'll bet something's gonna come through."

"What are you saying?" the priest asked, blinking to focus.

Pepa shrugged. "I'm just saying there might be something down the road, someplace where you might be needed."

"Like what?" he asked, still blinking.

"Like, no sé," Pepa replied. "I can't say, because I don't know. Maybe we're going to need your help with esa pinche winery Gilbert Cordóva's got planned. We might need one of those holy power speeches you guys give in church." She waited for his reaction.

He grabbed his empty glass and tapped it on the table. "Can you give me a little more to go on?" he asked.

Pepa shrugged. "No, because I just thought of it. But like I said, maybe down the line we might need you."

"But what about what we just talked about?"

"Padre, you're the one who's going to have to figure out if there's a God or some other power. Don't all priests do that?" Pepa sighed and leaned back in her chair.

"Yeah . . ." He reached for the bottle, but Pepa pulled it away.

"No. No more." She chain lit another cigarette and blew smoke toward the ceiling. "Padre, you never feel you're good enough, and you want to know why?"

He didn't answer.

"Too chicken."

He cut his eyes at Pepa. "I'm not a chicken."

"Yes you are! I just figured it out. You never take risks. I'm giving you a chance to do something with your life, something that will help the people here, and you want everything laid out. The only kind of people who work like that are chickens—well, maybe politicians." She flicked her ash into the frog mouth.

The padre picked up his glass and looked into it. "It makes sense that anyone would want to know more. It doesn't mean you're a chicken."

"Tell you what, forget it." Pepa waved him away. "We won't bother asking you for anything. That way you can keep squawking through your boring life." She tapped her watch. "Bueno, our time is up. I have to close the clínica."

She went over to her jars of hierbas and mixed seven together as a tea to calm his stomach. Then she gave him another mixture that would provide clarity and spiritual strength.

Priest or no priest, Pepa still charged him for the session and took away his car keys.

The padre shoved the hierbas into a backpack and headed toward the door. He sighed and turned to face Pepa. "I promise to think about what you asked me."

"Bueno. Tell you what, if we need you, we'll let you know. Then you can say whether or not you'll help us. How's that?"

The priest thought about it for a second. "No pressure?"

"No pressure." Pepa kept her face neutral.

"OK," he said, with a slow nod. "We got a deal."

"We got a deal," Pepa echoed, shooing him out the door. "Good night, Padre." She stood at the window, watching the priest slowly make his way through her yard and down the smooth angles of her dirt-paved street. "Que le vaya bien."

7

THE FOLLOWING FRIDAY, Dr. Jules Johnson had a life changing epiphany. As a physicist with the Los Alamos Nuclear Lab, he was well aware of the kind of work he'd been employed to do. But as he learned more of the lab's history and the mental gyrations the scientists took to justify their cause, he became increasingly agitated, losing sleep like a sad, guilty soul, night after night. His high security clearance enabled him to locate several documents supporting a long-held belief that the nuclear testing conducted by the lab in 1945 was far more destructive than they'd ever let on. Digging further, he searched for the specifics on radioactive fallout, knowing the Alamogordo test site released more than had publically been reported. What he managed to find, in a not-so-routine visit to the archives, made him absolutely sick. Large swaths of land, people, and animals had been contaminated or killed—leaving paths of destruction across the lower half of the state. It was at that exact moment, when he finished reading, that he finally decided he could no longer work for the lab. After handing his resignation to his dumbfounded supervisor, he danced a slow jig out the gated east door.

As he drove down the mountain, he noted his favorite parts of this very last drive. Though the drudgery of slogging up and down the wind-streaked highway could swallow the spirit of any soul, he never tired of its beauty. He continued driving, following the afternoon light as it blazed across peach-colored rocks, reflecting back glorious bits of tawny, gold, and pewter.

Jules blitzed through Española, feeling amazingly comfortable with not having a job anymore. He owned a small home in Dogtown, two bedrooms and an office, tucked away tight on a bare quarter-acre. And despite the neighborhood's poverty, the dogs and the roosters, there was nothing that could top that prime view of the land.

Jules rolled into town and stopped on a whim at the Rosario Cemetery. He parked his truck and began walking past the headstones, nodding his condolences, as he often did, to the people who'd perished in the prime of life, most during the late forties; grave after grave, men and women, some of them children. He closed his eyes and cursed his complicity. These deaths were just a drop in the bucket.

What he needed now was to locate anyone doing research on atomic history. He knew there was probably someone who might have a good idea about what really happened during New Mexico's nuclear testing so he headed off toward the library to begin his search.

After finding several antinuclear groups, Jules rubbed his face—bleary eyed from reading. He closed his notebook and called it a day. After all, it had been a very significant day. Taking a slight detour back to Dogtown, he stopped off at the Saints and Sinners Liquor for a bottle of whiskey. Arriving home, he kicked off his boots, toasted himself, and guzzled it straight.

8

On a bright May morning, Pepa rose early and stopped at Irma's to pick up Chica. The little pit bull, once fat and lazy, had grown to love the daily jaunts with Pepa and Joaquin to the top of the mesa.

Irma, now free of her cast, pulled up her pants to show Pepa her leg. "Mira," she exclaimed, "it's all shrunken, como un pygmy."

Pepa noticed one leg was clearly thinner than the other.

"Don't worry, mujer, it'll grow back. Just give it some time and make sure you exercise it." Irma had mentioned the cast was coming off, so Pepa had brought over a salve to heal the dried skin. She massaged the salve over the leg, knowing it would help it feel better. "And don't overdo it too much. Start slow, and in a few weeks your leg will grow back just like you had it." She smiled at her friend and waited for her to retrieve the pit bull's leash.

"Venga, Chica. Let's go." The dog bounced around the door and gave Pepa's dog a quick lick. "I'll be back in a little while," Pepa yelled over her shoulder. "Y ponte la medicina two times a day. Your leg looks like a dried up turkey neck."

Pepa and the dogs trotted down the street. Turning the corner, she heard a robin singing from a tree. She continued walking, greeting Lucky and the other dogs from the neighborhood. Noticing the smoke streaming from Mrs. Madrid's horno, she made a mental note to stop by on her way home to pick up a loaf of bread.

Waves of sage scented air intermixed with cooking-stove piñón smoke, as she started up the trail. Despite the early hour, everything felt hot and dry;

much like it'd been for the past six months. Pepa sighed, wishing it would rain. New Mexico, still in a drought, hadn't seen a rain drop in months. Many of the piñón trees dotting the mesa were withered, with others so brown they were clearly dead. As she studied the trees, she heard an unusual bird call, one she remembered hearing long ago. She continued her walk, and the bird called again.

"I gotta remember to ask somebody what the hell kind of bird that is," Pepa said to the dogs, who responded by cocking their heads as if they too were listening.

"It's a blue grosbeak," said a soft voice from out of nowhere.

Pepa looked around, but couldn't see who was speaking.

"Who's there?"

"It's not common. And it's also strange that it's here in the first place. It must've gotten separated to come this far from home."

"Come out where I can see you," Pepa demanded.

A young man emerged from the bushes, carrying a small cloth satchel.

Pepa stepped back, eyeing the clean-shaven traveler, wondering why he looked so familiar. "Mira, I walk this trail every day. And I know the people who come here, but I don't think I know you."

He didn't answer.

"Or do I?"

"I'm from the place you went to when you were young."

Though thin, he carried himself with a strength Pepa rarely saw in others.

The dogs, suspicious, pranced close to Pepa, the hair on their backs standing on end. "What's your name?" she asked.

"Me llamo Camilo." He held out his palm toward the dogs and whistled softly. They both quieted and came to him. He squatted to pet the animals, who now seemed completely at ease. "I don't know if you remember me. I lived with Don Gabriel, my great-grandfather. He told me there was a problem and sent me to help you."

Pepa straightened her shoulders. "Don Gabriel? Pero he's dead."

"Sí," said Camilo, still petting the dogs. He stopped, then stood, and met Pepa's eye.

Pepa said nothing for a good ten seconds. Then she slowly greeted him with a big, fat grin. "Ay, qué bueno . . . qué bueno!"

9

NINA PULLED HER OLD FORD F-150 into Pepa's large driveway. Faded political bumper stickers dotted the back end. She had just gotten off work, and bits of powdered sugar still clung to her face. The heat of the hot grease from the doughnut shop had caused the spikes of her hair to stick up even straighter. With her clinic hours over, Pepa had asked as many people as possible to join her for a community meeting. A small crowd, maybe twenty people, gathered outside Pepa's house, where she and her new apprentice, Camilo, had set up benches and chairs. It was a clear and balmy May evening, with a half-moon just beginning to rise.

Nina ran her hands through her hair, trying to shake off the sugar. She waved hello to her neighbor, Ben Quintana, who sold jewelry at the Santo Domingo store, and spotted Father Miguel from the St. Francis Cathedral, along with Myrna and Jaime García, a newlywed couple who lived around the corner. She didn't recognize the big gabacho in the back. He looked like a spy. That's the problem when you use a phone tree to call a meeting. She marched right past him, giving him a fish eye greeting. Whatever. They were here to talk about tough news. Not even the press had gotten wind of the winery, so this was going to be one hell of a surprise.

A few more people trickled in, including Pepa's daughter and her neighbor Irma, hobbling around with a stick-type cane. Camilo stood on the perimeter, eyeing the crowd. Nina had detected something different about him when she first met him, all immediately explained, of course, when he introduced himself as Don Gabriel's great-grandson. Camilo glided around like a dancer, except with a strange sinewy strength, as if he could leap over a six-foot fence without breaking stride.

Locating Tala, who seemed to be studying her notes, Nina paused to shamelessly ogle her girlfriend's cute face, not to mention the rest of the package. "You have the most luscious ass," she whispered as she gave Tala a hug.

Tala brushed the powdered sugar off Nina's face. "Mmmm. Yours isn't so bad either . . . I missed you today. Any chance you can stay with me tonight?"

"How could I resist?" Nina's eyes sparkled at the thought. They'd been together five years yet kept separate places. She relished her tiny cottage with an art studio in the back, and though she loved Tala like crazy, she most certainly didn't want to leave it. Her art was too important and she'd had several shows in town—no easy feat in a city full of artists. Tala's house, on the other hand, was old, creaky, and sweet, with a big inner garden of trees, flowers, and cacti—not to mention her rooster, hen, and clown of a dog. And God knows Tala loved those animals, bringing one or two into work every day. The critters were used to it, and the feed store customers loved it. Sometimes Nina wished she and Tala *did* live together, just so they could have a little extra time with one another. But right now this was how it was.

Pepa stepped up to the podium that was a rickety fruit box on top of a card table. A candle with some kind of saint on it sat burning on the table and funny-smelling incense smoked next to it on a bed of coals. The incense permeated the meeting space, lending a funky aroma to the air.

"Bueno, let's get started." Pepa looked around the yard and then began. "We called you to my house today because we have something important to tell you." The neighbors, who up until then had been catching up on chisme, hushed, and quickly settled down.

"For the sake of time, I'm gonna cut to the chase." She paused to look around the yard. "We want you to know that Gilbert Córdova, hijo de Vicente and Cleo who own the feed store, wants to buy our houses so he can knock them down to grow grapes and make a winery." A murmur of discontent swept through the crowd which had grown to about twenty-five people.

Nina noticed Domingo Salazar and his son walk in.

"Tala Córdova, hermana de Gilbert, who is also opposed to the winery, is gonna say a little more."

Nina's eyes caught Tala's as she walked to the podium followed by her dog. Usually her eyes sparkled like brilliant green garnets. But today they looked sad and puffy. Her steps were slow and guarded. Nina knew Tala had never publicly opposed her family. All their fights, and there were plenty of them, had been conducted under the roof of their house. Now she stepped into a more public place of pain. Tala smoothed her shirt, hands quivering.

"OK, well, this isn't exactly easy to talk about." She paused to pet her dog, now leaning against her. "My brother wants to buy our land and homes—homes where many of us have lived for generations. Now you and I know Dogtown's the only place left that hasn't been taken over by the ricos. And despite the city's negligence, it's what we call home. The streets are dusty in summer, muddy in winter, and dogs run around like they own everything . . . Yet suddenly we've got my brother talking to the mayor and all the right people so he can come in and force us out. Why? To grow grapes."

"No way, man! He can't do it!" yelled Benny Lucero from the crowd.

"But he can," continued Tala. "He's got a lot of people behind him: the chamber of commerce, most of city council—excepting Domingo Salazar," she said, glancing his way. "The mayor, my family, and at least one local lawyer. Not to mention the lawyers he's got in California. And, I kid you not, he's got a truckload of money he'll use to make you an offer."

Tala glanced at Nina, who nodded in support. "But there's a catch. It won't be enough to buy a new house or guarantee any kind of future for your old age. What he's going to do is send his little money crunchers to come up with a plan, ladle it out with just enough honey, and then you'll need to move. Maybe to the low-cost houses they're building near Española or the new trailer court the mayor plans to build out by the Motel Six. But it won't be the same, and you'll only get a portion of what your house is worth."

"This is impossible to believe!" cried out Opal McGee, a retired faculty member from the Santa Fe Art Institute.

"Believe it! They're saying since it will improve the area, they can use eminent domain. And on top of losing your homes," she paused, fighting for composure, "we'll lose our neighborhood. Mrs. Gallegos won't have her store. Papa Chick won't have the Laundromat. Benny Lucero won't have the cafe. And I won't have a home for my animals. Those of you who are artists, good luck finding affordable studios."

"We can't let this happen!" Benny Lucero said, scanning the faces around him.

"That's right!" said Opal McGee.

Nina gave Tala a hug and then took over. She studied the charged-up crowd. "I'm here tonight because I don't want to lose my house. Where would I go? I don't make good money like the mayor. I have what he calls a limited income." Several people chuckled. "This mayor's going to do his best to make the whole thing sound ass-kicking good. Good for the city, good for the people; you know, all that BS we typically hear. So what *we* need to know, right now, is how many of you want to fight?"

Most, but not all, the hands shot up.

"You guys who didn't raise your hands, do you mind telling us why?" Nina crossed her arms and waited. Out of the corner of her eye she saw Camilo and Tala also watching.

Jaime García, Nina's neighbor, stood up and took off his hat. Dressed in scuffed work boots and clothes from his construction job, he spoke slowly, choosing words carefully. "Well, me here and my wife are renters, so we don't have much of a say in this." Other people murmured in agreement.

Dora Cabrillo, single-momming five kids, stood up. "First of all, if my landlord wants to sell, I gotta go. And with all these kids, I don't know where that's gonna be."

Nina stifled her true thoughts about Dora and Jaime's sell-for-the-money bullshit and took a deep breath before she spoke. "Look, I'm a renter, but that doesn't mean we can't talk to our landlords and give them the four-one-one about how much money they'll lose. Even *they* won't want to sell when they see what'll be offered."

Domingo Salazar spoke next. "Oye hombres, mujeres. Miren. This is a helluva serious situation. I'm on the council, and I know how these people operate. They don't play when it comes to money. And we're talking big money here. Gilbert has gotten all the backing he needs to make this happen. Tala's right. Once Gilbert gets going, most of you will lose your homes—even you renters," he said, looking at Jaime.

"I'm a proud man, and one thing I don't believe in is getting stepped on. And just in case you haven't figured it out yet, you're gonna get stepped on mighty hard. I'm willing to fight this. But I gotta tell you it'll be an uphill battle, and we're gonna need to work together. I'll do my part, though I'm pretty sure I'm the only one on the council opposed to this pinche plan. So we're gonna need every one of you to do your part." Domingo sat down, with several around him offering an enthusiastic thumbs up.

For several seconds no one said a word. Then the big gabacho stood up. Nina noticed he was easy on the eyes, a mix of gray-blond locks curling around his neck. "My name—" he cleared his throat, "is Jules Johnson, and I live over on Taos Avenue. I used to be a physicist at the lab but I quit . . . I came today because I like living here. You can count on me to do whatever's needed to help." He glanced at the people around him, nodded, and sat down.

Nina caught Pepa's daughter Luz staring at the gabacho. She couldn't keep her eyes off the big man in the cowboy boots and jeans. Nina wondered about the state of physicists today, since he sure as hell didn't look like any physicist she'd ever seen.

Opal McGee stood up next. "All you people who just want to sit there and let these people take your houses can leave right now! The rest of you who want to fight this, meet at my house at 238 Santa Clara, same time, same day, next week. If you forget where I live, just ask Miss Pepa, she knows how to find me." People clapped in response. Tala mouthed a "thank you" to the feisty old lady.

Nina spotted Father Miguel standing in the back with a giant grin across his face. "Next week at Opal's we'll start organizing," she said. "I'm passing around a sign-up sheet. If you're interested in helping, put your name and number on it. We'll call you. Gracias for coming."

Nina noticed almost all the people attending the meeting that night had signed the sheet. She paid careful attention to the ones who hadn't.

10

ROLANDO REYES, NEARLY SIXTY and mayor of Santa Fe, felt pretty damn proud of himself. His parents, both schoolteachers, had encouraged him to set his goals high. Rolando did and succeeded at everything he set his mind to. He put himself through UNM and obtained a law degree from Stanford. He returned home on a quest to become someone people would ideally look up to, hopefully respect, or at the very least, fear. Up until his election as mayor, he ran a successful law practice with a management style much like that of a patrón.

Unlike most New Mexican men, Rolando stood 6' 2", with two-hundred-fifty pounds of former muscle. He liked how his size made small men look up and the weaker look away. He didn't know, of course, that almost everyone referred to him as el Bollo or, if they were kind, simply Rolo. He himself was not kind, though he did his damnedest to try. He went to church regularly and, out of respect for his wife and kids, kept his extramarital affairs private. Unfortunately, his quest to be kind, coupled with arrogance, gave him a blustery, big-shot quality. Pepa's description of the mayor fit best: "Most people who do politics around here are muy chingones. And the pinche mayor leads the pack."

On this mid-May morning, Rolo was meeting with Gilbert Córdova and his lawyer, Bill Takash. Excited about the winery proposal, Rolo wanted details on how it would work out for the Dogtownies. He knew he had to handle things carefully, since kicking people out of their homes was a little bit delicate. On top of everything, he had to make sure his personal investment stayed hidden.

Rolo walked out of his office into the waiting area where his assistant and the receptionist worked, and where Gilbert and Bill waited. He shook hands and asked the men to join him in his office, which he strutted into like an oversized rooster. The old City Hall building, considered a historic landmark, was in reality crumbling and leaky. His control of the city council and his connections throughout town did nothing to speed any movement toward getting a new building erected. Yet despite this, his personal office remained sleek and refined. He'd worked hard to outfit the rather large, drafty room with a sizeable collection of Santa Fe art and Navajo rugs. The office essentially functioned as a tribute to his accomplishments: pictures with several dignitaries, various honors and awards, and a wall filled with degrees and certificates. Eschewing the small conference table in the center of the room, Rolo herded the men toward a leather sofa and chair.

"Come on in. Dahlia, hold my calls." The mayor grimaced at his assistant, who, fighting the effects of age, reminded him more of a praying mantis than the once pretty homecoming queen she'd been. But bad habits and difficult men had left their marks, so she fought back with surgery, botox, and starvation. Twice divorced, and in debt up to her ears, she was hired as a political favor to a big donor, an act Rolo instantly regretted. It wasn't that Dahlia didn't do good work. It was more the fact that she had fallen for Rolo and doted on him throughout the day with her sticklike mantis hands. Rolo wanted to fire her, but knew at the moment his own hands were tied.

The mayor's time was tight and, as always, he preferred to get to the point. "Bueno hombres, tell me what you got. I want to make sure this goes as smoothly as possible."

Gilbert took a deep breath as Bill opened the portfolio. He placed a poster-sized map of Dogtown on a portable tripod. "We'd like to buy out four businesses, thirteen rental units, and twenty-seven owner-occupied houses." Gilbert pointed to the outlined area. "There's an old dog-patch park and three vacant, city-owned lots adjacent to the homes I'd also like to purchase. This section here," he continued, "will be used for the winery, picnic grounds, and parking lot. The rest is for growing grapes. I'll also import grapes from the southern tier of the state."

"You think that's a good idea?" asked the mayor.

"It'll be fine. We'll give people the impression the wine's grown from grapes in the Santa Fe area, with a few imported varietals. This way I still get the better grapes from down south, and Santa Fe gets the promotion." He gave Rolo an ain't-I-clever look.

Ignoring the look, the mayor nodded. "Go on."

Bill handed out a copy of the purchase plan as Gilbert continued. "This plan gives you the details, but I basically want to pay the renters a three-thousand-dollar move-out fee, and what I think is fair compensation to the home and apartment owners based on square footage and sub-prime value."

"It all works out to be approximately thirty dollars a square foot," said Bill.

"OK, so give me some examples." Rolo eagerly rocked back and forth, his girth making the leather squeak.

Bill passed him a sheet of calculations. "Let's say a house is eleven hundred square feet, which is small but typical of a home in that area. An owner would be compensated thirty-three thousand dollars. Added on would be a lower rate for surrounding land. Outhouses are a liability, so that would be a deduction."

"Go on."

Bill took a deep breath and continued. "A house with fifteen hundred square feet would get forty-five K. Something slightly bigger, like two thousand feet, would get sixty, and so on. Keep in mind that the school in this neighborhood is terrible, and the majority of houses are dilapidated, representing a fairly depreciated market value."

"In short," added Gilbert, "nobody wants to live there."

The mayor squeezed the arms of his chair and eyed both men. "You mean nobody except the people living there want to live there."

"Well—" Gilbert hesitated, glancing at Bill.

Leaning forward, the mayor focused on Gilbert. "How much would this whole thing cost?"

"Our estimate—"

Bill interrupted him. "I can speak about it. We estimate that, based on city planning information, it'll cost two-point-six or seven million to buy out the homeowners, rentals, and renters, and a couple hundred thousand to buy out the businesses."

"That's everyone?"

"Everyone," confirmed Bill.

Rolo eased his body back and folded his hands in front of him. "This won't work." He turned to Gilbert. "You're fucking these people with that kind of offer, and you're fucking with me. Come see me when you're really serious. What do you take these people for, imbeciles?" Rolo got up, indicating the meeting was over. "Look, I like this plan of yours, but you sure as hell better do something better. You can't just screw people 'cause they're poor, at least not in this town."

"Mayor Reyes," Gilbert said, still seated. "We're giving these people a fair deal. That whole neighborhood's been circling the drain for years. You're as aware of that as I am. They're all getting cash for trash. You should also know I'm not into screwing anyone since my own sister lives there."

Rolo studied the eyes of a man doing his best to look sincere. "Nope, I don't think so. No deal." He ushered the men to the door. "You're going to have to pump this up some more, hombre. Otherwise the city will crucify it and me along with it. Oh, and one last thing," he said, tapping Gilbert on the chest, "when you *do* get something realistic together, you better make *it*, and me, look good."

Speechless, the two men gathered their papers and hustled out.

Ten minutes after the meeting with the mayor, Tala got a phone call from her brother. "Feed Your Steed, this is Tala."

"I need to see you."

"Hmm. Guess you had a meeting with the big bollo, huh?" She picked up her rooster Otis and set him on her lap.

"Yeah, and the fuckhead backed out on me."

"He did? That's a surprise." Tala gave him the calmest voice she could muster. "Let's meet for lunch. You pick."

"Coyote at noon."

"How 'bout someplace else? I kinda hate it there." She rubbed Otis's back as he cuddled up against her.

"Why, too many tourists?"

"No, too much chipotle."

"Very funny. Look, do it for me. They've got a good wine selection, and I want to drink a whole lot of it right now."

Sensing there might be progress, Tala relented. "OK, see you then." She hung up the phone and gave Otis a kiss.

Facing the bathroom mirror at the Coyote Cafe, Tala wiped away the smirk on her face. "This acting shit is tough," she said to herself. "Next time Jane Fonda walks into the store, I'll have more respect."

She waited for her brother at the entrance. "Wow," she said, as he slinked into the restaurant wearing his fancy clothes. "You look good, but sad. I haven't seen you look this sad since Mom took away your BB gun and sold it at the flea market."

They were seated immediately. Gilbert perused the menu. He'd grown a goatee which, coupled with his chubby cheeks, reminded Tala of a muskrat. He ordered a bottle of Sauvignon Blanc, instructing the waiter to pour them each a glass. Tala didn't normally drink at lunch, but Gilbert was too upset to quibble over one glass of wine. After he glanced at the bottle and took a sip, he recapped his conversation with the mayor.

"I don't know what made him change his mind," he said, gulping down a corn fritter. "I had given him all the preliminary figures, and he'd made it sound like it was a go."

Tala listened as she scooped chicken fajitas into a tortilla. She took a big bite, momentarily surprised by how good it tasted.

"I guess he wasn't paying attention to the details," Gilbert added, refilling his glass.

"Maybe," Tala replied, her mouth full. "What he probably wanted to see was whether you could raise enough dough to pull it off. Anyone, even people with connections, can talk. Rolo-man wanted to see the cash, which brings us back to my proposed deal."

Gilbert closed his eyes, then took another sip of wine. "OK," he said, pursing his lips, "I'll give you fair-market price."

"And don't forget we're giving each other information," she replied, pouring salsa into the guacamole. She grabbed a spoon and stirred the two together.

"Wait, tell me why I'm doing this? So you can let the neighborhood know what I've got planned?" He picked up a chip and shoved it into the salsa-laced guacamole, leaving it there.

Tala grabbed the chip and slipped it in her mouth. "Yeah, but I give you information in return. To put it mildly, your buyout proposal is pretty iffy.

And you can come off looking like a bad boy if you don't do it right." She took a deep breath and let it out with a long, slow release.

Gilbert picked up another chip. "I'm still not sure about this little bargain. I'll have to ask my lawyer."

Tala eyed her brother, wishing she had something stronger than wine to drink. "Are you purposely forgetting that you're kicking me and all those poor people out of our houses?"

"Come on, Tala, I'm not dogging you," he said with a laugh, "but that place you call home should be condemned. Dogtown needed revitalization thirty years ago. I don't see why you want to stay with all that junk around, the trashed cars, the unpaved streets."

"It's not all junk. And the neighborhood's peaceful—one of the few spots in town without a million tourists running around in it. Plus it's a good place for my animals."

"Yeah, but don't you think it's time you got a nicer place anyway?"

Tala picked up a knife and cut her fajitas into tiny pieces. "I don't exactly have a rich wife who can help me march up Canyon Road and slap down the bucks for one of those fancy-ass adobes."

"If you're implying I married Claire for her money you're totally wrong, because I didn't even know she had it when I met her."

"I'm not implying anything, Mr. Defensive. I'm just stating a fact. I also think it's lame that I have to insist on fair-market value. And, Mr. Moneybags, you can't just take advantage of people no matter what positive change you think you're making. Rolo basically told you the same thing this morning."

Gilbert's jaw hardened.

"Look, sorry Rolo was rough on you." Tala forced out a softer tone. "But I don't want to leave my house, and I'll bet most of the Dogtownies won't either."

Gilbert poured the last of the wine into both of their glasses. He swirled his around and took a sip. "All right, it's a deal."

"Good." Tala patted the table, relief flowing through her.

Gilbert fingered the rim of his glass. "But we're going to do this without a contract."

"OK," Tala said, wondering why he wanted it this way.

"We in agreement?" he asked, finishing his wine.

"I suppose we are."

11

EVER SINCE THAT FIRST MEETING on the future of Dogtown, Pepa'd been working her tail off. Thank goodness Camilo stepped in to assist her—something she hadn't experienced in all her thirty years of work. It was a good thing, too, since people were appearing not only in droves, but with all kinds of ailments. Cleto Salcido, old, thin, and tough as a bullwhip, was one of them—dragging himself in, hat in hand. Pepa noticed a scrawny dog had followed him over to the clínica, moving almost as slowly as Cleto.

Pepa herded the viejito into the exam room. "This is my helper, Camilo," she said, introducing the young acolyte. "Great-grandson de Don Gabriel."

The old man stared at Camilo who nodded a greeting as he pulled up a chair.

"Y cómo 'stá?" asked Pepa, noting the mossy look of Cleto's eyes. "What brings you here today?"

The viejito turned his attention back to Pepa. "Bueno, Señora, I'm not feeling too good. I haven't had a decent shit in two weeks, my mouth feels dry as a lizard, and the gas in me could fill a hot-air balloon."

Pepa listened, suppressing a smile.

"On top of that, I haven't slept worth a damn since we found out about that pinche winery. I don't know what the hell I'd do if I lost my house. It might be an old shack, but damn it," he said, tapping his chest, "it's *my* old shack. Can the city really let them take my home away?" Tears welled up in Cleto's eyes. "I mean, what kind of country is this that lets people do that?"

Pepa gave him a hug and held his hand. "Camilo, dame un poquito de cáscara sagrada," she instructed, since it looked like that the old man needed a good purgative.

"Bueno Señor, esta winery is a big problem. Pero, we're gonna fight it. We're not letting el Gilbert sell us down the river. And I'll be damned if that cabrón gets my house."

She mixed the hierba into the portion he needed. "Here. You have a bad case of bilis cuajada—too much bile in your stomach. Take this and mix two teaspoons in a glass of water. It's gonna make you go to the bathroom a lot, but we need to clean everything out. OK?"

Cleto took the hierbas and nodded. "Gracias, Pepa. I hope this helps."

"Take it once a day for three days. You're gonna feel better. Pero, Cleto, don't just sit home worrying. We need you, entiende?" Pepa tapped him on the shoulder.

"Sí, Señora. Count me in." He peered into the bag of hierbas and slowly pulled out a tattered wallet to pay her.

"No, no." Pepa pushed it away, knowing the old man needed every one of his social security dollars. "You can pay me by bringing some yerba buena when you get a chance."

"Gracias," he said, sliding the wallet back in his pocket. "I'll get you some tomorrow."

"Good," Pepa said, smiling as the three walked out the door. "Leave it on the porch if I'm not here."

"You got it," he said. He called his dog over, who slowly pulled herself to a stand. "You people ever work with animals?"

"Pues nooo," answered Pepa, who sometimes wished she did.

"What's wrong with your dog?" Camilo asked, squatting next to her.

"No sé. I think it hurts her to walk."

Camilo held out his palm and let the dog sniff it. "Let me see," he said, running his hands over the dog's body, settling on the back right leg. "Is this where it hurts, girl?" The dog held still, letting Camilo probe the leg until he found the area that seemed to be the source of pain. He laid his hand across the leg and gently massaged it, holding the dog close. After about a minute he let the dog go. Wagging her tail, she ambled over to Cleto, her leg now appearing free of pain.

"I'll be a son-na-va-gun . . ." The old man cast Camilo a curious look before bending over to pet his dog. "It looks to me she's better."

"Seems so," said Camilo, looking pleased. "It's nothing special, just a little trick I do."

"That's one helluva trick," Pepa said, shifting her gaze between Camilo and the dog, not exactly sure what she just witnessed.

Cleto put on his hat. "We'll take tricks like that any old day, won't we, girl?" he said, petting his dog. "Bueno, Pepa, I better get going. Gracias por todo . . . Y tú," he said, placing his hand on Camilo's shoulder. "Thank you for helping my little girl."

"I'm glad she's better," Camilo replied, offering a shy grin.

The two healers stood on the porch watching Cleto trudge out of the yard in a slow, painful gait. "Oiga, Cleto! Don't forget to take your medicine!" Pepa ordered. The viejito stopped and waved before turning the corner. "Que le vaya bien," Pepa said, walking back in the clinic, shutting the door.

12

TALA LOOKED UP FROM A STACK of kitten chow and noticed a slender brunette gazing through the window. She did a double take, realizing it was Gilbert's wife, Claire. Surprised, she waved her in and did a quick scan around the store for her animals. She spotted Bess, the hen, in the back pecking at some crumbs, and Lisa, her slobbery sweet Boxer, trotting up to the door to greet Claire. She recalled her sister-in-law being a tad nervous around the animals. Tala figured it was probably due to her typically having the kids with her, preferring they stay away from beaks and teeth.

Dressed in fashionable jeans and sporty cowboy boots, Claire stopped midstride and stared at the dog's black and tan face. "Does he bite?"

Tala paused with her pricing gun poised over the chow. "No, *she* doesn't. Come on in! Good to see you." She wondered what the heck Claire was doing at the store, since she rarely came by and, with her kids and job, always seemed too overwhelmed to spend much time chatting. Tala scanned the store, searching for other customers, spotting Mrs. Silva by the dog food and Mr. Baca jabbering to Marcos, her assistant.

Tala gave her sister-in-law a hug. "What brings you by?"

Claire shrugged, her face reddening. "I had to come out and look at soil samples. Gil wants vines that can thrive here so we hired a geotech firm to pull some samples out by the park and several other spots. I know you're busy, but I wanted to stop in and say hello, pick up some food for those cats your mom likes to feed."

"Yeah, well don't let my dad know. It drives him crazy that Mom feeds all those strays."

Claire scratched her head. "You mean your dad doesn't know?"

"To tell you the truth, I'm not sure. I think he just likes bossing her all the time. She stands up to him, though, says it's her money and she'll spend it however she pleases." Tala rubbed a sore wrist she'd been nursing for over a week. "You look good . . . How're things going?"

"They're fine. Lots of change happening . . ." Claire replied, looking down. "The kids are getting big, but I suppose that's to be expected." She met Tala's gaze. "Jesse's starting kindergarten. Can you believe it?"

"Wasn't he just born last week?" Tala teased.

"It'll be five years in June," Claire replied with a smile. She started digging through her purse. "I usually have a picture or two, but I think I left them at your mom's."

"I'm sure I can look at hers or get one from you later." Tala noticed her dog Lisa standing behind Claire, who had picked up a shopping basket. "Bueno, I'll leave you to your shopping. Let me know if you need anything."

"OK." Claire meandered down the aisle. When she stopped at the cat food, Lisa nearly ran into her. "She's not a guard dog, is she? She seems to be following me."

"No, she just likes girls," said Tala, with a snicker. She patted her leg. "Lisa, come here, girl. Leave Claire alone." The dog reluctantly ambled over to Tala. As she paused to pet her, Tala spied Bess slinking slowly behind Claire.

"How do you feel about chickens?"

"Chickens? I don't know, why?"

"'Cause you got one right behind you."

Claire turned quickly, which startled Bess, making her jump in a loud swoosh. Claire yelped in fear.

Laughing, Tala went over to retrieve the chicken. "Ven, Bessita. Come here, Baby." Picking her up, she stroked her head, and turned toward her sister-in-law. "Sorry about that. I think you scared Bess more than she scared you, though. She doesn't do well with sudden movements." Tala paused to study Claire, wondering what she'd really come here to say. "Do you want to go sit in the office in the back?"

Claire brushed a feather off her shirt. "No, it's OK. I love looking around these old feed stores, especially in New Mexico . . . I don't know what it is. Maybe it's the smell of the grain or the old floorboards. Something about these stores makes me happy."

"I guess I feel the same, since I spend so much time here."

Two people were in line at the register. "Let me help these folks. Just give a holler if you need anything." She carried the chicken with her, paying little attention to the heads turning to her as she sweet-talked Bess.

The noon hour neared. Tala knew in a few minutes she'd be hopping with the lunch rush. She rang up Mrs. Silva's dog food.

"And your mom and dad, how're they doing?" Mrs. Silva asked as she pulled out her credit card.

"Oh, they're fine. They're going to Las Cruces next week for a cousin's wedding." Tala glanced at Claire who seemed to be studying everything in the store.

"They liking retirement?"

"Oooh, yeah. They're loving it." Tala watched Claire sidestep the dog who had gone back to following her. "I'm glad, too, because both of them worked hard and everything. They should take a real vacation like to Hawaii or something, but they won't go for some reason."

Mrs. Silva nodded. "Well, you know how it is. Sometimes if you're not used to traveling, it can be a little hard. Me and Roberto went there a long time ago for our honeymoon. Eeee, it's so purty. Some day I'm gonna go back, but I gotta get ese huevón I have for a husband off the couch to go with me again."

Tala laughed and checked the status of her in-law. Now she was handing Lisa a dog biscuit. The dog snapped it out of her hand, making her jump with a start.

"Bueno," Mrs. Silva continued. "I gotta get home and feed the dog. Don't work too hard."

"I'll try not to. You need help with that?"

"No, no. I got it. I'll see you later." She grabbed the bag and walked out the door. Tala picked up the chicken and put her on the counter. "Look at all that chicken feed Mr. Baca has," she said to Bess. "Maybe if you're a good girl I'll give you your very own chicken McNiblets. What do you think about that, huh?"

Claire had moved to the salt licks, her shopping basket full of cat food. Finally, she sauntered to the cash register and hefted the basket to the counter.

"You know I'm not going to let you pay for this." Tala rang up the food and wrote the total on a pad of paper.

"No, no, I insist." Claire reached into her purse and pulled out her wallet.

"Sorry," said Tala, as she bagged up the cans. "Store policy."

Claire paused, resting her hands on the wallet. "I guess it wouldn't do me any good to argue."

"Nope," Tala said, grinning.

"Thank you." She looked down, then glanced around the store. "I uh . . . I wanted to tell you . . . that I'm not happy where Gil wants to build the winery."

Tala raised an eyebrow. "No?"

"No."

"I tried talking him out of it—tried to get him to buy other land." She stuck her wallet into her purse. "I told him it didn't make sense to drive people out of their homes, especially since there's plenty of open country—not here of course, but other places. I don't know why he's got a one-track focus to stay here." She stared at the counter, rubbing two fingers across it. "So I came to say," she met Tala's gaze. "That I was sorry." She let out the words with a sigh. "Sorry, because I have to support him—he's my husband. But more sorry because it's hurting you—you and Nina." She looked around again, "And God knows who else."

Shocked, Tala reached for the register and knocked over a stack of bags. She and Claire bent to retrieve them.

"I got it." Tala gathered the bags and tossed them on the counter. "Thanks," she said with a nod as she quickly wiped away tears.

Claire grabbed Tala's arm and gave it a squeeze. "I'm so sorry . . . I guess—I guess I better go. I just needed to tell you how I felt."

"Sure." Tala crammed her hands in her pockets. "Thanks."

"Well, you make sure to take care of yourself during this mess, OK?"

Tala nodded.

"Call me if you need to talk or anything."

"OK." Tala looked away.

Claire held on to Tala a moment longer. Finally, she grabbed the cat food and hurried out the door.

As she slowly made her way back to where she had been tagging chow, Tala watched Claire hustle toward her car. Claire crossed the lot, digging into her purse for keys. Finding them, she got in the car and rested her hands on the steering wheel. Tala looked away, confused about what had just happened. In a flash, she grabbed a bag of chow and heaved it down the aisle. The impact broke it open, spilling kitten food across the floor. Cursing under her breath and thankful no one saw her childish display, she found the broom and began sweeping up the mess. She paused to see if Claire had lingered, wishing for some reason that she had. But the car was gone, leaving nothing in its place except empty space.

13

JULES JOHNSON PULLED HIS TRUCK into the parking lot of the What A Jerkee store. He was in a celebratory mood since his Aunt Tutti had just sent him a check for ten thousand dollars. Her note to him said she'd heard he quit the lab, and figuring he could use a few dollars, sent him some of the proceeds from a piece of rental property she'd sold. Jules knew she was really rewarding him for changing his line of work. She had never liked how he'd been making his living and had not so subtlety been trying to get him to do something else.

Jules cut the engine and hopped out of his truck. Though it was a Friday afternoon and nearly quitting time, the lot had a bevy of parked cars. A "Yes We're Open" sign beckoned him in as he ran his hands through his hair, hoping he looked presentable. He entered the store, inhaling the dusky scent of dried meat and seasonings, taking comfort in an ocher and black tapete hanging across a saffron-colored wall. Jules's gaze shifted to Luz, who stood at the counter ringing up orders.

He liked jerky OK, but ever since he'd seen Luz that day at Pepa's, he'd become a devotee. A couple guys told him Luz had a poor track record with men—especially white guys, but he obviously didn't care. There was something about her that ransacked his senses. It was as if Luz possessed a strange pheromone that penetrated his skin, zapping him hard, like nerve gas.

Luz seemed to notice him but kept her distance. She nodded when he walked through the door, but never touched him when he handed her money. And when he went to the counter to order, she stood back so far it almost seemed unnatural. Yet Jules kept on coming; the jerky accumulating from the cupboards of his kitchen to any open space in his house. Not knowing what to do with all the dried meat, he started walking around the neighborhood at night, discreetly feeding it to the dogs. He loved traipsing through Dogtown after the air had cooled and the scent of sage from the surrounding mesas drifted through town. The residual heat from the streets had a warming effect—compelling him to wear nothing more than jeans and a T-shirt, with a backpack over his shoulder stuffed with jerky. After several nights, he knew where most of the dogs lived, stopping now and then to toss the dried beef to any roustabout in need. Several tagged along as he journeyed back home, hoping for a few more pieces, which he usually obliged. Later, he'd sit on his porch downing a San Miguel and letting his thoughts of Luz go unbridled, allowing himself to fantasize about her kiss—or touch—along his body.

Now that he'd quit the lab, he'd been spending more time at the library, historical archives, anywhere he could get his hands on material related to New Mexico's nuclear testing. His luck had been mixed, and he often appeared bleary-eyed when he went to the store to buy more jerky. Everyone seemed to know he'd been a physicist at the lab, which he heard was a giant no-no for Luz's mother, but he'd quit, right? So that made him an ex-physicist as far as he was concerned.

On that particular day, he walked into the store after several hours of reading, and Luz asked him out of the blue, "Why are your eyes always red?"

"My eyes?" Jules, taken aback by her question, wasn't exactly sure how to respond.

"Yeah, your eyes." Luz peered into his bloodshot orbs. "They're about as red as quasars."

Jules instinctively touched his cheekbone. "Quasars? Hmm, well I've been doing lots of reading, I guess." His hair was now long enough to pull back into a ponytail. This he grabbed next.

"On?"

"On nuclear history. I . . ." he paused, seeing Luz draw back from the word *nuclear*. He'd become used to people's reactions to the word, especially in the political circles of some of his friends. He knew it was loaded and it usually guaranteed a reaction bordering on a cross between saying *child molester* and *serial killer*. Swallowing hard, he continued. "I quit the lab and have been investigating cancer from nuclear fallout." Luz's face began to soften. "I've been suspicious of it ever since hearing stories of people dying in their prime from leukemia, thyroid, and other cancers." Jules stopped. He could easily talk about this for hours and had to hold himself back.

He watched Luz study him with a slow rise of her chin. He hoped she saw he was sincere. So many people were on some kind of health kick or self-important campaign in this town. The rest of the state sometimes thought they were a little off-center, "Fanta Se," they'd say and laugh. Luz might think he was nuts, too, since he'd given up a high-paying job for a personal crusade. One, he might add, that would never implicate the government for its offenses. If she knew this, she might think he'd really gone loco.

"I close the shop at six. Want to get something to eat?"

Jules did a double take, followed by an immediate pull in his groin. "Sure," he said, trying to calm that happy boy down. Luz wasn't a beauty. Some might say she wasn't pretty at all. She sure as hell reeled him in, making him wonder where his head and his dick had been all these years. Married to his job, he thought. Well, no job stopping him now. Which he could honestly say he was totally looking forward to.

14

Tala eased herself into a minty-green booth at the Hungry Chula Cafe. Nina and Pepa followed, the three ordering iced tea and tacos de cabrito. Benny Lucero, owner of the cafe, prided himself on serving typical New Mexican food, but it was usually the kind tourists knew little of, like roasted cabeza de vaca, cabrito, and flat enchiladas with an egg on top. Tala, Nina, and Pepa ate there often, and the three of them were meeting for dinner to catch up on winery news.

"Rolo kicked the Vino Latino out of his office because the deal he set up was too chintzy." Tala took a bite of taco, its contents dripping juice across her chin. "Gilbert wanted to give everyone a bare-bones minimum based on some kooky-ass formula his accountant worked up." She took a napkin and wiped her face.

"Yeah, Rolo surprised the shit out of him by not liking it," added Nina.

Tala added green chile to her taco. "Plus, his caper was a little too transparent, and he thought he could get away with it." She always loved it when her brothers did dumb things, especially since they always thought they were smarter than their non-degreed sister.

"And so what's gonna happen?" Pepa asked, spooning salsa into her taco. Benny kept a slew of salsas on the tables along with a bowl of chopped green chile.

"I don't know," Tala answered. "He's gotta come up with more money. And Rolo will still have to OK it."

"Yeah, the big man wants everything pretty, but it's a bit hard to do that when you're kicking poor viejitos out of their homes." Nina licked taco juice off her fingers.

"So, Pepa, I want you to know," Tala's tone grew more serious. "That I talked Gilbert into giving me market rate for my house and regular updates on what he's planning. In exchange, I give him updates on what we're doing."

Pepa added more salt to her chile and set the shaker down. "Explain to me how he can give people less money than what our houses are worth?"

"He says people should get a lower rate because the neighborhood's all shot to hell. I told him it's not fair, especially since he's kicking people out of their homes, and he'll run into more trouble by trying to scam them."

Pepa put her food down, giving Tala her full attention. "Bueno, can he do this?"

"I don't know. He says he can—that it's totally legal, but it sounds kind of fishy to me. That's why I want us to exchange information so we both know what's going on. Of course, I don't see us telling each other everything. It's worth a try though to get more info out of him."

"He's got a lawyer helping him, so it seems to me," Nina replied, looking at both Pepa and Tala, "that we need a lawyer, too." She tapped Tala's arm. "What do you think about asking that ex of yours if she'll take the case pro-Sonny-Bono." She gave Tala a wink.

"Who?" Pepa asked,

"Elena Luján," answered Nina.

"Ay, chingao, she's tough," Pepa said, nodding in agreement. Then she gave Tala a double take. "I didn't know she was your ex."

Tala rolled her eyes. "We lasted maybe three months."

"*I* heard it was six," said Nina, giving Tala a teasing smile.

"Depends on who's doing the counting."

"Oye, chicas," Pepa interrupted. "Can we get back to business?" They both smiled and nodded. "I think we need this lawyer. You can't fight these things by yourself. Pero, do you think she'll do it for free?"

"I can ask her. She would get a lot of press for taking the case . . . Then we'll really see if Gilbert will cough up his information." Tala finished off the last of her food.

Pepa crinkled her left eye as she scrutinized Tala. "You think el Gilbert will tell you the truth?"

Tala shrugged. "It's hard to say."

Benny sauntered over with a pot of coffee. Pepa waited till he finished filling her cup before she responded. "Bueno, this might be a little hard for you. Y también, I don't think you should be hanging out with us too much in public—" she looked around the grungy old restaurant with its worn tables, cracked vinyl booths, plastic glasses, and old stacks of newspapers—opposite anything Gilbert or his friends would go to—"except maybe here."

Tala watched Nina fold a napkin into an origami design. "So tell me what's been happening with the people coming in to see you?"

"Eee, I've been so busy," Pepa said, drinking her coffee. "So many people with susto, or one thing or another. They're worried about este problema because they're scared they're going to lose their casitas."

"So you think most of the people are still against this?" Tala felt hopeful.

"I think so," said Pepa. "Where else are they going to go?"

Nina nodded, "Yeah, that's what I've mostly been getting from the land of lard, too."

Tala looked at Pepa, "OK. So let's plan what we're going to do next."

※

Tala gazed out the window of the feed store. She loved Santa Fe, especially Dogtown, in the spring. Even without rain, the light glimmering off the adobe or ricocheting across the mountains could stop hearts. And the whirling winds powered through the valleys, plucking thistle and sagebrush, tumbling them through the streets like a roving band of marauders. She pulled herself from the window and marched to the back office to phone Elena. One of the best lawyers in the city and tough enough to take on the mayor, Elena was the hands-down favorite to help them. Tala recalled meeting her when she was still an undergrad. Both uninvolved at the time, they'd had a hot and heavy affair. That is until Elena decided she wanted to be straight. Now married to a guy who'd been after her since high school, she seemed happy, though Tala always wondered where she'd pocketed those old desires.

Tala arranged an appointment at her house later the next day. Elena told her she'd heard about the winery and wanted to drive through Dogtown to get a better feel for the neighborhood. Tala escorted the well-heeled lawyer to the courtyard adorned with desert plants and a babbling fountain and served her iced tea. The garden surrounded a table and chairs set beneath a gorgeous cottonwood tree. The afternoon was warm, and the animals, after saying their hellos, went back to napping. Elena sat down, took a sip of tea, looking like she hadn't changed from the last time Tala had seen her. She gave the lawyer a lingering glance and noticed Elena still had that smile that could slay armies and, evidently, her husband. But a closer look revealed something had changed. Her eyes. Tala remembered them as bright bits of amber with warm, honeyed flecks. Now they seemed dull and burdened with fatigue. Too much work, thought Tala, feeling slightly bad about asking her to take on more. She noticed she still had the wedding ring. And thankfully Tala was no longer attracted to her, so she could concentrate on business. She filled the lawyer in with the details, outlining the support they'd gotten from Pepa and the residents, as well as the publicity campaign they were about to launch. She told her that they had no money, but she felt this case could receive national attention, particularly since it was in Santa Fe, and people would see what the poor folks in town were contending with. She halted her spiel and left to refill Elena's glass. When she returned, Elena gave her a fat grin and said she'd take the case.

"Thank you. Thank you so much," said Tala. "We've been working at a grassroots level to fight this, but we really need your help." Her gaze shifted briefly to her dog lying under the shade of the tree, the chicken scratching for bugs. She worried that she'd lose her little oasis and hoped Elena could truly help them. "I'm sure you know not just any lawyer can do this, especially with the mayor's talons wrapped around the project."

"That guy's a son of a bitch whose only concern is himself. He's had his priorities backwards since he's been in office," said Elena. "And his political machine has only made it worse. I'm taking this case pro bono because I'll be damned if he kicks you and these people out. Unfortunately, it won't be easy, and . . . of course I don't have guarantees. But you can rely on me to help to the best of my abilities."

"Thank you," Tala nodded, humbled by Elena's sincerity. "We really appreciate this." She set her tea down, and brushed several pine needles off the table. "I need to fill you in on a bit more."

"Bueno, talk to me." Alert, she gave Tala her full attention.

"It's important word doesn't get out I'm involved in this anti-winery fight. If anyone asks, tell them it was . . . the Canine Underground Resistors."

"The CURs?"

"Yeah, sort of what you'd call our Dogtown winery opposition team. I just made it up." Tala suppressed a smile. "You think of something better, let me know."

Elena tapped her finger to her lips. "It's got a nice ring to it. And no worries about keeping you out of this. Hell," she said with an exaggerated shrug of her shoulders, "I'm not even here today."

"One more thing," Tala continued. "My brother and I are supposed to give each other inside information on his plans and the Dogtown opposition."

"Uh-huh," Elena said, sensing something more.

"Well, it isn't right for him—and my parents, who support his little project—to just kick me and all these people out of our homes. It's as if who I am and where I live doesn't matter. So I also asked him for fair market value, that is, if this deal goes through, since he's trying to give everyone a lower market rate." She paused to study Elena's reaction.

"That's not very nice."

"Right. Since we're *family*," she gave the word quotations, "we made a deal to give each other information that I'll heavily censor, of course." Tala grabbed a lock of her hair and unconsciously pulled it. "It won't be easy doing this." She slumped lower in her chair. "I sort of feel like I'm in one of those twisted Shakespearean plays, except I don't know if I'm the victim or the idiot."

Elena leaned over and petted the dog, who had stuck her head under her open hand. "My guess is you might be both . . . I'm sorry you have to go through this." She returned her gaze to Tala. "I haven't driven through the neighborhood in a while, and it *is* looking pretty shabby. But I can see that despite the junked cars and all the mess, it still has its own particular charm—dogs running everywhere, viejitas baking bread or drying chicos in the hornos, and you can't beat the view. So I don't blame you. I'm just not sure I would have had the will to play nice with Gilbert, especially after all your family's given him and your brothers. You're tough," she said, her eyes dancing across Tala. "But that's what I've always liked about you."

Surprised by the flirtation, Tala chose to ignore it. "Yeah, tough or maybe stupid. But I gotta admit it's more than us losing our homes . . . You know, Gilbert was always teased by my father and brothers for being too sensitive.

And I'm the one who stuck up for him. So now that he's finally been accepted into the man-club—"

"And forgot about you. You're doing payback."

Tala clapped her hands and the dog ambled over. "No, I wouldn't say that." She ruffled the dog's fur. "It's all the stuff I told you already, plus showing him and my family that me and Nina matter."

"You do," said Elena.

"So, back to the legalities?" Tala needed to move on. "There's a chance with some fundraising we could rustle up a few dollars to pay you, but it'll be small potatoes. This is going to be a hell of a fight, and more than likely all you'll get is good publicity out of it."

Elena nodded. "I understand. But this is important. And I'm honored to do it."

Tala smiled. "Thank you."

Elena looked around Tala's garden, the babbling fountain, the fecund growth of plants and cacti, and the various animals among them. "Bueno," she said, rising. "I guess I'd better get to work."

15

Tala decided their fight had to go subversive. Thank goodness they had Elena now who could help them with the legal issues. But they needed a covert group of trusted "doggies" to work on the tougher matters of finding out the mayoral secrets and backroom deals supporting the winery. This covert group naturally included Nina, Pepa, and Camilo who met at the Hungry Chula to plan their first task: spying on the mayor. Their mission was to find out not only what he thought about Gilbert's project but, more importantly, how he was involved. Nina suggested, since no one knew Camilo, that he be elected first spy.

"No problem," said Camilo, looking around the table. "I was sent here to help Pepa, so put me to work."

During the meeting, which continued over dinner, Tala said she also wanted Jules added to the group since she felt they might need someone with technical skills. Pepa balked since he was an ex-lab physicist and now dating her daughter, but the other three overruled her. They put Jules through a tough grilling, and once it was determined he could be trusted, he, too, was added.

☀

Word on the street was that Rolo's terrible temper kept the office in such a state that few beyond Dahlia stayed longer than a paycheck. Camilo applied for an open receptionist position, and Dahlia hired him despite his limited typing skills. His job was to greet the mayor's guests and keep his appointments.

By the end of the week, Camilo—a quick study—knew the mayor's favorite restaurants. And, by the second week, he knew both his wife and mistress. Another week or two and he'd hopefully get the information they needed.

It had taken extra time, but Camilo's insistent questions uncovered a Dahlia-derived fact: the mayor not only supported the winery, he'd also lobbied several council members to support it.

Camilo set out to confirm from the big oso's mouth if what Dahlia told him was true. He cornered the mayor while she was away on break.

"Excuse me Mr. Mayor, but I'd like to ask you a question about the winery Gilbert Córdova is planning for Dogtown."

The mayor, walking at a fast clip past Camilo's desk, stopped and faced his assistant. "What is it you want to know?" he replied, his eyes bulging with suspicion.

Camilo flattened his hands on his desk. "I just wanted to make sure I'm on the same page with everyone here about you fully supporting the project." He offered a benevolent smile.

"Let me put it this way Mr.—what did you say your name was?"

"Camilo."

"Mr. Camilo. If I thought this was any of your business I would have scheduled a private meeting and told you about it. Since it isn't, I've nothing to say. Entendido?"

Camilo calmly returned Rolo's gaze. "Then you should know, sir, I've been receiving calls from the governor's office, city council, the media, residents of Dogtown, and a lot of people you refer to as big shots, about the project, so it seems to be part of the office's business, which I believe, makes it part of mine."

Rolo gave his mustache a momentary scratch. He followed with a full ratchet of his shoulders shifting forty pounds of panza into Camilo's face. "You know, you don't look like you've been off the tit long enough to talk to me like that. It seems *I'm* the goddamn mayor of this city and that makes me in charge of what's your business. Keep this up and I'll have your scrawny little ass out of here so fast, you won't even remember working for me."

Camilo didn't blink. He stood up and faced the mayor. "There's no reason for you to speak to me in this manner . . . sir. It's not very nice, especially since I simply asked you a business-related question." Out of the corner of his eye he spotted Dahlia returning to her desk with an open can of root beer. She had inserted a straw into the can and took a long, long sip before stepping between the two men.

"Uh, gentlemen, is there something I can be of assistance with?"

Rolo waved Camilo away. "You deal with him. I don't have time for this insubordinate crap." He marched to his office, opened the door, and slammed it.

"What happened?" she asked, her chin shifting upward with concern.

"I'm not sure," Camilo replied, truly confused. "Does he always respond to business questions with such fury?"

Dahlia lowered her chin. "Only if they're direct. Look," she whispered, glancing at the mayor's door. "Don't take it personal. He's like this with everyone." She paused. "Well, maybe not with me." She swallowed more soda. "Hey, why don't you go on a break? On second thought," she peeked at her watch. "Maybe you should just go home early. We can count it an eight-hour day, huh?" Smiling, she tapped him on the shoulder.

Camilo countered with his own look of concern.

"Go on," she continued. "Everything will be fine. He has his moments. When you come back tomorrow, he'll act like nothing ever happened."

❀

Tala called the CURs to an emergency meeting at the Hungry Chula. To give them privacy, Benny Lucero gave them the small banquet room in the back. Paneled with wood, the room was dark, but Benny loved candles and made sure there were always several lit on the table. He'd also hung papel picado across the ceiling, adding cheer to the place. Tala felt better that they were meeting in a private room since her parents or their friends would be less likely to see her with the other CURs.

"The Vino Latino's meeting with the Rolo ball in a couple days." Tala pulled out her meeting notes. "Cam, as the mayor likes to call him," she said, nodding toward Camilo, "found out Rolo's on board with the winery—even lobbied other council members to support it."

Everyone looked at Camilo, who nodded in agreement. "Y también, not only do they support it, they'll all get three cases of wine every year just to help him make it happen. It's not much, but when I checked the city charter, it's technically against policy."

"What are their names?" Pepa asked between bites of frijoles.

Camilo paused to think. "I don't know, but it's all of them except Domingo Salazar and Darlene McCorkle."

"McCorkle?" asked Nina, looking surprised. "She's got more ovaries than I thought."

"Either that or she's just not part of the men's club," offered Jules.

"Speaking of men, Cam, can you change the oil in my truck? I could use some help now that Tala's spare time is so occupied." Nina playfully batted her eyelashes.

"Claro que sí," Camilo replied with a deep he-man voice. "Right after I learn how to drive."

Everyone laughed.

"Would you two stop! We're trying to have a meeting here." Tala, slightly exasperated, took a sip of coffee and looked back at her notes. "Gilbert's spending tons of time on this project—most of it with Bill Takash and investors. Bill's got most of the i's dotted, and I have to meet Gilbert after he sees the mayor to give him an appraisal of what the Doggies are doing. If I can get Nina and Camilo's attention, perhaps we can work out the details . . ."

The meeting continued another hour. As they wrapped things up, Jules looked worried. "I don't know," he said, speaking softly. "We've been kind of light about this tonight, but from the looks of it, Gilbert might have this thing in the bag."

"Not yet," countered Camilo.

"Camilo's right. We're not giving up without a fight," added Pepa.

"Then if you all don't mind," Jules paused, glancing around the table. "I'd like to make an announcement."

They immediately halted their tasks to listen.

"I recently received a small amount of cash from my Aunt Tutti."

"Good for you," said Nina, giving Jules a happy pat on the back.

He smiled at Nina and continued. "She's getting up in age and sold a small piece of property, sent me part of it as a gift. It wasn't a lot—to be honest, it was ten thousand dollars. But I'd like to donate half of it to our cause."

"You what?" said Tala. "Aren't you on a zero income?"

"Yes, but this is a windfall. Plus I can get a job teaching or something. I just see us needing a jolt of cash to help us with publicity, a Web site, photocopying, whatever. It's not much, but it's something I'd like to do."

No one said a word.

"Uh, so, are you OK with this?" He looked around the table.

"Pues, sí," answered Pepa. "We need the money."

"We do," added Camilo.

"Then it's done." Jules grinned. "And if you all don't mind, I'd like to be more active with the CURs. I'm not sure of what I can do to help us, but I learn fast, and like I said, I'm willing to do whatever it takes."

"Bueno, then. Thank you," said Tala. "That's very generous. We'll open a CURs bank account tomorrow in your Aunt's honor. What's her last name?"

Jules blushed. "It's Taylor. She's on my mom's side of the family."

"OK. Let's keep it simple. How 'bout if we call it the Tutti Taylor Terroirists fund?"

Everyone started laughing.

"Sounds great," said Jules, grinning. "Sounds really good."

Three days later, Camilo called Tala with the news. "Your brother left the mayor's office this morning with a big smile on his face."

Tala sighed. "Well, I guess Rolo went for it."

"I have to tell you," Camilo added, "I don't think I've ever seen anyone leave his office with a smile."

"I'm sure we'll find out later what they're offering." Tala looked at her watch. "I'm meeting the Vino Latino now for lunch. Thanks for the heads up."

Gilbert sat at the table grinning as Tala rushed in to greet him. "He went for it. I'm in, man. I'm in!"

Tala, her acting skills considerably better since their last encounter, smiled brightly. "Good for you, Bro."

Not seeming to notice the irony of Tala's comment, he looked around for a waiter. "This calls for a celebration. How 'bout champagne?"

"Sorry, no can do. I have to get back to work. I was nearly useless the last time I drank with you at lunch." Gilbert gave her a hurt puppy dog look, a face that used to work its way into Tala's soft spot, but she kept her emotions in check. "Sorry, Gil. Mom and Dad will want to celebrate with you. Take them out tonight. They'll love it."

The two of them ordered. This time Tala insisted on their meeting at the Cowgirl BBQ. The bar itself was a beautiful hunk of cottonwood, and the owner had added wapiti antlers on the wall above it. Everything felt festive and alive with colored lights strung inside and out. The added bonus, which Tala neglected to mention, was the beautiful waitstaff consisting entirely of tough femmes, Tala's favorite.

"Let's see," Gilbert said, examining the wine list. "This place serves good barbeque, so I should probably get a Zin." He perused the menu, set it aside, and gestured toward the waitress. She hurried over, and he ordered something that seemed to make him happy. "So, what's new in the land that time forgot?"

"Very funny," Tala replied. The waitress returned, showed Gilbert the bottle, and patiently held it for his approval. He nodded and she opened it.

Tala put her hand over her wine glass. "I'm not drinking." The waitress smiled, put the bottle on the table, and took away the glass.

"Sooo," Tala continued, pulling out a notebook. "No surprise, but the people in Dogtown have already heard about the deal. And the majority don't want to leave."

"And you ascertained this by—"

"Hiring DeLoitte and Touche." Her brother almost believed her. "By phone calls and meetings, how else would we do it?" She took a drink of water. "Anyway, I also spoke with the four business owners there, and they said they're not leaving either."

Gilbert took a sip of wine. "And these are?"

"Benny Lucero of the Hungry Chula—"

"Roach-laden dive."

"Mrs. Gallegos of the Ojos del Rey—"

"Store from the dark ages."

"Papa Chick and his Laundromat—"

"Washing machines that don't."

"And Pepa Romero of—"

"Old school hocus pocus."

Tala gripped the chair under the table, doing her best to stay in control. "You know, these businesses, especially Pepa's, are vital to the community." She took another drink of water. "Pepa's been healing people for three decades."

Gilbert, chewing on a tortilla chip, nearly choked. "She's a quack, man! Besides, she's been ripping off the town since time immemorial. They'll probably thank me for putting her out of business."

"On second thought, I think I'm going to have some of that wine of yours." Tala drained the last of her water and reached across the table to pour wine into her now empty glass.

"You know if you drink wine out of its proper glass it tastes better." Gilbert looked appalled.

"This one's working fine." She drank several gulps, which made her brother cringe.

"How can you do that to a good glass of wine?"

"Do what?" Tala replied, setting down the glass.

"Uh, can we talk business now?" Gilbert asked, his voice on edge.

"You're the one talking about how I'm drinking wine." She took another drink. "Go ahead."

"OK," he continued, eyeing Tala's glass. "So the way I see it, none of these businesses amount to much. We'll make them offers so they can either retire, since most of them are up in age, or render enough cash to move their businesses some place else. Problem solved." He talked like a magician showing off a new trick.

Tala studied his fancy jacket and Rolex watch. She recalled him always being careful about his appearance—especially when he'd left for college. He had said he was entering a white man's world and needed to dress the part. "And what are you proposing for the people who actually *live* there?"

Gilbert took another sip of wine and held the glass up to the light before answering. "This wine's got nice legs . . ."

"Gilbert."

"Huh? Well that's a little more complicated," he said, setting down his glass. "It's based on whether they're owners or not, have mortgages paid off, or are simply renters. The planning consultant I hired worked out a deal based on fair market value—"

"Good!"

"Well, fair market value for the area."

"Is it better than your first proposal?"

"Yeah, it is," he said, raising a hand to hold Tala back. "The details are in his report. But I'm pretty sure everyone will be happy with what we'll offer them. Heck, some of them might even get a job out of this. So, in a sense, I'm giving back to the community." He shrugged a half smile.

"I'm not sure I understand this kind of giving." Tala finished her wine and reached for the bottle.

Gilbert grabbed it first and, hoisting it high, signaled for the waitress. "Excuse me, Miss, could you get her a wine glass, please? It seems she's changed her mind about drinking." The waitress eyed Gilbert and left.

"Seems like my glass is awfully important." The waitress returned with both wine and water glasses. "Happy now?" asked Tala.

"Like I said, a proper glass will correctly enhance the nuance of the wine."

"Is it similar to the nuance of jerking people around?"

"Come on, Tala! Those Dogtownies are a bunch of dust motes. They wouldn't move if their life depended on it. But I guarantee you, once they see the cash, they'll jump ship."

"No, they won't because you're forcing them to leave."

"No, I'm not! They'll elect to move on their own. People move all the time. Hell, I moved three times before I found a house I liked. Everyone moves. Even you'll move to hopefully a nicer place. You and some of these people are making this out to be a bigger problem than it actually is. You know," he said, smacking the table, "it's such a pain in the ass doing business here! Everyone hates change, even when it's for their own good! You'd think I was doing something bad to these people! The whole neighborhood's going to profit on this!"

Tala noticed a few heads turning in their direction.

"I mean, hell. I've been totally on the up and up with this. Totally legit!"

Now the waitstaff had stopped what they were doing to see what was wrong.

"Gilbert!"

"What?"

"You're talking loud enough for the cooks in the kitchen to hear you. Would you cool it?" Tala gulped down half of her water. "Try to put yourself in their place. How would you feel if you were getting kicked out—"

"Bought out," he said. "There's a difference, you know."

"OK, *bought* out of their homes. People don't like to be told they have to leave, even if they are living in what you call dives or getting what you think are good offers."

"They *are* good offers."

Tala shook her head in dismay. "You know what's wrong with you? You've been gone too long and don't know what it's like to make a living in this town now. How hanging on to your home—as old and decrepit as it is—might be all that's keeping these people alive."

"Oh, brother." Gilbert threw his napkin on the table. "I thought you were a capitalist, not a social worker."

Tala felt her face flush with anger. "I don't know who you are anymore. And you're not hearing anything I'm saying because you only see what *you* want."

"And what about you? I don't feel any support coming from you, and you're my sister. You could be helping me out a little more with this, you know—help us as a family."

Tala stared at her brother as if he'd just spoken a strange, new language. "That's interesting. I've never heard you refer to me as being part of this 'us' before." She leaned forward, elbows propped on the table. "The way I've seen it, 'us' has only meant the men in the family. So when you say I should do this for us, I get a little confused. Because us is not working at the feed store. It seems I am. And us isn't helping out Mom and Dad with things they can't do anymore. So even though I know you really want this winery, I have a hard time thinking I'm part of the 'us' team since I wasn't asked to be part of the deal in the first place. The only reason you seem to be calling me an 'us' person now is that you have to kick me out of my house, and my being your sister complicates it."

"I'm giving you a fair market rate," he replied, pointing. "And in my book that makes you a partner."

Tala laughed. "I'm not sure what business school your consultant went to, but that doesn't make me a partner."

Gilbert's jaw muscles flexed. "Well, I guess I know where you stand."

"Likewise," Tala replied.

Gilbert picked up his napkin and set it back on his lap. "I swear I didn't include you in the plan because I honestly didn't think you'd be interested."

"Really? So it had nothing to do with me living where you want to build it?"

"I—well, forget it. It's water under the bridge. You're living your life now and so am I." The waitress appeared with their lunch. "Look, this thing's important to me." He studied the platter of ribs in front of him. "But it doesn't mean I don't care about the people who need to leave—or about you, because I do."

Tala felt completely confused. "What?"

"I'm not a mean, heartless ogre, you know." He picked up a rib then set it down. "But what I want—actually, what I *need* from you is to see this from my perspective, see how much it means to me."

"And what if I don't?"

"Then you and I are going to have really big problems."

16

TALA PARKED HER TRUCK across the street from Pepa's house, tucked her rooster under her arm, and pulled her dog along by the collar. Neither pet took kindly to staying cooped up in the truck. With Otis squirming to get free, Tala walked into Pepa's yard, pausing to watch her light five urns with incense. After each was lit, Pepa placed them around the perimeter, blowing softly on the coals to make sure they stayed alight. The slightly bittersweet aroma drifted throughout the courtyard, circling worried faces and lending dusky anticipation to the evening's meeting. Tala figured the incense was Pepa's attempt to keep everyone calm since the CURs had called the meeting to prepare Dogtowners for the mayor's announcement.

Tala noticed several white candles flickering along the faded rail fence. A few people brought their own chairs, tethered in the beds of pickups. Tala let the rooster go and surveyed the worried crowd that had grown considerably larger from their first community meeting. She saw Nina and waved, then waited for Pepa to give the signal to begin. Pepa blew on the last bit of incense to make sure it was going before giving Tala the nod.

"We called this meeting today to update you on the winery situation." Since they couldn't tell anyone Camilo was spying, the CURs decided to give rough estimates of what the mayor was going to propose. "Renters will get a flat fee. Owners will get what the city *considers* fair market value." Tala scanned the worried faces. "All of you will probably get more money than what you paid for your house or business. But it will be less than what your home is truly worth. They're saying we live in a 'dilapidated community,' so fair market value might not sound so fair."

Opal McGee stood up. "Who's saying we live in a dilapidated community? I have a sweet home on a street where I can look out and can see the Sangre de Cristo Range. What the hell kind of dilapidated is that?"

Papa Chick stood up next. His faded blue overalls were covered with a coating of white dust. Tala nodded to the grizzled old man, knowing he had probably been working on some kind of upgrade at his Laundromat. Her dog stood quietly at his side sniffing him. "So you telling me we're not getting what we think our businesses are worth? I just spent two days putting up drywall trying to keep things looking nice."

"And from falling down," snickered someone in the back.

Papa Chick looked around to see who had said it. Not seeing who it was, he shooed the dog away and continued, "I ain't too pleased with what I hear you saying." He eyed Tala, then turned back, still searching for the smart-ass in the crowd.

"Y yo, I can't start over," said Mrs. Gallegos, leaning on the chair in front of her. "Where would I go?" She looked over at Papa Chick. "*Some* of the people here might want the money, pero some of us don't."

"Hell! I didn't say I wanted the money!" answered Papa Chick, glaring now at Mrs. Gallegos. "Don't be putting words in my mouth, woman!"

Tala signaled Nina to speak next. She walked to the front of the crowd, dazzling in tight jeans and T-shirt. Tala watched her survey the audience, hands on narrow hips.

"None of the people working on this deal live here. The way I look at it, we got just as much right to live here as anyone else." Right then Otis hopped on the podium and crowed. Everyone laughed. Nina rolled her eyes and continued. "But these guys got some sneaky-ass lawyers." She paused to smile at Elena Luján. "And they're gonna try to find some kind of Manifest Destiny way to kick us out."

"Thank you, Nina, and thank you, Otis." Tala returned to the podium, picked up the rooster, and set him down. She felt it was time to move the meeting along and signaled to Elena to step up. "Now, I'm pleased to report that we have the fabulous lawyer, Elena Luján, representing our cause. And Elena, I might add, is working pro bono on the case." Several people clapped and cheered.

Elena gave a grateful nod to Tala as she stood up to give her report. "Right now I can't do much of anything until Gilbert sends you an offer, which, as you know, he intends to do soon. However, since he's attempting to build a winery in a residential zone, he needs the city to make a zoning change to allow commercial development. Once the city goes about doing this, I'll file a complaint saying your due process rights were violated, which is your right as residents to present an objection to the change. I'll get the complaint ready and will file it as soon as the city acts."

"Then what?" asked Opal McGee.

"Then we try to keep the zone residential so he can't build here."

"Will it work?" asked Tala.

"I'm not sure. It depends on how far we can take this and, if so, what kind of judge we're assigned. We may not even get assigned to a judge, in which case the city can go ahead and make the zoning change despite our objection. Still, it's the first step, and it's an important one."

"What happens if ese zoning change gets the go ahead?" asked Cleto Salcido, petting Tala's dog, who had moved to a person with a more active petting hand.

Tala noticed a brief glimmer of worry flash across Elena's face. "Well, this isn't the first time something like this has happened. In fact, it's happening more and more every day, particularly in poor communities. We'll just keep fighting till we win." She raised her fist up, and the crowd gave her an enthusiastic response of claps and whistles.

"Bueno, then, sí se puede, no?" asked Cleto, looking around.

"Sí, sí," was the reply to the old man, complete with a few chuckles.

"I mean we gotta believe we can fight this, que no?" Cleto continued.

"If we don't believe, then it doesn't happen," Elena replied, stepping back from Otis, who had swooped up again to the podium next to her. The Dogtownies seemed to agree, at least for the moment, and the meeting was adjourned.

"I feel more optimistic," Tala said to Elena after the meeting.

"Why's that?" Elena asked, gathering her papers.

"I don't know. I guess having a lawyer—especially having you—makes me feel a little more empowered." She smiled hopefully.

Elena put a hand on her shoulder. "You know if that were true, I'd be a hell of a rich woman." She lowered her hand, then stepped past Tala without looking back.

17

TRUE TO HIS WORD, THE MAYOR, in conjunction with Gilbert Córdova, called a meeting a week later with the residents of Dogtown. Since there wasn't a hall big enough in the neighborhood, the two of them thought it best to have the meeting at the Rancho del Rio Park. The "park," set in the far west corner of Dogtown, was no more than a patch of dirt and four raggedy barbecue pits. Several dried up cottonwood trees flanked the pits, giving off a slim memory of shade. The mayor hadn't been out this way in a while, and couldn't recall it ever looking so bad. Gilbert informed him, however, that this was one of the prime areas he wanted to develop, which pleased the mayor, since he wouldn't have to comment on improving it. Gilbert had decided at the last minute to rent chairs as a goodwill gesture. He checked his watch, pacing back and forth as he waited for the mayor. Glancing at the sky, he searched for any clouds on the horizon. Seeing none, he continued gawking above him since he felt the sky was one of the best things about New Mexico. Almost a day didn't go by where it didn't offer a stunning performance. Yet, as he studied the dusty terrain and sunburnt trees, he wondered if the place was ever going to see rain again.

The mayor arrived later than expected. Gilbert pulled him aside to tell him the residents weren't happy about the winery. But in typical fashion, the mayor brushed it off. So after he proposed the "new partnership between Gilbert and Dogtown," what he heard in response was immediate grumbling.

"What the hell's going on?" Rolo whispered to Gilbert during a passionate speech by Opal McGee. "I thought they'd be going for this."

Gilbert shook his head. He had been troubled ever since his sister told him it was going to be a tough sell. He had secretly hoped the mayor's power would help persuade, or at least coerce, the residents to go along with the project. Now he only saw distrust and anger. He'd been reasonably warned but couldn't help feeling frustrated. His intentions were clear and about as fair as he could make them. It's true he wanted to develop the land where these people lived, but what did they expect for a bunch of rundown houses anyway?

While the mayor answered the old lady's questions, Gilbert looked around to see who else was there. He spotted a priest and a tall white guy he didn't know, along with Pepa, Nina, and Domingo Salazar. With Gilbert's mother home nursing a headache, his father had joined him in support. Seated across from him was that pain in the ass lawyer, Elena something or another. Bill had warned him about her, said if she got involved it was going to be a tougher go. Way in the back, standing next to a cop, was his sister, watching the proceedings. He hoped, despite her misgivings about the winery, that she would come on board with the project. He needed her to convince these diehards to move.

Sweating despite the evening's cooling air, the mayor asked for everyone's patience so that Bill Takash could present the details. Bill gave the figures, finishing to cold stares and hisses.

It was apparent that the town hall was a waste of time, and Rolo twirled his finger around, saying "let's wrap it" to Gilbert and Bill. The Dogtownies looked tired, and the wind had picked up, rustling through the desiccated branches overhead. Before Rolo could end things, though, their lawyer rose to speak.

"Mayor Reyes," Elena said with the smooth cadence of practice. "My firm has offered to represent this group of citizens during these proceedings. They've met with me in anticipation of Mr. Córdova's proposal. In this spirit, though they have yet to receive official offers, I should inform you that the majority of the people living within the perimeter of Juanita Street, Salazar Avenue, Camino de Angel, Taos Street, and Santa Clara Boulevard, commonly known as Dogtown, are opposed to this development. They are unofficially notifying you that they reject this offer and will choose, instead, to remain in their homes and businesses."

The crowd let out a big cheer. Domingo raised his fist in the air, while Nina gave the lawyer a thumb's up. Gilbert looked for his sister, wanting to see her reaction. Instead, she was staring straight at him with an I-told-you-so face.

Having nothing to lose, he rolled back his shoulders and asked the mayor to stand next to him as he proceeded toward the mike. He unbuttoned his jacket, took it off, and tossed it over an empty chair. "Señores y señoras," he paused to look everyone over. "Soy un Manito, a native New Mexican, just like most of you here. What I'm asking you to do today is listen for a moment. I know this is a tough thing to consider. I, too, grew up in Santa Fe and feel where I lived is very special."

"A lot nicer, too," someone heckled.

Gilbert continued with barely a glance toward the heckler. "But I worked hard to raise the money, not only for the winery, but to fairly compensate you all. This includes not only those of you who own homes and businesses, but the renters, too. I believe this project can be an opportunity, obviously not only for me, but for all of us. Where else in town would you be able to see an entire community make a new beginning? The money I'm paying you will allow some of you to buy a new house or a new business. And, for those of you who don't own homes, an opportunity to have enough for a down payment on something you can call your own."

"You forgot to say where they'd be living," Elena called out.

Gilbert ignored her. "This winery will be something wonderful for Santa Fe. Not only will we be able to make the best wine in the state of New Mexico, we'll be creating new jobs. A winery doesn't run itself. It needs people to run it—people like you. So before you reject my offer I ask that when you receive it in the mail, to think carefully and consider this a chance for a new beginning. Gracias." He looked up and saw Tala still watching him.

A stunned silence followed. Gilbert nodded and waved goodbye. As he walked away with the mayor, Rolo turned and gave him a half smile. "Oye, hombre, where'd you learn to talk like that?" The two paused near the mayor's car. "That was a good speech, man." He touched Gilbert's elbow. "Most of the people I deal with talk out of their assholes. You got talent. Let me know if you ever think about running for something."

Gilbert bowed his head and smiled. It was the last thing he'd want to do. He still felt worried about his argument with Tala and scared about his winery. And he was completely frustrated with all the mayor's bullshit. "Thanks, Mayor Reyes, I'll be sure to let you know."

18

PEPA CLOSED HER DOOR and gratefully turned the key. The day, finally over, had been too goddamn busy. Ever since Camilo had begun his spy work on Rolo, she'd been putting in longer and longer days at the clínica. She hadn't realized how much she'd grown to depend on Camilo and looked forward to his return. As luck would have it, the CURs felt he had garnered enough information, at least for now, so he gave a two-week notice and quit in good standing. Despite his poor typing skills, he was a conscientious worker, which pleased Dahlia, who told him she was sad to see him go.

Pepa and Camilo spoke about his work on a hike up the mesa the Monday after he'd quit. "Eeee, Pepa," Camilo said, kicking aside an old pinecone. "That mayor is awful. I've never seen anyone lie so much. I don't think he even knows *how* to tell the truth. He always changes a story just so that he gains some kind of advantage. He wants everyone, especially white people, to look up to him, como un gran patrón."

"He doesn't like gabachos?" This was perplexing to Pepa since she knew that having the support of ricos, who were primarily Anglos, was a key component to acquiring power in the city.

"Oh, no. He has to meet with them and everything, of course, and he never says bad stuff, at least not directly. But I can tell by the way he acts that he doesn't like them. And I noticed he doesn't hire white people if he can get away with it—just a few here and there. That way no one accuses him of favoritism. Pero, I can't believe no one's caught on. Even his mistresses aren't white—every other color—given what I saw come into the office, but definitely not white."

"Hmmph, can't say it's a surprise." Pepa stopped to look for any clouds. Seeing none she continued. "Hay mucha gente aquí who don't like gabachos. Pero, hay muchos gabachos who don't like la gente, tampoco. I'm not sticking up for him. All I'm saying is it's too bad he's that way, too." Pepa wondered if people would ever really stop the age-old anti-gabacho, anti-Chicano prejudice in this state.

"Sí, and he sure doesn't want anyone to know it."

"Pero it's not a secret anymore, is it?" Pepa said, smiling. She threw a stick for the dogs, who grabbed it in a tug-of-war. "Y esta winery del Gilbert. The mayor's a personal investor, que no?"

"Well, yah. We know he put in his own money, but we don't know how much. So I worked late one night and went through the winery file and found an anonymous investor who put in fifty thousand."

"You think it was him?"

"Probably. I can't find his name anywhere, but I'll bet it's him. And unless Rolo's lying, several city council members put in at least ten thousand each. He told me himself, once he started to trust me, that they'd invested as silent partners."

"De veras?"

"Sí. They figure they'll make a nice percentage of the profits once the winery gets going."

Pepa watched her footing, as this part of the trail, now parched and dry, was more treacherous. "Bueno, we have to make sure that lawyer, cómo se llama?"

"Elena Luján."

Pepa nodded as she walked. "She needs to know that mayor is a cabrón, y también a lying one."

Camilo started laughing. "Pero, don't you think everyone knows that?"

"No, I think they only know he's a cabrón. I don't think they know how much of a lying one he is."

"What do you mean?"

Her eyes followed the mesas to the mountains. "The mayor thinks only about the mayor." She turned to face him. "He doesn't care about other people, not the city—not even his wife." Her eyes crinkled with concern. "One look at him and you can tell he likes to—cómo se dice?—" she paused, "call the shots. With his power, even his big gut." Camilo laughed. "Don't laugh, because that man has a hole in his heart. And those kinds of people hardly ever change."

They arrived at the top of the mesa. Pepa lit a cigarette. Her eyes drifted away, absorbed in thought. She sighed, then carefully tapped her ash. "Bueno, you ready to start helping me today?"

"You bet," Camilo said, smiling. "I like being your assistant."

"You know you're more than that." Pepa finished her smoke, then the two began their descent.

"I came here to help you. And that means doing whatever you need." Camilo threw another stick for the dogs.

Pepa studied the man, wondering what other things he could do. They left the trail and entered the neighborhood, encountering the usual pack of street dogs, half of which swarmed Camilo like a new age St. Francis.

"I think los perros are glad to have you back, too." Pepa watched them prance about. "I don't think I've ever seen these dogs so happy."

Camilo squatted and petted every dog. Some actually looked like they were smiling.

They continued walking. Turning the corner on to their street they saw several patients waiting. "I sure am glad you're back, mijo." Pepa grabbed Camilo and gave him a hug.

"So am I."

19

JULES NEVER REALIZED HOW quitting his job would keep him so busy. He'd been spending hours in libraries or on the web, pursuing all the clues on nuclear fallout he could find. He'd also toured numerous cemeteries throughout the state, recording who had passed away during the 1940s and at what age. Before leaving the lab, he had tried his best to acquire as much information as possible on fallout drift during the testing phase of the atom bomb, but he found it difficult to obtain everything he wanted. The data, considered top-secret, had been sequestered away in an onsite, but off-limits, location. Still, he was relentless, searching for anything related to nuclear testing or worker illness, using the Freedom of Information Act to the best of his abilities.

What kept throwing him off, though, was not his research, but this woman, Luz. They started dating, slowly at first, their attraction growing as they began spending more time together. Jules had always regarded himself as a steady, even-keeled man. His passion had been dedicated most of his life to his work. Most women found him handsome, but boring. The second he saw Luz, though, something inside him jiggled free. Just looking at her aroused him. And even when he wasn't with her he found himself doing things he'd never done before, like cooking, writing poetry, and playing salsa music. After successfully baking his first chocolate cake from scratch, he realized he'd been in suspended animation for most of his thirty-eight years. When he found himself smiling for what appeared to be no reason, he finally had to admit that he might be falling, or at least stumbling, into love.

Luz, on the other hand, who'd given up finding a Mr. Mediocre, much less a Mr. Right, had been thrown a left hook. Usually, she went for short, brown, and outgoing, but she had been completely taken by this tall, quiet, gabacho. Was it his smile? His jeans? Scruffy cowboy boots? Quién sabe, pero it drove her beyond cultural control. And she especially liked how he listened to her when she talked, his eyes glimmering with attention. Yet it was more than this, something she couldn't explain. Being around Jules pushed her to examine the landscape of New Mexico in ways she hadn't thought of much before. The mountains stunned her, even the desert night sky. More puzzling was the big smile now greeting her in the mirror each morning. And the colors had changed, from red, yellow, and blue to vermilion, ocher, and sapphire. Fantasizing most of her life about wanting to paint, she decided to make it happen, marching over to the Art-Mart to sign up for a watercolor class. She was almost scared to admit, as she purchased her brushes and supplies, that she might be falling for this good-looking güero.

Given all the love fireworks, Luz could barely concentrate. She had put off sleeping with Jules, telling him she wanted the timing to be perfect. Though, truthfully, she was a teensy bit nervous. But the day arrived when she found herself lying next to him, naked in bed. Luz eyeballed the long, lean, freckled body alongside her and realized she was going to have to adjust her man-looking lenses. Truth be told, she had never lain so close to skin so white and blond hair so plentiful on one man's body.

As she and Jules ogled each other, her thoughts flashed to the story of *Moby Dick*, a book that had been assigned by her teacher in high school. She never forgot how Moby's whiteness thrust from the black sea and wondered why Ahab couldn't have chased some other giant, colored whale. Surely, there were plenty of other colored whales around, maybe some bigger than even Moby. Yet Ahab wanted only the white one. Luz had written a term paper on the book, and with the exception of the small detail of Ahab's leg getting bit off, she stated that he only wanted the whale because he was white. She remembered thinking the book was simply a story about a white man obsessed with himself, only bigger. Luz's teacher told her she was way off the mark and handed back her paper with a big, fat *D*.

And now, as Luz looked at her love lying beside her, with skin so milky it almost appeared blue, she faced her own Mobyfied challenge. If she'd been given a choice, she would have chosen a color easier on the eyes, maybe caramelo, cinnamon, or walnut. Instead she had a Moby, and she sure as hell wasn't Ahab.

She took a deep breath and ran her fingers across Jules's chest . . . There. That wasn't so hard. It still felt manly and chest-like. She stroked his arm . . . No problem there, either. It was like a lot of other arms she'd felt in the past. She glanced at his belly and took another breath. Well, no use holding back. She reached out and felt the muscles on his stomach, startled by the brown of her hand against his skin.

Jules, touch-starved muchacho that he was, felt like Luz was doing a slow, sexy inflammation of his senses. He felt the heat rise in him with each touch of her hand. He hadn't been caressed by a woman for so long, he was embarrassed by all the things that started to take off. He cared about Luz, and this only accelerated his desire.

Sensing his heat, Luz countered with a shift in her own body. Slowly, she saw a new kind of beauty in him, something fun, sexy, and sweet. She grabbed his face and kissed him hard. As she felt him against her, her desire thickened, and she knew he'd be OK, Moby skin and all. I can get used to it, she thought, kissing him again. I could.

✺

Pepa was the first to notice something peculiar about her daughter. Over at Irma's one Saturday morning, as she attempted to fill her in on the latest Dogtown chisme, the two sat jabbering in Irma's Lay-Z-Boys, a table between them stocked with coffee and bizcochitos. Irma loved cartoons, and the TV blasted an old Bugs Bunny number, but the two barely glanced at the rabbit's latest caper. Pepa told Irma about the town hall meeting with Gilbert and the mayor. Then she checked on Irma's leg, which looked almost good as new.

"Changing the subject, you seen Luz around lately?" Pepa sat up straight in the Lay-Z-Boy and lit a cigarette.

"As a matter of fact, I saw her yesterday at the Paisano Market. Her hair looked different. She cut it?"

"No." Pepa narrowed her eyes. "You notice anything else?"

"You know, now that I think about it, she smiled at me."

"She's different, no?" Pepa eyed her friend as she exhaled her cigarette.

"Well, now that you say it, I thought there was something about her I couldn't quite put my foot on." Irma bit off another piece of cookie and chewed.

"You noticed, right? She's changed. And it's been since she started dating that gabacho."

"¿Quién?"

"El Jules . . . el hombre who worked for Los Alamos. The one who's helping us con esta pinche winery. "

"¿El güero?"

"Sí. At first I didn't say nothing, because it was making me kind of mad."

"¿Por qué?" Irma said, snapping what was left of the cookie in two.

"Bueno, because he worked at the lab. But since I couldn't say nothing to Luz, I asked Camilo to give me a limpia. Y también, I was drinking lots of té de manzanilla . . . and well, a little wine, you know, to help make me más tranquila."

"And?" Irma popped the cookie in her mouth.

"OK, it helped. I felt a little better." Pepa put out her cigarette and immediately lit another. "I think la Luz likes este hombre a lot. I mean a lot, a lot. And I think he likes her, too. I've never seen her like this. She's happy. Now, you might remember that girl has never been happy. When she was little she cried and cried and cried. And when she grew up, she still cried. But now, she smiles all the time and gives me jerky for free. She even gave a bag of rejects to my dog, when I know she used to sneak them into what she sold her customers. And, on top of that, she's painting. Painting! Sunsets, sunrises, cats, trees, even dogs. A qué cabrón I thought when I saw one of her dog paintings. 'Cause let me tell you, I don't think I've ever seen her pet one! And she's good, too. All this time, who knew she could paint! And that smiling's done something to her face. She used to be so mad her face sagged like a thirsty iguana. Now she looks like she had a face-lift! She even walks different."

Irma slurped her coffee. "Well this is good, que no?"

"Yah, sí it's good, it's good." Pepa waved her hand in the air. "But I think the real reason I started liking este Jules was not because he's good for my daughter."

"No?"

"No . . . Well, a little, I guess."

"Was it because he gave you guys five thousand dollars? That's a lot of money."

"No, that's not the reason either, though I'm glad he gave us the cash." Pepa inhaled her cigarette and released a long stream of smoke. "I gotta tell you that the reason I like him is that he studies what happened when they were making the bomb and what happened when they were testing it."

"De veras?" Irma poured them both another cup of coffee. "You'd think he already knew that stuff."

"No, hombre, they hide it, even to their own workers." She added sugar and absently stirred her coffee. "I think they'd be scared if all the cats on that one got out of the bag."

"But they got that bomb museum in Albuquerque."

"Sí, pero they don't say everything they did. El Jules is trying to find out the same things I've been looking for. And he says he's been thinking about it a long time."

"Qué bueno."

"Mmm-hmm," Pepa replied, then bit into her bizcochito. The cookie's soft crunch released the sweet aroma of anise.

"Maybe you and him can work together?"

"Maybe," Pepa said with a shrug. She grabbed another cookie then got up to change the channel. "We'll see."

20

GILBERT CÓRDOVA PRACTICED HIS new signature over and over till he got all the loops and angles perfect. He thought his name looked pretty damn good in this new style and absolutely gorgeous when he signed it at the bottom of his hot-off-the-press winery stationary. He gave his assistant all the signed letters, instructing her to send them to the residents registered mail. He'd made every resident what he considered a decent offer. True, it wasn't fair market. But it would be ludicrous to give them more. Even that pompous-assed mayor was finally satisfied. He looked out the window, studying the rolling hills of grapes. Hell, it was going to be hard to leave California. Still, he knew, this was the right decision. Now, all he had to do was wait.

Nina tore open her letter and read the first paragraph. "We're in trouble," she said to Tala who was peeking over Nina's shoulder on her front porch. "He's offering me three thousand to move out, which I personally have never seen except in the form of a loan check. Can you imagine what some of the people here are going to do when they see this?"

"He really did it, huh?" Tala read the letter herself. "Oh God, we *are* in trouble. Let's get on the phone to find out who got offered what."

Nina called Pepa, Jules, and Opal, who told her their offers as owners were based on their homes' square footage, with Pepa getting extra for her business. All were given forty dollars a square foot. Nina and Tala continued the phone tree then called up Domingo Salazar and Elena Luján, asking them to a meeting with Jules, Pepa, and Camilo at Pepa's house that evening.

The early summer air remained hot. Pepa raised the windows in the kitchen and opened the front and back doors so the cross-breeze could help cool things down. She lit three white candles and placed them beneath her mother's picture, hoping her spirit would guide them with her wisdom. After pulling in extra chairs, she lit lavender-scented oil to keep everyone calm.

Pepa's dog barked out a greeting at the sound of Tala and Nina at the door. The two walked in with Tala's dog in tow. The dogs loved playing together, and the animals were let loose in the kitchen, while the three stood watching them play. When the others showed up, Pepa shooed the dogs into the waiting room. She offered everyone iced tea, adding cinnamon to her own for an extra punch.

The soothing scent of lavender soon filled the kitchen as Tala started the meeting.

"We've phone-treed most of the neighborhood," she said, as she looked at her tally sheet. "We didn't talk to everyone, but those we did speak with are getting the same offer."

"What's your view about how everyone feels about this?" asked Elena.

Pepa noticed she was still dressed in her business suit. All the phone callers looked at their notes. "I'll go first," said Camilo. "I got three renters out of four interested, and one owner out of five." He glanced at Elena, who had started a tally sheet.

"I called twelve people," said Jules in his soft baritone. "Four renters out of five want it, not a single owner of the seven I talked to did. I'll try the rest tonight." He glanced around the room, then studied the picture of Pepa's mother on the altar.

"Y I called ten people, and six said they're thinking about taking the money. Five of five were renters and one of five were owners." Pepa gave her report then stood next to the back door and lit a cigarette. She held the cigarette toward the screen then exhaled through the gray mesh.

"As for me and Tala," Nina said, "we talked to seventeen people. Six renters out of seven, and two owners out of ten are interested. We also called Papa Chick, Benny, and Mrs. Gallegos. None of them want to go." She got up to refill her glass, then went around freshening the others.

"So it looks, based on your sample tally, that eighteen renters out of twenty-one, and four owners out of twenty-seven are interested in Gilbert's—"

"Ay, Elena, it's Mr. Córdova," Nina corrected with a smile.

"Perdón," said Elena with a lilting tilt of voice. "Mr. Córdova's offer. If this sample is any indication of what the rest of the people feel, then most of the renters and at least fifteen percent of the owners seem interested."

"I knew those assholes would take the money. They ain't got a pot to piss in in the first place, and now that they got a chance to get a few dollars, they're all for signing on the dotted line." Domingo's eyes flashed with anger.

"I didn't think el Gilbert had that much money," Pepa said, rejoining the group. She moved the lavender oil closer to Domingo. "And let me tell you, we'll probably get more owners who'll want to move. The people who live here don't have money. So right from the start I was worried about this. They can take that money and go put a down payment on a trailer or pay off some bills. Or maybe they can use it to move away." Pepa thought about some of her patients whom she called "lost souls." They always seemed to be searching for a purpose in life.

"Well, that's why we're having this meeting," said Tala, petting one of the dogs who'd wandered back in. "We need to know," she said, looking at Elena, "what happens if some of the people want to accept and some don't? And what if it's more renters than owners?"

"That's a really good question," Elena replied. "Gilbert needs *all* the land for this to work out. He can't just create a winery in sections. Having the renters exit makes it easier for the owners to consider selling since they don't have to deal with evictions. Yet the way I look at it," she said, eyes on Tala, "he needs the whole community to buy in."

"Unless," Jules continued, "he gets a significant number who accept his offer. In which case he can level the house and create enough blight to compel others to sell."

"And don't forget he said there were going to be jobs," Camilo said, balancing his chair on two legs.

"I don't know," said Domingo, more controlled now. He grabbed the oil lamp, held it under his nose, and inhaled the lavender-scented air. "If most of the renters want to go for the money, that's still less than half. We got more owners here. He can knock down a house or two, but I think it would take more than a vacant lot to get someone to sell. Where the hell they gonna go?"

"He'll put pressure on everyone and for sure will get the mayor to help him," said Camilo, with the added authority of knowing Rolo. "We just have to convince people not to do it."

"He's right," said Tala looking around.

"Yah, sí," added Pepa. "He is."

Elena took the oil candle from Domingo and stared into its flame. She was silent for a moment, then shifted her gaze back to Tala. "You realize, of course, that doing so will be far easier said than done?"

21

Tala needed to see her parents. She closed up the store, hopped in her truck, and headed for their house. She'd only had Otis in the store that day, and the rooster rode in the front seat, sitting on his favorite towel. For the past several weeks she'd done her best to dodge her feelings about her parents'—or at least her father's—support of Gilbert's winery. But after the offer letters went out, she felt heartbroken over the real possibility of losing her home and seeing the Dogtown residents lose everything. Tala drove through her old neighborhood, the streets quieting as the evening approached. As she turned off Galisteo, the fading sun cast glitter-lit chevrons across the surrounding adobe walls. She couldn't help but think of the changes that lay ahead, the confusion in the eyes of old Mr. Lucero, who couldn't understand why he would have to leave, and the loss of income for Mrs. Gallegos, whose little store was all she had. By the time Tala arrived, she was already in tears.

She parked in the shade, leaving Otis in the truck with the windows cracked since her parents absolutely forbade her to bring in chickens. She wiped her eyes, blew her nose, and knocked on the door. Her mother greeted her with a hug, studying her closely. "Bueno, tell me," she asked, "what's wrong?"

Her father, perhaps hearing her mother's words, came out of the den. He gave Tala a quick once-over. She stood in the living room, shifting slightly from foot to foot. She heard the TV blasting in the back and caught the fragrant scent of beans cooking in the Crock-Pot. But this evening she had no appetite. She glanced at both parents, almost frantic. "Gilbert made an offer to everyone in Dogtown, forty-three renters and owners. Most of the people are sad and scared, and I feel terrible because it's my own brother who's doing this."

Her parents glanced at one another, surprised by her outburst.

"Don't you care about this?" Tala asked.

Her mother led her to the couch, left the room momentarily, and returned with a glass of water. Tala nodded a grateful thank-you and drank it down in one long gulp.

Vince sat in a chair across from Tala, his brow furrowed with worry. "So how do you know so much about this?"

"Well I haven't exactly kept my head in the sand. A lot of people will take the offer because they think they have to or because they need the cash."

"Honey, have you figured out who really wants to leave? Maybe most of them won't go." Tala's mother glanced at her father again.

"We haven't asked everyone, yet, but we think most of the renters will." Tala picked up an ashtray from the coffee table and spun it around. "But lots of people still don't want to move. We had a meeting the other night and some of them were crying and wondering what they were gonna do."

"Tala, cálmate. Your brother doesn't have a done deal, yet. He still needs the city council, the mayor, and everyone who lives there to go along with this." Vince leaned back in his chair, putting his hands behind his head. "I have to admit I think it's a pretty good plan. Gilbert has this idea and he's actually raised the cash. He even says he can give people jobs."

"It's *not* a good plan, Dad," Tala replied. "I can't believe my own parents support my brother doing this." She gave the ashtray another spin.

"Now hold on there, I didn't say I'm totally behind it. You're making me think about this a little more." Vince took a cigar out of his pocket, lit it, and sucked on it for a few seconds. "Have you talked to your brother?"

"Yeah, but he's really set on it—even Marty and Junior gave him money." Tala stared at the ashtray, feeling the impact of straddling between obligations to her family, her neighbors, and her own home and life.

"Honey, maybe we should talk to him? Tala's mother grabbed the ashtray and set it on the coffee table. "Maybe he can go someplace else?" She gave Tala an affectionate squeeze.

"He wants it here because he wants to call it a Santa Fe wine." Vince puffed his cigar. "On top of that, he wouldn't be able to get any of the deals the city's setting up for him, and the ricos, Indians, or government's got most of the other land tied up outside of town. Nah," he took another puff, "Gilbert was in a tough spot, and thought this was the best deal to go with."

"Tough spot? What tough spot? How 'bout losing your home or business? That's what I'd call a tough spot, not making wine."

Vince puffed out a cloud of smoke. Tala hated his stinky cigars. She didn't know how her mother could put up with all that stink inside her home.

"You want more water?" Cleo picked up Tala's cup.

She shook her head as she scrutinized her father. "I know you want this. And it doesn't seem to matter to you that all those people, including me and Nina, will have to move."

"I said I was thinking about it," Vince replied, his eyes hot.

"Yeah, but I can tell you're proud of your high-rolling son and his little backroom deal. Especially since that pinche mayor supports it. You think it's going to make you and Gilbert look good."

"I actually think you better watch how you're talking to me, young lady."

Tala sighed, disappointed. "'A man of la gente,' you always told me, and I believed you. Now I guess I know what gente you're really talking about." Tala got up to leave.

Vince set his cigar in the ashtray then stood up to face her. "Now that I'm thinking about it," he crossed his arms, "it doesn't seem like such a bad deal, except for maybe you, Nina, and a few others. I really think the people in Dogtown, and of course the city, will basically profit from this."

Tala looked, tears in her eyes. She walked toward the door and turned to face her mother. "Mom, thanks for listening."

"What are you going do?" Cleo asked. "What do you want me to do?"

"I don't know," Tala replied, shoulders hunched as she walked out the door. "Find a way to get Gilbert to listen. Or pray for a miracle." She gave her mother a hug, the sun's golden remnants caressing her face. Their eyes momentarily met. Then Tala turned and walked away.

❁

Nina flashed Tala a gap-toothed grin after ordering at the Vita-Eat-a-Vegamin, a new vegan restaurant off Agua Fria. The restaurant had caught on quickly with the locals. Rainbow-hued rebozos and Oaxacan rugs were hung across peach-colored walls. White tablecloths and candles upped the ambience and, to Nina's dismay, the price of the place. The two had just received their drinks when she saw Luz and Jules walk in. Spotting Nina and Tala, the two stopped by their table to say hello.

"How're you all doing?" asked Luz, her eyes sparkling like freshly watered grass. She had added gold streaks to her black hair, giving her a bruja-like quality.

Nina couldn't help staring. "Us?" She glanced over at Tala. "Other than the prospect of losing my house and studio—I can't complain."

Nina switched her gaze to Jules whose hand had been grazing Luz's backside. He looked as if all the creases on his face had melted, like someone had taken putty and smoothed them over.

"Yeah, isn't this whole thing awful?" Luz took off her jacket. "My mother has patients coming out of her ears. They've got susto, telele, stuff she hasn't seen in twenty years. I even have to go over from time to time to grind a few things just to give her and Camilo a hand."

She turned to Jules and gently stroked his face. "Even my poor amorcito had his share of nerves. Didn't you honey?"

Jules nodded, looking embarrassed.

"Well, we're all upset by this," Nina replied.

"You got that right," said Luz, looking like she'd be happy to talk about it for the rest of the evening.

"Honey, you want to sit down?" Jules rubbed her shoulders as he looked around the restaurant for an empty table.

"Yeah, Baby." She squeezed his hand. "Bueno, you girls take care of yourselves. You look so cute together." She patted Nina's arm. "I'll talk to you later."

"Alrighty," Nina replied.

They walked toward an empty table on the other side of the restaurant.

Nina leaned her chin on her hands. "Ever see so much love?" she whispered.

"Is something bothering you?" Tala couldn't help smiling. They glanced at the couple, clearly enmeshed in their oyster-shelled world. "You gotta admit, both of them have changed for the better. Luz actually seems nice."

"Uh-huh," Nina replied, sipping a freshly squeezed limonada.

"And, even though I never knew Jules before all this winery mierda, he does seem more relaxed. Love will do that, you know." Tala smiled as she caressed Nina's hands.

"Yeah, it will, Miss Gotta-Admit. But—OK, I just have to say it." She glanced surreptitiously at the couple now happily kissing each other. "It's a cliché."

"What?" asked Tala, sipping a Bohemia.

"You figure it out." Nina stabbed her vegetarian frijoles.

"'Cause of the white man, brown woman thing?"

"Duh."

"And now that the previously unhappy Luz who's dated hundreds of Chicano guys finally finds love in a big güero, you're having a problem?"

"Yeah. I guess so." Nina glanced around hoping no one was listening. "I mean, I believe in the beauty of love and everything. Plus, who am I to judge who can love and not love, especially given who *I've* chosen to love, but it's a pinche cliché! And not just an ordinary one! It's a Malinche-Pocahontas-Sally-Hemmings-combined cliché."

"You're kinda focusing just on the women, you know." Tala eyed Nina and took another sip of beer.

"Yeah, but it's our own homegrown Dances with Wolves!"

"Nina, can you cool it a little? Any louder and we'll have one less physicist we can count on."

"OK, OK." Nina let out a long, slow breath. She asked the waiter to bring her a margarita. Then she folded her hands on the table in a concerted effort to calm down. "I guess I get worked up a little over these things."

"Not to mention judgmental. Jeez, Nina, I totally agree with you about this cliché thing, but you can't control desire. If that was the case, I'd be with men."

"What?" Nina asked, shocked.

Tala started peeling the label off her beer bottle, studying it like a thirsty sailor. "I would. Everything would be easier. Mom and Dad would quit quibbling about the Church. Relatives would stop whispering behind my back. And I could get married, get tons of free presents, and bask in thousands of heterosexual perks. It's easier being straight. But it just so happens I love you."

"Is this a speech I should be proud of?" Nina asked, rolling her eyes.

"No, Miss High-and-Mighty." Tala took the strips of paper she'd peeled off and wadded them up. "I'm just saying I can't control who I love, just like we can't control who Luz and Jules love."

The waiter brought Nina her drink. She thanked him, took a sip, and sighed. "I guess you're right. I'm just so tired of the white-man-as-savior syndrome."

"It *is* tiresome," Tala agreed, biting a piece of bread "buttered" with tofu spread. "Think we'll ever see a man of color as savior?"

"We already have." Nina picked up the spread, sniffed it, then set it back down.

"Who?" Tala slathered more of the tofu on her bread.

"The Hulk," Nina replied, laughing.

"Very funny."

She took another sip of her margarita. "But you're right. It's really not for me to say who we can and can't love."

"Right," Tala replied, looking more relaxed.

"Doesn't mean I have to like it, though," Nina said, pointing.

"No, it doesn't. And stop pointing."

"I'm not pointing. I'm just making a point."

This time Tala rolled her eyes.

"And it doesn't mean I have to go to their wedding if they get married."

"No, it doesn't because we don't go to weddings anyway." Tala tapped Nina's finger.

"True," Nina nodded. She paused, then returned her gaze to Tala. "You know I love you, Baby. I love you a lot."

"I love you, too, Honey." Tala grabbed both of Nina's hands and held them gently. She glanced over at Jules and Luz. Luz's head was thrown back in laughter.

Nina looked, too. "Shit, they look happy. I guess that's all that matters, no?"

"Absolutely," said Tala, then she gave Nina a kiss.

❈

Two days after Tala and Nina's dinner at the Vita-Eat-a-Vegamin, Tacho, on break, stomped into Pepa's treatment room and demanded that she tell him what was *really* wrong with him.

Pepa gave the once-over to her poor patient. She noticed he looked good, smelled good, but appeared agitated, gripping the handle of his police baton like he'd actually like to use it.

"I was hoping maybe you'd figure that out yourself. It'd be better if you did." Pepa lit a lavender-infused candle and set it on the table. She sat down across from him, her hands folded in her lap. The stern look of her mother's picture seemed to cast a disapproving glance.

"But I don't know what to figure out." Tacho pulled the baton out of his belt and rolled it against the chair beside him. He took off his hat and laid it on the table. "I don't know what I think or feel or nada. I get up each day, do my job, but something doesn't feel right. My mother told me to go see a priest, pero I don't think a priest would help me very much."

"Pienso que it would depend on the priest," Pepa replied, her face crinkled with concern. "Pero, I think your problem, if you want to call it that, can't be helped by the Church."

"No?"

"No."

Tacho leaned in. "Bueno, dígame," he said, gesturing for her to hand him the truth like he was asking for her driver's license.

Pepa rubbed her face, trying to think of the best way to say it. But she was tired. And being tired left her little patience. Finally, in a fit of exasperation, she blurted it out. "Bueno, Tacho, you've been coming to see me every week, but you're wasting my time and your money. I've been trying to get you to look into your heart. Pero, you don't want to. So I'm just gonna have to tell you, I guess." She stood up in front of him, placed her hands on her hips, and looked him straight in the eye, "Bueno, hombre . . . you're gay."

"I'm gay?"

"Sí, you're gay."

"You mean queer gay—" he flattened his palm and waved it—"not happy gay?"

"Well, you could be a happy gay," said Pepa. "I guess it depends."

"Depends . . ." Tacho looked like he'd just fallen out of a tree.

Pepa softened her voice. "This can't be a surprise, que no? Didn't you like boys when you were little? And don't you like men now?"

Tacho's body tensed. He cleared his throat and tapped his fingers on the table. Pepa laid her hand on his arm. "Mira, hombre, it's OK, you know. It's not a bad thing. Lots of people are gay. Gay and proud! People you love. Even cops! All it means is that you love men." She kept her hand on his arm, willing him to listen. "Maybe now you can finally open your heart."

Finally Tacho smiled, his eyes tearing. He stood up and hugged Pepa.

"I guess it makes sense," he said, still holding her close. "I have to do some thinking."

"Just make sure it's good thinking." She grinned and then pulled herself away.

"Gracias for telling me."

"And gracias for not being mad that I did." She squeezed his arm again. "You're gonna be happier now, I promise you."

Tacho wiped his eyes. "I hope so," he said, nodding, "I truly do."

22

"OYE, CAMILO." Pepa spooned a heaping mound of chokecherry jam on her toast and took a big bite. "I just figured out how este Padre Miguel can help us." Finished with their morning walk, she and Camilo were having breakfast in the kitchen, as the delicious aroma of fresh coffee and toast filled the room. The morning sun peeked over the curtains tumbling in golden strands of light.

"Sí?" Busy eating, Camilo put down his toast to give Pepa his undivided attention.

"Bueno, el padre wants to do something more to help people. Not too long ago he told me he wanted to find una causa importante. So why don't we get him to talk to people about este problema con Gilbert."

"Sounds good," Camilo replied. "We can have him tell people at the church it's a bad idea." He picked up his toast again.

Pepa chewed and talked. "He can try it, no?"

"Sure," Camilo said, nodding. "Let's go see him."

Pepa stopped chewing. "Today?"

Camilo checked the clock. "Sí. Let's go to his Mass."

The two of them drove to the ten o'clock Mass in Pepa's old Buick. The car sputtered and huffed as they meandered toward the church, but they got there in time, seating themselves in front. Father Miguel, dressed in his priestly garb, strolled to the altar, appearing a little surprised by the presence of the two. Pepa waved to the priest, who looked embarrassed by the unconventional attention, though he discreetly waved back. The two of them watched him as he conducted the Mass.

"You think he's acting?" whispered Pepa.

Camilo raised his eyebrows and shrugged. "No sé."

During communion, the two decided to join the procession. The priest noticed Pepa in line and shot her a look of concern, since she'd made it perfectly clear from their past conversations that she had never stepped into a confessional booth.

"The body of Christ," the priest said, with a look that asked Pepa if she was truly going through with this. Camilo stood behind her as a long line of people waited their turn.

"Padre," Pepa held up her hand, "we need to see you after Mass."

"Bueno," he replied. "I'll meet you out front when it's over. The body of Christ."

"No, no, in your office. Dónde 'stá?"

People were beginning to wonder what the holdup was. "Pepa, take the host. I'll meet you in the back of the church, then, OK? The body of Christ."

"Over by that old shed that looks like a chicken coop, or by the nun house?" Heads were now jutting out in all directions.

"Pepa, please take the host!" The priest commanded. "I'll wait for you in the back. The body of Christ!"

"Bueno," Pepa agreed, nodding.

"Say, amen, take the host, and put it in your mouth."

"Oh, yah, yah, I forgot. It's been a long time since I did this." She looked at those in line behind her and smiled. "Bueno, amén." She pulled a host out of the chalice and popped it her mouth. Turning around, she faced Camilo who had been patiently waiting.

"Oye, Camilo," she said with a grimace, "I don't think you want to eat one of these papelitos." She took out what remained in her mouth. "They taste awful and stick to your teeth."

Camilo nodded, waved to the priest, then followed Pepa back to their pew. She picked up her purse. "Vamos, let's go outside and wait for him. Then I can have a smoke while he finishes."

They sat on the steps outside Father Miguel's residence until he showed up.

"Hola, Padre." Pepa waved, another cigarette in hand. "Hijo, I don't remember Mass taking so long. Did you guys start making it longer?"

"No," said the priest, waving off Pepa's question. "Who's your friend?"

"This is Camilo. He's the great-grandson of Don Gabriel, the old curandero from San Geronimo. He sent Camilo to help me."

The priest stopped and stared at the young man, looking both frightened and curious. "Fuh—forgive me," said Father Miguel. "I must've forgotten my manners because I—well, isn't Don Gabriel dead?"

"Sí," said Camilo, nodding. "But he talks to me."

"Really?" The priest glanced at Pepa, then back at Camilo. Finally, he stuck out his hand. "Well, it's nice to meet you."

"Same here," said Camilo, shaking his hand.

The priest gave Pepa a wide-eyed look and opened the door to his office. "Come on in."

The two followed him into a small, cluttered room. The walls were thick and dusty. An undersized window near the ceiling cast a small amount of light. The priest gestured toward two battered chairs, took off his chasuble and laid it across his desk. Then he sat with a big sigh in the desk chair and rubbed his face. He had bags under his eyes. "So what is it you'd like to talk about?" he asked, blinking with fatigue.

Pepa leaned in toward the priest. "We need your help now."

"You do?" He scratched his head, then opened a mini-refrigerator, pulling out two beers. Pepa and Camilo declined the one he offered. Shrugging, he shoved it back in the fridge and unscrewed his own, taking a long swallow. "I don't usually drink before the noon hour, but today I feel the need."

Pepa studied the priest. She watched him take another pull from the bottle. "Bueno Padre, we came to you today to ask you to start talking to la gente about Gilbert's winery."

"Can you give me a little more to go on?" asked the priest, stifling a burp.

"Well, the people outside of Dogtown need to see we're losing our homes to big business."

"Like a new age Manifest Destiny?"

"I think they call it gentrification. Pero, you can call it what you want," she replied. "And some of the Dogtown people are taking Gilbert's money, which is stupid. Tú sabe. You were at the meetings."

The priest pursed his lips then took another swig of beer. "How can I convince them it's bad," he said, waving the bottle around, "if some people don't think it's that bad? Plus, I don't think I'm a good enough speaker. You heard me today, right?"

"A little," Pepa shrugged, not recalling anything the priest had said since she was making a shopping list while he spoke. "Pero, it doesn't matter if you can't talk good. People listen to priests." She glanced at Camilo. "Well, most people do." Pepa noticed political posters on the walls: César Chávez, Nelson Mandela, and Rigoberta Menchú. Pictures of Jesus were missing. "Mire, Padre, you're not a normal priest. But you have a good heart. And all we need is for you to talk from it. César Chávez didn't go to college," she said, pointing to his poster, "but what he said mattered because he spoke," she tapped her chest, "from here."

"Well, I'm no César Chávez," the priest replied, eyeing the poster, "but it's true, he did speak with passion."

"It's what made him so powerful." Camilo blurted out. He hadn't uttered a word since they'd walked into his office. "I saw him give a talk once and never forgot it."

"You can do it, too, Padre," said Pepa.

"Well," the priest paused to drink more beer. "We're not supposed to mix politics in with our homilies—"

"Since when?" Pepa said, giving his shoulder a playful shove. "Don't you priests talk about este right to life, and the death penalty, and anything you want all the time?"

"Sometimes, but—"

"And didn't Jesus talk a lot, especially about the poor?"

"Yeah, but he was preaching."

"Well, it's the same thing." Pepa took a cigarette out and put it behind her ear.

"I suppose so," he said rubbing his chin.

"We need you to get the word out on this." Camilo laid his hand flat on the desk. "Starting with your next Mass."

The priest looked uncertain.

"Bueno, didn't you tell me you needed to do something important with your life?" Pepa pulled the cigarette from behind her ear. "Well, this is it, hombre," she said, pointing with the cigarette.

"I don't know," said the priest, still looking doubtful. "It's not exactly what I had in mind." He raised the bottle, checked its contents, and finished it off.

Pepa picked up the empty bottle and sat on his desk. "Padre, do you want to die as an alcoholic who never did anything? Or an alcoholic who did?" She tapped the empty bottle with her finger.

The priest focused on the bottle, his face reddening.

Pepa waited patiently, watching his eyes shift from her, to Camilo, then back.

"Alright . . . I'll give it a try."

"That's the spirit." She affectionately patted his wrist.

"I'm glad you're helping us," added Camilo.

Pepa peeked at her watch. "Ay Dios, we gotta go. We'll come in next week and sit in on one of your lecturas, give you a few tips. Oh, and, uh, you think maybe you can get some better body-of-Christ papelitos? Those ones you give out taste terrible. I don't know how people can eat them."

The priest looked like a hurricane had just worked him over. "So what happens if no one listens?"

"Ni modo," Pepa replied, sliding the cigarette into her mouth. "We'll try something else."

Jules drove his truck to Pepa's early one morning unannounced. He climbed out of the cab carrying a backpack, wearing his normal attire of cowboy boots and jeans. Wiping the dust on his boots on the back of his legs, he walked toward Pepa's front door and knocked. Pepa answered, surprise registering on her face.

"Hello, Mrs. Romero. I know this might not be a good time since you're probably working, but I was wondering if I could come in and talk to you."

Pepa gave him a once-over, and after appearing to think about it for several seconds, gestured for him to enter. "Venga," she said. She led him past the waiting and treatment rooms into her kitchen, pointing to a chair.

Luz had given Jules the four-one-one on Pepa's house, but nothing could really prepare him for the first time. He took in the details of both the waiting and treatment rooms. He'd never seen such an intricate altar, and the egg-rolling station Luz told him about made him wonder how many eggs were actually dropped, since it looked like it could handle an onslaught. Luz had said Pepa was always busy, yet there wasn't anyone around. Wondering where her patients might be, he glanced at his watch and noticed the date stamp said Saturday.

"I, uh . . ." he pulled out a chair from the kitchen table and sat. "I wanted to talk to you about the research I was doing on nuclear testing and cancer." He paused to look around Pepa's kitchen. The dried herbs hanging from the beams provoked his curiosity. He'd love to know what each one of them did, but that's not what he was here for today. His hands shook as he took his notebook out of his backpack. He placed it on the table. Pepa sat on the chair facing him. "I know you and I spoke a little while back about our mutual interest in this subject. So I thought since maybe you might be seeing a little more of me 'cause of Luz and all, that we could put our heads together and help each other out."

Pepa folded her arms across her chest. "You want to talk about nuclear testing?"

"Yes," Jules replied. He felt nervous—unsure how Pepa would regard him. "If I could have just a few minutes of your time. Would that be OK?"

Pepa looked away, then agreed.

"Well," he continued, his gaze intent on Pepa. "It seems the US has been testing weapons of mass destruction for many years on all kinds of people across this state and other states, most notably Nevada and Utah."

Pepa nodded. "Yah. The people who made these bombs son muy cabrones." She still had her arms crossed.

"Right, but I found out the US often authorized scientists to conduct testing without a clue of the aftermath. They—"

"Didn't give a damn about anything," Pepa interrupted with a flip of her hand, "just their bombs. This is why so many people got cancer. My mama tried to help mucha gente who were sick with it. They came here," she stabbed the table with her fingers, "coughing and pissing blood, eyes bulging out, in so much pain I would just watch them and cry. I hid in a corner so I could see how Mama worked on them. Some were even carried here on stretchers." Pepa rubbed her fingers together. "My mama tried, pero there was nothing she could do. The people were so sick, it was too late for most of them. Some got operations and lived, but not many. I remember this nice man came in to see Mama." She paused in an effort to remember his name. "Mr. Ortiz," she said, nodding. "He had the prettiest blue eyes and, can you believe, seven kids! He was only thirty-nine, pobrecito. Dead with cancer in three months. His wife had to raise those kids by herself."

Jules let out a big sigh. "That's very sad, Pepa. Your mother must've felt terrible not to have been able to help him."

"Sí," Pepa replied, now rubbing her hands against her legs. "Mama was so mad she talked to the police, then the mayor, then the senator—even wrote him a letter. And all they said was . . . well, they said nothing! She even wrote the president to ask him to stop making bombs. He wrote her back, can you believe it? But he said we need these bombs for the future of our country and for everybody to be safe . . . from what?" She glanced at Jules, then rested her hands on her thighs.

Jules knew of countless statistics of people getting cancer, but Pepa's personal account added a human dimension he'd never seen. He pulled out a pen from his backpack, still focusing on her words.

"What made it worse was that everybody went about their business, kids were outside playing, people went to work, and the whole time the government was dropping their pinche test bombs across the state. And you know why people let their kids go outside?"

"Because they didn't know," answered Jules.

"That's right!" Pepa said with a slap to her knee. "They lied about everything. Even the milk we were drinking was bad." She sighed and looked away, tears in her eyes. "I think my mama died from a broken heart. They said it was cancer." She bit the inside of her lip. "But I really think she couldn't look at those people suffer anymore."

"I'm sorry," Jules said, breathing softly, moved by Pepa's words. "It must've been hard on your mother . . . The research I've looked at seems somewhat inconsistent . . . people in the wrong place at the wrong time . . . that kind of thing. I've been trying to verify the fallout and downwind patterns but I couldn't get the lab, or the government, to release the information. Almost everything related to nuclear development in this country remains hidden. And you know what the sad thing is?" He tapped his pen on his notebook. "Even if we were to prove what the government did, there isn't a damn thing we could do about it."

Pepa sat back, surprised. "Why?"

"Because the US government has sovereign immunity—a congressional doctrine that protects it from any suit. It doesn't matter that it acted irresponsibly by killing all those people in Japan, or that it lied to its citizens, or even had its own workers die from radiation. All that matters to this country is the successful production of lethal weapons."

"It's different now, que no?"

"No." Jules waited for the inevitable question.

Pepa squinted at him for a good ten seconds. "So if you care so much about it, then why did you work for them? You had to know what you were doing."

Jules shifted in his seat. "It's hard to say. I grew up in Maine. My dad was a fisherman, but he didn't want me to follow him, said it was too damn hard to make a living. I liked math, so I ended up going to MIT on scholarship. It was there that I fell in love with physics and became so immersed in it that I got excited only about new possibilities. I can't say I'm proud of this." He averted his eyes. "And I didn't think much about the consequences of my actions. I figured Uncle Sam had done good things for me and that I owed him." Jules knew Pepa probably wouldn't want to hear his next words, but he felt compelled to say them. It was the only way she might give him a chance. "We were told the new developments we were working on, the underground testing, lasers, cluster bombs, were to protect our national interest. I bought the whole thing hook, line, and sinker." He finally brought his eyes back to Pepa's. "I can't say I was naïve, because you're right, I did know what I was doing. I'm not sure why I believed in it so much. Somehow I equated making weapons with serving the country."

Pepa rubbed her forehead, looking confused. "Pero, so many people think like you. And it's not just gabachos either. I know people—even from this neighborhood, Chicanos, Indios, who work at that lab." Pepa lit a cigarette, exhaling toward the ceiling. "How you figure Indios can work there, when the lab is built on sacred ground, especially when those bombs destroyed their land, water, and people?"

Jules shrugged. "It *is* the damnedest question." He watched her smoke. "I'd wager, though, that the Indians who owned that land had it taken from them. And you're right, there's all types of people working there. And every single one of them—except for maybe a couple—believe what they're doing is right."

Pepa sighed. "So what made you change?"

"I had high-level clearance. After that I got to work on the most," he raised his fingers in quotations, " 'exciting projects.' We were developing a new laser—something the military wanted, and everything was supposed to be a big deal. One day, over lunch, one of the older guys started laughing about our 'secret project,' saying it was like designing a toy compared to what his father had worked on in the forties. He said they tested bombs all over New Mexico way before the Trinity project. Said people right and left, even physicists, got their asses charred by all the stuff that was going on.

"Something about what he said chewed at me. So I began seeking information the public had no access to: secret testing, workers exposed to radiation, and the cancers, birth defects, and diseases caused by toxic exposure. I found out bombs were exploded next to Indian reservations, sources of water, towns created to house workers, or places where there were so few people, the government felt no one would care."

He leaned forward in his chair, looking directly at Pepa. "And it was eating me alive. I started getting sick—stomach problems, headaches. The more info I found, the sicker I got. After a while, I couldn't ignore it anymore. That's when I started going to the cemeteries." He paused, remembering the first of many he visited. "There were countless people, in every cemetery, who had died in the prime of life."

Pepa got up to give Jules a cup of yerba buena tea. "Sí, I know about this." She set the tea in front of him. "So what is it you want from me?"

Jules shrugged. "I'm not really sure . . . but I want to do something about it. I know there's plenty of other people here and other organizations opposed to nuclear development. But Luz tells me you have lots of stories, and you even know survivors. I don't know anyone, at least not in New Mexico, who has your experience."

Pepa put out her cigarette, then folded her hands on the table.

"So, Mrs. Romero, will you work with me?" Jules placed his hands next to hers. He was ready for the answer, knowing she'd tell him right to his face whatever it was going to be.

Pepa studied him with eyes that could melt steel. Jules waited, listening to the wind rustling through the trees. A rooster—late for this time of the morning—crowed mournfully in the distance.

Finally Pepa blinked. "Bueno," she said, her eyes softening. "I guess we can try."

23

THE CURS NEEDED A NEW SPY. Someone who could delve deeper into the mayor's activities, become privy to his desires, mine his well-kept secrets. For this, it had to be a woman, and it could only be Nina. She had logged in seven years at the doughnut shop and was ready for a change, and though she sometimes appeared a little brusque, she could be good with the public. The CURs originally thought the mayor might recognize her, but reconsidered, figuring a wig and a makeover could pull it off.

But being a spy wasn't Nina's only mission. Pepa and Camilo had other plans—plans they deemed a bit more challenging, plans they needed to discuss in private.

Nina sat in Pepa's kitchen and dropped her backpack at her side. She crossed her legs and leaned back, suspicious. The afternoon air, still hot, parched everything in its path. The sun jetted through the cracks in the cu-randera's window blinds, obliging the three to lean at an angle till they found respite from the light.

Pepa set a pot of tea on the table. Nina leaned over it and sniffed. It smelled vaguely familiar, yet she wouldn't put past the curandera to throw in something funky.

As if reading her mind, Pepa remarked that it was only chamomile. She poured the tea into three cups, then settled in her chair. "Mira, Nina, you know this mayor is mean and sneaky." Pepa opened the sugar bowl and ladled in two teaspoons. "He don't give a damn about anything unless it makes him look good. So even though you only have to spy on him, me and Camilo want you to do something else, something más importante."

"And that might be?" said Nina, growing antsy by the moment. Pepa was starting to look a little fox-like herself.

"We need you to bring him here to the clínica—only once."

"Why?" Nina fanned her tea, then added sugar. She wished Pepa had at least iced it. It was too damn hot to be drinking steam.

"Bueno, so we can . . ." Pepa sniffed, then glanced at Camilo. "So we can . . . Bueno, so we can help him." She gave Nina a Mona Lisa grin.

Nina studied the curandera. Needing gum, she reached into her backpack, pulled out a stick, and popped it in her mouth. A glimmer of a smile folded across her lips. "OK, so you want to *help* him," she said, chewing. "And for some truly obvious reason you want me to bring him here. Why? Shouldn't we be bringing Gilbert? Isn't *he* the man who wants to make the wine?"

Camilo nodded. "That's a good question. Pero el Gilbert thinks only about the winery, and nothing else. The mayor's the one we want because he's the linchpin, the mero-jefe. He goes by popularity—"

"Or greed," added Pepa.

"Sí, or greed." Camilo sipped his tea. "Hijo, Pepa, it's hot." He looked at Nina's untouched tea and got up to retrieve three glasses and a tray of ice. "You know, the whole time I worked for him I could never figure out what he cared about, except, of course, himself." He plunked the ice into the glasses and transferred the contents of each cup. He handed Nina's glass to her and took a sip from his own. "Ahhh, that's better." He took another sip. "Bringing him here might show us a side of him we've never seen; give us a clue on how he bends. Drink your tea. It's actually refreshing."

"Cut the crap, Camilo. You know as well as I do the only thing that'll be bending will be us taking it from both him and Gilbert." Nina popped a bubble. "This is ridiculous. He'll never come here. I mean, look at this place. You're surrounded by weeds dangling from rafters, a gazillion candles, water bowls, and half a farmer's market of vegetables and eggs. And that doesn't even count all that weird stuff on your altar. Even if I get him here, he'll think what you do is either whacked out, Old World, or a combo of the two. And more important, he'll think I've lost my mind dragging his ass over here. Why can't you do whatever you need to do someplace else?"

"Because we need him here." Pepa clasped her hands, then folded them in her lap.

Nina rubbed her neck, then sipped her tea. "Look, I can do the spy thing, but I can't promise you anything else. It's a lot to ask."

"Bueno, that's fine." Pepa grabbed Nina's arm. "Do whatever you can." She smiled, giving it a squeeze. "I'm not going to pressure you. It'll be hard enough to work for that cabezón."

Nina smiled, grateful Pepa understood.

"Pero, would you at least think about giving it try?"

Pepa's hand remained on her wrist. She felt the force of the healer's grip; the veins along her arm crinkling up like a fault. Nina knew the two were working her, but felt they probably had a good reason.

Camilo crossed his arms and angled his body toward the sound of a mockingbird singing in the distance.

Nina pulled the gum out of her mouth, wadded it in its wrapper, and powerballed it into the trash. "I guess if you want it this bad, then I'll have to give it a shot." She finished her tea. "But I honestly don't know if I can pull it off."

"Bueno, that's OK," Pepa answered with relief. "We think you can."

"How's that?" Nina asked, curious.

"No sé," Pepa cast a sly glance at Camilo. "We just do."

※

Nina felt Pepa and Camilo's request was impossible or, at minimum, a long shot. But she didn't like to do anything half-baked, so she made up her mind to give it her best effort. For this, she needed help.

Calling out the big guns, Nina contacted her old friend Francine LeCroix. On top of looking exactly like a real-life version of Disney's Pocahontas (which Nina never failed to mention, despite Francine's being from Brussels), Nina knew her friend could pull off an ass-kicking makeover. Some women naturally gravitate toward femininity, and Francine most certainly did. But she attributed her ultra-femme styling to her mother who dressed in silk caftans, chanclas, and hairpieces. Francine, always a quick study, learned enough from her mother to work as a make-up artist for Big Sky Entertainment, an Albuquerque production company known for daytime TV. The pay wasn't great, but it was a good job, and Francine loved the work. In fact, it was probably the only thing Francine did love. That is, until she met Silver. Now Silver, an aptly named, slim-hipped Muscogee, also worked for Big Sky, and spotted Francine one day doing a comb-out on a hairpiece. Stopping mid-stride, Silver did a double take then introduced herself. Poking and prodding to ascertain Francine's dating logistics, she found out she had a boyfriend but wasn't in love, therefore, in Silver's eyes, open for pursuit. Francine, a life-long heterosexual, never thought much about women as lovers till Silver dogged her enough to try. Possessing a fine set of womanly attributes, Silver *did* please Francine in that proverbial no-man-had-ever-done-before kind of way, instantly converting Francine to the lavender life.

Time passed, and Francine became spiritual. She broke up with Silver and moved to Santa Fe, swearing off all modes of meat, make-up, and chanclas. She changed her name to Ciel, which she felt more fitting for someone practicing a daily meditation, and landed a job as a receptionist at the Santa Fe Zen Center.

Nina knew Ciel still had the talent for makeovers and, handicapped by spiky hair, T-shirts, and jeans, she called up her friend, who enthusiastically accepted the challenge.

Luckily, Nina was skinny. Even more luckily, Ciel was sentimental, having stashed a number of skirts, heels, and blouses in the back of her closet. Rejoicing over the secret cache of femininity, Nina dove into the makeover. Ciel tossed in a black wig, make-up, and nail polish, transforming the tough-looking gurrl into a rough-looking diva.

Ciel insisted that Nina wear heals and practice walking in them till she could climb stairs and sharpen pencils without wobbling. As a final touch, she gave Nina elocution lessons.

"From now on, at least around the mayor, you'll need to talk different."

"Why?" Still dressed in her high-femme outfit, Nina couldn't stop running her hands up and down her newly shaved legs.

"Because you can't wear that getup," Ciel said, pointing, "and talk the way you do." The two of them were drinking ginger tea on Ciel's couch after the makeover. Nina noticed several Buddha books on the coffee table.

"Why not?" she asked, holding out her hand to examine her nails.

"Because the two don't match. Plus men like women who talk sexy." She paused to think. "Kinda like doves."

"Doves? The only things doves do is coo."

"That's right."

"What do you mean, that's right?" Nina set her untouched tea on the coffee table, spilling it in the process.

"That's pretty much what I mean." Ciel grabbed a towel to sop up the mess. "So I want you to start talking sexy. Now repeat these words after me." She closed her eyes, concentrated, then spoke. "Heloh Misterh Mayorh."

Nina could only stare.

Ciel opened her eyes. "Now come on, I'm serious. If you really want to get this guy, you have to talk sexy."

"But I don't want to talk sexy. I want to talk—well, like me. If he thinks it's sexy, then cool. If not, too bad. Y'know?" Nina sipped her tea, made a face, then looked around. "You got any beer?"

"No. Now come on, you look fabulous." Ciel inhaled the tea's aroma. "Half the population would sell their souls to look like you. But you'll spoil it if you talk the way you do."

"What's wrong with the way I talk? Tala likes it." Nina pushed the tea away. "I think you just want me to talk like some of those Buddhistic people you hang with."

"Buddhistic people don't talk sexy." Ciel paused. "At least not the ones I know. Look, I know Tala likes the way you talk, but men like the mayor usually don't go for women who talk, well, like cholas."

"A chola, huh?"

"Would you trust me? I know what I'm talking about. You need him wrapped." She held up her pointer finger. "And if you coo just right, you'll get him that way. Look at it as acting." She patted Nina's hand.

"This totally sucks."

"Come on, Nina, just give it a try. Trust me . . . Heloh, Misterh Mayorh."

"Hello, Mister Mayor." Nina rolled her eyes.

"No. No. It's Heloh, Misterh Mayorh." Ciel tapped her knee for rhythm.

Nina took a deep breath. She was starting to hate Ciel. "OK, I'll try again. Hellow Meester Mayor." She looked at Ciel for approval.

"Something's off," Ciel said, staring at Nina's mouth. "It's your tongue. The stud. It's gotta go."

"What?"

"That earring in your tongue. You need to pull it out."

"I can't just take it out. It's embedded," Nina crossed her arms and pouted.

"Just a minute." Ciel left then returned with a couple tissues. "Sorry, but it's blocking your diction."

"But I like it." Nina stared at the tissues. "Plus, it'll leave a hole. Then if I eat or drink anything it'll leak through."

"That's not true and you know it. Now come on, open up." Ciel tapped Nina's jaw. "Let me unscrew it."

"I can't believe I'm letting you do this." Nina felt like she was donating a kidney.

"Hang on to the top part." Ciel gave Nina a tissue. "Now roll up your tongue, and I'll unscrew it." Nina went along, only because she was trying to make it hard for Ciel. She'd taken the stud off by herself plenty of times.

Triumphant, Ciel took both parts and set them on the tissue. "Now try it again."

Nina rolled her tongue around and gave Ciel a dirty look. "I hope you know this is compromising my feminist ethics."

Ciel laughed. "This is only the beginning. Now come on."

Nina swallowed a couple times then cleared her throat. "Heloh Misterh Mayorh."

"Much better!" said Ciel, clapping. "Now say, 'I'm a leetle newh at this, but I'h lerrn fast.'"

Nina crossed her arms. "You didn't say I had to play a ditz."

"You're not playing a ditz. You're playing a diva."

"I prefer one with brains." She reached under her wig to scratch her head. "This thing itches like hell."

"Try not to do that."

Nina finished scratching.

"OK?"

"All right." Nina cleared her throat again. "I'm a leetle newh at this, but I'h lerrn fast."

"Wow, perfect. You're a natural." Ciel went to her bookshelf and pulled out Hemingway's *A Farewell to Arms*. She opened the first chapter and gave the book to Nina. "Now practice reading that paragraph."

Nina looked at the cover. "You been keeping secrets?"

"No." Ciel looked embarrassed.

"I would've thought maybe Alice Walker, Julia Álvarez, Linda Hogan, or Amy Tan."

"Read!"

"Or even Oscar Wilde. But *Hemingway*?"

"Just read!" Ciel commanded. "It's from a writing class."

Nina eyed her friend, wondering what else she'd been hiding. She took a deep breath, then began reciting the lines in the coo dove voice. "'In the lateh summerh of that yearh weh lihved in a househ in a villageh that lookedh across the riverh and the plaain toh the mountains. In the bedh of the riiver thereh wereh pehbbles and bouldehs, dryh and whiteh in the sun, and'—this is boring, Ciel—"

"Read!"

"'The waterh was cleear and swiiftly movingh and blueh in the channels.'" She looked up. "Don't you think it sounds like I have a speech impediment?"

"No. Now I want you to practice reading and talking like this for a half hour every day. The only way to get the voice down is to practice. If you need a model, think of Marilyn Monroe."

"But I hate her," Nina scrunched up her nose. "And I especially hated how she talked."

"It doesn't matter," said Ciel. "Men lost their minds, their sense of reason around her, even the most powerful ones. Remember?"

"Yeah." Nina felt depressed.

"I rest my case."

Nina practiced for a week without Tala around so she wouldn't laugh at her. She got so good at the M-speak, she could yell, sing, or mumble without breaking cadence. At the end of the week she invited Tala, Ciel, Pepa, and Camilo to her house for the unveiling. It was after dinner, the air only starting to cool. Chucho, Nina's Shepard-mix, sniffed the guests as they arrived. He wasn't a friendly guy, except of course to Camilo, who had to put up with his stinky breath as the dog snuggled against him.

Nina served everyone beer, then retreated to the bedroom. As the guests visited and chatted, Nina changed clothes. Twelve minutes later, she announced she was ready.

"Attention please," Ciel stood up like a game show host. "May I now introduce, Miss—Nina—Le Chic—López!"

The door opened and Nina stepped out, repackaged in black skirt, teal blouse, heels, and a sexy cabrona wig. Her eyebrows had been shaped into refined arches, and her face tinted with the soft glow of foundation. She looked professionally stunning, like a cross between a newscaster and a soap star.

"Heloh, Misterh Mayorh. I'h was wondering if I'h might apply forh a job hearh?"

"Holy hell," said Tala, doing a double take.

"You got that right," echoed Camilo, who jumped back and startled the dog.

Pepa grabbed the bridge of her nose, stifling a laugh.

"Uh, in case you forgot, it's still me, OK?" said Nina, looking around the room.

"Meyowww." Tala fanned her crotch.

"You look—well, you look hot, like you could be on TV," Camilo blurted.

"Oh no, she looks much prettier than what's on television," said Pepa. "What a miracle, que, no?"

Nina smiled, pleased. "I'll tell you one thing. I sure as hell never thought I could look like this." She looked at Tala and grinned.

"Neither did I, Amor." Tala still looked dumbstruck. "You're killing me, you look so fine." She cleared her throat and looked at the others in the room. "That is, in that classic, oppressive-to-women kind of way."

"Right," Camilo added, petting the dog. "Completely without a feminist consciousness."

"Well, this is what we wanted, right?" Ciel asked, looking around. "I mean, isn't she perfect Rolo bait?"

Pepa gave Nina the once over. "Bueno, you better get ready, mujer, because from now on, you're going to have the mayor and half the town after you."

"Maybe Chucho can be your bodyguard," said Camilo, rubbing the dog's head. "On second thought, doesn't Jules need a job?"

"Are you serious?" Tala replied. "Luz would skin him alive." Everyone laughed.

"Wait, there's one more thing." Ciel reached into her shoulder bag and pulled out a bottle of Chanel No.5. "Spray some of this on before going to work."

Nina shook her head. "Nix on that, girlfriend. I'm in killer drag, and that's good enough. Plus, it happens to be what my mother wears!"

"Your mother. My mother, and millions of other successful women. Use it," Ciel commanded, "and I guarantee it'll be the coup de grace."

"Coup de grace for me from smelling it all day." Nina took the bottle, opened it, and sniffed. "Well, I guess it's not that bad," she said, grimacing. She let Tala sniff it, then Camilo, who sprayed some on the dog.

"Very funny." Nina grabbed the bottle back and offered it to Pepa.

She shook her head, refusing to come close.

Camilo sniffed the dog. "He smells like he could get a boyfriend, too." The five of them laughed again.

"Thank you, Sweetie," Nina said to Ciel. "I know I kicked and screamed all the way through this. But you hung in there and made me a femme."

"Honey, I hate to break this to you," Ciel pulled Nina close. "But you already are one." She smiled and gave Nina a hug. "I just hope it works."

24

PEPA AND CAMILO STARTED GOING to Father Miguel's Masses to see how his lectures were going. It was two weeks after their last talk, another dry day, with just a hint of piñón smoke in the air. Father Miguel had been at St. Francis for twelve years and, given his current faltering of faith, had altered all his sermons. In the past, he had preached standards, such as "The Power of the Holy Spirit" or "Love Can Conquer All." Now, he had changed everything to reflect his own position of doubt, such as: "Where Is the Love?" and "Is God Letting Us Down?"

The people who attended his Masses listened politely to his new sermons, though some thought he was reading too much nonfiction. Others figured he might be having a midlife crisis. Still others wondered if he was in trouble, like many other priests around the country. The day Pepa and Camilo showed up, Father Miguel was attempting his anti-winery sermon, "Will Making Wine Make Us Greedy?"

Pepa decided, since she and Camilo were sitting in the front row, that they needed to be more covert, so they only nodded to the priest when he approached the altar. They tried to go through all the kneeling, standing, and replies to the padre's call outs but ended up bungling most of them, so they gave up and simply mumbled and squatted. Pepa was relieved when the priest got to the sermon part of the Mass. Father Miguel stood at the pulpit, looking grave and serious. After a brief introduction where he recited some part of the Bible, he got right to the point.

"Now some of you may be wondering what we should do about the proposed winery on the outskirts of town. I know a few of you are looking forward to receiving the money since you think it will bring excitement or change. I, for one, know the Catholic Church could probably use a few extra dollars, especially with all the legal issues we're confronting. But the Church wouldn't take this money.

"The people who live in Dogtown have lived there for generations. Many are workers who clean, cook, and care in some capacity of service to our city. Most of these jobs are not high-paying, and Dogtown is one of the few places where it's still affordable to live.

"Recently, everyone living within a certain area of Dogtown was given an offer to sell their homes." The priest looked across the rows of parishioners. "This, for lack of a better word, is simply a bribe. Not an ordinary bribe," he said, pausing for effect, "but a bribe directly from the devil." A small intake of breath erupted collectively from the audience. "Yes, I said the devil. For only when the heart opens itself to evil does it make it susceptible to greed. It's the oldest trick in the book. Jesus knew that money corrupts a soul. But we, like Jesus, are not those kinds of people."

"Yes we are!" Someone in the back yelled. Pepa darted a quick glance to Camilo, then turned around to see that it was Jeff Díaz, a former meth addict. A low rumble started throughout the church. People looked at one another, mumbling various things in response to both the priest and the man who had spoken.

"I don't agree," Father Miguel countered. "We must resist this onslaught of temptation so that we can keep our homes and our future. Dogtown belongs to the people. Not to Santa Fe. And not to the winery. We ask that God guide us through these times like he guided Jesus when he chased the moneychangers out of the temple. Your home is your temple—"

"Then you sure haven't seen mine!" answered Jeff.

"Bueno," said the priest. "You can disagree with me, but I only ask that you think carefully about what you desire. The Lord's Prayer speaks of leading us not into temptation. I ask you all to recite an extra Lord's Prayer during these difficult times . . ." He paused again. "To give you extra strength."

"Let's go," Pepa said, glancing at the red-faced priest. "Time for Plan B."

The next morning Pepa and Camilo waited for Father Miguel outside his office. "Sister Teresa said he usually shows up around now," Pepa said, looking at her watch. Sure enough, the priest appeared, shuffling toward them with a cup of coffee, and sporting a San Diego Padres baseball cap.

"Hey Pepa, Camilo. How are things?"

"Oye, Padre, I like your hat." Pepa had never seen a baseball cap with a bat-swinging friar. "Can we talk to you for a little bit?"

"Sure, sure." He opened his office and let them in. The priest plopped down on his chair and gestured toward the other two in the office. "Have a seat."

Pepa noticed a layer of dust on all his books and papers. "Mind if I smoke?" she asked, pulling a cigarette out of her purse.

"I kinda do," he said, taking a sip of his coffee. "But I'll make an exception." He got up to open a window. "So what's up? What did you think of my sermon yesterday?"

"We thought it didn't go too well," said Camilo. Pepa liked how Camilo never beat around the bush.

"No?" the priest looked surprised.

"No," said Camilo.

"In fact," said Pepa, lighting up then exhaling. "We thought it might have made things worse." She looked at Camilo who was tapping the tips of his fingers together.

"Well, I didn't think it was so bad," said the priest. "It's just that every once in a while you get a heckler." He took off his hat, ran his fingers through his hair, then put the hat back on.

"Mmm-hmm," Pepa eyed the priest as she inhaled and exhaled quickly. "Mire, Padre, I get people who are crackpots in my house pretty often. I don't know a lot about church, but me and Camilo asked around, and no one said they've ever heard of anyone talking back to a priest, at least not in Mass." She stared at the light in the window; the dust motes flickered slowly in the haze.

The padre sniffed, then rubbed his face. "I suppose you're right," he said, sighing. "So now what?"

"So now we have to do Plan B," said Pepa.

"Plan B?"

Camilo pulled a bag of hierbas out of his jacket. "These are special herbs we'd like you to use with some of that incense you burn." He placed the bag on the padre's desk. The priest opened it and took a whiff.

"Whew! What's in there, hypnotizing powder?"

"Not really," said Camilo, straight-faced.

"Well maybe just a little," said Pepa, averting her gaze.

"Hmmm," said Father Miguel, taking another whiff.

"Padre. Estas hierbas will help us a little bit. Pero, it's you we really need. People will listen to you because you're a priest." Pepa exhaled smoke out of the corner of her mouth. "Pero, they're a rough crowd, and it couldn't hurt to burn a little of this during your lectura."

The priest looked troubled, as if he might be committing some kind of sin. Pepa saw the look and waited.

"You know, you're asking me to do something very serious—something so unusual it goes against the oath we take."

"Sí." Pepa replied, watching the priest lecture her in his Padres baseball cap.

"Well, yeah," he continued, "burning personal herbs in Mass. It doesn't take much to understand all the implications." He picked up a book and flung it across his desk.

Camilo sneezed from the dust.

"Sorry," the priest said.

Camilo pulled a tissue from his jacket pocket and blew his nose. "Padre, these herbs won't hurt anyone. And we wouldn't ask you to burn them if we didn't think they were safe. But we and you need help making the people see how this deal from Gilbert is wrong."

"OK, let's say I burn these herbs, maybe because I trust you. But we don't burn incense except on special sacrament days like Christmas and Easter. This would be considered highly unusual, not only by the clergy, but by the monsignor. Plus, I'm sure they'll smell funny."

Pepa tapped her ash into his trashcan. "Bueno, just add a little frank-incense."

"But we only use that on special occasions."

"So what?" said Pepa, with a shrug. "I'm sure you can think of something. Look, we need you to burn it for la causa. You said you wanted to help us and do something that mattered. Well, now's your chance."

"But you haven't told me what they're gonna do."

"OK, those herbs," Camilo said, pointing, "will help people think better."

"More clearly," added Pepa, exhaling smoke.

The priest pressed two fingers against his forehead. Pepa waited and looked around his office. She wondered if he ever cleaned it. The place looked like it could use a good going over. Camilo took the tissue he used, folded it into little squares, and placed it in his pocket.

"Alright," said the priest. "I'll do it. I guess I can tell them I'm burning incense as an extra prayer for world peace. That will probably work, don't you think?"

"Absolutely," said Pepa doing her best to look solemn. "Absolutely."

☀

That same week, Camilo got a call from Dahlia at the mayor's office who told him his old job was currently open and would he consider coming back. Camilo told her no, of course, but was sending over his good friend, Nina, whom he highly recommended.

"All right," said Dahlia, sounding disappointed. "She can always fill out an application. You don't know any more guys like you who might be interested, do you?"

"No," said Camilo, "I truly don't. Any idea when Mayor Reyes will be in?"

"Hang on, I'll check his schedule."

Of course, Camilo timed it so that Nina applied for the job while Rolo was in the office. Predictably, and overruling Dahlia's authority, he hired her on the spot.

Nina quit her job at the doughnut shop and started work the next day. Rolo, instantly smitten, struggled to hide his attraction, but his body gave him away. Nina watched him trip over steps, bump into furniture, and even slam, full face, into a wall. She heard the man was brilliant, but everything about him appeared the opposite. He lost track of time, forgot what he was saying, and bungled key appointments. Aphrodite herself couldn't have done any better.

Relaxing in bed, Nina and Tala recapped what had happened after her first week of work. "Y, este mayor, what a baboso." Nina stretched, then propped on her side facing Tala. She wore a tight T-shirt with Go Fish across the front. "He can't take his eyes off me no matter who he's talking to. Then he tries to hold in his big gut whenever he walks by. When the suits come in, especially white guys, he shows me off like a little boy in charge of a play army."

◀ 120 ▶

"Hmmm, how 'bout la Dahlia?" Tala traced her finger down Nina's arm. "How's she been treating you?"

Nina scrunched up her nose. "You mean the little CP?"

"CP?"

"Well, you know how I hate the C-word? And how I always want to punch out anybody who uses it?"

"Yeah," Tala replied, eyes alert. "I distinctly recall seeing that reaction before."

"Right. Well Dahlia is so horrible to me that I actually have to give in to the word. But since I can't really say it, I call her a cunty-poo."

"A cunty-poo." Tala seemed to suppress a smile.

"It kinda mellows it just enough," Nina held two fingertips together, "so I can almost get away with it."

"Uh-huh."

"On top of everything, she's in love with Rolo's flabby ass."

"Nooo."

"Yes! And that's the other reason no one can last in that office, at least not anyone who's a threat to her."

"Which is why she liked Camilo."

"Exactly. And why my bimbo suit makes her foam at the mouth."

"Too bad," sighed Tala. "It's hard enough having to work around Rolo, and now you have to put up with all that hateful cunty-poo hostility." She smiled, then gave Nina a kiss. "I bet you make that big doughnut walk around with a boner all day."

"Eeeww, stop." Nina playfully slapped Tala. "It's hard enough working with him. Now I have to think about his boners."

"Shit, I'd have a big braunschweiger if I had to work with something like you in the office." She laughed as Nina picked up a pillow and threw it at her.

"The sad thing is I know if I walked in wearing my real hair and clothes, he wouldn't give me the time of day." Nina scratched her head, then began peeling off her T-shirt. "Which, when it comes down to it, tells you what he really thinks of women."

"So what's it feel like, Amor," Tala caressed the half-naked Nina. "To be transformed into a feminine mystique?" She kissed her neck and ran her hands down her thighs. "Do you feel, like a vixen . . . or a vampire," she asked as she continued kissing, "in those spiky heels?"

"Mmm, no, I'd say a little more like a Jodie Foster." They both laughed. "You know," Nina bit Tala's lips, then stopped abruptly. "It's kinda weird. I never played up that feminine wiles bullshit before. And I hate the way I have to act to get his pigified attention. But I'm kinda liking his slave-like devotion. I sorta feel like a low-grade dominatrix."

She kissed Tala, who failed to respond.

"What, you don't want to kiss me now 'cause of what I just said?"

"No, I'll kiss you." Tala didn't sound convincing. "I'm just realizing what your real mission is. I don't think this is going to be easy for you. Pretty soon, he'll ask you out. Then it's gonna get harder."

"Yeah, it will." Nina watched Tala's eyes darken with concern.

"Just don't let him mess with you. Find out what you can, and if you can bring him to Pepa's, great. Pero, don't kill yourself over this. It isn't worth it."

Nina climbed on top of Tala and studied her troubled face. She ran her pinkie over Tala's lips. "Hmmm, is my weetle Amorcita getting just a weetle bit jealous?"

"Nooo," said Tala. "Pero, if I do, I'll let you know."

"You don't have to worry, Amor. I'm not interested in him."

"Good, 'cause I don't want you liking it when he comes on to you."

"I only like it when *you* come on to me." Nina put her arms around Tala and held her.

"You're playing with me now."

"I am." Nina replied, biting the back of Tala's neck.

"That's OK. Keep doing it."

☀

The skirts, heels, and wig worked their mojo, and it wasn't long before Rolo asked Nina out. Dahlia was on her lunch break, and the mayor thought there was no time like the present.

"Nina, I was wondering," he asked, handing her a letter he had signed, "if you're not busy Friday night, would you like to accompany me to the current Teatro Sabor show?"

Nina looked up from her work, captivating him with those stunning brown eyes. "Teatroh Saborh? Wellh, Misterh Mayorh, I'm not shurh I'h know much about this showh, but tell meh a little morh."

"Bueno, ahem." Sweating from excitement, he forced himself to stare at the wall so he could focus. "It's uh, a theater group known for their innovative shows. I think avant-garde is the term people use to describe them. You never heard of them?" He walked over to the window and adjusted the blinds where the sun was poking in Nina's eye. "How's that?" he asked.

"Better, thank-youh."

He didn't know that Nina knew the group well, particularly since she had painted a set for one of their previous shows. "Nowh thath I'h think abouth it, I recall hearingh something abouth them."

"So, would you like to go?" The mayor pulled out a handkerchief from his jacket and wiped his face. "Their new show is called *Atole, Chauquehue, y Qué?*"

Nina chuckled.

"It's funny, no?"

Nina was still laughing. "Is it goodh?"

"Oh yeeaaahh," Rolo replied, having absolutely no idea. His only concern was taking Nina to a place they'd least likely be sighted. Afterward, they could go to his favorite hotel for a drink. An added perk was that the Teatro Sabor attracted a hip, younger crowd—a place his wife, or any of her friends, were unlikely to appear.

"Wellh, OKh," She looked down at her desk, then back at him. "But sirh, yourh wife?"

Rolo sucked his lips. Shit, this girl didn't miss a beat. "Well, me and her have a special relationship. We, uh, we have an agreement when it comes to entertainment."

Nina looked surprised. She dropped a pen, spending a few seconds in an effort to find it. Retrieving it, she straightened herself and laid it carefully on her desk. "Reallyh?"

Rolo shrugged. Why was he feeling so nervous? "Bueno, she doesn't always like going out, especially to the theater. So, we kind of do our own thing—with entertainment, that is." He leaned a hand on her desk. "She's shy, so the lack of privacy is an issue."

"Ohh?" Nina took out a notepad. She wrote the date in the corner, then jiggled the pen in her hand. It looked like she wanted to get back to work.

"Well, it's the part of being the mayor's wife she doesn't care for, since I always get a lot of attention, and she doesn't care for the intrusions. Sometimes she just likes to stay home and read a book." He wasn't completely lying. He actually saw her do it once.

"No kidding?" Nina replied, now doodling on the pad.

Rolo noticed she was drawing a man with a long nose and whiskers. "Oh yeah. She's a bit old fashioned, I suppose. She grew up in a very religious house, always going to church and all. Doesn't really like the limelight."

"Hmm," Nina said, still drawing.

Rolo thought she had just put some long teeth on the man. "Believe me, you'll see it when, I mean if, we go out. Sometimes, even *I* wish I could just wear a disguise and go out so no one recognizes me."

"Then dooh."

"What?"

"Then dooh. Whyh don't youh wearh some kindh ofh outfit. Maybeh a cowboy or, waith, I knowh, a hell's angel guyh. If you put on a fakeh beard, and leatherh no one willh be able to tellh it's youh."

Rolo studied Nina, wondering what kind of girl she really was. It was making her sound even more exciting. He felt his dick start to throb. Shit, he didn't want to get hard in front of her. His heart started picking up the pace. "Bueno. So, you'd like to join me?" Shit, he was already at half-mast. "That is," he suddenly remembered Nina might have a boyfriend. "If you can."

"Shurh," Nina replied, as she looked him straight in the eye. "But onlyh if yourh in disguiseh."

Rolo thought perhaps it wasn't such a bad idea. He could inquire at a local costume shop about a disguise and simply tell them it was for a private party. "Sí, cómo no? I'll give it a try." He arched one brow and winked.

"Nowh that's theh spirit."

25

FATHER MIGUEL, IN AN EFFORT to atone for his weakness, decided to burn the herbs Pepa had given him the following Sunday. He insisted, however, that neither Pepa nor Camilo be present.

Instructing his server to set up the censer before Mass, he carefully sprinkled the herbs among the resin. He hoped this stuff worked, since he was risking more than his trust of Pepa. At ten o'clock, he lit the incense then carried it down the aisle, making sure to give the chains holding the container good strong shakes in order to spread the slightly foochi smell throughout the congregation. Finishing, he brought the censer to the center of the church, where he set it down in its place near the baptismal.

He began Mass, and as usual, halfway through, started the homily. It was the speech Pepa and Camilo had written for him. The two of them had decided to write it so that it cut to the chase—stating the basic facts of why the winery wasn't good for the people. They omitted all the Gilbert as Devil language, figuring a straightforward, just the facts approach, with a little help from the herbs, would better incite the congregation to abandon Gilbert's proposal. The priest, proceeding, yawned and shook his head, feeling a little groggy.

"Whenever we've been met with challenges to the soul," the priest continued, stifling another yawn, "We find our best efforts are not always the correct ones. Today we burn incense for peace, because peace does not reign in the world, nor for that matter, in Dogtown. Rather," he looked up from his notes and noticed several people nodding off. "Rather, we sometimes have to do the right thing, and not—" He glanced at the server, who resembled a dozing penguin, "—the thing we think is best for our bank accounts." For some reason he was having a hard time concentrating. He also noticed most of the congregation was either glassy-eyed or nodding off. He was surprised since he hadn't been speaking long. He gathered his notes, shook his head again, and continued.

"The light in our hearts beats with the faith that God will be the true judge of our sins, and even . . ." he paused, yawning once again, "our mistakes. We cannot afford . . ." Damn, he was suddenly feeling very tired—"to make judgments that benefit our pocketbooks, when this, in turn, hurts others. We have a chance . . ." The deacon's head now slumped face down in the missal—"to do the right thing. And we ask you to look to God, and into your hearts, to do not what will help only you, but what will help . . . all of us. We ask you this, through Christ, our Lord." It was probably one of the shortest homilies he'd ever given. Typically, he elaborated on his notes. But this morning he just couldn't do it.

"Through Christ our Lord—" he repeated, waiting for the amen, yet the congregation sat strangely silent. A closer look revealed that every single person had fallen fast asleep. The server had folded himself around his bells. Children were zonked out in their parents' laps, arms akimbo like dolls, while their mothers and fathers slumped over, heads rolling to the side. Old people slept with mouths open like gargoyles. Even the typically amped teenagers were still, eyes shut in angelic beauty.

The priest left his pulpit, grabbed a container filled with flowers off the altar and poured some of the water into the still smoldering censer. It went out in a loud hiss. Then he pulled the bells from beneath the altar boy and went back to the pulpit. He rang them loudly and managed to wake enough people to finish the Mass. He was certain no one had heard a word he'd said.

"Bueno . . . Bueno . . . Bueno, Padre. Lo siento, eh? Lo siento. We're sorry, we were trying something new and—" Pepa held the phone away from her ear, doing her best to calm the angry priest. She looked at Camilo, who stood beside her listening, and rolled her eyes. "No. No. We weren't trying to sabotage you. No, hombre. No . . . Porque we wanted them to listen to you. Bueno, these things happen . . . It was a mistake, we feel bad, pero las hierbas didn't work like we planned . . . I understand, pero . . ." She grabbed her cigarettes. "We could probably fix it . . . What do you mean never again?"

She set them down. "We didn't do it on purpose . . . Bueno, can you at least think about it?" Camilo brought Pepa a cup of manzanilla tea. She nodded her thanks. "This isn't exact science . . . Padre, don't give up on us . . . We need you . . . Los pobres and viejitos . . . Sí, los chiquitos, también . . . Sí . . . Sí! Bueno, if you can let us try it again, we'll test it first . . . No, on ourselves . . . No really, just ourselves . . . Mire, don't worry. We'll let you know . . . don't worry . . . Bueno gracias, Padre. Gracias. Bueno . . . bueno. Sí . . . OK, ba-bye."

26

Nina heard the car pull up and peeked through the blinds. "He's driving a TP Cruiser," she said to Ciel, who was sitting on the couch, waiting with Nina till Rolo arrived. The date, arranged to maintain Nina's identity with a pickup at Ciel's, was now set in motion.

"A what?"

"You know, one of those flashback to the forties cars."

Ciel squinted through the blinds. "That's a PT Cruiser."

"That's what I said. Think it's his regular car?" Nina scratched her scalp through her wig.

"Hope not," Ciel replied, eyes wide with worry.

"Oh—my—God," Nina caught sight of a large man slowly maneuvering out of the car. He had on a T-shirt, leather vest, jeans, and a baseball cap. On his face was a fake beard, and, as he approached the house, Nina thought he was wearing some kind of boot-like clogs. She turned toward Ciel. "What did I get myself into?"

"It's OK, Honey, just go with the flow." Ciel waved her hands in large circles. "You told him to come in disguise. He's just doing what you asked, except for maybe the shoes. Now, in order for this to work, you have to make him feel good in his little tough-guy outfit."

"Easy for you to say, you're not the one going out with him. I told him to dress like a biker, but he looks more like a cross between a mass murderer and an Oakland Raiders football fan." Nina clasped her hands and sighed. "I was sort of kidding when I told him to do this but he went kinda overboard, don't you think?"

They were still peeking out the window. "Yeah, I suppose," said Ciel. "He does look a little mass murderer-esque."

Rolo was almost at the door. Ciel gave Nina a peck on the cheek. "Remember, it's for the cause." She gave her a quick once over and wiped a smudge of lipstick off her face. "You look good, Honey. Hang in there. You'll do fine." Then she disappeared into her hiding spot.

Done up in her wig, low-cut black sweater, jeans, and sling-backs, Nina took a deep, long breath. She heard a soft knock, then released the breath as she opened the door.

The two drove in Rolo's car to the theater, a gutted and refurbished commercial bakery. A banner with *Atole, Chauquehue, y Qué?* hung across the entrance. Darkness had fallen, and little white lights were aglow in the surrounding trees. Nina had remained torn, up to the last minute, about whether she should give a heads up to the people at Teatro Sabor, but decided, after talking it over with Tala, that it was best not to raise attention. She didn't want anyone to blow her cover. Besides, she was nearly unrecognizable in her wig and make-up, except for her gap-toothed grin, which she figured she could hide. She bought a pair of slightly tinted sunglasses to help conceal her face, telling Rolo she needed them to see distances.

It actually hadn't been so bad on the drive over. Rolo, nervous in his costume, didn't want a tour of the house. He told her she looked nice and asked her what she thought of his outfit. Up close was even worse. His fake beard looked old and tattered, and he actually *was* wearing a baseball cap with the Raiders' insignia. His belly protruded through the leather vest, and his jeans and shoes looked like he had purchased them on the drive over.

"So you think anyone will recognize me?" he had asked, exiting Ciel's house.

Nina shook her head. "Not a chanceh." And it was true. He didn't look anything like himself.

"I even rented a car, just to be thorough. Thought the PT Cruiser would go with the image." He opened her car door for her. "You ever ride in one of these?"

"Noh, can't say I have," said Nina

"They're kind of kooky looking, but fun. Not as fun as my Mercedes, but it'll do for tonight." He looked at her and winked.

As they walked into the theater, they got the once over from nearly everyone they encountered. Nina figured it was because she was with an older man—a very weird-looking older man. She recognized various people from the teatro, and ducked or looked the other way when they began staring a tad too long. Rolo's middle name was Manuel, and he told Nina she should call him Manny for the evening. Nina nodded as they wrestled through the lobby noting the curious glances tossed in their direction.

Manny still carried his "in charge" mayor's personality, which caused people to stare all the more since they thought he was somebody famous. The theater was stuffy, and Nina started to itch under all her fake hair. She subtly scratched her head, wishing now she had told the mayor she didn't date bosses.

She looked around the lobby and asked Manny if he could go get her a Coke.

"Sure," he replied. "I'll be right back."

As he waddled away, she caught Tala watching her out of the corner her eye. Her outfit was '80s gaucho, as she stood with her hat tilted, pretending to read a program. Frowning, Nina mouthed the words, "What are you doing here?"

Tala smiled and mimed, "Watching you."

Nina turned and went over to Manny who was still standing in line. "I'm goingh toh the ladies roomh. I'll beh right backh." Manny nodded as Nina scampered away. There was a line of women waiting for the five stalls. Nina walked past the line over to the mirror and pulled out her lipstick. Tala joined her within seconds.

"You shouldn't have come," Nina whispered.

"I wanted to make sure you were OK," Tala replied, readjusting her hat.

"No, you didn't. You wanted to keep an eye on me, which is stupid. I already told you not to worry. Plus he could recognize you, you know." Nina gave her girlfriend an angry look.

"So what? He sees me at a play. Big deal. I have to say, though," she said, compressing a smile, "he's got a pretty funny outfit on. Sorta like a cross between a biker and a wrestler."

"Yes, I know," Nina huffed, shoving her lipstick back in her purse.

"Don't you like my Santa Fe señorita look?"

Nina narrowed her eyes. She thought Tala was acting like a wiener. "You blow it for me, and you blow it for everyone. And," she said, with a sigh, "you distract me. This work isn't easy, you know. You think I want to wear all this shit and look at him with goo-goo eyes all night? Besides, I'm fully capable of taking care of myself."

Tala looked hurt, but Nina was too mad to care. "Bueno, I gotta go." She exited the restroom and saw Manny waiting for her with the Coke.

"Thank-youh," she murmured, eagerly downing the soft drink.

"Shall we go inside?" Manny led Nina by the arm toward their seats. Nina caught a glimpse of Tala quietly slipping into her chair. "Something the matter?" he asked.

Nina took a deep breath. "Noh, noh. I'm fine." Settling into her seat, she let out a long, silent sigh as the performance began.

The play turned out to be funny. Really funny. Sitting in the theater's darkness, Nina relaxed enough to pay attention to something besides Rolo and to calm down about Tala. Rolo, on the other hand, wasn't paying much attention to anything except Nina. She felt his come-on vibe; the way he leaned in toward her, how he smiled, took care of her needs. She knew she had to keep him at bay, yet at the same time, keep his interest. So she forced herself to look at him, willing herself to smile.

She got a break at intermission. Thank God for long bathroom lines. This time Tala backed off and didn't join her. Nina spotted Ana, the Teatro's set designer, fixing her hair in the mirror. Nina averted her eyes, but not before Ana caught sight of her.

"You seem familiar to me. Do we know each other?" Nina shook her head. "I'm an artist. Visual, you know. I never forget a face." She scrutinized Nina. "I know you're somebody I know."

Nina had worked closely with Ana during the Teatro's last theater show. She had that I'm-a-better-artist-than-you arrogance that grated on Nina's nerves.

Nina, sweating profusely now, felt as if the plastic part of the wig was melting to her scalp. She desperately wanted to scratch her head, but that would have been a giveaway to the astute Ana.

"I got it! You're Dara Velásquez," she said pointing. "I can always place a face. I haven't seen you in years, since we did the *Channeling Grace* show. What've you been up to?"

Nina stifled a smile. Dara Velásquez was an artist known throughout town for her macabre performance art. Nina played along, focusing on the irony since she herself was one of Dara's biggest critics. During Dara's last exhibit of menstrual blood paintings, Nina had told her she thought she was "unoriginal, and frankly trying too hard," which of course made Nina a mortal enemy.

"I've been traveling," said Nina, fake-frogging her voice. "Sorry, I, I have a little cold . . . Yes, well, I had a group show in LA, and a solo in Soho. Then I lucked out and won the *Art World* New Faces Prize. It's kept me hopping. How about you?"

Ana crinkled an eye. "Really?"

"Mmm-hmm. It's been a fab year." She checked her lipstick.

"Well, I, uh, I've been doing the art direction here. What do you think of the set?"

"It works." Nina folded her arms and gave Ana her own version of Ana's well-practiced arrogance.

Ana cleared her throat. "Right. Well." She looked at her watch. "I better get going. Second half is about to start." She scooted out the door.

This time Nina couldn't keep from laughing. Serves her right, she thought. Rolo looked happy when she finally returned. Once the second half started, he tried putting his arm around her but she gently shook it off. Part of Ciel's lessons were never to let a man think you're easy.

When the play was over, everyone got up and flowed out of the theater. Without a hitch they were back in his car. "So how'd you like it?" he asked.

"Ih lovedh it. It was a lot funnierh than Ih thought ith was going to be."

Rolo nodded, unconsciously scratching his fake beard. "Yeah, these guys here do a good job. I'm pleased you enjoyed it." He started the car. "So," he continued. "Would you like to go for a drink?"

Nina took a long, slow, deep breath. "Whath I'd really likeh is a physich healing."

"A what?" he asked, looking at Nina like she had just spoken pig latin.

"A physich healing." Hell, Nina thought, if he thinks I'm weird, then I might as well go for broke. "I've beenh feelingh kind ofh stressed lately. Ih guess with the newh jobh and everythingh. I thinkh it would beh good forh meh to seeh Pepah Romero for a limpiah, you knowh, a healing." She batted her eyelashes at him, looking as coy as she was capable. "Will youh take meh?"

Rolo studied the dashboard, clearly disappointed. "You really mean it, don't you?" he asked.

Nina nodded like a happy puppy. Rolo sighed, took a lingering glance at Nina, then answered, "OK." He put the PT Cruiser in gear and headed off to Pepa's Charm House.

Alrighty, thought Nina, here we go.

Warned that Nina might be bringing the mayor over that evening, Pepa and Camilo had everything planned, particularly around the fact that they would technically be treating Nina and not the mayor. Camilo hid in the back bedroom, and Pepa, hearing their approach, peeked through the window. Catching sight of the two in the yellow haze of her porch light, she nearly fell out laughing. Nina knocked on the outside door, and Pepa let her in, with the recalcitrant mayor trudging stiffly behind her.

"Hi, Miss Pepah," said Nina, giving the curandera an innocent-looking smile. "Meh and my friendh Manny here were outh at the theaterh and wellh, even though it's a bit lateh, I've beenh kindah stressed andh wondered if youh could maybeh give me a limpiah?"

"Bueno," Pepa said, folding her arms across her chest in an effort to contain her laughter. Now that she thought about it, Nina looked exactly like Cher, and Rolo a chubby Sonny. "Un momentito." She gestured toward two chairs and walked out of the waiting room. "I'm gonna be right back."

The Mayor and Nina sat down while Pepa continued through the treatment room, then into her house. She snatched a pillow, went into the bathroom, and shut the door. Burying her head deep into the pillow, she let the laugh she'd been stifling for the past two minutes into the pillow's polyester. The combination of her hyena-like laughter, and the pillow created a sound more akin to crying. Camilo tapped on the door, and Pepa let in her worried-looking assistant. Quickly shutting the door, she remarked, "I just couldn't hold it anymore." She sat on the toilet, clutching the pillow tightly to her chest.

"Hold what?" Camilo asked, still concerned.

Pepa, smiled, then wiped her eyes.

"Wait, you're not crying, you're laughing." Camilo looked both angry and relieved.

Pepa nodded. "Sí, they're both in costumes, and they look just like Sonny and Cher, pero un Sonny muy feo." She started laughing again, then took a deep breath in an effort to quell it. She rinsed her eyes with cool water and wiped off her face. "Wait till you see 'em." Then she realized, as she exited the bathroom, that he was probably too young to even know who Sonny and Cher were. Still chuckling, she went over to her bureau and pulled out an old mantilla that had belonged to her mother. It was in a plastic bag and in perfect condition. She placed the cream-colored veil on her head, figuring it would generate a sense of holiness about her and hopefully soothe any feelings of unease in her guests. The mantilla still smelled faintly of her mother, chamomile and lavender, bringing Pepa back to the seriousness of the moment. She remembered how her mother used to wear it during limpias with tough patients, said it was her good luck charm. Now focused on the purpose of the evening, Pepa walked out to greet her guests with the holiness of a Carmelite nun.

"Bueno," she said, as solemnly as she could, since the mere sight of Nina in her tight jeans and wig, and Rolo in his leather vest and beard, made her close to losing it again. "Venga conmigo." She gestured toward the treatment room where she was already burning calming hierbas.

Nina got up but the mayor stayed put. "Hey-uh, if you don't mind," he said, lifting his cap up and down, "I'd like to stay here. I'm sure you probably want your privacy and all." His eyes flitted from Nina to Pepa.

"Oh no, Mannyh. I want youh with meh." Nina gave him her practiced Marilyn Monroe pout, which Pepa watched in admiration.

"Uh, this stuff gives me the heebie-jeebies," he said, scrunching his shoulders. Pepa noticed he was starting to sweat, which made him look like a nervous billy goat.

"Ah, come onh, don't be a scaredy cath. I need big ol' youh with meh in case I fainth or somethingh." Nina gave Rolo another kitten face.

He lifted his baseball cap to scratch his head. "Well—OK. I guess I can stand in the doorway."

"Thank youh, Mannyh." Nina smiled at the mayor as the two followed Pepa into her treatment room. A Hopi chant with soft, rhythmic tones played on a hidden tape deck. Rolo looked around the room, his eyes stopping momentarily on the statues of the Virgen de Guadalupe and San Martín de Porres. Pepa had added a few things to her altar, such as shiny metal hearts and heads, and tiny statues of Zapotec gods. This was in addition to what she normally had, such as the hierbas burning in a metal container and various candles. Rolo's eyes wandered across the candles, black rocks, crystals, and the oils in different shades of green.

As Pepa set out several bowls of specially prepared hierbas, she glanced at the new additions above her altar: a photograph of Don Gabriel that Camilo had brought her, a faded picture of Shiprock she'd found in Taos, and a flat piece of wood etched with the face of Jesus. She'd made the Jesus face herself with a home wood-burning kit. An attempt, she thought, to comfort the anxieties of the more religious patients. Camilo remarked that it looked like a fourth-grader had done it, but Pepa dismissed the criticism, saying it was rough-looking on purpose, just like a real-life milagro. The photos of Don Gabriel and the other of Shiprock were added for Pepa's own spiritual guidance, especially since she felt she needed extra help for what she was about to embark on.

Breathing steady, Pepa focused on the task at hand. She and Camilo had prepared long in advance of this evening and felt determined to make the procedure they were about to begin a success. Nina sat on a chair. Rolo stood close by. Pepa took Nina's pulse, looked under her eyelids, and felt her forehead. "Está poquito caliente. What happened to you? Why are you so hot?"

Nina shrugged, then continued in her Marilyn Monroe voice. "Well, I've had a lot on my mind lately like a Ferris wheel inside my head. I don't know if I'm coming or going. My boss hates me—not you, Manny," she whispered, glancing at him. "—My supervisor Dahlia. I don't make enough money, and I'm sometimes overwhelmed by too many people wanting too much from me." She looked at Rolo again. He cocked his head, appearing concerned.

Pepa wasn't completely sure whether Nina was acting or telling the truth. She snuck a glance at Rolo. He looked tired. She gestured toward another chair in the room, and he gratefully took a seat. Of course the chair was placed directly in front of the burning hierbas. Pepa knew the hierbas would work quickly to relax the two. She looked at Nina's tongue. Truthfully, she thought Nina could benefit from the limpia no matter what they did to Rolo tonight. She began massaging Nina's hands, rubbing in one of her homemade salves. It smelled of lavender and rosemary. Nina smiled—her face and body began to relax.

Pepa walked over to check the burning hierbas, then added a little more. Due to their relaxing nature, both she and Camilo had taken an elixir to counteract their hypnotic effect.

"What're those for?" asked Rolo, pointing to the hierbas.

"These are for la mujer," Pepa answered, angling her eyes toward Nina. Satisfied with the simplistic answer, he crossed his arms and watched Pepa.

The treatment room had already gotten hot. The hierbas burning around Rolo had begun to make him sleepy. Pepa saw how he watched her massage Nina's hands. He probably wished he was doing the massaging. He closed his eyes, then opened them again, fighting to stay awake. He took off his hat and unsnapped the buttons on his vest. Pepa rolled a raw egg over Nina's body. Rolo's eyes widened.

Nina smiled when the egg touched her breasts, but Pepa didn't stop since she was concentrating on performing a true limpia. She figured why not kill two birds with one stone. She shot another glance at Rolo and saw him start to nod off. That's one tough bastard. Most sonavabitch's would've fallen asleep by now. She recalled the first time she met the mayor and had been taken aback by the hardness in his eyes.

She was almost done with the egg rolling. Nina, awake but relaxed, looked like a moldable Barbie. No wonder este cabrón mayor has the hots for her. Pepa set down the egg and half-carried Nina to the pallet she pulled out from under the altar. She helped Nina settle in and glanced at Rolo again, almost willing the big chingón to fall asleep. She closed her eyes, concentrating on the mayor. After a minute she opened them, then cracked the egg into a glass of agua preparada.

And as if by magic, Rolo keeled over.

Pepa made sure the now dozing Nina was comfortable and shifted her attention to the mayor. He had slumped halfway down the chair. But to make sure he was out, she waved the hierbas under his nose for another minute. He fell into a deep sleep with a soft purr of a snore. Satisfied, Pepa eased him to the floor, and placed the burning hierbas next to his head. Then she walked back to the bedroom and signaled Camilo to come out. He did, wearing a disguise of baggy pants, do-rag, and sunglasses, just in case Rolo awakened.

Pepa returned to her altar and lit her own candle for guidance. Her practice through the years had always been to heal, supported by her own desires, and the strong wills of her teachers. Yet the malpuesto she and Camilo were about to perform was contrary to everything she, and most certainly Camilo, had been taught.

Rolo's quest for power had hurt many of the people in town. And his support of Gilbert's winery could affect many more. Their lost futures were too much to ignore. This was an occasion where they had to make an exception. From everything she'd heard, Pepa knew Rolo was a bully. One look at the way the big oso swaggered told her he especially enjoyed scaring smaller men. Camilo, skinny as he was, had never been afraid of him. He said it had driven Rolo nuts since he couldn't, for the life of him, figure out why.

Pepa scrutinized the heft of the mayor's gut and the size of his overly padded shoulders. This man loved throwing his weight around, and that had to stop. "Bueno, cabrón, first thing we're gonna do is put you on a diet." She took some hierba del trueno, which was a stimulant, a pinch of the purgative, cascara sagrada, and handful of canchalagua to induce weight loss, and mashed them in her molcajete. Then she added prune juice and let the hierbas soften. Keeping an eye on Rolo, she snuck a quick look at Nina. "Go ahead and take off his jewelry now." Pepa gestured toward Rolo, and Camilo carefully removed a gold bracelet and his watch. Nina had already been instructed not to wear jewelry. Both noticed Rolo wasn't wearing any rings.

Pepa lit three purple candles, which she placed in a triangle around Rolo's body. Their purpose was to attack bad spirits, of which Rolo had plenty. She then took a clean turkey baster and dipped it in the prune juice mix, making sure she had sucked up all the hierbas. Camilo took Rolo's head and lifted it. Pepa recited an inaudible chant as she slowly dripped the juice down his throat.

"Bueno, 'stá bien," she said, removing the empty turkey baster. "Now comes the tricky part." Pepa recalled Camilo's saying that the mayor boasted he feared no one. He remembered once seeing Rolo embarrass the governor, then laugh out loud when confronted over his actions. Pepa knew this arrogance made Rolo blind to the pain of others—something she knew she needed to change. She grabbed popotón, chicolote, chayo, and pájaro bobo—all hierbas she'd gotten from a botánica in Oaxaca. Pepa was certain, though she'd never done this malpuesto before, that this combination of hierbas would add fear or, at the very least, greater sensitivity to Rolo's cold-hearted spirit.

Camilo brought out a small wooden box. Inside, wrapped in plastic, were dried, green buds. "This is hierba del coyote," Camilo said, handing one to Pepa. "Don Gabriel gave it to me before he died. He said it will add strength to whatever we use. The mayor has strong energy, so I want to make sure what we do tonight works."

Pepa trusted Camilo, who, after all, had studied far longer than she with their old teacher. She sprinkled her hierbas into a small pot of boiling water, then stood aside while he added his. Their harsh, metallic smell surprised her. To prevent any loss of potency, she covered them with a lid. While they boiled, Pepa turned her attention back to Nina. She examined the egg in the water, noting the color, contour, and shape. It seemed to indicate unease, a restlessness of spirit, which Camilo also agreed with. Pepa felt Nina's soul had been damaged from something in her past, something that had hardened her, since the sadness appeared so deep. Retrieving a bowl of agua preparada, Pepa rubbed lemon verbena oil into her hands, then immersed them in the water for a full minute. She dried each hand, then placed one on Nina's chest and the other on her stomach, gently working to remove the pain still present in her body. Moaning from Pepa's touch, Nina began weeping, her eyes tearing with relief. Pepa knew Nina needed more than a single limpia, but for this particular evening it would have to suffice.

Camilo lit three green candles in a triangle around Nina, while chanting the Twelve Truths of the World. The candles were to protect her from further harm and counteract the damage that had already been done. Nina's spirit needed extra strength now that she was working for Rolo, so as Pepa focused on drawing the damaged energy out of Nina, Camilo took a branch of albaca and swept it over her body. Nina's eyes flickered, and she smiled when the hierba brushed her face. She stayed in the trance, breathing softly as the candles shimmered around her.

When the boiled hierbas were ready, Pepa poured everything into a bowl of flour de maíz, stirring until it was thoroughly mixed. She took it outside to cool and set it on one of the benches. It was a moonless night, the sky covered in clouds. Pepa couldn't remember the last time she'd seen so many clouds. A soft roll of thunder rumbled across the mountains. The sky lit up as lightning flickered a moment later. In a matter of seconds, rain began to fall. A wide grin broke across Pepa's face as she listened to the drops popping against her tin roof. She walked through her yard, arms spread with joy, and smelled the heady combination of water on parched earth. Nowhere did she know a fragrance so lovely. Had the drought finally broken? She glanced at her cooling poultice and noticed rain splattering the steaming concoction. No importa, she thought. A little bit of moisture from the sky would do no harm. If anything, it was a good sign.

She went inside to check on Rolo and Nina. The air in the treatment room was thick with the pungent odors of the hierbas. Camilo was keeping close watch on everything, his eyes blinking away the acrid smells around him. "'Stá bien?" Pepa asked.

"Like sleeping little lambs," Camilo replied.

"Hear the rain?" Pepa gestured toward the ceiling.

Camilo nodded and smiled. "It's hard to believe, que no?"

Pepa checked both Rolo's and Nina's pulses. Satisfied, she walked back outside.

As she stood next to the cooling poultice, she let the rain fall on her, each drop its own caress. She and the mantilla she wore were getting wet, but it felt so good she didn't care. She waited another minute, then picked up the bowl of the now lukewarm poultice, and returned to the house.

Camilo had rolled back the mayor's shirt to expose his chest and stomach. He also removed Rolo's shoes and socks. Pepa put on latex gloves, placed the poultice on top of a cutting board covered with wax paper, and separated it into several pieces. Still warm, it glistened from the moisture of the rain. She took each poultice and pressed it on Rolo's chest, stomach, palms, and bottoms of his feet. Heavily sedated by the hierbas, he slept through it all. Droplets of water from Pepa's hair fell over Rolo's face as she applied the poultices. The patter outside decreased. Pepa chanted prayers to the spirits around her to guide this task and instill power to the hierbas. She hoped they would see that the intention of the malpuesto was only for greater good. Camilo added more trance-inducing hierbas to those burning near Rolo. It was important to keep him still during the process. Nina slept peacefully while the candles around her burned.

After twenty minutes, the poultices had completely cooled and were somewhat hardened. As Camilo removed each piece, he said his own prayers in a combination of Spanish and Náhuatl. Pepa took warm water and carefully cleaned off any residue. She rubbed diluted lemon verbena oil on all the spots. This would clear the mind and cover the smell of the hierbas. She also dabbed a bit on Nina's forehead and along the base of her neck. They put Rolo's clothes and jewelry back on and propped him back against the chair. Camilo blew out the candles and took them outside. Then he returned to his hiding place.

Pepa extinguished the trance-inducing hierbas. She opened all the doors to clear the air. When the couple began to stir, she closed the doors and burned dried peppermint to wake them. Finally, she took sahumerio de San Cipriano—a specially prepared hierba for cleansing—and placed it in a small metal bowl. She lit it and instructed a groggy Nina to take several deep breaths.

Nina leaned over the bowl, inhaled the sahumerio smoke, looked up at Pepa, and smiled. "Wow, I feel calm, lighter, like I've had a long vacation."

Rolo woke and rubbed his eyes. "I must've dozed off. How long was I out?"

"Not very long," Pepa said, studying Rolo while assisting Nina.

Rolo unconsciously rubbed his stomach, then burped. "Excuse me," he said, as he pulled himself back on the chair. He adjusted his beard, and glanced around. "It smells like lemons," he said, sniffing. He looked confused. "I don't remember you using them, but I know I can smell them." His tone was more curious than expectant, already a notable change.

"Bueno, sí," replied Pepa, completely at ease. "I put aceite de lemon verbena on Nina, and a little on you. It purifies the body. You needed it, too, since you were in the same room with her. It could take away all the work I just did if I didn't give you any. It won't hurt you. Mire." She took the vial of lemon oil, opened it, and rubbed some on her wrist. Then she let Rolo sniff it. He took a whiff and nodded.

Satisfied, he stood up, buttoned his vest, and put on his hat. "Bueno, so she's done now, eh?" he asked, rubbing his stomach again.

"Sí," said Pepa, stifling a yawn. "She's all done. She's gonna feel real good now, I guarantee it." She smiled, thinking how he'd feel the opposite.

Nina adjusted her wig. Pepa noticed she looked hot under all that hair "Bueno, gracias Pepa. What do I owe youh?"

"Forty bucks," said Pepa, as she snuffed out the San Cipriano hierbas. "Late-night discount."

"Looks like it rained a little," Nina remarked as they walked to the car.

"Yeah, it does," answered Rolo. He opened Nina's car door, and the two drove to Ciel's without a word. Rolo parked the car and remarked that he had an upset stomach.

"What did you eat?" Nina asked.

"Just a bowl of menudo—might've been some bad tripe, though."

Nina didn't want to hear more. "Well, I hope you feel better."

"Oh sure, I will," Rolo said, with a shrug.

"Thanks for the nice evening," Nina still felt light. "And thanks for coming with me to Pepa's. I can't believe how great I feel." Rolo looked at her with twinkly eyes, then leaned in for a kiss. Anticipating this, Nina pulled away. "Uh, I don't think so."

"You mean I had to look at your pretty face all night and can't even get a good-bye kiss?"

"That's right," said Nina, forcing a smile. She grabbed the door handle and opened it. Rolo tried to touch her face, but she managed to scramble away. "Bye bye," she said, slamming the door.

It was nearly midnight, but Ciel was still up. She peeked through the curtains after Nina walked in. "He's gone," she said, then sat on the chair facing her. "How did it go?"

"Well, it's over," said Nina. Then with a grunt she pulled off her wig. "I was kinda in a trance so I don't know what Pepa and Camilo did to Rolo, but *I* feel pretty damn good. I didn't think they were gonna do something to *me*, but it looks like they did since I feel so good now." She ran her hands through her hair, scratched her scalp, then collapsed on the couch.

The telephone rang. Ciel picked it up and said it was Tala. "Tell her to come get me," Nina yelled across the room. "And to bring some beer!"

27

THE FOLLOWING MONDAY ROLO, still nauseous, and Nina, forewarned that he'd feel crappy, took advantage of the situation while Dahlia was on break. Nina sought the names of editors and TV station managers he'd told earlier not to run any news on the Dogtown residents. Camilo said Rolo had threatened them all with some kind of payback. Nina wanted to see if some of Pepa's magic had worked.

"Mayor Reyes, don't you think it's funny no one's written a story about how the winery will affect the people living there?" Rolo looked surprised about her question but seemed too sick to care.

"Yeah, maybe, I don't know. I guess so." He rubbed his belly, his face a sallow green.

"Why d'you think?" Nina, still talking in her "Marilyn voice," gave him her coy muchacha look—something she'd mimicked from a Mexican panadería wrapper. She eyed the clock, knowing Dahlia was due back soon.

"I don't know. They're all a bunch of shit-disturbers. Everything they write makes my job harder. We got their names in a file under media assholes or something." He gestured toward the file drawer. "But fair's fair, I guess. Maybe you should contact them." He burped, then disappeared into his office.

Nina used her lunch break to happily type memos to those same people, saying Rolo had changed his mind. She copied the mayor's ostentatious signature across the bottom of each letter and faxed them all off.

In a matter of what seemed like minutes, the mayor's blackout of Dogtown news had been lifted. Domingo Salazar called for an emergency meeting at Opal McGee's house, and formulated a plan. The CURs wanted Benny Lucero, Mrs. Gallegos, Opal McGee, and Domingo to do the first round of talking to the reporters. All that had been stated by the media so far was how wonderful the winery was going to be, how great the wine would taste, and how many jobs the winery would provide. In addition, a native New Mexican—a Hispano—was establishing the winery, an accomplishment many were proud of. Gilbert Córdova, at least in the public's eye, actually had the knowledge, desire, and money not only to make great wine, but also to put New Mexico on the winemaking map. The full impact of people losing their homes and businesses was of course minimized. The Dogtown folk had a different angle to present to the media. Everyone received a list of data points to study before their interviews with reporters, and they all spoke not only the facts, but also with their hearts.

❋

The media's effect was immediate. Profits made by the Indian tribes who had developed casinos around Santa Fe had been good. There were several tribes, however, who hadn't erected casinos and were hurting for cash. One tribe, who asked to remain anonymous, heard about the proposed winery and offered Gilbert an opportunity to lease some of their land on the outskirts of town. In return Gilbert would pay a leasing fee and give the tribe a share of the profits.

Tala urged her brother to accept the offer. The two were having their monthly lunch at the Plaza Cafe, filled to the gills with tourists and locals. Hungry, Tala ordered a hamburger with green chile, french fries, and a Coke. Appalled at Tala's choice of lunch fare, her brother requested a Cobb salad with a glass of Pinot Grigio.

"I'd go for the tribal offer, if I were you," Tala said, taking a bite of hamburger. "This way you avoid the hassles with the Doggies. They got Elena Luján for a lawyer y'know. One of the best." She dipped a french fry in catsup and popped it in her mouth.

Gilbert chewed his salad, not bothering to conceal his disdain. "That land shark's got a snowball's chance in hell of beating me, and you know it."

Tala's face reddened with anger. "Hey, cool it with the names, OK? She's a friend of mine."

"Sorry," Gilbert said, rolling his eyes. "Anyway, *lawyer* or not, I got everything taken care of *and* the zoning changed." He took a sip of wine, eyes focused intensely on his sister.

Tala noticed his hard little stare and took several gulps of Coke. "Yeah, OK, but wouldn't it be cool if you got your winery without a fight? The Doggies amped up their publicity, and I just heard *60 Minutes* might pick up the story. If they do, you're gonna come out looking like a burnt sopapilla."

"What do you mean?" Gilbert asked, fork suspended in front of him.

"You know, brown all around but white when you bite."

"That's crazy," Gilbert said, shaking his head.

"It's not," Tala replied, her eyes gleaming with excitement. She picked up another french fry "This is a great op for you to bow out gracefully. You save face by helping the Native folks," she said, pointing with the fry. "The Doggies get to stay, you get your winery, and you still make a profit. What's there to lose?" She took another drink of Coke and eyed her brother back.

Gilbert threw down his fork. "Wait, whose side you on, anyway? You've been trying from day one to get me to pull out of this."

"And I've also told you from day one how I felt about losing my place, but that doesn't seem to matter. What I'm telling you now, though, is good business logic."

"And what I'm offering you is fair market value."

"Which is still chump change when it comes to what I'd need to buy another house." Tala sighed in frustration. "Plus, this tribe is making you a good offer." She paused to study a family of tourists eating plates of flat enchiladas. All of them seemed happy, as if they actually enjoyed being with each other. "Look, you love wine," she said, turning back to her brother. "You love drinking it, and all you really want to do is make it. So why do you have to make it in Dogtown? Rolo has you brainwashed thinking it's the only place you can do it. It's doesn't make sense to have it here, or for that matter to keep that blowhard happy."

Gilbert looked like he was holding something back.

"What?"

"It's not just the mayor who wants it here . . . It's me."

"But why? Nothing about this makes any sense." Tala honestly couldn't figure out why Gilbert needed his winery in city limits.

"I want to make wine. You're right, that's what I primarily care about. But I want it here so I can be closer to home. Up until I got the tribal offer, I didn't have many options. Rolo liked the idea of Santa Fe wine—said it'd be good for sales, which I happen to agree with. Plus Claire says the terroir is surprisingly good." He folded his napkin into long, thin rectangles.

Tala stabbed four french fries and let the fork stand on its own. "That soil is desert. Claire will need to shove compost in from half the state just to get anything to grow. The plain and simple is Rolo wants taxes and profits, but he especially wants to bulldoze the poor side of town. What better way to do it than with your project and your money?" Tala couldn't help speaking sarcastically. "You've been had, Gilbert. Just like everyone else who deals with that mayor."

"You don't know the whole story." Smug, Gilbert waved off Tala's comment. "And you don't know *half* the things Rolo's done for me. He's backed me up on this almost as much as Mom and Dad."

Tala picked up the fry-laden fork, willing herself not to fling it. "Well, I am so impressed. You've got all your connections, favors from the mayor, Mom and Dad's blessings, and approval from our big brothers, not to mention their money. And you're going to do all this just so you can make wine at the expense of people who can't afford to move anywhere else."

Gilbert sighed. "How many times do we have to go over this?"

"You don't care, do you? Not about me, not about those—"

"If I have to hear you say *those poor, innocent people of Dogtown* one more time, I'll—"

"What, Gilbert! You'll what?!"

"I don't know what I'll do," he said, clenching his jaw like he actually would do something.

"That's it then." Tala threw her napkin on the table. "I don't have to deal with your threats or listen to you spew your coldhearted crap every time we meet, especially while I live next to the very people affected by your self-serving project. I'm not doing this anymore."

Gilbert's eyes narrowed. "What did you just say?"

Tala saw the anger on his face, yet continued. "You heard me. You keep refusing to see how these people will be—actually are being hurt by this plan of yours. I had naively hoped you'd change your mind from our meetings together. Hoped that you might see how much this is hurting everyone—

especially me." She paused, holding back her tears. "But now that you're a member of the big man club there's no going back."

Gilbert stood up, crimson splotches erupting across his neck. "So that's what this is about."

The derision in his voice felt like a slap. "Yeah, that and a whole lot more," Tala said. "I've been trying to explain what I feel to you. But you're not listening. You don't even see me! All you see is what you want."

"Oh really? I think I'm seeing things pretty clear right now. And that's that I have a sister who cares more about other people than her own family."

"That's a bunch of bullshit and you know it. *You're* the one who doesn't care about the family. You only care about yourself! That's your real story, isn't it, Gilbert? Isn't it?"

"You know what Tala? Go to hell!" He reached in his wallet, pulled out a twenty, and threw it on the table. Then he marched out of the restaurant and cut across the plaza, never once looking back.

Despite all her anger, and there was certainly plenty, Tala couldn't help recalling the brother he once was. "But I'm wasting my time because that man doesn't care." When the server returned she ordered a pint of Dos Equis—just like their old times on hot, summer days. Now, sitting alone, she raised the glass in a toast: "To my assholian brother! May you someday see who you now truly are." She took a long swallow of beer, wiped her lips, and hoisted the glass again. "And to me and you, and to what we once were. May *I* finally accept who you now truly are." She took a longer swallow, then another for good measure. "That ought do it," she said, to no one in particular. Then she tossed down more money and walked out of the door.

28

DESPITE THE BAD PUBLICITY, twenty residents accepted Gilbert's offer. Word spread like an oil slick, with almost all signers remarking that they had attended Father Miguel's Mass during his "sleepy-time sermon" two weeks ago.

"It was as if I'd been in a bad nightmare and, bueno—I woke up," said Dora Cabrillo, who was overheard by Irma, Pepa's friend, talking about it at Chick's Laundromat.

"Qué bad nightmare," commented Pepa, as she and Camilo hiked up their favorite trail shortly after they'd heard the news. The Sangre de Cristos glowed hazy purple in the early morning light. Pepa's dog, Joaquin, walked ahead of them, marking the trail, while Irma's dog, Chica, followed close behind. "The only bad nightmare esta Dora has is her own making. I knew she'd sell out." Pepa kept a fast pace, making it hard for Camilo to talk.

"Sí, pero, what about the others?" he asked, breathing hard. The morning air, still cool, enveloped them like a blanket. The rain that had fallen the night of Rolo and Nina's "treatments" occurred only for that evening. The September day ahead would be exactly like the spring and summer preceding it: hot and dry.

"It's hard to believe twenty people sold out just like that," Camilo said, snapping his fingers. "It was like the hierbas we burned were some kind of truth serum, que no?" He stopped, leaning over to catch his breath.

Pepa noticed several white datura flowers had bloomed, reflecting the sky's golden light. She loved watching how different flowers bloomed over the seasons, even more amazed that they persisted despite the drought.

Camilo continued, "We were trying to get everyone to listen to Father Miguel. But maybe what they were really doing was listening to themselves."

Pepa stopped and faced Camilo, the simplicity of his words caught her attention.

"I think you might be right. If we gave them a truth serum, like you said, then maybe this is it, que no? Maybe everyone else will stay?"

Camilo shook his head. "Oooh no, because not everyone went to Mass that day. All I can say is, if we do the hierbas again, we should practice on a few people first. Either that," he said, looking off toward the mountains, "or we better think of something else."

They were almost home when Pepa saw it first. Camilo, following close behind, nearly ran into her as she stopped to gape at the huge sign in front of Dora Cabrillo's home. Somehow, during the past twenty-four hours, Gilbert's contractors had erected a large, colorful sign, stating "Future Home of the Sangre del Sol Winery." On it was a generic-looking hacienda, complete with grapes, workers, and the New Mexican state symbol.

"A qué cabrón!" Pepa stood, transfixed.

Camilo grabbed both the dogs and leashed them. "He went and did it, didn't he?"

Distracted, Pepa didn't notice Jules had pulled up in his truck, climbed out of it, and stood alongside her.

"This is a sad day," he said, shaking his head.

"Stupid me," Camilo replied, eyes tearing. "And here I thought we still had a chance."

Dora lived on a corner lot at the edge of Dogtown. Her house, old and dilapidated, had a large porch with several steps leading up to it. She lived on the main drag, and anyone driving down it passed her house with hardly a blink. Today, however, was a different story. A large group had gathered at the bottom of her steps. Tala, on her way to work with her dog and rooster, saw the sign and braked so hard the poor animals slammed into each other in a loud flurry of howls and screeches. Luckily, both of them had survived similar mishaps before. Still, they were upset and decided right then to raise a fuss. Tala parked in front of Dora's house, too angry to pay more than cursory attention to the pets. She checked to see if they were OK, and seeing that they were, left them inside. In her haste, she forgot to roll up the window.

Tala spotted Dora on her porch, sitting like a queen on an old, tattered couch. Her five children stood around her. The eldest boy held the baby, and the younger three huddled quietly behind the couch. Tala's dog, unhappy to be left in the truck, leaned halfway out the window, barking in furious yelps, while Otis, standing on the seat beside him, bellowed an incessant siren of crows.

Nina, on her way to work, pulled over, and Tala ran over to join her.

"That pinche cabrona sold us down the river." Nina hit the steering wheel, glowering at the contented-looking Dora.

Leaning against the car door, Tala crossed her arms in disgust. "How 'bout my pinche brother?" Their relationship, what was left of it, seemed completely shot to hell. She looked around to see who else she recognized in the crowd. "There's Jaime and Myrna." Tala jerked her chin toward the couple.

"I'm sure they sold out, too," Nina replied, eyes hard with anger.

"And I see Pepa, Camilo, and Jules across the street."

Nina grabbed Tala's arm. "Well, Amor, your brother's clearly playing hardball, so we better figure out what we're gonna do next."

Sighing, Tala nodded. "Yeah . . ." She glanced at her watch. "Hey, you're gonna be late. Call me, OK?" She tapped the truck as Nina put it in gear and drove away.

In the meantime, Pepa noticed the growing crowd had begun harassing Dora, calling her names, including a money-grubbing sellout. "My kids need a future," she hollered at their taunts.

"Bet you weren't thinking that when you were making them," yelled Papa Chick, hands cupped around his mouth, body stooped and gnarly as an old manzanita bush.

"Shut up, you old fart! It's none of your damn business what I do in my private life!" said Dora.

"What private life?" he replied, laughing. "Everyone knows all your doings."

"Since when did you get appointed Pope?" Dora responded, pointing at the old man.

"Wasn't it just yesterday you found who the real daddy was to your oldest boy?" Papa Chick slapped back.

"Cállese hombre!" Pepa yelled, worried.

But the old man paid no attention. "And I heard it was a double sad day, since it turned out it was your own daddy."

"You sonavabitch! I ain't letting you get away with talking to me like that!" Dora vanished into the house.

"Uh-oh, I don't like the looks of this," said Jules.

Pepa agreed. "Este cabrón is just going to stand there and piss her off till she does something stupid." The three planted themselves against an adobe wall. Pepa lit a cigarette and saw that Dora had returned with a shotgun.

"Now let's see you talk!" she said, loading the gun.

"Ay, no," exclaimed Camilo. "Somebody better call the cops."

Right then, as if on cue, a police car drove up. "Ahí viene el Tacho," Pepa said, eyeing her former patient.

Tacho took one look at the situation, and talked into his radio.

"And here comes the shit kickers," added Pepa, watching a group of worried Dogtownies drive up with an angry-looking Domingo Salazar. The flurry of activity was accompanied by the cacophony of the dog and the rooster, both of whom had jumped out of Tala's truck and were now roaming through the crowd.

Dora cocked the gun and fired it into the air. Everyone screamed, clearing a wide circle around her. Her kids, looking well experienced in motherly instability, stepped closer to the front door. The rooster, frightened by the gunshot, ran around the yard raising more of a fuss. Tala tried to catch him and her dog, who had stormed to the bottom of Dora's steps and started barking, chest out with teeth bared. Dora pointed her gun at the dog and screamed, "Get this goddamn pit bull outta here, or I'm gonna kill it!"

"I got her! I got her! Don't kill my dog. She's not gonna do nothing to you!" Tala abandoned the rooster, caught the dog and dragged her back to the truck, shoving her inside. This time she rolled up the window high enough so she wouldn't escape.

Tacho and his newly arrived police pals had their guns drawn. Dora's kids looked frightened and confused. "I want you to put the gun down, Dora," said Tacho, his voice calm and soothing. "No one's gonna hurt you. But the gun has to go."

"These people are nuts," hollered Dora. "They got something to prove.

Well, I ain't letting 'em. It's a free country and too goddamn bad if they don't like it." She pointed her gun at the crowd. Several people screamed.

Pepa held her breath, praying for Dora's sanity. She saw Domingo wave to the cops, then slowly walk to the bottom of Dora's steps. "Oye, mujer."

"Don't 'oye mujer' me. Get the hell off my property!" Dora glared at the councilman.

"What's he doing?" whispered Pepa.

"I will. I promise you I will, but could you at least hear me out?"

She didn't shoot, but stood, rigid with anger, finger on the trigger.

"Look, you know me, right? You know how I feel about este winery. Pero, I've always been up-front with you, que no? With you, and with everyone else." He gestured toward the crowd. "As your councilman, my job is to insure your constitutional rights. And that's freedom of speech and freedom to sell your own damn house, if that's what you want to do."

"'Cept she don't own it," shouted Papa Chick.

"Quiet!" Domingo yelled, eyes still on Dora who had swiveled the gun toward the old man.

"Hold on! Hold on!" Domingo continued, pressing his hands downward. "Don't pay him no mind."

"I'm going to tell Tacho to get rid of that pendejo," said Pepa, standing.

"Oh, no you're not," said Camilo who grabbed her arm and held her back.

Dora, gun still leveled at Papa Chick, looked like she might be listening.

"I know we disagree on this winery mierda," Domingo added, "Pero, I know damn well I can't tell you how to live your life. And that goes for everyone here." He gestured toward the crowd.

"Errr-errr-errr-errr-errrrr," crowed Otis, now pecking at the ground in front of Dora's steps.

"Tala, you better get that bird," Domingo yelled.

"Otherwise she might kill it and eat it," whispered someone in the crowd. Several people chuckled. Domingo glared at Papa Chick.

"Hey, it wasn't me," he said, taking a step back, waving toward the ground. Camilo still hung on to Pepa.

"Bueno," Domingo continued, looking at the crowd. "You all know Dora isn't the only one who said yes to Gilbert. And given it's a free country, all of you'd be just as pissed off as she is here if this situation was reversed. Am I right?" Several people in the crowd nodded. "I said, am I right?"

"Yeah," added a few souls.

"So, Dora," he said, turning back to her. "Put the gun down. No one's gonna hurt you. Some of these people here might be pretty damn mad. But it's your goddamn God-given right to give up your property. Maybe the whole pinche problem will be settled in the courts. But I can't tell you what to do, just like you can't tell me. And neither can anyone else, not even Papa Chick." He gestured toward the still defiant old goat. "So put the gun down, mujer. Put it down."

Papa Chick folded his arms across his chest, almost daring her to shoot him. Dora licked her lips, the gun still aimed in his direction. Finally, after glaring at the crowd, she slowly—so slow it was almost painful—lowered the shotgun. When it was finally on the ground, the crowd released a collective sigh. Tacho tiptoed to Dora and grabbed the gun. Trembling with relief, she gathered her kids around her.

Pepa released a big breath and settled back against the wall.

Domingo walked away, and Pepa signaled him to join them. He'd worked up a sweat and wiped his face with the palms of his hands. Standing next to Pepa, he pulled a cigar out of his pocket. "Tell you one thing, that's one woman in the neighborhood I won't miss."

Pepa handed him her lighter. "Oye, Councilman, that was a pretty good speech you gave." Pepa eyed Domingo as he lit his cigar. She waited till he had it good and lit. "You believe all that crap you were saying?"

Domingo puffed out a big cloud of smoke, glancing over in Dora's direction. The cops had gathered around her, filing reports and waving away people. "Ah, hell no," he said, grinning. "All I was doing was giving her my best bullshit so she'd drop that gun."

29

Elena Luján opened the morning paper and let out a barely audible "crap." "Woman Defends Right to Free Speech" was splayed across the front page, with a shot of Dora standing on the porch surrounded by her kids, gun in hand. Elena stared at the picture, shaking her head, wondering sometimes why she had ever pursued the line of work she was in. She threw three sugar cubes instead of the usual two into her coffee. It was uncanny how people could twist the facts. She took a sip, grimacing because it was now too sweet. She grabbed the phone and gave Tala a call.

"Hi. I read what happened in the newspaper today. Any chance you and I could meet to discuss this?"

"I'm slammed all day," said Tala, "but I can get together tomorrow."

Impatient, Elena didn't want to wait. "I was thinking more like today, like after work, at the Railyard. What do you think?"

"Uh, I was going to work on inventory, but I guess it can wait."

"OK, let's meet at, say, seven?"

"See you then."

Satisfied, Elena finished reading the article, wadded it up, then shunted it across the room.

With the same newspaper article spread across his desk, Gilbert pumped his arms back and forth with ecstatic little jabs. He knew people would react to the sign he erected, but he couldn't have scripted a better result. "Pure, absolute gold, pairing the winery with free speech," he muttered to himself. He'd been so preoccupied with putting up the sign, he couldn't tell anyone, not even his family, about it, but now that that loca Dora had gotten him so much positive press, he was damn glad he'd done it. He reread the article, then took the paper and folded it into a glider. Hoisting it to his head, he let it go with a flick of his wrist and watched it sail over his desk, across the room, and out the window.

Tala walked into the door of the Railyard and saw Elena waiting for her at the bar.

"Hey, good to see you." She gave her a hug. "Saved you a seat." She pulled her briefcase off the chair next to her.

"Thanks." Tala noticed Elena had on a sexy black dress, with enough cleavage inside to challenge any good intention.

"What would you like?" Elena asked, signaling the bartender.

Tala stole another look, her breath growing shallow. I'll bet that cabrona wore that dress on purpose. "A Bohemia would be great."

Elena ordered herself a martini and the beer for Tala. "Listen, I want to thank you for getting together with me," she said, flashing those million dollar eyes. "I was pretty upset about that article and needed to talk."

The bartender brought the drinks, and the two did a quick toast.

"That's understandable," said Tala, knocking back a long pull. "I'm still pissed about it too."

"And thirsty, by all appearances."

"You got that right," Tala said, trying not to stare. "Dealing with all this crap can really take it out of you."

"So, uh," Elena placed her hand on Tala's wrist. "Do you mind filling me in on what exactly happened?"

Tala wondered if Elena's hand was simply being friendly. She slapped herself back into focus and concentrated on recapping what had occurred at Dora's house, tossing in a few choice words about her brother. "I swear," she said, finishing the story, "I really didn't know if that crazy loon was going to pull the trigger."

"Thank God she didn't," said Elena, laughing. "Though Gilbert probably would've found a way to exploit that, too." She paused, suddenly realizing she'd just spoken ill of Tala's brother. "I'm sorry, I didn't mean to . . . it's just that martinis have this way of bringing out the truth."

"Then you of all people should avoid them."

"You got that right," she said, leaning in, brushing her chiches against Tala's arm. She lifted her beer bottle. "Hey, you're almost empty. Would you like another?"

Tala couldn't figure out what the hell was going on, and she certainly didn't think it was a good idea to stick around to find out. "You know, normally I would," she replied, checking her watch. "But I—uh think I'd better not."

Elena looked disappointed. "Can I get a rain check?"

"I'm totally sure that you, me, and all the others will have plenty more opportunities to drink." Tala gathered up her things. "Thanks for the beer. I'll talk to you later."

❀

Nina pulled up at Pepa's house and wiped the sweat from her eyes. The CURs had called an emergency community meeting. As usual, the drought-driven heat dried everything in its path. Nina exited her truck and felt a slight zip of a breeze, which brought only hints of relief to her and the heat-soaked crowd. The meeting, once again in Pepa's yard, was set up with benches, chairs, and a makeshift podium—a wooden crate covered with a serape. Nina noticed Pepa had lit copper urns again around the perimeter of the yard that burned a mixture of sweet smelling hierbas. She recognized the scent of lavender and sage.

Domingo, Elena, Benny Lucero, and Father Miguel had come to the meeting, as well as several people from the neighborhood. Papa Chick arrived with a young-looking dog—some kind of shepherd mix, from the looks of her. Maybe he was feeling the need for protection. Luz and Jules walked in wearing matching boots and cowboy hats. Their cream-colored hats, with brown feathers on the side, were complimented by turquoise Quetzalcoatl birds etched across the toe of each boot. Nina restrained herself from rolling her eyes. Out of disguise and in her usual attire of T-shirt and jeans, she volunteered to be the facilitator. Tala stayed in the back.

"What we have here," Nina said, glaring at the people around her, "is a state of emergency. Gilbert got himself a few sellouts and, on that basis, put up his pinche sign in front of Dora's house advertising his Sangre de Asshole Winery." Papa Chick clapped, giving her a tooth-missing grin.

"Now I know how a lot of you feel about this. But what we need to know tonight is if you're still willing to kick some Sangre de Pinche Sol butt?" She looked around and noticed most everyone nodding. "Can I get a show of hands of people willing to go down to the wire on this?" All hands present went up. "Good," she said, nodding. "Now here's Elena for the legal stuff. "

"As most of you know," Elena began, "our complaint with the city for an infringement of our due process right to retain Dogtown as a residential district was dismissed." Papa Chick and Opal McGee booed. "Knowing how well connected Gilbert is I expected this. In which case, I have now filed a suit against Córdova Enterprises in an effort to stop him from building the winery. The suit contends that living here is historically protected and that losing your home is an infringement of your human rights. The city of Santa Fe and, by proxy, Gilbert Córdova, will ultimately try to establish, but should not have, eminent domain rights to take your space."

"That's right!" shouted Nina, fist in the air.

"Still, what I think and what I filed does not necessarily mean we'll win. In the end," she said, returning her gaze to Nina, "it could depend on the decision of a judge."

Nina looked down, shaking her head.

"What we need," Elena said, "is even more publicity."

Pepa placed one of the urns with the burning hierbas closer to Elena. She added more lavender, then blew on it to get it going.

"So when this goes to court, people will see what all of you will lose." Elena sniffed, then frowned at Pepa's close placement of the hierbas. She coughed, then took a step back from the billowing smoke. "This calls for petitions, a web page, signs, and strategies to get publicity that helps *us* since Mr. Córdova is getting a boatload of good press over Dora's little Annie Oakley show."

Opal and Papa Chick hissed.

"I call it boatload of bullshit," Nina yelled out to the crowd.

"Call it what you want," said Elena, "but we need to get people to see our side of the story. We need people with connections to the media and people who are willing to go door-to-door. Everyone needs to explain what's really going on and how your rights are being threatened."

"We can do this!" Nina said, pounding the podium, moving closer to Elena.

"And we need signs in every yard, bumper stickers for our cars, radio and television spots, press releases, and more. These things cost money."

"And we're not talking about bake sale money either," added Nina.

"That's right," said Elena. "We're going to have to start a fundraising campaign—get things going to bring in cash. How about somebody organizing a big fundraiser, get some local artists to donate pieces for an auction, big-name writers who'll read, some prominent people who'll either donate or speak for our cause."

"Like Shirley MacClaine!" someone yelled.

"Yes, like Shirley MacClaine," Elena answered, searching the crowd. "Who's willing to head up the fundraising campaign?"

"I will," said Jules, who removed his hat and stood tall, looking around the yard. "I got enough time to do it and enough people I know here in town, Española, and Albuquerque, plus a few other places."

"But do you know Shirley MacClaine?" asked Domingo.

Jules offered a shy smile. "Can't say I do, but I can ask around till I find someone who does."

Elena flashed a wide grin. "Thank you, Jules. It's a big task, and we appreciate it."

Nina watched her work the crowd, admitting she *was* cute. No wonder Tala had gone out with her.

"OK, we're doing good," Elena continued. "But we need a better space for organizing. Let's settle that now. Can anyone donate a room to our publicity campaign?"

"They can use my dining room," said Opal McGee. "And my house is right in the middle of all of you," she said, pointing to the crowd.

"Wonderful," said Elena. "Let's give a big thanks to Opal." Several people cheered. Nina gave her a thumbs up. Elena hesitated, then continued. "I have one last thing to say."

"Hey! Quiet, everybody, she's not done yet!" Nina rapped on the podium. The mood shifted back to serious. Even Papa Chick kept silent, his dog settling down next to him.

"This fight's not going to be easy. And . . ." she rubbed her forehead, focusing on a blazing candle of San Martín . . . "it could get pretty nasty."

"Well, we're not giving up!" said Nina, taking over the podium. "Ain't that right?"

"That's right!" said Pepa, clapping. "Sí-se-pue-de. Sí-se-pue-de." Others chanted and clapped with her until the entire crowd erupted into a raucous cheer.

After Dora's little incident, several more Dogtowners gave in to Gilbert's offer. It was as if Dora had become the Pied Piper for the Sangre del Sol Winery. People who had been fence-sitters in the past decided to accept Gilbert's offer simply because they perceived the "attack" on Dora as an attack on their free speech. Conservative columnists picked up on the story and wrote about it in several big papers. The bad publicity for the Canines was damaging their cause, since those who weren't close enough to the actual problem were more easily duped by the poor-Dora angle.

"Next thing you know, they'll have Clint Eastwood doing a gig for them," grumbled Nina, as she and Tala watched the evening news. Exhausted from trying days at work, the two had splayed themselves across the couch, knocking back bone-cold Bohemias. Nina had typed a gazillion letters for Rolo, who was capitalizing on all the publicity to raise money for his re-election campaign. It didn't matter that the election was two years away. Rolo told her that starting to bankroll a big war chest now would ultimately pay off down the line.

A commercial came on, and Nina's attention shifted back to her job. She'd never before had to work for somebody she didn't respect. Even Mingo, the cheapskate owner of the Donut Time, had political convictions. Rolo was a whole different ball of mierda. After their date together, and finished with the task of getting him over to Pepa's house, Nina put her foot down about going out with him again. It had been too taxing to play the vixen in the wig after hours. Her job was bad enough. Fending off the horny Hulk from Hispanola (as she liked to call him, though he appeared to be shrinking by the hour) was enough to try even the most committed soul.

Nina took another swig of beer and looked over at Tala. Damn, that woman was fine. How'd she get so lucky? And not only that, Tala was smart, too. But Nina's thoughts flashed back to work. She knew that despite Rolo's hatefulness, her only job now was to spy, which didn't entail much more than looking at Rolo's schedule and taking notes for him during meetings. He was still an idiot around her, showing her off, taking her everywhere, all with the hope that it'd make his associates jealous. This allowed her access to most of his business, making her privy to far more of his goings-on than Camilo ever had. She took another drink of beer. She couldn't get over how

Rolo handled his job as mayor. Almost everything he did was some kind of setup to advance himself or one of his partners. This required payback of some kind, which made Nina all the more sick. No wonder Camilo needed several hundred limpias to get well after working for the lug.

Tala finished her beer and set the empty bottle on the coffee table. "You know, Gilbert and I haven't spoken since our last argument."

"Yeah, well, it makes sense, given how mad you two were." Nina rolled her feet in tight little circles. The girly-girl shoes killed her ankles by the end of the day.

"I only see him now when we're at our parents' house. He loves rubbing in that damn winery. If I have to hear him say 'the Sangre is really moving along' one more time, I'm going to give him some real sangre to deal with."

Nina looked up from the TV news and smiled. "Just tune him out, Sweetheart. He's just a baby-man and needs to grow up. He knows you're against the winery, so he's gonna slap you with it every chance he gets."

"But the whole thing is so hateful. I feel this winery thing has cost me not only my family but a person I was close to most of my life."

Nina gave Tala her undivided attention.

"I mean me and Gilbert had a special connection—did everything together as kids, stuck up for each other. Poor guy spent half his life trying to please our father, not to mention dealing with Junior and Marty's teasing all the time."

Nina turned off the TV. "So are you're feeling sorry for him now?"

Tala shook her head. "No, not sorry. Just sad . . . I guess people change. I have to say, I'm mad, too."

Nina held Tala's hand. "So here's what I think you should do." She slid closer to Tala. "Every time you hear him start the sparkly winery speech, just put on a claymation face and think of me." She leaned over and kissed Tala softly on the cheek.

"Think it will work?"

Nina nodded.

"Can I think of you in that skirt and black wig?" Tala winked.

Nina got up and straddled Tala, who up until then had been too tired to think straight. "You can think of me any way you want." She kissed her on the forehead. "With the wig." She kissed her on the nose. "Without the wig." She kissed her on the neck. "Or maybe just plain naked." This time she kissed her hard on the mouth.

Tala reached behind Nina and lovingly squeezed her ass. "I like thinking of you in that wig," she said, breathing fast.

"I guess I better grow my hair for your little pigified ass."

"Would you?"

Nina gave Tala a playful slap. "Anyway, I think any of these mechanisms are perfectly good ways to deal with the Vino Latino, don't you?"

"Absolutely, mi amor," she said, kissing her again. "Absolutely."

30

SINCE HE LIKED TO USE his Hulk-heavy bigness to intimidate people, Rolo had been in complete denial about his shrinking belt size. His stomachache had continued after the night out with Nina, but he'd attributed it to heartache over unrequited love. He did, however, go to a doctor who gave him a battery of tests and told him that, aside from his cholesterol level and high blood pressure, he seemed generally healthy. Rolo, of course, couldn't tell the doctor about his love for his secretary, so he walked out of the office feeling like a schoolboy, hands crammed in his pockets.

At the end of the day he headed home and poured himself a glass of tonic water. He gave his wife Christina a peck on the cheek. She placed a steaming platter of enchiladas in front of him, but he could only eat a few bites.

"Bueno, hombre, what's wrong with you?" Christina asked, more annoyed than worried. "I asked Andrea to make these enchiladas to try to get you to eat, and you don't even give the work she did justice."

Rolo shook his head as he pushed away the beautiful plate of food. "I don't know," he said, taking a sip of tonic. "My stomach hurts, pero the doctor says I'm healthy. I don't have cancer, I don't have an ulcer, I don't have gout, gas, or gastritis. I just don't have an appetite. He thinks it's all in my head—"

"He told you that?" Christina Reyes looked taken aback.

Rolo gave his wife a weak smile. "Bueno, no, he didn't say that. He just said there wasn't anything wrong with me, at least not physically."

"That doctor's too goddamn old to be practicing. I've told you that for years. You're not eating. And for you that means something's not right."

She placed her hand on his forehead to check for a fever. Feeling none, she lowered it. "Other than that, you're still the same old cabrón." She smiled and pinched him affectionately on his cheek. "Well," she continued, now serious, "we'll go to another doctor and get a second opinion."

Rolo shook his head again. "Nah, I'll just hang in there. Maybe I'll start feeling better soon. Give me some of that yerba buena tea your mother makes. Maybe that'll help."

When Rolo stepped out of his office the next day, Dahlia looked up from her work, squinted her left eye, and remarked, "You're losing a lot of weight, sir."

Nina shot him a look. Rolo noticed, but tried to ignore it. He leafed through a stack of papers and pursed his lips. "My doctor told me I should drop a few pounds. Said it'd be better for my health. How's the council agenda coming?"

"I'm working on it right now." Dahlia crossed her hands on top of her desk and continued her study of him.

"Good," he said, feeling a bit uncomfortable under Dahlia's scrutiny. "Did you put in enough time to talk about all the crap from Gilbert's pinche sign? This stuff is making us look like the goddamn poster child for the NRA. Who the hell was the dumbshit who sold her the gun in the first place? Find out and get somebody here to check on that bastard and every other place we sell guns. I don't want the FBI or whoever coming back to haunt me with any crap about selling guns to felons."

Dahlia checked the agenda. "I gave you twenty minutes to talk about it," she said, looking him up and down. "And it seems like you're dropping weight fast. You aren't on one of those liquid diets or those Dexatrim mess-up-your-metabolism things, are you?"

Rolo figured it was natural to worry since he'd shed about twenty pounds pretty damn fast. Nina continued typing, which—even Dahlia had conceded—had improved since she'd started working. Rolo was glad since the pressure was off about hiring an unqualified worker. Now Nina could actually do some aspects of the job she'd been hired for.

Rolo glanced over the agenda. "Me? Nah, I'm just watching what I'm eating instead of garbage-canning everything into my mouth. It's amazing what changing your diet can do." He rebuttoned his jacket and glanced briefly at Nina. She didn't notice.

"Well, I think you look good," Dahlia said, with a nod of approval. "It's just that it seems to be happening awfully fast. I would hate to see you lose all this weight and then . . ."

"And then what? Get fat again? Not a problem. I'm changing my attitude around food, health, exercising. Don't worry about it." He gave his assistant a smirky half smile. "Speaking of food, I've got a lunch meeting with the tourism board. Could you get me the notes on it so I can read them before noon? And don't forget to get me the update from public works. I need to check on how we're doing with this damn drought."

"OK," Dahlia said, giving him that squinty, I-wish-you'd-cut-the-crap-and-tell-me-what's-really-going-on-with-you look.

Rolo hated when people wanted to know too much—especially Dahlia. He gathered his papers, glanced at Nina again, walked into his office, and shut the door.

❄

Gilbert studied the latest piece of legal mierda that damn Dogtown lawyer had filed. Things had been progressing at a steady pace despite his sister backing out on him, that is until this new legal glitch. Elena Luján's latest caper was to sue the city of Santa Fe for impinging on the right to live without encumbrance to one's home, whether owned or rented. Gilbert shook his head. What the hell was that? Every lawyer's got some trick up their sleeve to get what they want. She'd try anything to keep him from building his winery. Why the hell were people against this when anyone could see how they'd benefit? Where else would people without a pot to piss in get good money for houses that are trashed or shot to hell?

He called in Bill Takash to talk about this mess. Gilbert's Santa Fe office was now covered with final-phase architect's plans, in addition to showboating a scale model of the winery on an adjoining table. He directed Bill to a couple of leather chairs next to an inlaid coffee table.

"Jesus Christ, man! Why are these people so driven to keep me from building a good, solid redevelopment?"

"What Elena's filed is a long shot," said Bill, clasping a cigarette.

❦ 163 ❧

Gilbert glared out the window. The drought had shriveled the leaves on the trees. The air outside, so long without moisture, exuded a popcorn-hot dryness. The city had even instituted water rationing. The hottest months were over, yet there was no hint of rain in the forecast. Maybe he *was* foolish to plant a vineyard here.

"She's scrambling for an angle."

"You ever heard of that kind of suit?" asked Gilbert, lighting a cigar. It was a new thing for him. Helped calm his nerves.

"Once. They tried it over in Vegas when they were putting in a highway overpass."

"And?"

"Eminent domain. But they gave them enough cash to keep people quiet."

"Can we do that?"

Bill rubbed his chin. "For a winery, eminent domain would be a long shot. But, since it's urban development, so to speak, we could give it a try. We got nothing to lose, especially since the city's behind us. But they would need to back us up on this. We couldn't pull that one off without them," he said, grinning.

Gilbert nodded. "If Elena can grab at straws, so can we." He glanced at the architect plans. "We got something good happening here. We can't let one measly shark—no offense," he said, looking at the lawyer, "keep us from getting this." He rolled the ashes off his cigar into the ashtray.

"She's got nothing to stand on." Bill inhaled his cigarette, then exhaled while talking. "The judge will take one look at that and throw it out."

"No jury trial?"

"I seriously doubt it."

"Then why is she doing this?"

"Delay tactic."

Gilbert looked out the window again. He hated this stuff. If these dinosaurs would just come to their senses and accept his offer he could start making wine. "Delay tactic?" He returned his gaze to his lawyer.

"We use them all the time. It lets us gather information—you know, interview people, get more data. It usually helps us in the long run to strengthen our case. Sometimes we can even prove the suit is irrelevant if enough time passes."

Gilbert puffed his cigar. "Well that woman's an ass-kicker, so I'd feel a lot better if you consulted my lawyer in California." He got up and poured two glasses of sherry. He believed Bill but he wanted to make sure, and his California lawyer was one crafty guy.

"Be happy to," Bill replied, taking a sip of sherry.

"Just run it by him," Gilbert said, with a flick of his wrist. "No big deal, especially if you think it's penny ante."

Bill nodded and stubbed out his cigarette.

"How long you think she can do this?"

"Depends. Since you're ready to go on this, it obviously doesn't serve us to delay. I figure she's got six months, max." Bill pushed away his sherry.

"Shit. And I'm doing everything by the book. Been totally up front." Gilbert shot a lean eye at the lawyer. "Well, almost. But hell, it's no wonder this damn state is stuck in the dark ages. I swear I can drive to some of those hamlets up in the mountains and aside from all the drugs and the rich gab-achos buying property, there isn't anything different from what everyone did a hundred years ago."

"Hang in there, hombre." Bill jerked his chin with a confident purse of his lips. "Sooner or later you'll get your winery." He lit another cigarette. "Besides, you got new people taking you up on your offer every day. Give it a little time and Elena might not have enough folks living there to even warrant a suit."

Gilbert wondered if Bill was right. He'd known the guy since he was a kid, and he hired him because he understood New Mexico. But hell, this winery was his baby. He had planned everything, clear down to the type of glasses he wanted in the tasting room. "Just a few months?" he asked.

Bill nodded, exhaling smoke across the room, tapped his ash, and nodded again.

31

JULES HIT THE PRINT BUTTON, yawned, smiled, and stretched. He watched the printer zip out an article he and Pepa had just cowritten on the latent effects of nuclear testing. He rubbed his eyes, knowing he should call it a night, but he could hardly contain his energy ever since he and Pepa had started collaborating. Reluctant at first, she quickly warmed up to him when she read his first attempts to patch something together on the historical price nuclear development exacted across the state. She gave him information on people she, her mother, or Don Gabriel had known whose bodies were riddled with cancer—cancer most likely the result of being in the wrong place at the wrong time. He couldn't believe Pepa had agreed to work with him, but it went to show you people can change.

His office door opened, and Luz walked in with a cup of tea. She grinned when she saw him, set the tea down, and gave his shoulders a rub.

"Thanks, my love," he said as he pulled her in for a kiss.

"It's chamomile." She wrapped her arms around him. "So you can relax, get off that computer, and come to bed with me. I don't like it when I'm in bed and you're not." She looked over his shoulder at the computer screen. "You still working on that piece you're doing with my mom?"

"Uh-hmm," he said, pulling Luz onto his lap and nuzzling her neck.

"Mmm, you feel good, cabrón. Stop all that pinche writing and come to bed."

"OK, OK," he replied, feeling a lot more awake than he had a minute ago.

She wrapped one arm around him and picked up the article. "How many does this make you've written?" She scanned the title and the first few lines.

"That one," he said, gesturing with his chin, "makes three. So far *The Dallas Morning News* is the only good response we've had. They seem like they're really interested in our story, and they're a good paper. I'm sending something like it to a couple more mags who might bite." He paused to inhale Luz's perfume. Faded now, its spicy scent still lingered enough to slightly divert his attention. "I got an email today from an editor who accused me of being anti-American. And, even worse, not a single paper in this state expressed any interest."

Luz turned to face him. "Pssh, are you surprised? I don't want to pop your bubble, Amor, but my mom raised all kinds of hell thirty years ago when my grandmother died, and nothing came of it except some folks around here saying she was a Communist. Hijo, that practically killed her."

This caught Jules's attention. "That they called her a Communist?"

"No, not that, though she isn't. What drove her crazy was that no one seemed to care about people getting cancer—Americans dying all over this state, on top of all those people they killed in Japan. And the lab was still making even bigger bombs. She wouldn't shut up about that, either."

"I didn't know Pepa was such a radical."

"Was and is. And when she puts her mind to something, look out."

"I noticed," he said, smiling. "Maybe having her cowrite these articles will get us some attention."

Luz gave him a quick kiss on the cheek. "Don't count on it. Almost everyone has their head in the sand around here. Now come to bed."

❀

Luckily Luz was just a little bit wrong, as Jules received a call from Toni Pearlman, the science editor at the *Washington Post*. She told him she saw the piece come over the wire from the Dallas newspaper and wondered if they might talk about the possibility of speaking to a cancer survivor.

Jules called Pepa and gave her a quick rundown of what the reporter had asked. He could hardly contain his enthusiasm as he explained it.

"Y esta mujer, can you trust her?" asked Pepa.

"I suppose . . ." Jules scratched his cheek. "It's hard to say. She said that article we wrote got under her skin—that she tried to ignore it, saying it was old news, but couldn't, since you had personalized the story with real people."

"Hmmph."

Jules heard rustling in the background, knowing Pepa had probably started looking for notes from patients she'd treated long ago.

"She said she wanted to come out and interview you and any survivors."

"Bueno, that might be hard, because I think people might not talk, pero," she paused, "I guess we could ask."

Two weeks later the reporter and her photographer showed up at Jules's door. "I'm Toni," she said as she gave his hand a firm shake.

Small and thin, she had an air about her that exhibited both warmth and impatience. Jules hoped she was on the up and up since he didn't want to do anything to jeopardize his relationship with Pepa. Yet as the reporter spoke, she quickly conveyed that she had done her homework and seemed excited about what she'd come to investigate.

Toni introduced Bill, her photographer, a young Latino guy who didn't talk much, though he often stood around gazing at the landscape.

"We're not in an area that gets much action from tourists, are we?" he asked.

"No, I wouldn't say we are," Jules replied with a grin. "Let's go take a drive. I've already contacted Pepa, who you'll meet later. In the meantime, I want to show you a couple cemeteries, since it's a good way to introduce you to what we're talking about."

The three of them hopped in his truck, and they drove out to several cemeteries in Santa Fe and Española, continuing up the road to Los Alamos. He pointed to the graves of people who had died young—children, women, and men. There were also those who would have been too old to serve in the war, but had died in their thirties and forties.

"I'm surprised to see how many people died in their prime," remarked Toni.

"It's actually worse in other parts of the state," Jules said. "People in some of the towns and reservations downwind from White Sands and over by the Nevada border really got it bad." He walked them through the cemetery. The photographer snapped several pictures of the headstones.

A while later, after they finished the cemetery tour and had a late lunch at Dolly's in Española, they drove back to Dogtown and met up with Pepa and

Luz. The five strolled through Pepa's garden and clínica, then settled in the kitchen. Toni pulled out a tape recorder and asked Pepa if she minded being recorded. She agreed, much to Jules's relief. The reporter took off, asking Pepa a steady stream of questions.

Luz had agreed to help Jules while they were at her mother's house. He gave her a wink as she made a fresh pot of coffee, grinning over the extra effort she took to set out a few gingersnaps from the old tin Pepa kept in the cupboard and, of course, some of her jerky. Jules served the coffee while Luz brought the milk and sugar. The whole time he kept a steady eye on Pepa, hoping she'd like the reporter.

"I'm thinking of calling this story 'Deadly Downwinds,'" said Toni. "I was struck today by all the graves I saw of people who'd perished at such a young age, and I'm baffled that no one seemed to pay much attention to these lost lives—or so it appears. I didn't find much from the archival searches I did. I suppose the difficulty around finding information here was that everything had to be top secret."

"I suppose," said Pepa. "Pero that's why so many people got sick. They didn't know the air they breathed would hurt them."

"Did you find that some people didn't become ill till much later in their lives? Maybe ten, fifteen, or even twenty years after exposure?"

"Oh sí," answered Pepa. "Many of them were kids when those winds hit. A lot of them got cancer in their early twenties."

"Do you know any people who were ill and are still alive?"

"Sí," replied Pepa.

"Any way some of them might talk to me?"

Pepa hesitated then looked at Jules. "Bueno, I guess we can ask."

☀

Pepa called up people she knew who had survived thyroid cancer, which was one of the most common ailments. Because they trusted Pepa, three of them agreed to let the reporter talk to them. The photographer took candid portraits of the scarred survivors, the youngest of whom were now in their late sixties. Pepa made sure to tell Toni what happened to the Native tribes in the region since the government had used their land, contaminated their water, and ignored them when they asked them to stop. Pepa watched the care and respect the reporter gave to the people she spoke with. She didn't have much hope that anything would come out of this story, but she was damn glad someone had finally decided to write it.

Jules gave the reporter the Los Alamos Lab's PR contact, since she had hoped to find someone who would speak to her about past testing practices. They declined, saying it was against policy.

Toni looked flummoxed. "Geez, they got that giant museum in Albuquerque, and they don't want to talk to me? What more have they got to hide?"

Jules simply grinned.

"Lots more?"

He nodded.

"Is there more you can tell me?"

He grew serious. "Unfortunately, no. I told you everything I know. I'm certain it's just a portion of what happened."

During some down time, while they were sipping ice tea in Jules's backyard, he took the opportunity to speak to Toni about the winery situation, doing his best to convey the exploitation connection. Aside from several concerned head nods, he got little response.

When he pressed further, Toni finally replied, "Hey, I hear you, and we all know exploitation comes in every shape and size. But this winery issue doesn't fit my story. I wish you the best, though."

Can't say he didn't try.

A week later, Toni emailed Jules a copy of the "Deadly Downwinds" article scheduled to run in the following Sunday's *Washington Post*. "We did it," he hollered to Luz, who grabbed him and gave him a big kiss. "I'm so happy," he said, his eyes glistening with tears.

"And I'm glad Mom and all those people are part of the story. She's the one who saw so many suffer."

Jules gathered Luz into his arms and held her. "Honey, you know there won't be any reparations, and probably not even apologies. But," he pulled back and kissed her on the nose. "At least the lab's dirty little secret is finally out in the open."

"Then it makes everything you've done worth it," said Luz. "Now let's go get Mom and celebrate."

32

TALA DECIDED ON A NEW TACTIC: being nice to her parents—which meant inviting them over for dinner. She admitted their siding with Gilbert had pissed her off to no end. And Gilbert, of course, had bad-mouthed her as a sellout to the family. But Tala desperately wanted her parents to see her side of the story. And desperate people do desperate things.

That evening, the temperature lingered in the high eighties. Any cool breeze that scratched its way through the screen door was simply a false hope. Tala had asked Nina to join her, wanting to showcase not only their relationship but how losing their homes would impact their lives. A tall order for the evening but Tala figured she had nothing to lose. Nina couldn't cook, so she'd been instructed to come early to do galley-slave duties. Tala checked her watch. Nina still hadn't shown.

Vince and Cleo arrived on time but her father seemed nervous, pacing throughout the house while Cleo relaxed in the kitchen. As Tala sliced vegetables for a salad, she heard her dad walking from room to room, commenting on whatever caught his interest—a photo on the mantle, books on the coffee table, art on the wall. She wouldn't be surprised if he was going through the bank statements on her desk.

"Hey, who painted this sad-sack skeleton you got hanging out here?" Vince hollered from the dining room.

Tala figured he was referring to Nina's painting of a Frida Kahlo calavera holding a calavera baby. "You mean Frida with the baby?"

"I guess."

"Nina did," Tala answered from the kitchen. "It's cool, isn't it? On the surface, it's a statement reflecting Frida's inability to have children." Tala paused, holding the knife midair. "But if you go deeper, it's a critique of how Latina women are pressured to find fulfillment only as mothers."

Tala heard no response so she resumed slicing.

"Seems like it goes a little overboard, don't you think?" said Vince.

"Well, it won the City of Gold art competition, so I guess not everyone thinks so."

Her father strutted into the kitchen, grabbed a slice of cucumber, and took a bite. "I know I'm no art expert . . ."

"But?" Tala interrupted, hackles raised.

"Vince, cállate!" ordered Cleo. "You always have something to say, even when you don't know what you're talking about."

Vince pulled up a chair and sat, craning his neck as he studied the masks, papel picado, and painted saucers hanging on the walls. Tala forced herself to remain calm. She figured her father wanted to say a hell of a lot more and no doubt received a lecture from her mother telling him to stay on good behavior. She had to hand it to her mom who never stopped trying to keep the old man in line—usually to no avail.

"Well I wasn't exactly born yesterday, and from living in this town I think I can say I know a little bit about art . . ."

"How 'bout a beer," Tala interrupted, handing her father a Tecate. She offered her mother a rum and Coke, which she surprisingly accepted. Tala shoved the guacamole and chips, and jícama doused with lime juice and chile, closer toward her parents. She grabbed a bag of roasted pepitas and tossed them in a bowl. "And here's a few snacks. Please eat."

"Qué rico!" said Cleo, taking a bite of the jícama. "Oye," she said, nudging her husband, "make sure to eat so you don't get drunk."

Vince examined the spread in front of him, grabbed a chip, and scooped up guacamole. Facing Cleo, he shoved the whole thing in his mouth.

The front door opened and Tala's dog, who had been sequestered in the backyard, barked through the screen door. She settled down immediately when she recognized Nina's voice.

"Hi, everyone!"

"Hi, Honey. We're in the kitchen!" said Tala. "Do me a favor," she whispered to her father. "Don't talk about that painting, OK?"

Vince stabbed the guacamole with a jícama strip and gave his daughter a fake smile.

Nina marched into the kitchen, her cheeks rosy. Tala watched her scan the mood in the room. Seemingly satisfied, she gave a quick peck on the cheek to Tala's parents and began unloading a grocery bag, pulling out beer, sparkling water, and raspberry liqueur. "I'm sorry I'm late. The store was packed to the rafters like it was the Arts Fest or something. I knew we needed more beer, and, Cleo, I wanted to get you your favorite drink."

"Mom's drinking a rum and coke now," said Tala, who gave Nina a wide eyeball.

"Sí, pero I'll have some as soon as I'm finished." Cleo held up her glass, graced with a sprig of spearmint. "That was nice of you to buy me that raspberry stuff."

Nina glanced at the Coke, then back at Tala, since the two knew Cleo usually didn't drink. "Well, I know you like it. Let me get my beer and start helping."

What Nina couldn't do in the kitchen, she made up for in her ability to talk. A schmoozer when she wanted to be, she soon had Tala's parents talking about the local arts scene, the Teatro Sabor's next play, and her own current art project. Tala watched in awe as Nina moved the conversation deftly through moments of difficulty, working to keep things light, despite the obvious pall of the winery and the disagreements between Tala and Gilbert. Finally, after a wonderful dinner of grilled chicken, asparagus, and polenta, they moved to the backyard so Vince could smoke his cigar. The evening air had cooled, and the fountain bubbled a soothing beat. The animals settled in as Tala served everyone chilled moscato with homemade bizcochitos.

Vince puffed contently on his cigar, then stopped suddenly, as if remembering what he'd clearly been wanting to say all evening: "I need to ask you something . . . and it's not easy to talk about, so I'm just going to ask it . . . Do you think you and Gilbert can figure out a way to work out your problems?"

Caught by surprise, Tala turned to her mother for salvation. Cleo shrugged and raised her eyes like she hadn't a clue what to do.

Vince rolled his cigar around in his mouth. "You kids didn't use to fight—at least not when you were little."

"You mean they actually got along?" asked Nina.

"Oh yeah! Those two were like two baby goats. Always running around with twinkly smiles on their faces." He turned to Tala. "Shit, remember when you two went with me to drop off some hay at your uncle Jake's?"

Tala nodded, not sure where this was going.

"I think you guys were probably around seven or eight."

Nina leaned in, interested in the story.

"Well, your uncle Jake had a ranch about five miles outside of town. And he had this old caretaker there who lived in a shabby little shack. Mr. Ben Lomo I think was his name." Vince set his cigar in the ashtray and folded his arms behind his head. "I remember it was around lunch, and he was cooking something that smelled damn good in the oven."

"I have a funny feeling where this might be going," said Nina, crossing her legs.

"So I was shooting the shit with your uncle and saw you two jabbering to Mr. Lomo. And I think it was you," he said, pointing at Tala, "who asked him what he was cooking. That guy . . ." He paused to chuckle. "That guy had nothing but cows all around him, so anyone would figure he was cooking some kind of beef. And it did smell good, too, like maybe he had a nice roast going. So he answered and said he was cooking a cow head. Well, you two just fell out laughing," he said, sipping his drink. "And Gilbert, you gotta hand it to him, didn't believe him. So he told the guy, 'You're not cooking a cow head.' And the old man said, 'Yes I am.' You must've thought he was playing with you, too, Natalia, because you asked him if he was faking. And he said, 'No, no, I'm not. Look!' So he opened that oven, and sitting there on the pan roasting and crackling in the heat, was a big ol' cow head! And that sucker was so damn ugly with its eyes popping and tongue dangling, that the two of you thought you'd seen the devil himself. Then you both took off, screaming bloody murder out of that house."

"Both of them?" asked Nina.

"Both of them. Now that I think about it, Gilbert was in the lead." Vince retrieved the cigar and relit it. "And those two wouldn't take a single step back inside that shack neither, hungry or not."

"Pobrecitos, you should have brought them a sandwich," said Cleo.

"Yeah, I probably should have."

"Is that why you have a cow head in the store window, Honey?" asked Nina.

"Kind of," Tala answered, giving Nina a "let's-not-go-there" look.

"You two did a lot of stuff together when you were kids. And since you're my youngest—well, I've got a particular attachment to you both. So your fighting causes me and your mother a lot of pain."

"Dad, I don't want to fight with him. It's just that he's only seeing things his way. And *you're* only seeing things his way. That's how it's always been."

"I know, I know. And I have to admit, I did help him with this. But can't you two work something out?"

"I could have supported him," Tala said, though she knew it stretched the truth. "But the more I saw what was going to happen to everyone, including me and Nina, the more I couldn't. Plus, I've got a nice house here. I mean, look at this place." Tala gestured toward the house and yard. "See how happy my animals are? And all the work I've put into the interior and the landscaping? Plus I wouldn't be able to buy anything close to what I've got, not in this town, and not even with Gilbert paying me market rate. And Nina's got a cute duplex with a studio in the back, which she rents for a pittance." Tala paused and glanced at her mother who looked like she was listening. "I just can't bear to see a bulldozer level this."

The dog got up and moved close to Tala, worried over the tone of her voice. She leaned against her, eyes shifting between Tala and her father. "Don't worry, Baby. Everything's OK," Tala said, petting her.

"That dog's smart," Vince said, pointing. "I saw how she came to you just now."

"I guess she knows when something's not right, que no?" asked Cleo.

"I'll say," said Nina.

"Look," Tala folded her hands in her lap. "I want you to know I didn't desert our family. And I'm not even opposed to Gilbert building a winery, especially since I know how much it means to him. I just want him to do it someplace else. Is that asking too much?"

"I guess for him it is," answered Vince.

"Is there any way you two might look at my situation? See what I've got to lose instead of everything coming from his angle?"

Vince tapped his cigar ash in the ashtray. "Bueno, you got a point. The only thing I can tell you is that I hear what you're saying."

"And how about you, Mom?"

"I hear you, too." Cleo said, staring at her husband. "I'm just not sure if anything will change."

33

PEPA SAID GOODBYE TO THE last patient of the day, closed the door, and gratefully retreated to the kitchen. She opened a bottle of merlot and poured herself a glass. Camilo washed his hands, grabbed a couple ice cubes, and tossed them into a glass. He filled it with tonic water and splashed it with Campari. The two had gotten so damn busy lately with all the sick people they'd been seeing, helping the CURs, as well as all the antinuclear work, that Pepa had thought about hiring a personal assistant como la J. Lo. She chuckled to herself and drank some of the wine, her thoughts turning to the mayor. She was still stymied over the fact that, aside from him losing weight, the treatment she and Camilo had given him two months prior seems generally to have had only mixed results. Pepa hadn't seen Rolo lately, but according to Nina, he appeared to be a little bit nicer but hadn't shown any major personality changes, which is what they had hoped for. She said people now greeted him with comments like "you look great" and "what's your secret?" But then they'd ask her later on if he had cancer or AIDS. "It's a sad state of affairs that you can't lose weight nowadays without people thinking you're dying," Nina said to Pepa, with an innocent batting of her eyes.

"Sí," Pepa agreed. "Very sad."

On Saturday, two weeks after their last CURs meeting, Pepa and Camilo sat down for breakfast. Pepa put sugar in her coffee, stirred it for a few seconds, then stopped and placed her hands flat on the table. "Oye, Camilo, we've got to try something else."

"Yah?" His eyes flickered to attention.

"Yah. Pero, what we have to do isn't here. We need to go to San Geronimo."

"A la casa de Don Gabriel?"

"Sí."

"Pero, what's there that we don't have or know of already? We get a few hierbas there, and Don Gabriel's house is empty."

Pepa knew Camilo would ask these questions, but she didn't really have an answer. "No sé, pero I just think we need to go. And you for sure have to come."

Camilo looked down at his coffee. "Mira, Pepa. I know you think there's more up there than what me and you know, but I lived with him all my life. And—"

"And that's why you have to go with me." Pepa pounded her finger on the table. She slurped her coffee then set the cup down so hard she spilled it. "Bueno, will you come?"

Camilo let out a long, tired sigh. "OK."

Pepa rolled her old sleeping bag into a tight little bun. She expected to spend the night, so she instructed Camilo to bring a sleeping bag, change of clothes, and anything else he needed. She also packed a shopping bag with a few utensils and provisions, making sure to bring her notebook, tattered from many years of writing down hierbas and potions.

Kicking the tires of her old Buick, Pepa decided it was too risky to drive to San Geronimo, so she bought two bus tickets to Las Vegas, figuring they'd catch a ride from her friend Moisés, who lived in Old Town. Pepa met Moisés when she'd studied with Don Gabriel thirty years ago. Moisés had injured his elbow in a factory accident and sought the curandero's help. Don Gabriel healed the elbow, restoring it to full function. In the meantime, Moisés and Pepa became friends, instantly taking to each other. The relationship could've gone farther. But Pepa was too distracted, grieving the loss of her mother and focusing on her apprenticeship with the curandero, to accommodate anything more. Still, her friendship with Moisés grew, and though they went their own ways and married others, they kept a special place in their hearts for one another.

"Oye, hombre, where have you been? We've been standing here in the hot sun for over fifteen minutes waiting." Pepa shielded her eyes from the sun's afternoon glare as Moisés pulled up to the two of them in a new Chevy pickup. The two had parked themselves in front of the Plaza Hotel, sitting miserably on the steps.

Moisés, tall and flaco, with a long, craggy-cut face, looked at his watch. "Hijo! Lo siento. I was at the Piggly Wiggly getting some slippers for Merlene, and it took a little longer than I thought." He opened the door of his truck and motioned for Pepa and Camilo to hop inside. Camilo threw their bags in the back and got in after Pepa.

"Bueno, what's wrong with Merlene's arms and legs that she can't buy her own slippers?" Pepa asked, as Moisés started the engine. "We need to stop at Lutie's so we can get some Cokes and chorizo." Pepa looked at her watch then back at Moisés. "And how come you're always late, eh? Every time I ask you to do something for me, you're late. I think it's because you want to be late, que no?"

Moisés put the truck in gear and hit the gas. "Pues nooo, I saw they were having a sale on those slippers Merlene likes. And since you were taking the bus, you didn't tell me exactly when you were coming. You know Merlene just had gallbladder surgery."

"Sí, I know. I'm the one who told her to go to the hospital, don't you remember?"

"Bueno, sí, pero I wanted to get those slippers and some candy for her since she can't drive, either."

Pepa gave Moisés a dirty look. "I can drive. I just don't have a good car."

"Ahem," Camilo cleared his throat. "Pepa." She didn't respond. "Pepa, I don't know your friend."

Pepa shifted her attention back to Camilo, his hair blue-black in the sunlight. "You don't know Moisés?"

Camilo shook his head.

"Pues, lo siento, I thought you knew him." She jerked her thumb toward her friend. "This is Moisés. And this," she said with a jerk of her chin, "is Camilo. He works with me. He's the great-grandson of Don Gabriel, hijo del Faustín y Graciela Archuleta who used to live in San Geronimo."

"Oh, sí?" Moisés replied, glancing at Camilo as he circled the plaza, then headed up through Old Town toward Lutie's.

"Sí, mi papá y mamá moved to California when I was ten, but I wanted to stay with Don Gabriel."

"You lived with him at his house?" Moisés turned into the grocery store's parking lot.

"Pues sí, he raised me."

"And that was OK with your mom and dad? I mean he must've been up in age."

"Oh, yeah. They knew I didn't want to leave. And they figured I'd be in good hands. He was definitely old," Camilo said, nodding, "but he taught me a lot. And he could still cook."

"Yeah, I heard the old man could make good beans and tortillas." Moisés killed the engine, rolled up the window, and grabbed the door handle.

"He could," Camilo replied, nodding. "Pero, he taught me more about healing. I thought he was going to live forever, the way he was going. People said he was one hundred and twenty when he died."

"De veras?" Moisés halted midstride.

"That's what they said."

"We all gotta die sometime," said Pepa, glaring at Moisés.

"Pepa, I got one of these cell phones now," he said, pointing to the phone attached to his belt loop. "I'll give you my number so you can call me next time I'm late. Better yet, call me ahead of time to remind me so I won't be late."

Pepa huffed all the way into the store. She purchased water, Cokes, tortillas, cheese, and chorizo. Then they piled in the truck and headed out to San Geronimo.

On the drive up, Pepa, calmer now, feasted on the agate blue sky. The sharp scent of wild sage greeted her with its warm embrace. She loved the land up here—stark and rugged. She wore an old shirt and jeans as well as her hiking boots, just in case they had to walk. She instructed Camilo to do the same since she wasn't sure where they were headed or what they would find. Moisés and Camilo chatted amicably, with Pepa stuffed between the shoulders of the two men.

Their journey continued up a rutted dirt road meandering toward hills covered with dry grass. As the truck climbed upward, the landscape filled with piñón trees and aspen. Pepa knew Don Gabriel's house was abandoned, for he had instructed that all his possessions be donated to those in need. He wasn't a man of many words, and he most certainly didn't write much down. Instead he kept his vast knowledge of the ways of healing and the uses of many plants and hierbas in his head. Whatever made Pepa decide to come here on this day, she couldn't say. Maybe it was his spirit she needed, since his presence had always comforted her in the past. Maybe it was just a hunch. What mattered was that she and Camilo were here.

The truck turned into Don Gabriel's driveway, and his old wooden house greeted them at the end of a gravel road. Pepa thought the house leaned more than she had recalled in the past—the result of a collapsing foundation. Two stories tall, it looked battered from the harsh New Mexico weather. The windows were covered with faded blue shutters. Pepa walked around the house, happy there were still no other houses nearby, at least none she could see. She was glad Don Gabriel's children didn't sell the property to developers, not that any would be interested. Most of the people who lived in San Geronimo had long ago abandoned the tiny hamlet, seeking new lives, jobs, or simply a change from the ways of their ancestors. Those who remained were few, mostly viejitos who refused to leave. This made taking care of them all the more difficult since their children had to drive up the road every few days to see how they were doing and take them into town if the need arose.

Don Gabriel was one of the viejitos who had refused to leave, but he had Camilo with him and moved with the fluidity of a man half his age. This house once held Don Gabriel's family—three girls and a boy who'd also followed the desires of the young, leaving San Geronimo many years prior. None of Don Gabriel's children had taken on the work of healer—that is, except for Pepa, who never got a straight answer as to whether the old man was really her father. The curandero was so wrinkled, Pepa couldn't spot physical characteristics in him that resembled her own, with the exception of his hands. Both the viejito and Pepa had beautiful hands, long fingers, with lovely oval nails. Other than her skills as a curandera, she didn't see anything else.

In any case, after the curandero died and Camilo left, the children abandoned the house. They took all of Don Gabriel's furniture and donated his books and papers (what little there was) to the University of New Mexico.

None had intentions of moving back, yet the only thing they could agree upon was keeping the house as an investment.

"Let's go inside and see how it looks," Pepa said, walking up to the porch. "I hope it's in good enough shape to stay the night."

As expected, the house wasn't locked—at least none of the windows were. Camilo opened the shutter, then the window, and climbed in with a boost from Moisés. He went to the front door and let the other two in.

Pepa looked around, noticing the dust on the floor, rodent droppings in the corners, and the stale smell of a house that had been sealed up for a while. Still, the familiar scent of hierbas infused the air, as if permanently bonded into the very pores of the wood. Leaving the front door open, Pepa walked into Don Gabriel's treatment room, big enough back then to hold an altar, two chairs, and a bed. He always hung the hierbas from the rafters overhead to dry. Pepa saw they had been left hanging, though most had fallen now, forming dusty piles on the floor.

Camilo joined Pepa, squatted on the floor beside her, picked up a handful of hierbas, and brought them to his nose. "He told me to leave the hierbas where they were."

"Can you smell them?" Pepa asked, rubbing the hierbas together to bring out their scent.

"Poquito. Can you believe it?" he brought several more handfuls to his nose, smiling happily. He stood up, then left the room.

Pepa examined Don Gabriel's handmade altar—nothing more, really, than slabs of wood over four posts. It was heavy, hewn from the trees out back, the wood glistening from the touch of the curandero's hands. Pepa ran her fingertips across the altar. Don Gabriel's family had decided not to take it, probably thinking it was both cumbersome and worthless. Pepa lingered in the room, recalling when she had sat in the corner as a young woman watching the curandero work. She remembered how he pulled the hierbas from the rafters with quick snaps of his wrist, then ground them in a metate, prescribing their use in his soothing baritone. Pepa looked around the room, eyes blurry with tears. Running her hand once more along the altar, she turned and walked out.

Dirty and creaky, the house still gave off a solid feeling. There was a functional outhouse, and the creek running beside the house gurgled with clear mountain water. An old wood-burning stove stood in the kitchen, a few pieces of cut wood stacked on a small porch in the back.

Camilo looked puzzled. "I wonder why they didn't take the stove?"

Moisés, who had been walking through the house, rejoined the two. "No sé," he replied. "Maybe it was too heavy." He examined the stove and opened the oven door. There was an old cast-iron pot inside it. "They probably tried to lift it with this inside," he said, pulling it out. "Hijo, it's heavy."

"Bueno, I guess we can boil water from the creek to wash our faces, use the outhouse, and sleep on the floor for one night. We can even heat up water to make tea. What do you think, Camilo?"

Camilo shrugged. "Sí, cómo no? We brought sleeping bags, and drinking cups, so it's kinda like camping." He gazed at Pepa with sad, sweet eyes. She wondered how he felt coming back to the place he'd called home for many years.

Pepa looked around the living room, appearing satisfied. "Bueno then. Let's do it. Moisés, can you come back and get us tomorrow around ten?"

"Pues sí. And I promise to keep an eye on the clock," he said, tapping his watch. "Let me help you." He grabbed one of their bags and took it inside. "You think you'll be OK?"

Both Camilo and Pepa nodded. "Oh, yeah," said Pepa.

"We'll be fine," added Camilo.

"Bueno." Moisés walked outside and got in his truck. "I'll see you both mañana."

Pepa tapped her watch. "Don't forget, ten o'clock."

Moisés grinned. "How could I?" He put the truck in gear and slowly drove away.

Pepa eyed the dusty floor in the living room. Knowing she had to make do, she went outside and pulled a small branch off one of the trees. She shook off the dried pine needles, then used it to brush away as much dust as she could off the stove, as well as the floor where they would lay their bags. Camilo took the heavy pot to the stream and rinsed it out. Then he brought it back filled with water. He gathered wood for the stove. Pepa watched him collect a few small twigs, stacking them with a bit of paper in a small pyramid inside the stove. Soon, he had a fire going with the help of her lighter. After a few minutes he put the pot of water on top to boil.

"We've got bottled water for drinking, but we'll want this for tea," Camilo said, adding bigger sticks to the fire. The wood popped and fizzed, sending the sweet smell of piñón smoke into the air. "Y también, it looks like it might get a little chilly tonight." He crammed his hands into his pockets.

The sound of the wood burning reminded Pepa of her evenings around the stove with Don Gabriel. She took the lid opener, hoisted the lid open, and tossed in a bigger log. "It's getting a little chilly now," she said, as she rolled out both her and Camilo's sleeping bags in the living room. She noticed the fading light. "Why don't we go explore the house before it gets too dark." She retrieved a flashlight from the bag of supplies and put it in her back pocket.

Camilo followed her as they began wandering from room to room. Pepa poked her head into the three dusty bedrooms, smiling over the familiar texture of the hand-hewn pine still gracing the walls. She opened the closets, hoping for something the curandero would have purposely hidden. Seeing nothing, and sneezing from the dust, Camilo went back to his satchel in search of tissue. Pepa ventured into the curandero's treatment room again, stopping in front of the altar to pay tribute to the old man. Still finding nothing more than the spilled hierbas on the floor, she squatted down, picked them up, and inhaled their scent. She recognized the faded but unmistakable aromas of anís, altamisa, and oshá. The room was dark, but a small window let in what was left of daylight. The barren altar looked strange without the familiar items she recalled Don Gabriel having. She gathered the hierbas that had fallen on the floor and spread them over the altar, then went back to the living room to retrieve a candle from her supplies.

Camilo knelt on his sleeping bag, blowing his nose. He nodded and smiled through watery eyes as Pepa returned to the altar, cleared away some of the hierbas, and lit the candle. She felt a strange sense of longing as the dusky glow from the flame emanated throughout the room. Focusing her thoughts on the curandero, Pepa sprinkled bits of crumbled hierbas into the flame, momentarily sending their combined scent into the air. She savored the burning hierbas, each one bringing back a host of memories as they crinkled into ash. She recited a silent prayer to the curandero for guidance, for the spirit of his love to help the Dogtown people with what they needed. The floor squeaked. Thinking his spirit might have joined her, she laughed when she saw it was only Camilo. He studied the hierbas Pepa had strewn across the altar and stood beside her.

The two remained silent, concentrating on the candle, the hierbas, and the sanctity of the altar. After some time, Pepa felt a sense of warmth in the room, a presence and power alongside her and Camilo. She added more hierbas, inhaling their scent as she watched them burn. After about twenty minutes Camilo raised his head and exited. Pepa followed him. "Did you see him?" she asked, as they returned to the kitchen.

"No," Camilo replied. "But I felt him with us."

Pepa nodded slowly. "He's here," she said. "I felt him, too." She walked outside to smoke a cigarette, respecting Don Gabriel's request to never smoke in the house. She smiled, recalling his daily cigarette scoldings, eyes bright with anger, as he spoke of the irony of her habit.

"Bueno, you're right," she'd replied, then promptly lit another. She sat down on the old porch steps and glanced at the moon that had slowly begun to appear over the Mineral Hills. She exhaled a plume of smoke through the trees. A slight breeze rustled through them, stirring, swaying with deep familiarity. She wondered if Don Gabriel's spirit would come even closer, as she absolutely needed him now. She had faith—faith that the strength of her and Camilo's calls to him would bring the curandero back. She finished the cigarette and went inside, threw the butt in the fire, and checked the water on the stove. "It's boiling. Quieres té?"

"Sí." Camilo relaxed on top of his sleeping bag. "What do you think we'll find here?" He unlaced his boots, but didn't remove them.

Pepa poured hot water into the two cups she had brought with them, the yerba buena tea released its minty fragrance. "No sé," she said shrugging. "Maybe nothing. Maybe something." She brought the tea over to Camilo, who nodded his thanks. "Maybe what we need. No sé."

She spread a clean towel over the floor, pulled out a little chopping board, and sliced up chorizo and cheese. She opened a pack of tortillas, and the two ate their cold meal with gusto. The yerba buena's calming effects started to make them sleepy.

"We should've brought some beer," said Pepa with a grin.

Camilo glanced at his watch. "Eee, Pepa, it's only eight o'clock. I can't go to sleep this early."

"Maybe you can read with candles. I brought a lot. Why don't you light a few around your head?"

"Candles?" He looked doubtful.

"Sí, what've you got to lose?"

Camilo grabbed several votive candles and arranged them in a halo around him. He lit them and actually seemed to have enough light to read a book on el Niño Fidencio he had brought. "What're you going to do?"

"I'm gonna lie here and think. I'm too tired to read anyway."

In about ten minutes, both of them were asleep.

During the night the wind picked up, and by daylight storm clouds had gathered in a roiling flurry. Pepa woke around six. Somehow Camilo must've remembered to blow out the candles as they were all neatly gathered to the left of his head. She smiled, gently nudged him till he awakened, and the two pulled themselves out of their sleeping bags. After washing their faces and brushing their teeth, they grabbed their jackets, and walked outside. It had begun to rain—a sprinkle really, only the second break from months of drought. Pepa studied the steel-colored clouds fomenting across the hills, squinting through the wetness as it brushed across her face. She paused, relishing the heavenly aroma of newly dampened earth.

Pepa ruffled Camilo's hair, now moist from the rain. "Let's go for a walk, eh? Have a look around."

Camilo nodded and followed Pepa around Don Gabriel's property, the two noting the sagging back porch and dilapidated roof. Lightning flashed overhead, followed by a low rumble of thunder. Pepa looked at Camilo, his eyes wide with excitement. Smiling, the two sauntered down a trail they'd often taken to gather hierbas.

"We need anything?" Pepa asked, pulling a plastic bag out of her pocket. She always kept one with her since she never knew when she might need it to collect hierbas.

"Creo que we're getting low on a couple things," replied Camilo, scanning the trail ahead. "Let's see what we find."

As they ventured farther from the house, Pepa noticed the storm clouds growing denser. "It looks strange seeing clouds when all we've had is so much blue."

Camilo glanced at the sky, then put a handful of sage in the bag. "Ya sé" he said, watching the clouds transform themselves into a deeper gray. "I'm so happy it's raining. Maybe if it rains enough the trees will live."

In short time they made it to the village of San Geronimo. There were no people around, probably due to the early morning hour. Turning past the old church, simple—yet built with loving determination—Pepa noticed it sported a face-lift, as its adobe exterior was painted with a new shade of cocoa, most likely from its devoted group of patrons. Despite the rain, the tin roof glimmered, and the window frames glowed with a fresh coat of turquoise. As they got closer, Pepa watched a slew of red ants crawl up the steps leading to the church. The ants, glistening with rain, looked like shiny bits of desert paintbrush.

After a quick jaunt around the church, the two continued on toward a large mesa where the town's cemetery stood and where Don Gabriel was buried. "We need to go to his grave," Pepa said, pulling Camilo along.

"OK," he replied, following.

At the cemetery's entrance, a rusted gate leaned slightly to the side. It yielded with a gentle push. Barbed wire surrounded the cemetery, nearly invisible as it succumbed to the mass of overgrown weeds. Pepa searched the graveyard, noticing several headstones stretching up through the grass. It was hard to tell how many people were actually buried there since those who were poor had only rocks for markers.

As they made their way toward the curandero's grave they trod with careful steps, eyes alert for rattlesnakes. Pepa saw several grave mounds newly adorned with cut PVC pipes filled with plastic daisies. She almost bypassed Don Gabriel's grave, failing to recognize its new headstone and surrounding black iron fence.

"His daughters—and my mom—did it," remarked Camilo, leaning on the fence, watching the rain pockmark the dust across the grave. "They didn't like him having just a rock with his name."

Pepa studied the headstone. At the top were two hands carved into a handshake.

"Who you think he's shaking hands with?" asked Pepa, wondering why the hell they'd picked that kind of headstone.

Camilo smiled, shaking his head. Inscribed below the hands were the words, "Querido padre, Gabriel Ortiz, 1875–2000, May He Rest In Peace."

"Y también, how did they know when he was born?" Pepa continued her scrutiny of the gravestone.

"They probably just made it up," said Camilo. "I don't think anyone knew when he was really born. You didn't, did you?" he turned, facing her.

"Me? No. I heard he was muy viejo, pero quién sabe? I don't think anyone really knew." She laughed. "But it didn't matter, because he stayed sharp up here," she gestured toward her head. "All the way until he died."

"You know what else he had until he died?" Camilo's eyes were playful.

"Qué?"

"A girlfriend."

"Quién?" Pepa replied, aghast.

"Candelaria."

"No."

"Sí."

"Her?"

Candelaria, at least fifty years younger, had a reputation for having lots of boyfriends, some of them still married.

"Sí. She lived in her own house. They saw each other two or three times a week. That's the way they liked it."

"I can't believe esa cabrona was his girlfriend. What did he like about her?"

"Ay, Pepa, weren't you the one who said love conquers all?" Camilo replied, eyebrows raised.

Pepa pushed him playfully. "Ay! Don't talk to me like that. I can't take it." She couldn't figure out what the old man saw in Candelaria, and for that matter, what Candelaria saw in the old man.

The two of them were silent for a moment, eyes returning to the gravestone.

"That sonavagun . . ." Pepa grabbed the iron fence around the grave and leaned her head against it. She jiggled the gate open and stepped inside. Kneeling at the curandero's headstone, she grew quiet. "Camilo, give me some of that sage you picked, por favor."

He knelt next to Pepa, pulled out the bag of sage, and handed it to her. Pepa dried the herb on her shirt, took her lighter, and lit it, sheltering the herb from the rain with her jacket. She blew on the sage, sending the sweet smoke across the grave. Holding the sage, Pepa prayed to the curandero to come to their aid, to help them through this difficult time. She closed her eyes and called to his spirit. The musky smell of the rain hitting the parched earth around them complemented the pungent sage, which continued to burn despite being damp and green.

Pepa opened her eyes and glanced at Camilo kneeling silently beside her, his lips moving in prayer. She turned back to the headstone. The wind had shifted, now coming from the mountains. She felt a pocket of warmth embrace her. Smiling, she tossed the still burning sage on the grave, across what she hoped was the curandero's heart.

"I never asked what he told you on his last day," Pepa said, still kneeling, now eyeing Camilo.

"He didn't say much." Camilo opened his eyes. "I knew he was dying and actually thought he was dead when I went to look for him. I told you he wasn't in his bed, remember?"

Pepa nodded.

"When I found him sitting outside the house, over by the big tree, in the back he looked, bueno, I guess you could say—at peace. His hands were on his lap, and when he saw me he smiled. I tried to get him inside since it was kind of cold, but he wouldn't move." Camilo's eyes reddened with tears. The rain made soft pit pats against the weeds. Pepa watched Camilo as his face shifted with emotion. "Then he said, 'Mijo, remember the answer is always inside you.' He smiled again. And he died."

Camilo lifted his face to the sky. It began raining harder. "We're gonna get soaked."

"That's OK," Pepa said, studying the rain on her hands and on Camilo's face. "It's what we came for."

34

RIGHT AROUND THE TIME the rain was beginning to fall on Pepa and Camilo in San Geronimo, Rolo was enjoying a productive business lunch at Pasqual's. Two men from the city manager's office accompanied him, as well as a local developer, and Nina, of course, to take notes. As they finished their meeting, Nina glanced out the window and noticed a pile of ash-colored clouds moving in, Santa Fe's first storm of the season. The clouds looked heavy, big enough to blow in a lot of rain and, thankfully, break the drought. Despite living all her life in Santa Fe, Nina still loved the magic of New Mexican storms. They could rush in like a train or cloak themselves over the mountains, so you could see them coming for miles—curdled black clouds, scraggly lightning bolts, and bone-crushing thunder.

This was the latter kind of storm, giving everyone fair warning. Nina and the mayor had left the office without umbrellas, him, because he was too busy talking, and her, because she didn't think a big-throated storm would actually hit them—too many months of cloudless days ingrained in her psyche. As they walked to the restaurant, Rolo spouted off a long-winded speech about why he had to convince the big-shot developer to go along with a new project he was proposing. Nina couldn't believe how much Rolo talked. "Habla y habla y habla," she thought, as the mayor droned on. He didn't even glance upwards when she remarked about the weather.

The meeting started promptly. Nina felt that aside from a few disagreements between Rolo and the developer whose face reminded her of an old medicine ball, it had gone well. As the check was being settled, she glanced out the window, and saw the rain falling in fat, heavy drops. She nudged the mayor, pointing to the rain.

"Hey, that's great," he said, with a wink. "Gentlemen," he continued, "I think our drought is officially over. May I suggest you look out the window?" He gestured toward the window as if he himself had something to do with it.

The developer raised what was left in his wineglass and offered a toast. "To Santa Fe's future."

Nina ignored the toast and gathered her notes, worrying how her wig would hold up under the weight of water. She hoped it wouldn't stick together in thick, heavy glops. Or worse, part itself across the middle and expose its little stitches like an oversized doll head.

She needn't have worried. As she and Rolo stepped out the door, the rain hitting them like heavy, wet slaps, she noticed the oddest thing. Rolo was acting—well, strange. Not the kind of strange you see in scary movies when something evil is about to happen. Or the he-ain't-right, village idiot kind of strange. This strange was when you think you know someone well, and then they do something so completely out of the ordinary that you stand back, speechless. What Nina saw in Rolo's face as the rain hit it was what she'd seen in the office on other men, in one form or another, nearly every single day: fear.

Now since she hadn't seen this particular expression on Rolo before, she first thought he might be sick. "Excuse me, sir," she called to him in her "M" voice, but it seemed he didn't hear her. Nina trotted alongside the mayor, inhaling the rust-scented New Mexican soil. Despite her wet clothes and wig, she relished this delicious treat from the sky. Rolo, on the other hand, acted like he was escaping an acid-tainted deluge. He upped their pace to almost a jog. The rain pounded them harder, leaving splotches of water across their skin. Lightning streaked over the plaza, followed by a thick pulse of thunder across their backs.

Rolo still seemed stuck in his own world. "Mr. Mayor!" Nina cried. "Mr. Mayor!" Rolo turned toward her, speechless, eyes consumed with panic. He reminded Nina of men she'd seen in war movies having flashbacks. Except Nina knew Rolo worked at the Fort Dejeune disbursement office, cutting checks when he was in the service. The closest thing to a traumatic event he had would have been losing a poker game or getting slapped in the face from a woman refusing his come-on.

"Are you OK?" Nina asked as they continued jogging. Rolo glanced at her, but didn't reply. He kept looking at the clouds, lips curled up in fright.

"We gotta get outta this rain!" he finally blurted over his shoulder.

Rain? He's upset about the rain? Nina wondered if it was because of his Versace. The suit was new since he'd dropped a ton of weight, probably close to forty pounds. Now that she thought about it, she didn't recall seeing Rolo eat much at lunch that day. Was he wasting away like Karen Carpenter? She indulged in a luscious fantasy of watching an anorexic Rolo crumble under the fist of a bigger man. Or maybe, ha! even under her own fist. She gave him a long eyeball. On top of that he wasn't even cute. She remembered seeing a TV show about heavy people losing weight, unmasking model-like features. But Rolo wasn't cutting it. He still looked like a rottweiler with a goatee, only minus the jowls.

The rain felt cool, like a shower after a workout. Rolo grabbed Nina's elbow, pulling her along at an even faster pace. Running any farther in the chintzy heels she'd picked up at an Albuquerque discount store wasn't an option.

"Sorry, Boss. You're gonna have to go ahead on your own," she said, gasping and wobbling. "I can't run in these heels. Go on without me. I'll see you back at the office."

Rolo was still trying to drag Nina along. "You sure?" He looked desperate.

"Yeah, go, go. I'm gonna stop by Walgreen's anyway."

"OK," he said, clearly relieved. He took off running, dashing through pedestrians without a backward glance.

When Nina returned to the office, flushed and soggy, Rolo's door was closed. Dahlia, as usual, wouldn't look at her—working, it seemed, on something important. Nina wanted to ask her if she'd noticed anything strange about Rolo, but figured it was futile. Dahlia always acted like she didn't know anything, even though she was so attuned to Rolo she reminded Nina of a cockroach, waiting and watching for the slightest tidbit of food. Dahlia thought no one knew how she felt about Rolo, but all the building workers talked about her, following their comments with a headshake or snicker. The nicer ones simply shrugged and said, "Pobrecita." Nina watched Dahlia pull Rolo's schedule out of the printer with her roachified arms. Then she walked past Nina's desk with her nose bent sideways. Pobrecita, my ass.

"What's the mayor's plans for the afternoon?" Nina forced out the best honey-lamb voice she could muster.

"He's canceled them all," Dahlia replied, eyes glued to the computer.

"He not feeling well?"

"That's what he told me. I'm going through his itinerary now. Call these people." She laid a piece of paper with several names and phone numbers on her desk. "And tell them the Mayor took ill and has to reschedule. Then get their availability so I can squeeze them in over the next couple of weeks."

Returning to her desk, Dahlia studied her computer screen. "The problem is," she added, "I don't know how I'm going to do it."

"What's he sick with?"

Dahlia finally looked at her. "It's really none of our business, is it?" Her fuck-you-and-your-little-black-skirt reply hit Nina like a slap. She punched the telephone buttons with hard, pointed pecks. It was either them or Dahlia's eyes. Truthfully, she didn't know how much longer she would last. It took all her willpower not to tell Dahlia what she thought of her. She heard the phone at the other end ringing, the voicemail picking up her call. She smiled to herself, marveling at this change in her personality. Maybe it was because she was more mature. In the old days, she would've just let go. Nina waited for the beep and left a message. Well, I didn't hit her or tell her off. And I don't even want to egg her car. Nina hung up the phone, glancing again at Dahlia's arms. I guess I am more mature.

But it was clear Rolo was acting weird. "He said he wasn't feeling well," Dahlia whispered, almost like a confession. Then she turned back to her computer screen. "Hope it's not the flu since it would set him back. He's too busy to get sick." Nina watched Dahlia study his schedule. "Criminy," she added, shaking her head. "He just pushes himself. It's probably why he got sick."

Nina nodded, wondering what the hell was really going on with Rolo. "Uh-huh. Maybe he'll feel better tomorrow. Why's his door closed?"

"He said he had a few things to finish up."

"Okey-dokey." Nina shrugged, then continued calling his afternoon appointments. At 1:38 pm, Rolo opened his door looking considerably calmer. She glanced out the window and noticed the rain had stopped. He put on his jacket and grabbed the big umbrella he kept in a stand next to the coat rack. Nina put on her *I care* kitten face. "I heard you're feeling poorly." She knew he was a sucker whenever she doted on him.

He turned, looking both defiant and embarrassed, like a cross between a conquistador and a voice-changing choirboy. "Yeah, I, uh, didn't feel well after we left the restaurant. That's why I had to move fast. Probably something I ate." He rubbed his shrunken belly.

"Sorry you feel bad," Nina said with a purr. "I hope you get better soon."

"Me too," he replied, his face looking even sadder.

Nina actually felt sorry for the guy—at least temporarily. He looked like he'd been put through the wringer, his face flushed, cheeks drawn.

"Dahlia," Rolo buttoned his jacket, "did you cancel my appointments?" He patted his buttons, making sure all were fastened.

"Almost done," said Dahlia, pounding the keyboard. "I think I can fit them in this week, but it'll be tight . . . Uh, I know it's none of my business," she swiveled her chair, facing him directly, "but I was wondering if you might be working too much?"

Nina watched Dahlia place her hands under her chin, now looking dead-on like a praying mantis. Her eyes even had that same Jiffy-Popped look.

"What say a vacation?" Dahlia added. "You haven't had one in a while."

"Nah, it's just a bug," said Rolo. "I'll be back tomorrow. Besides," he said, opening the door, "I don't have time for one." Then he walked out and shut the door softly behind him.

Feeling pretty damn confused, Nina bolted over to the Feed Your Steed at five o'clock without even changing her costume. She needed to see Tala, who was ringing up a brisk, after-work rush accompanied by her chicken, Bess, and her dog, Lisa. Nina watched Bess peck into the cash register every time Tala opened it. The bird once had the golden opportunity of being around spilled sunflower seeds that had accidentally fallen in. Now each time Tala brought Bess to the store, the hen lingered around the checkout stand, still searching for seed fragments.

Ignoring those in line, Nina rushed to the front, picked up the chicken and tossed her gently to the floor. "I gotta talk to you," she exclaimed over the chicken's loud protests. Her wig, lopsided from both the rain and the rush over to the store, now leaned over her left eye.

"Sweetie, can it wait a minute?" Tala gave her the I-am-busy-being-a-professional-eyeball. "We can talk at six." Nina noticed several customers telegraphing long-nosed looks. They had gotten used to dogs in the aisles and chickens in the cash registers, but apparently not to hot-looking lesbians in high-heels and miniskirts.

"Can't you just take a quick break? I really need to talk to you. Something weird's going on with Rolo. It'll just take a minute." Tala's eyes shifted. Nina followed them and realized the entire line of people waiting to pay were ogling her and Tala. "Uh, never mind, I'll talk to you after closing. Meet me at the girly-girl," which was their fun word for the Cowgirl BBQ. "Wait till I tell you what happened." Nina raised her eyebrows to emphasize her point.

"OK," Tala replied, eyes wide with curiosity. "I'll see you there soon."

☼

"It's a malpuesto," Tala said over a steaming bowl of posole. Seeing the state Nina was in, she had locked the doors early and hurled through traffic to meet her.

Nina, working on her second margarita, and now happily out of costume, sat back with a jolt. "A mal what?" She'd ordered a salad, but it lay untouched on the table.

"A malpuesto," Tala replied after slugging back a long pull of Bohemia. "You never heard of one?"

Nina shook her head.

"It's when a bruja or brujo," Tala said, thinking of Camilo, "puts a hex on someone to make them sick."

Nina paused to think. "I think that's what Pepa did about him not eating. I mean, she basically told us that. So him losing weight wasn't a surprise, but this rain thing is really weird."

"Why?" Tala slurped down her posole.

"Because he wasn't sick. He was scared. Really scared. Scared like I've never seen him before."

Tala put her spoon down and leaned in closer. "You said his face was splotchy and his eyes buggy."

"Right, just like that tough guy from the movie *The Birds*. It's the same look I always see in the poor jerks Rolo slam dunks at the office every day." Nina sipped more margarita.

"Maybe this is payback." Tala's eyes danced with sarcasm.

"But this was even worse. You know those scary movies where there's always a monster who chases a guy and then he gets mashed into pâté? And right before he dies the camera zeroes in on his face and it looks sweaty and death-rowified?"

"Yeah?"

"Well, substitute the rain for sweat and that's exactly how Rolo looked." Nina stabbed a tomato, taking a quick bite out of it.

"Like in *Jurassic Park?*"

"Yeah, like that," she replied, chewing.

Tala drank more beer. "Doesn't it seem fishy that he's weird about rain? Who the hell ever freaks out over rain? I mean people are scared of dogs and snakes. But when do you hear about people freaking over rain?" She stopped to think for a minute, barely noticing two cute girls who had just walked into the bar. "You never saw him act this way before?"

"Never." Nina took a whole piece of bread, slathered butter over it, then set it back down on her plate.

"Has it ever rained while you've been working there?" Tala rubbed the tips of her fingers together, a nervous habit she developed in high school.

"Just the night of our date, but it had already stopped when we left Pepa's."

"Hmmm. Did he ever talk about being tortured?"

"Are you serious?" Nina smirked. "I think the only thing that's ever tortured him was when he didn't get his way. That guy was so scared today he left me alone just to bust ass back to the office." Nina concentrated momentarily. "Maybe he has some kind of complex." She took a small bite of the bread. "Or a hang-up."

Tala rolled her eyes over Nina's outdated terms. "Complex or hang-up, he's still a macho. Tell me when you've ever heard of a man being afraid of rain."

Nina wrinkled her nose as she bit into a green bean. "Maybe he was worried about his new suit."

"I doubt it. I think Pepa and Camilo did something more than put him on a diet." Tala grabbed Nina's hand. "Do you remember anything else that happened the night of the limpia?"

Nina shook her head. "I had some kind of lemony-smelling oil on me, but Pepa said it was for cleansing. I was kinda sleepy, though. I think it was from the heat, or that damn old wig I used to wear. It always made my head so hot it felt grilled."

"Yeah, you always yelled when you took it off." Tala touched Nina's nose.

"Did not. I was just expressing relief," she said, brown eyes flashing.

Tala bent over to kiss her. "My poor little baby has had to suffer so much."

"Yeah, so I think I was sleepy and maybe dozed off for a sec. But I don't remember Pepa doing anything different than what you've said she's done to you when you get limpias. When I left her house, I felt calm. Peaceful, y'know?"

Tala paused. "Now that I think about it. I *have* noticed a change. You don't seem to get as mad at things."

"Maybe it worked." She gave Tala a kiss on the lips. "Do you like me in my new-mad mode, or my old-mad mode?" She kissed her again.

"Depends on what you're mad about," Tala smiled, then leaned in close. "All I can say is that Pepa must've done something big-time to Rolo while she was treating you."

"Yeah, too bad I don't remember anything." Nina finished her margarita.

Tala grabbed Nina's hands. "Did you notice anything else, I mean anything at all?"

Nina squinted in concentration. "The room had a funny smell . . . and Rolo was moving kinda slow and," she snapped her fingers, "remember I said it had been raining?"

"After your limpia?"

"No, during, because there were drops of water on the car when we left."

Tala finished her beer. "I think we need to pay a little visit to Pepa."

❋

Pepa filled four of her special crystal glasses full of brandy. Setting them down on the kitchen table, she concentrated on keeping her on-trial face innocent. "I don't know," she said, glancing at Camilo. Tala and Nina had stopped by unexpectedly, their faces marked with concern. Gathered in Pepa's kitchen, they drilled for the truth. "We didn't do nothing more than we planned, que no?" said Pepa, sounding weak.

"Sí," Camilo added. "We just gave him a treatment to make him feel kinda sick so he wouldn't eat." He sipped his brandy. "But that was just to make him lose a few pounds."

"Yah, well that's worked. He's about as wide as a maple bar now. Have you seen him lately?" Nina swirled the brandy in her glass.

"No." Pepa hadn't seen him in several weeks.

"Just wait," Nina continued. "You probably won't recognize him."

"Really?" Camilo asked, getting excited.

Pepa noticed and secretly kicked him.

"Man, whatever you guys used on him you should market, 'cause you'd be millionaires," added Tala. "That asshole came into the store the other day to buy a few things for his dogs, and I thought he was a government agent. I kept wondering who the hell he was, but it wasn't till he whipped out his card that I saw it was him."

"So tell me, did you guys plan for him to lose all that lard?" asked Nina.

"Nooo." Pepa shook her head. "Pero nothing we do is what I call exact science." She rested her hands in her lap.

"Sí," Camilo continued, eyes steady on Pepa. "We just wanted him to stop feeling like he could go up to people and stick his big panza in their faces." They all laughed, breaking the tension.

"Well, his stomach's gone, but he still looks like a barracuda, except for yesterday." Nina gripped the table edge. "I mean it was so weird because he actually cringed when the rain hit him, like it was something painful. And his eyes puffed out like a chameleon, and his lips were curled, like Chucho's when he doesn't like you." Nina demonstrated her dog's snarl, making everyone laugh again.

Pepa held herself still, concentrating on Nina's words. What in the hell had they done? And, more specifically, what did she and Camilo do to screw up? "And how was he today?" she asked.

"Well, it didn't rain, so he was fine. Totally the same." Nina took another sip of brandy. "You think he'll be scared again when it rains?"

Pepa shrugged. "No sé. I guess we'll just have to see, que no?"

"You're not worried?" Nina pressed.

"Bueno, it's a little strange, but it doesn't sound like he's gonna die or anything. You said he was back to normal today, no?"

"Yeah," Nina shrugged.

"Bueno, so let's not worry now." Pepa forced a smile.

"Anyone know the forecast for tomorrow?" asked Tala.

"Yeah," Camilo said, grabbing the paper. "Rain."

35

"Híjole, I've never seen so many people eat so much jerky in all my life." Luz, on her lunch break, parked herself at Pepa's kitchen table the day after Tala and Nina's visit. The rain had stopped, but a pocket of clouds had settled around the town, giving cool relief to the sun-stroked land.

"You want a limpia?" Pepa thought Luz looked a little tired.

"Maybe later, Mom. Phew," she said, rubbing her forehead. "Ever since you and Jules started writing your bomb articles, business has been crazy. Now explain that one to me." She removed her shoes, massaging her feet.

"No sé," Pepa replied, with an impish grin. "Maybe people think if you can make good bombs you can make good jerky."

"Very funny." Luz rolled her eyes. "But, you know, now that business is good, me and Jules are gonna find a place together."

"Really?"

"Yup." Luz set silverware and two plates on the table, while Pepa warmed leftovers from the night before. She took the remains of a baked chicken out of the oven, then turned the heat off a pot of calabacitas.

Pepa eyed her daughter as she stirred the vegetables. Aside from looking a bit tired, she seemed calm, almost serene. Luz had always seemed a little bitter, frayed like an old cord. Pepa never thought she would heal. Now she was seeing a side of her daughter she'd never known before.

"Why doesn't el Jules just move into your place? Or I guess you could move into his, since his is bigger."

Luz served herself some food, then took a bite of a chicken leg. "Oh no, we can't live together now."

"Por qué? You like each other, no?"

"Sí, pero we don't want to take over the other person's space."

Confused, Pepa asked, "Space? Qué space?"

"Well, our houses are filled with just our own things." Luz took another bite of chicken, chewing while she talked. "Jules has a big library with tons of books on physics and bombs, you know, things he studies. And I don't have room in my house for a physics library—or any library—now that I think about it."

"Yah, well he can box up some of those books, no? He doesn't study el physics anymore, so he doesn't have to have all those nasty books around anyway. That'll solve your problem." Pepa sucked in her lips. She'd just as soon cart those books off to the dump herself if she had her way.

"My house is too small, Mom, even if he did box everything up. We're gonna see how things go with us, then we'll play it by ear."

Pepa took a big bite of calabacitas and chewed the mix of corn, squash, and chile. "Well, if we can keep esta winery out, then maybe you can move in with Jules and build an addition?"

Luz sprinkled salt on her food. "Like I said, we'll have to see. Jules is the first guy I've wanted to live with since I was married. Did you know that?"

"Kind of." Pepa knew full well the extent of Luz's poor track record. "He good to you?"

"Yeah. He's good, and fun—well, funny." She paused. "A little weird," she said, chewing.

"Weird? Como qué?" Pepa tore a tortilla in half with one swift motion.

"You know, nerdy, I guess. Maybe that's a better way to describe it. Sort of a geek."

Pepa let out a long, slow breath.

"But I like him 'cause I can be myself around him." Luz finished off the chicken leg.

"You think you'll get married?" Pepa didn't know how in the hell she was going to deal with having a Los Alamos scientist for a son-in-law, even if he didn't actually work there anymore.

"No, probably not."

Pepa let out another long, slow breath.

"We don't think we need a marriage to be together," Luz continued, spreading green chile on a tortilla.

"Ya sé. Nowadays no one gets married anymore, anyway."

Luz nodded.

"Y . . ." Pepa hesitated. "How you feel about him being a . . . a . . . well, a gabacho?"

Luz got up to get the coffeepot, pouring coffee for both her and Pepa. "You know, it was hard getting used to in the beginning. I remember when I first saw him without a shirt and thought egad, this guy sure is white. But, after looking at him for a little while you start getting used to it. Y, bueno, I guess when you love someone you take them as they are, freckles and all."

"Bueno, I guess that's good." Pepa added sugar to her coffee.

"And he has to, in turn, deal with who I am, you know, as a Chicana and everything."

"Chicana, huh?"

"Yeah."

Pepa couldn't remember if she had added one or two teaspoons. She shrugged and added another. "Como?"

"Well, he's never had a Chicana for a girlfriend before, so he has to under-stand the brown woman in white society thing . . . Then there's the fact that I sell jerky for a living, and I don't have a college degree. And . . ."

"Sí?" Pepa lit a cigarette and inhaled. She hoped this guy wasn't one of those scientific know-it-alls. Just what she needed.

"Well, there's also the fact that you're a curandera, y—well—y todo eso."

Pepa released a plume of cigarette smoke. "Sí. Some people are afraid of my work." She tapped her fingernail against her teeth. "Pero, what do you mean 'y todo eso'?"

"Bueno, nada," Luz scratched her leg, "except maybe . . . well, you're not a typical mom. The kind that stays home all day and cooks."

"Pues what's he looking for, a TV show? Is it because I buy store-bought tortillas?" Pepa couldn't think what else made her atypical. Sure, she smoked, cussed, and drank, but so did lots of people.

"No, not that," Luz waved her hand in the air. "It's more like you don't go to church and you make money curing people with hierbas, candles, and oils."

Pepa smiled. "Well, at least I make them feel better. Plus you gotta admit I'm not boring."

Luz nodded. "You got that right. So, he's got a few things to get used to. Pero, in general, it's been pretty good."

Pepa tapped the ash from her cigarette with slow, steady pats. "'Cause he's gabacho?"

"Oh, no." Luz waved away the comment with a flick of her wrist. "I like him because he's just easy and fun. And—" she paused—"I think he brings out my best."

"And I gotta say he works pretty hard on all that nuclear stuff we're doing," Pepa admitted.

"Yeah, you two work together pretty good. I know your helping him really makes a difference."

"That's good," said Pepa. She never thought in a million years she'd have a nuclear scientist for a son-in-law, much less work with one so closely. "Maybe you, me, and Jules should go on Oprah?" Pepa put out her cigarette.

"Oprah? Por qué?"

"Because you opened your minds, and then your hearts changed, and then you changed—for the better!" Pepa gave Luz a sweet smile. "Y la Oprah le gusta people who do those things, que no?"

"Well don't kid yourself," Luz replied. "I'd go if she asked."

36

ELENA LUJÁN WALKED INTO THE courthouse impeccably dressed, accompanied by one of her legal assistants. She was about to present her case to the judge and had an entourage of Dogtownies who showed up to support her: Pepa, Camilo, Father Miguel, and Jules. Tala, after telling Gilbert her true feelings about the winery, knew there was no point posing as a neutral party anymore, so she sat with the rest of the Canines. Elena caught Tala's eye, and Tala flashed her a grin, raising her fist in solidarity. Gilbert and Tala's parents were seated several rows back, one on each side of the courtroom.

Bill Takash and a big, corn-fed looking guy from California comprised Gilbert's legal team, both moving with the confidence of a winning case. Gilbert sat directly behind them, and way in the back sat Nina taking notes for the mayor.

Elena caught it all in one sweep of the courtroom. She pulled her notes from her briefcase, knowing she was pulling straws to present a cogent case to the judge. Her plan, as she checked her notes, was to stall things enough to see if something better would arise. She remained hopeful that the negative publicity, petitions, fundraisers, web sites, and yard signs the Dogtowners had worked on would sway public opinion, and, as a consequence, the judge's. She knew she didn't have much of a chance to win this case. Gilbert's well-choreographed sincerity about being "up front and honest" with the Dogtown residents had created an amazing counter blitz. Elena was savvy enough to know everyone did backroom deals when they wanted something bad enough. What she hadn't counted on were some of the Dogtownies actually accepting the money Gilbert had offered them. She had erred in judgment, and it would cost her.

Now Gilbert was ready to slam-dunk the rest of Dogtown by forcing the resistors out. She was certain he'd find a way to get the judge to support an eminent domain request, something she heard was in the works. These things happen all the time, usually for new developments—freeways and shopping centers. But she never thought they'd try it for a winery. A pinche winery. It was too silly to ponder why Gilbert wanted a winery so close to the city limits in the first place, especially when he could have one without all the hassle just a few miles away. Elena stopped herself since she needed to stay focused. Going into the illogic of Gilbert's brain was a waste of time.

Elena curled her fingers in and out. She had to concentrate, psych up against Bill Takash and the California corn pone. To win, she'd have to do a real body slam, and even then still pray for a miracle since the judge was a crony of Rolo's. It was amazing how deep the mayor's tentacles slithered. Rolo's philosophy was simple: he did you a favor, so you owed him.

She smelled the peppermint-slicked breath of Gilbert's legal team. Noticed their nails were even manicured. Fucking land sharks.

"All rise," the bailiff announced as the judge entered. Everyone stood as the "honorable" Karl Carson walked in. Elena watched the judge assemble his papers, recalling what an asshole he'd been in past cases. She knew his self-proclaimed heir-to-Kit-Carson story was a load of horseshit. Judge Carson never proved he was a descendent of the explorer/Indian killer. A few letters ostensibly written by Karl's great, great-grandmother were all he had. Even *he* knew that wasn't much to build a legacy. When Elena stared at his drumette arms, comb-over, and eyes peeking through his glasses like black speckled eggs, she wanted to laugh.

After studying the case notes, the judge finally looked up. "Case Number 4423559, the People of the Mesa Azul tract, also known as Dogtown, sectored within a four block radius between Juanita Street, Salazar Avenue, Camino de Angel, Taos Street, and Santa Clara Boulevard, versus Gilbert Córdova Enterprises. May I speak with counsel?"

Elena and the two lawyers from Gilbert's team walked up to the judge.

"I've examined both your motions," the judge said in a harsh whisper, "and find the motion filed by Counselor Luján has little legal merit. You, Ms. Luján," he said, examining Elena over the top of his glasses, "may proceed with your arguments if you wish, but since this is not a jury-based trial, you have only me to convince. I can clearly see by the evidence presented that suing Córdova Enterprises on the grounds that your clients have the 'right to habitation in their current place of residence, etcetera, etcetera' has no legal precedent, nor any basis for argument, at least not as a court case." He looked like he was actually stifling a smile. "Ms. Luján, why are you wasting my time?"

Expecting this, Elena rolled back her shoulders. "Your Honor, I have evidence that states the contrary, if you will examine—"

"It doesn't matter what you have, Counselor Luján. The way I look at it, and I *am* the one who's looking at it, you don't have a case. What you have is garbage. And because I don't find your argument worthy of anyone's time, especially mine, my opinion is you should withdraw your motion." Gilbert's lawyers glanced at each other, eyes giving away their glee.

Elena, unfazed, stood her ground. "I refuse to do so on the basis as noted in the file." And, she thought, on the basis of attempted intimidation by a pissant chicken hawk.

Karl Carson shrugged. "As you wish."

Elena proceeded with her plan, citing coercion by Gilbert, conflict of interest by the mayor, and violation of due process rights concerning city zoning laws. The judge stonewalled the arguments one by one as if swatting gnats. When she asked for a decision delay, he nearly laughed in her face.

Elena gathered her papers, taking deep breaths to steady herself, as Gilbert's lawyers low-fived each other.

"This is a sham," grumbled Jules from the stands. "I can't believe we live in the twenty-first century. I'll tell you what, we're not through yet."

Pepa, Tala, Nina, and Camilo walked up to Elena, all remarking that, despite everything, she had done a good job. Tala gave her a hug, saying she was sorry.

"I gave it what I could," Elena replied, eyes clouding with emotion. "I honestly don't think we had anything else to go on."

"Bueno, let's get out of here." Pepa put her arm around Elena. "Why don't you come over and I'll give you a limpia."

Elena took a step backward. "Oh, gracias, Pepa, but you know I, uh, don't really believe in those things."

Pepa raised an eyebrow.

"I know they must work for some people, but I don't think they work for me—too damn rational, I think." She grabbed Pepa's hand. "No, what I need now, I have to honestly say, is a great deal of very pure alcohol. Thanks." She squeezed her hand. "And if there's anyone who'd like to join me," she said, glancing at the others, her eyes settling on Tala, "I'll be at the Railyard in twenty minutes."

"I'll join you," said Jules. "It'll give me a chance to learn a little more about this case."

"I'll go, too," added Father Miguel. "You shouldn't be alone right now."

Pepa, Camilo, and Nina said they were unable to join her. All eyes rested on Tala.

"I think I can squeeze in one drink," Tala said, examining her watch. She turned to Nina and gave her a kiss. "I'll talk to you a little later."

"OK," said Elena, feeling pleased about the company. "Shall we go?"

✺

Outraged by the previous day's events in court, Jules wanted a follow-up meeting with the Dogtown residents. He felt it was important to get the word out on what had happened and an explanation from Elena on their legal options. This way people would get the facts straight without having important items misconstrued through gossip. The rest of the CURs agreed, and they sent word out about the meeting through phone tree and their newly formed Listserv, Tutti'sTerroirists. As usual, Pepa volunteered her yard, and they convened the next evening.

Dressed in cowboy boots and jeans, Jules stood tall at the podium. "Good evening, everyone. Thank you for coming tonight. Our legal counsel Elena Luján had a court proceeding yesterday with Gilbert and his lawyers. As witnesses, we felt you should be fully informed so we can strategize on what to do next." He turned to Elena and gestured toward the podium.

"Thanks Jules. Bueno, yesterday did not go as well as I had hoped. So, without further ado, I'll get right to the point." She opened her notebook and quickly scanned the brief. "Gilbert submitted a request to the judge to evict all Dogtown residents, citing eminent domain under a theory of commercial investment. A court date's been set in thirty days. It pains me to tell you this but, based on our track record, Gilbert could possibly win."

Elena went on to explain what eminent domain entailed. "If Gilbert wins, then everyone will be given an official document declaring eviction from your property, which you can contest in a jury trial. If you decide against this, you'll receive a check for your home, business, or rental unit based on a formula agreed to by you and the city."

Jules studied the faces of those seated on chairs and benches in Pepa's yard. As usual, Tala had brought her dog and one of the chickens with her. The twilight hour sent in cooler air. The glow from the candles Pepa had placed along the fence gave off an almost comforting feel, in contrast to Elena's difficult words.

"You can fight this in court," she continued, "but I don't think you'll be successful, since Gilbert appears to have a judge in his favor. Still, I don't want to discourage you from fighting. If you chose to do so, make sure you don't cash that check."

"What happens if we stay?" Opal McGee stood up, hands on hips. Others mumbled in agreement.

"I can't say what will happen," Elena said, offering a compassionate smile. "Especially since I've never seen a case where so many people get evicted at one time. But according to Gilbert's lawyers," she paused to read from one of her documents, " 'Said parties who refuse to comply will be forcibly removed.'"

"A qué cabrón!" said Pepa.

"You can say that again," echoed Father Miguel, who, doing his best to be an ally, attended all the Dogtown meetings.

"I'll tell you one thing," Opal added, pointing to Elena. "It'll be a cold day in hell when they see me complying with that kind of mess . . . They'll have to tie my ass to a chair and carry me outta my house!"

Jules loved that old woman's spark.

"I should let you know," Elena continued, with a stern gaze. "That being forcibly removed means they'll arrest you and confiscate your belongings."

"Then they're just gonna have to rent a gym for all our stuff." Tala raised her hands outward like the Pope. Others cheered as her dog Lisa ran over to get petted.

"That's right, let 'em build a new jail to hold us, too!" added Nina. More cheers erupted.

"Don't give them any ideas," Elena replied, smiling sadly.

Jules, holding the chicken in his lap, set her down gently before standing up to speak. "They're not taking me, or my house."

"What, you gonna make a bomb?" asked Father Miguel with an evil-looking grin.

Jules turned toward the priest. "No, Padre, I'm not going to make a bomb. In fact, I don't know what I'm going to do. All I know is that I am going to fight this with every ounce of energy I got." His jaw muscles flexed with anger.

"Well, I ain't going either!" yelled Papa Chick, standing bowed legs and all, gnarled fist in the air.

"Ni yo!" yelled Irma, Pepa's next-door neighbor.

Looking worried over the resistance coming from everyone, Elena rapped on the podium. "Can I get your attention, please? Hello, everyone! Can I get your attention?" The crowd slowly quieted. "I don't want you all to think I'm advocating resisting eviction. A forced eviction is a nasty proceeding, and it can sometimes be dangerous. If the mayor thinks this will encompass more than the city can handle, he'll call in the state troopers. So if you decide to resist, I ask that you exercise careful judgment and extreme caution."

"Elena! Oye, Elena!" It was Pepa, yelling from the middle of the crowd. She stood up, gazed across the people assembled in her yard, then turned back to the lawyer. "Besides what we've tried in the courts, is there anything else we can do?"

Jules studied the feisty curandera. If there was anyone who could think of something, he knew it would be her.

Focusing her gaze on Pepa, Elena finally replied. "Nothing I can think of, aside from making Gilbert an offer he couldn't refuse." She nodded to the crowd. "Thanks for coming tonight. I'll keep you informed of any changes."

"Bueno, gracias," Pepa replied, directing a sharp look to Camilo.

Noticing their exchange, Jules felt too depressed to do more than wonder.

※

"We have to tell Tala and Nina something." Camilo walked around the kitchen, shoulders hunched, arms folded together.

Pepa noticed his agitation and set two glasses and a bottle of Don Presidente on the table. She offered the brandy to Camilo, who watched her pour it to the top of his glass. Then she lit a cigarette and blew the smoke toward the ceiling. "Mira, we can't tell anyone what we did, not even those two."

Camilo took a sip of brandy, grimacing as he swallowed. "Pues, por qué no? Don't you think they should know?"

Pepa drummed the table with soft little raps. "If anybody finds out we did something to that mayor, they'll come and throw our asses in jail. I think it's better if we say nothing." She took a slug of brandy, the liquid burning her chest. She sniffed, then absently flicked her ash, worried about what the hell she and Camilo had done to the man.

"Pero, we didn't plan for him to be afraid of rain." Camilo rubbed his face. "We just wanted him to have a little humility."

"Tell me what you put in that emplasto again." Pepa focused her attention on Camilo. His eyes seemed to lack their usual luster.

"Don Gabriel gave me a special hierba before he died, said he'd gotten it no sé where—I think it was from an old medicine woman in Jemez. He said to use it only when we were dealing with something evil, or someone very powerful."

"Sí, you said it increased the hierba's potency, pero did he tell you what it was?"

"No," Camilo replied, shaking his head.

"Did he tell you how much to use?" Pepa inhaled her cigarette, eyes steady on the acolyte.

"Kind of," he replied, staring at his brandy. "Well, not really." His eyes met Pepa's. "He said I'll know when I use it."

"And did you?"

Camilo drank, then slowly set his glass down. "Yeah, I suppose." He took another sip. "I used a couple pinches."

Pepa inhaled a long, deep pull of her cigarette, then tapped it into the ashtray with four steady pats. She tried to recall exactly what happened that night. "I remember I had to cool the emplasto so I took it outside."

"How long were you out there?"

She closed her eyes. "Not too long, maybe ten minutes." Then she opened her eyes and snapped her fingers. "It was raining, remember?"

"Sí."

"A few drops fell on the emplasto."

"How wet did it get?"

"Not too much. It was a little shiny when I brought it in, but since we'd mixed it with water, I didn't think nothing of it. Pero, maybe it did something." She put out her cigarette.

"But that doesn't make sense." Camilo looked doubtful. "Were you wet from the rain?"

"Sí, a little bit. My hair was wet. Maybe it dripped a little on him while I was working."

Pepa poured herself another glass, trying to comprehend what actually happened. "This is the first time it's rained since we gave him the malpuesto, no?"

"Yah." Camilo's eyebrows were crunched up like caterpillars. "Now what do we do?"

"Bueno, I guess it's out of our hands," said Pepa with a shrug.

Camilo blinked. "Shouldn't we try something to fix him?"

"No, because even if we did, we couldn't."

Camilo seemed mystified. "Why not?"

"Porque we gave him una hierba we don't know anything about. We were—cómo se dice?—Doctores de Frankenstein." She attempted a smile.

He picked up his glass, then quickly set it down. "How can you make a joke about this?"

"Bueno, hombre, I feel bad, but what am I gonna do? I just hope he doesn't get worse."

"Well, I'm worried. We might've really hurt him or made him into an even bigger monster."

"I don't think so," Pepa thought about the effects of the hierbas they had used. "Whatever we gave him worked . . . maybe just a little more than we thought."

"But we don't really know." Camilo folded a paper napkin into a tiny square. "Plus, he'll put two and two together and remember he came here."

Pepa sipped her brandy. She was beginning to feel more relaxed. "La mujer in Jemez, is she still alive?"

"I don't know." Camilo opened the kitchen door to let in the dog. He licked Camilo's hand as he walked by. "We can go look for her."

"We don't have a car that can get us there." She squeezed his arm. "Camilo, we wanted him to know what it's like to be afraid, and the way it's turned out, at least for now, is that he's afraid of rain. Let him go through this. If it gets real bad we'll ask somebody to take us to Jemez."

"OK, I guess." Camilo still looked worried.

"Pero, I need you to do something else."

"What?" he asked, alert.

Pepa studied Camilo, trying to shape what she had to say into something he wouldn't think were words of a madwoman. "I think you already know. It's why Don Gabriel sent you to live with me."

"And I've been helping you y todo, no?"

Pepa nodded. "Sí, you came to help me, and you have. Pero, I know you can do even more. I knew it the first time I saw you."

"When? That time I met you on the trail walking the dogs?" Joaquín jerked his head at the word.

Retrieving a white candle from the cabinet next to her altar, Pepa lit it then sprinkled lavender and rosemary over the flame, releasing their sweetness into the room. She sat down, folded her hands, and faced the young man she had grown to love.

"I met you when you were a little boy. No me recuerdo how old you were. You were already living in San Geronimo."

Camilo nodded.

"I stopped by the house to say hello. Then you came into the room and Don Gabriel said he was taking care of you, that your mama and daddy had gone to California and left you with him. But when I saw you there, I noticed something different about you. No sé qué. Pero, a few months ago when you came to live with me and told me Don Gabriel had sent you, I knew he'd sent you for a reason."

"You needed help."

"Sí, pero don't forget he told you this after he died. And you haven't told me why you're really here."

Finishing his brandy, Camilo held up the empty glass to the light. "Bueno, you have it all wrong. He did send me to help you, but he spoke to me in a dream." His eyes seemed to be searching Pepa's for confirmation.

"Don't play games with me, Camilo. You did something to the dogs when they first saw you. Recuerdas? I don't know what you did, but they liked you right away. And those dogs don't like anybody they don't know . . . In fact the whole time you've been here, you've done things no one else could do, not even me—special hierbas, cures for the animals, y más."

"Chhh, don't be silly." He leaned back in his chair, looking away.

"Pienso que," Pepa said, folding her hands together, "you have special power. Power that comes from someplace inside you. Ay, I sound silly." She waved her hand through the air. "But I know what I feel, and what I see . . ."

Camilo looked out the window toward the mountains. "I guess you see things different than me. I've done a few things here and there with the animals—helped you with patients. Pero it's nada. I just pick up their energy and use it to heal them, just like you and Don Gabriel. It's why I feel so bad about what we did to Rolo."

Pepa got up and put her arm around Camilo. "I'm worried about that mayor, too. But like I said, he has a big hole in his heart. And don't forget he's spent most of his life hurting other people. I think deep down there's something inside him he hates. Why else would he be so mean? So maybe what we're doing is helping him change into what he really wants."

"Which is what?" asked Camilo.

"To be a better man," Pepa said with a smile.

"I don't know." Camilo grabbed the arms of his chair, rocking back and forth. "I hate to say this, but this all sounds kind of like a crock of shit."

"Pero, it's not," Pepa sat close, facing him. "Rolo needs to open his heart. Once he does it he won't be afraid. He'll even eat again."

"But how do you know?"

"I—I guess I just do. Pero, until it happens, I need you to do something else." She leaned in closer, grabbing his hands.

"Qué?"

"Rain—we need more of it."

Camilo started laughing like it was the best joke he'd heard all summer.

Ignoring his laughter, Pepa got the calendar off the wall. "Today is September twenty-first. We need," she paused to look ahead a month, "it to rain every day, all the way through October."

Camilo looked at Pepa like she had lost her mind. "Besides the fact that I can't make it rain," he continued, "we already had a rainstorm. And it's supposed to rain tomorrow."

"Sí, pero it has to rain lots more. Every day and every night for forty days, nonstop."

"Por qué?"

"No sé, but when we were at the cemetery, it's what I knew we needed."

"Did Don Gabriel happen to channel his request from the grave?" He filled his glass again, corked the bottle, then took a sip.

"I'm not playing."

Camilo rubbed his eyes and stared at the floor.

Pepa got up and exchanged the brandy for a cup of tea. Then she brought over milk and honey. "Camilo, look at me."

He didn't respond.

"Camilo, por favor . . . Por favor, look at me."

Slowly, he lifted his face to Pepa's.

"I know I can sometimes be—" Pepa paused, "poquito chingona. And you're probably thinking I'm a little crazy, too. But I know, and I feel it in my heart, that you can do what I'm asking you." Camilo's eyes reflected back at Pepa, but they remained flat, like still pools of water. Pepa heard a mockingbird call in the distance. Her dog flicked his ears at the sound. She glanced at the burning candle on the altar, waiting for his response.

Finally, Camilo spoke. "I don't know if you've ever had this happen to you before, but this may be the first time you're wrong. No soy un brujo. I can't do what you're asking me. And even if I could, I wouldn't know how to begin. I'm sorry." He placed his hand on Pepa's shoulder, got up, and walked out of the room.

Camilo picked up his pillow and threw it hard against his headboard. He kicked off his shoes and fell back on his bed, the old springs squeaking. The evening breeze from the open window lapped against the lace curtain. He knew from experience that Pepa was rarely wrong. But where did she ever get the notion he was a brujo?

He lay on his bed trying to recall all the things Don Gabriel had said to him while he was growing up, telling him once that he thought he had "a gift." But he never explained what that meant. And the lessons he received throughout his life had focused on healing, not on his "gift," or of special powers, or brujería.

Camilo heard the door crack open, and Joaquín walked in. He sat on the floor beside the bed, leaning against it so Camilo would pet him. As he rubbed the dog's head, he wondered if Pepa knew something he didn't. She had a gift for healing he could only dream of matching. But this "make it rain" stuff sounded more like the rant of a crazy woman.

He got up and went over to his altar. On it were three purple candles, each surrounded by stones, crystals, and beads he'd collected from special places. As he lit each candle, he said a prayer, wanting to center his thoughts. He felt troubled by the things they'd done to Rolo and asked the spirits to guide him. "Help me stay true," he prayed. "Help me stay honorable and do what's right."

After finishing, he went back to his bed, letting the candles burn. The amber flames continued to pulse in the room's dim light. He was sleepy, so he closed his eyes and thought about what Pepa had asked him. "Don Gabriel, go to Pepa. Help her. I know she wants this, needs it, but I—I can't do it . . . can't do what she asks . . . She needs your help. So please, go to her . . . and help her . . . help her . . . help her . . . help her . . . please . . ."

Camilo fell asleep. Joaquín settled in, lying on the floor beside him. At some point in the night, Camilo turned over, unaware that the wind had picked up, gusting and winding its way through the Sangre de Cristo Mountains, gathering and pulling clouds out of nowhere, roiling with an intensity previously unseen. As he continued to sleep, the rain scheduled for the next day began to fall, its patter hitting the tin roof like soft little slaps.

37

JULES HEAVED A FROZEN SLAB of beef to his shoulder and walked out of the freezer. Lumbering under the weight of the meat, he made his way into the What A Jerkee's kitchen, laden by both beef and frustration. After he and Pepa had worked so hard to get the story in the *Washington Post*, he'd hoped it would become a breakout piece. But it had turned out to be nothing more than another saga of the government's infamous secrets. That it happened over fifty years ago only made it worse. People have poor memories. Even the victims poisoned by the bombs wanted to move on. One woman, who'd lost her husband, a physicist, to radiation poisoning, said that it had occurred so long ago, she had basically moved on with her life.

Sighing, Jules revved up the slicer and cut the big slab in half. He set the machine to automatic. Adjusting the width, he pressed start, and the slicer screamed to life as it bladed through the meat. He pulled away neat, even slices, stopping the machine from time to time to wipe off the residue. He was allergic to all types of gloves and had to handle the beef barehanded. Several minutes into slicing left his fingers covered with blood.

As he worked through the meat, he wondered if he'd been a fool. Though completely illogical, he had fantasized that something more might have resulted from his and Pepa's efforts—at the very least, a government apology. Nothing had occurred. He couldn't get over the fact that the stories of people who spoke of their illnesses, deaths of loved ones, or the damage the testing had done to the environment actually hadn't mattered, that is, unless you were a victim. Sure, he got letters from supporters who thanked him and Pepa for bringing to light another example of the US's secret practices. More were surprisingly angry for bringing up old news or failing to understand the sacrifices necessary for our country's greater good. Several said he had a chip on his shoulder or, even worse, was un-American.

Jules placed a new hunk of beef in the slicer. He'd even asked several law firms to file a class-action suit. But no one would take the case. Everyone knew the government was exempt from prosecution so even working for society's greater good would be a waste of time. And of course there had been no luck with their senator. Everything, start to finish, about this particular cause was an exercise in futility.

What a bunch of crap. Jules gathered the sliced beef and placed it on the dryer trays. Wanting to think of something more pleasant, he looked for Luz through the prep window. She had on the tight little jacket he'd bought her for her birthday, and her black pants nuzzled nice around her ass. Momentarily distracted, he stopped working and waited for her to catch his eye. But with her back to him, she remained focused on a woman picking up an order. He sighed again, slicing more beef. Outside, the rain had picked up, sending welcome relief across the sun-battered land. Jules heard the rumble of thunder and smiled. Well, I'm not giving up, he thought. I don't know what it is or when it'll be. But somehow, someway, something more's got to happen. He pulled the last piece of meat off the slicer, laid it on the dryer, then marched to the sink to wash off the blood.

38

RAIN PUMMELED THE WINDOWS. Nina glanced at the clock, Tala in the shower, then back at the mirror, resuming the task of plucking her eyebrows. Prior to working in Rolo's office she had never given them a second thought. Now plucking the two thin angles of hair over her eyes had become a hated daily ritual. Why do women do these things she wondered, her eyes tearing from the pain.

"Oye, Amor! After I'm done working for Rolo I'm gonna invite everyone over and have a sacrificial burning of my wig, nylons, bra, and these damn tweezers," Nina yelled so Tala could hear her. "How much longer do I have to work in that big cabezón's office anyway?"

Tala turned off the water and opened the shower curtain painted with Nina's version of a Tongan tapa cloth, replacing the usual fish with dogs and cats. "I don't know, Honey. I'm not sure how much longer this is going to go on." She grabbed a towel and began drying her hair. "After Elena got body-slammed, I don't know if there's much else we can do."

Facing Tala, Nina placed a finger to her lips. "Well, we can set fire to everything after he builds his little winery." She turned back to the mirror and plucked the top part of her left eyebrow. She had to focus since she'd mistakenly plucked too much one time and ended up looking surprised for a week.

Tala stepped out of the shower. "I think that's what fire insurance is for, darling."

Nina switched to the other eyebrow. "Well, I'm getting muy sick of the job. The money sucks, Dahlia's a dog-ass bitch, and I'm so over wearing this gooey femme crap. Plus, Rolo's a Night-of-the-Living-Dead weirdo now and isn't doing anything except rolling out the red carpet for Gil-hell-berto's stupid grape farm."

"Yeah, but I'd just hate to have you quit before it's absolutely over." Tala stopped drying long enough to kiss the back of Nina's neck.

Nina set down the tweezers. "Mmm." Turning around, she had another thought. "You probably don't want me to quit 'cause you like seeing me in this skirt everyday."

"Baby, you know that's not true." Tala wrapped the towel around her hair. "You *do* look as cute as a Barbie doll, but I know it's not you. Commere." She put her arms around Nina, pulling her close.

When clothed, Tala was hard to resist. Buck naked, she was nearly impossible. Nina caved in to her softness. "Well, I guess I can stick it out a little while longer. But I don't know how long I'll last." She gave Tala a kiss, then turned back to the mirror. "I'm gonna bring up my quitting at the next CURs meeting."

Tala squeezed lotion on her palm and began rubbing it all over her body. "We can talk about that and what else we're going to do—not that I can think of anything."

"Ouch!" Nina rubbed her eyebrow where a painful little welt had formed. "I can't believe your brother won. I thought everybody would see how unfair this is and then maybe Greenpeace, or whoever watches over unfair things, would help us. Pero nada. We're all losing our homes and no one seems to give a damn."

Nina lowered the toilet lid and dejectedly sat down. She stretched out a slightly tattered pair of pantyhose. "Hell, this one has a run." She studied her scruffy little bathroom decorated with her artwork, pictures of her dog Chucho and Tala. "I love my house." Her eyes teared again at the thought of losing her home—of seeing all the care she'd given it over the years leveled into nothingness by Gilbert's bulldozer.

Tala put on the robe Nina had stolen from a local B and B. "I'm sorry, Baby. I feel sad, too."

"Can't that lawyer ex-girlfriend of yours do something to help us?"

Tala knelt in front of Nina. "She's trying, mi amor, just like we all are. We just have to keep the faith."

"I suppose," said Nina. Chucho lumbered in and leaned his face on her legs. Nina petted him, comforted by the sweetness of his concern. She looked out the window, noticing the rain smacking against it and the moan of the wind pushing through the cracks of her doors. "You know, it rained all night."

Tala offered an impish grin. "Think the big baboso will come to work today?"

Nina shrugged. "No sé, José," she replied. "But if he does, he'll for sure be wearing foul-weather fishing gear." She examined her pantyhose again. "Rain's the shits when you wear nylons. Maybe I'll wear pants today so he'll be doubly disappointed." She paused, then smiled. "Yeah, I think I will." Wadding up the nylons, she sky-hooked them into the trash.

✳

At 8:45 the mayor walked into the office covered, as Nina had predicted, in raincoat, rain pants, waterproof boots, gloves, and a pith helmet—all this in addition to a golf umbrella. Muddling through her email, Nina could only sit back and gape.

"Morning," Rolo grunted, looking slightly rattled. Nina watched him stand next to the coat rack while he stripped off his outerwear. His hands shook as he removed each item. And his eyes, after he took off the pith helmet, resembled those of a cornered yard dog.

"Morning, sir," Dahlia replied.

Nina was doing her best to keep from laughing. "Morning," she peeped. She had to focus on the computer screen to retain control.

Rolo finished stripping, with the exception of his shoes, which looked like a cross between go-go boots and mukluks. Nina shook her head, wondering where the hell he'd found them. She glanced at her watch, knowing Rolo had a nine o'clock meeting with two guys from the planning commission. She assumed he'd pull her into the meeting as usual, but instead he asked her to venture to the Java Jolt to get him a latte. "Make sure it's full fat with extra foam," he ordered, "and come inside and join us when you get back, alright?"

"Alrighty," she replied, taking the three dollars he handed her.

"Stick in a couple sugars, will you, love?"

Nina nodded, ignoring the endearment. She couldn't understand why Rolo hadn't stopped by the Jolt to get his own damn latte like he normally did. She glanced at Dahlia, but the roach barely flicked her an eyelash. Nina grabbed her umbrella and raincoat and walked out the door.

❰ 219 ❱

Luckily, the coffee shop was across the street, but Nina quickly saw why Rolo had sent her on the errand. With so much rain falling, the gutters, overwhelmed by the water, had flooded. The lazy fuck didn't want to get his boots wet, Nina figured, as she attempted a leap over the raging torrent. She landed clear of the gutter, but the sidewalk claimed the extra runoff. She glanced down at what she had thought were her waterproof shoes, now soaking wet. "This is gonna be the most expensive latte Tuffy's ever gonna drink 'cause I'm hitting him up for these puppies." She dashed into the Java Jolt and ordered his latte. Throwing in two sugars, she stirred the contents a little too vigorously, spilling coffee over the sides. "Oh well, too bad." Nina pulled out the stir stick, covered the cup, and returned to the office.

The journey back was the same precarious gutter hopping, this time more difficult since hot latte would squirt out of the lid's slurp section. When she walked into the office and took off her raincoat, she noticed that, in addition to her shoes, her pants were now stuck to her like wet crepe paper.

"That was quick," muttered Dahlia.

"Not quick enough," replied Nina under her breath. She hung up her raincoat and wiped off her face. Then she grabbed her notepad, removed the lid on the latte, and walked into Rolo's office. Placing the dripping cup on a napkin, she sat back to take notes. With the meeting in full swing, Nina watched Rolo attempting a WrestleMania takedown.

"It doesn't matter what you think, that bid's full of crap! They won't keep it to budget, and you know it. We go at least a third over their bid every time we deal with them. Cancel the jerk! Thanks, Nina," he said, glancing briefly at the still wet coffee cup.

Flustered, but unswayed, one of the planning commission hombres wearing cowboy boots and sporting a long ponytail stood his ground. "Sir, we've dealt with this contractor before, and he always underbids the competition." He cocked his head with the classic slant of a know-it-all. "And you know, by law, we have to accept it."

"The hell we do! We don't have to bend over and take it up the ass with his manipulative bullshit." Both the planning men looked over at Nina. Accustomed to Rolo's rough talk, she didn't blink. "That fucker always grabs us by the balls and squeezes the shit out of them every time we try to build anything in this—ahhh!" Rolo had touched the coffee cup then drew back his hand in surprise.

"Sir?" asked one of the planning crew.

"No, no, it's OK. Nina, can you get me something to wipe this?"

"Did you burn yourself?" Nina handed the mayor several tissues.

"No, it's just dripping a lot. No big deal." He grimaced a smile as he dried off the rainwater.

Nina watched the planning commission members glance surreptitiously at each other.

Rolo scooted to the edge of his seat. "Now, like I was saying, I want you to cancel that contract. I'll massage whoever I need to in order to get us a better deal." Nina watched how he examined the cup looking, it seemed, for any signs of wetness. Finally, he took a sip.

"With all due respect," replied the hombre with the ponytail, "no can do."

"What do you mean 'no can do'?" Rolo leaned forward, his jaw flexing like a rabbit.

This caught Nina's attention since she couldn't recall people ever telling the mayor "no." Mr. Ponytail still hadn't replied.

"I asked you a question."

"And I've told you the answer," said the hombre, his eyes lasered on the mayor. "We can't cancel the contract. We'd get sued. You want to cancel, you do it. But for the record, we're officially opposed. And I do hope," he said, standing, pointing to Nina, "that your secretary here has that all down. This meeting's over." The two closed their briefcases and marched out the door.

Nina finished writing the hombre's last words. Rolo, listing slightly to the left, wavered as if hit by a stun gun. Hearing a soft trickle of water, Nina feared the worst, but saw it was only a leak that had formed over the left corner of the ceiling. She watched the water fall in a fine, straight line, and noticed the mayor had seen it, too. Still he hadn't moved. Something was definitely off. Yet, aside from the weirdness about the wet cup, he'd been his typical T-Rexified self. The only thing different was that the planning hombres didn't cave. Lightning catapulted itself into the room, followed by a loud punch of thunder. Rolo's latte sat cooling in a pile of tissues, its foam melted to nothing. Closing her notebook, Nina glanced once more at the ceiling, then limped out of the office. Her shoes, now stiff and cold, gave out brassy-toned squeaks, like shiny new announcements.

The rain, steady now for two and a half weeks, streamed like ribbons down the mayor's window. The leak in the ceiling hadn't been fixed, and Rolo had no recourse but to place a shiny tin bucket underneath it. To his dismay, he noticed another leak across the room, so he purchased another bucket and a portable stereo, playing classical music throughout the day in an effort to counter the continuous blips of water. Shuffling through the minutes from the city's newly formed Santa Fe Response Action Team, or SFeRAT, Rolo shook his head over the acronym, wondering if the team was either making fun of him, or were simply a bunch of idiots. In any case, he agreed with the members, comprised of police, fire, public works, and management, that the city could really use a break. Tourism had plummeted. People got stuck so often on I-25 from flash flooding that the state police had assigned tow trucks to patrol the area on a continual basis. And the rain, coming from God knows where, sliced at an angle, making it difficult to walk anywhere without getting wet, even with an umbrella. Santa Fe needed—depended on tourists. Without them, the city's economy and every business within a sixty-mile radius, would sink. Tarps that had been set up over the perimeter of the plaza, particularly where the Indians sold their wares, had become, he admitted, a silly act of despondency. Water overwhelmed gutters and sewer systems and, despite sandbags and plastic, the craftspeople still ended up leaving since they couldn't keep themselves or their jewelry dry. Even if they could, no one seemed to be shopping. The tribal leaders complained to Rolo about loss of income, but this was only a drop in his overflowing bucket.

Rolo continued reading the SFeRAT notes. Low-lying areas had metastasized into block-long lakes. The Santa Fe River, normally a placid trickle, thundered through town in a white-water rage. One of the bridges near the Plaza, weakened by the river, leaned so precariously the city had closed it, causing extra backups and delays.

Driving became a nightmare, unless you owned a four-wheel drive. The water's force elicited bouts of stupidity or wishful thinking, since people somehow thought their Acuras and BMWs could plow through water. Abandoned cars filled the streets, adding to the mess. Even more disturbing was that many of the city's ricos, finding it too hateful to stick around, had simply vanished.

Rolo tossed the SFeRAT minutes aside and turned on the portable television. He not only needed to keep an eye on what reporters were saying about the city, but he was to be featured that day on the evening news. Though he kept pushing the newscasters to focus on something besides the storm, the peculiarity and growing superstition of it all kept everyone transfixed.

"With a thirty-mile radius around Santa Fe declared the storm's eye, homes and businesses are facing more damage." A soggy reporter, hair slathered by the rain, stood next to a house cut in half by a tree. "We've got strong winds and a nonstop downpour that has uprooted trees, ripped power lines, and created flood damage, particularly in low-lying areas. It seems," she continued, pausing briefly to catch her breath, "that according to the National Weather Service, Santa Fe has its own peculiar system. Some have even said a continuous dark cloud."

"And fuck you, too," Rolo replied to the TV, knowing full well everyone loved making fun of his beloved city.

The screen flashed to the mayor garbed in so much foul weather gear a mosquito would have a hard time finding skin. "Santa Fe welcomes the rain," he told the camera. He had tossed the pith helmet, substituting a more stylish fedora. "Not only do we need it, we like to think of it as a big wet kiss welcoming everyone to our own special land of enchantment. We're open for business, and we've got plenty of hot, steaming red and green chili. Come join us! Just bring an umbrella!"

Of course Rolo made sure his carefully planned statement was filmed under an eave. He wasn't about to stand outside any longer than necessary since it would send a bad message to tourists, not to mention be completely intolerable for him.

Rolo turned off the TV and read the last of the SFeRAT minutes, which focused on new developments. Gilbert's new winery was delayed due to the rain and the people of Dogtown had to stay put, since no one could move in the deluge. The flooded streets and rusty red mud spreading everywhere like goo had brought both Dogtown and the rest of Santa Fe to a standstill.

⁂

Rain or not, Pepa's business remained steady. She was even able to continue her morning walk since her new Gore-Tex rain clothes, found at an outlet store, kept everything dry. The dogs, both used to rough New Mexico weather, didn't mind the rain and scampered about, nearly as happy as on a dry day.

Pepa's Dogtown clients, though grateful for the delay, still worried about their future. If the ultimate decision was that of being forced to move, most hadn't the foggiest idea where they would go. Some said they'd stay with relatives, or maybe get a trailer outside of town. The majority remained stymied over how the city could simply elect to take their land.

"Mira, you never heard of Manifest Destiny, hombre?" Pepa asked, as she palpitated Benny Lucero's belly, certain he had a gallbladder disorder. She had him laid out on the pallet, shirt off and belt loosened. The big guy must be feeling pretty damn bad to take off precious time from running the Hungry Chula. On this morning she worked alone, as Camilo had gone into town to volunteer at the low-cost pet clinic, which he liked doing once a week.

Pepa probed a warm spot on Benny's abdomen and he nearly jumped off the pallet.

"Ayy! Chingao, that hurts!"

Pepa figured Benny felt crappy from his gallbladder, but he seemed more upset due to the impending loss of his restaurant.

"And goddammit, I know about pinche Manifest Destiny," he said, holding his belly. "I just can't believe this town can still manifest its destiny on whoever it wants. It's like we simply don't matter."

"It's not just this town, hombre," replied Pepa, momentarily stopping her treatment to light a white candle on her altar. "It's anyplace estos cabrones want to build something, especially if they think it'll make money. Look at all the Walmarts going up everywhere. Those guys take over people's houses, schools, ranchos—whatever they want. And that's just the tip of the iceberg. No one even cares about the poor people. Why do you think it'd be different here?"

"Because it's Gilbert, Pepa," Benny said, sitting up straight. "He grew up in this town, and he knows us. Y también, you expect to get stabbed in the back from developers or cualquier assholes who aren't from around here. But not from your own kind. Hell, I guess I expected more."

"Sí," Pepa added with a sigh. "We all did." She lit a small amount of frankincense oil to calm Benny down.

"But the Chula's been part of this neighborhood for over six generations," Benny continued. "I'll bet it's even a historical landmark."

"Creo que sí." Pepa stopped what she was doing and pulled up a chair since it was clear the man wanted to talk.

"I sure as hell never figured this city would run me out of business, not after all these years. Y este cabrón, con his pinche winery isn't giving me enough to buy another place either, at least not around here." He rubbed his hand across his cheek. "You know I've been making my living on that little plot of land for over thirty years. I can't see the Chula going down—not for this." He sighed, wiping tears from his eyes. "It isn't right," he studied the candle on Pepa's altar. "It just isn't right."

Pepa squeezed Benny's hand. "No, it isn't," she said, still holding it tight.

Benny paused, then returned his gaze to Pepa. "Qué hombre? You're dealing with the same thing as me. I got so carried away about myself I forgot about you."

"It's OK." Pepa, softly patted his arm. "But I'm telling you, este cabrón's gonna have to send the whole police force over to get me. I'm gonna make damn sure of that."

Benny wiped his eyes and sighed. Pepa reached over to give him a big hug. "Don't you pack a thing. Let that chingón mayor and Gilbert come over and pack us." Pepa gestured dismissively toward downtown.

"Pero, you know they can still come and knock down our houses and haul us to jail." He paused and looked around the clinic, fighting back more tears. "At some point, we all gotta decide what we're gonna do."

Pepa got up to resume her treatment. "Well, when you got that one figured out, compa, you make sure to tell me."

39

ROLO'S WIFE CHRISTINA HAD JUST ABOUT had it with her husband. He'd been complaining for months about a stomachache, lost nearly sixty pounds and, ever since the rain began, developed a bad case of telele. One of the things she'd been most attracted to in him was his fearlessness. He'd tackle projects others would run away from, stand up to rich Texans, and speak so bluntly people thought he was gifted. He was a self-made and very powerful man. She liked the respect he garnered and secretly admired how everyone cowered in his presence.

But the flaco reading the paper now, forcing a few driblets of oatmeal down his throat, didn't look anything like the husband she'd married. Maybe he was having a nervous breakdown. Maybe the rain's constant drumming had gotten to him. The way he dressed to keep the water from touching his skin was nothing short of loco; plastic raincoat and pants, gloves, waterproof boots, pith helmet, and a golfing umbrella. How he talked now, and even the way he looked at you, seemed off kilter. Last week he'd called in sick when he just couldn't bear going outside, something she found profoundly disturbing.

She refilled his coffee cup and sat down beside him at the breakfast table. Their kids were in school, the house settled back into peace, with the exception of the morning news droning from the television in the breakfast nook. "What's on your agenda today?" Christina asked, stroking Rolo's arm.

"Huh?" Rolo's eyes remained fixed on the TV.

"Your agenda. I asked what's on your agenda?"

He took a sip of coffee. "Bureau of tourism and the pendejos from emergency services."

Christina noticed the weather report wasn't on yet, which is why he probably felt he could talk.

"You know," he said, scratching his chin, "sometimes this job isn't what it's cracked up to be."

"How so?"

"All these assholes I gotta deal with day in and day out. And for what? Lousy schools, overpriced developments, and a sewer system ready to blow. I got no big accomplishment I can call my own. Not a damn thing. Even la winery del Gilbert's been a helluva headache. I told that asshole to make me look good, but all I've been doing is dodging bullets over the crap that's resulted from it. And those pendejos in Dogtown would rather rot than move on to something better. Cabrones! And on top of everything—we got this." He gestured toward the television, the weatherman forecasting more rain. "Three weeks steady now!" He turned off the TV. "I'd better get going."

Christina watched him shuffle toward the coat rack where he kept his rain gear. He began with the pants.

"I wish to hell I didn't have to wear this crap either."

"So don't wear it," she said, "It's kind of over the top, don't you think?"

He stopped for a moment, staring at her like she was the crazy one. "I have to. I got on good clothes, and I don't like water."

Christina threw her hands in the air. "Honey, since when have you not liked water? Me and you own a damn swimming pool for chrissakes."

"Well, this is different," he said, looking out the window. "This rain gives me the willies."

"Does taking a shower give you the willies?"

"No," he replied.

"Then I don't get it. The rain's been falling for three weeks, we had a drought, and we need it. So why are you acting like this?" Her eyes flitted over her husband's skinny ass as he put on the rain gear he'd ordered from L. L. Bean. He slipped each piece of clothing on like he was preparing for war.

"I—" he stopped to think for a moment. "I don't know. I just don't like it." And with that he finished dressing. "I'll be home around six. I cancelled my meeting at the Rotary Club. It's too goddamn wet. See you later."

Christina raised her cheek for a good-bye peck. He ambled over, rain gear rustling like petticoats, leaned toward her face, and surprised her lips with a kiss.

※

Pepa gazed out the window of the Hungry Chula Cafe. She studied the pulse of the rain, how the wind slanted it across streets, buildings, and people, each marked with its own distinct imprint. On time for a pre-meeting dinner date with the normally punctual Camilo before the rest of the CURs arrived, she glanced at her watch, wondering where he was. The roof of the restaurant, older than Benny cared to admit, leaked in multiple places. Buckets, bowls, and pans placed strategically to catch drips gave the restaurant a Poseidon-like quality, which brought back memories of the *Poseidon Adventure* movie when Shelley Winters had kicked ass. Pepa watched with amusement how Benny ordered everyone around just like a Shelley Winters incarnate.

Pulling out her pocket calendar, Pepa checked the date. It was the twenty-third consecutive day of rain. The lakes around the region, nearly dry from drought, were now at full capacity. Though large, New Mexico lakes were never planned for flood control since it was unlikely the arid state would ever suffer from too much rain. But Pepa, even though she had wanted it, was becoming increasingly uneasy about all the water. On today's five o'clock news, local reporters had announced that with tourism diminished, most of the staff in the larger restaurants, hotels, and bars were being laid off. "Be careful what you wish for," she recalled her mother telling her as a child. Now seeing the effect of the deluge, she hoped she hadn't made a mistake by asking for so much rain.

Pepa noticed the roof and walls of the Hungry Chula were now so damaged by the water that Benny had to remove all the paintings and tapetes. The bare walls and peeling green paint gave the restaurant a barracks feel. Yet leaky roof and all, the Chula bustled. Having had a steady clientele, it was now, perhaps due to its possible demise, busier than ever. People stopped by Pepa's table, updating her on their jobs, complaining about an ailment, and anxious, always anxious, about the storm.

Pepa glanced at her watch again. Camilo was now fifteen minutes late. She ordered a glass of wine and thought about the folks from Dogtown.

Everyone, with the exception of the sellouts, seemed depressed. Pepa let out a big sigh. What the hell were they going to do if they have to move? Where would they go?

The door opened and Camilo rushed in wet and out of breath. "I'm sorry," he said, flipping back his hood. "The bus got stuck in the mud out by the 7-Eleven, and we all had to get out and walk. Good thing I had on my rain boots," he said, smiling. His eyelashes shimmered under the restaurant's lights.

Pepa smiled at her friend, then looked through the window at the steady downpour. "You know, there's a lot of goddamn rain happening."

"There is," said Camilo. He took off his coat and hung it on his chair. He grabbed several napkins and wiped his face.

"Been living here fifty years, and I've never seen this much water. It's starting to scare people," Pepa continued, studying Camilo.

"Stop it with the vieja talk. And in case you still don't believe me, I didn't make it rain." He looked around the restaurant to see who was there. Spotting Mr. Maestas, the artist of Pepa's favorite painting, *Old Blu*, he waved hello.

"Bueno," Pepa said, flicking her hand like it wasn't important. "It's just kind of funny the rain started to fall right after I asked you to make it happen."

Camilo took the wet napkins and squeezed them into a tight ball. "Maybe *you* did it," he said, pointing.

"Oh, no," Pepa replied, certain. "When it comes to helping people I can do a few things, pero not this." The waiter brought her wine, and Pepa gratefully nodded her thanks.

"I can't believe you don't believe me." Camilo seemed insulted. "Did you ever think maybe somebody else did it?"

"No," she said.

"I'm telling you it wasn't me."

"And pienso que it was."

Camilo opened the menu and studied it, which Pepa knew was unnecessary since he, like half the neighborhood, knew everything on it.

Pepa took another stab. "Pienso que you might of done it without knowing it. Maybe you got secret powers and you don't know you have them, como el Spiderman."

"Pepa, that's a comic book. Before I came to live here, I'd been with Don Gabriel most all my life. Don't you think he would have told me if I had secret powers like making it rain? We've had a drought. If I'd known I could make rain, I would have done it sooner."

Pepa gave him a fat eyeball. His gaze was steady, not a glint of self-doubt. She scratched her head. If it wasn't him, then who the hell was it? A zag of lightning knifed the sky, followed by a double blast of thunder. "Bueno," she said, "I thought it was you, because it happened after I asked you to do it. And no matter what Don Gabriel te dijo or not, I still think you have extra powers, or whatever you *don't* want to call them."

"OK, what if I told you I did."

This caught Pepa by surprise. "Qué?"

"I said, what if I told you I did."

Pepa folded her hands on the table. "Bueno, dime."

Camilo waited to reply, looking like he had to think about every word he was about to say. "What if I told you Don Gabriel said I had some kind of gift?"

"Like?"

"No sé." He studied the leaky ceiling, then listened to the drips ting-tanging into the pans. "He mentioned it once, but never said anything about it again."

"Do you remember what he told you?"

"He didn't say a whole lot. It's basically what I just said."

"Bueno, didn't you ask him to explain it a little?"

"Sí, pero all he said was I would figure it out someday."

"Y ahora?" Pepa sipped more wine.

"I'm not sure," replied Camilo, looking around the restaurant. "I never felt any different or thought about it much. But now I've been making some connections. And I think—or maybe feel—that I can . . . well . . . that I can talk to spirits. Including him."

Pepa felt relieved. "Qué bueno, no?"

Camilo still looked uneasy. "I'm just starting to see things more clearly, what I do with animals, things I happen to sense, and now this rain. It's kind of unsettling."

Pepa grabbed his hand and held it tight. "Mijo, I know you'll work this out. Y también, you have a good heart. Just follow what it tells you."

"It doesn't always mean I'm right," he said, glancing at the drops hitting the pans. "I mean look at all the water everywhere. It's way more than what we need."

"Mira, Camilo, no sé why, pero I think it's something we have to have." She looked out the window and saw a car spinning its tires in the mud. "Though I got to admit, that if it keeps raining like this, it's gonna get tough. I guess," she said, glancing at the waiter who was coming over to take their order, "we can always build an ark."

The rest of the CURs showed up on time for the meeting. Pepa grabbed her wine glass as she and Camilo moved to the table in the back room to join Tala and Nina. Jules stopped traffic when he walked in with a new hairstyle and goatee. His blond ponytail now chopped to a sleek cut gave his face a regal look. His eyes, more exposed without all the hair around them, sparkled bright like sea glass.

"Ayyy, look at el Chuck Norris," Tala teased as Jules pulled up a chair.

"Hey, who cut your hair?" asked Nina, reaching out to touch his shorn locks.

"Who's Chuck Norris?" asked Camilo.

"It's the guy who plays Walker the Texas Ranger," said Pepa. "I like him," she added, with a nod of approval, "because he's always—tough."

Jules stroked his goatee. "Think I should keep it?"

"What? The goatee or the haircut?" asked Tala.

"Both," Jules answered, his face reddening.

Everyone studied Jules's face. "I vote yes," said Tala. "It makes you look exotic."

"Exotic? He doesn't look exotic," countered Nina. "He looks more man-ified."

"Man-i-fied?" Jules looked confused.

"You know, butch."

"Oh," he replied, smiling. "Don't I have to be a lesbian to be butch?"

"Not today you don't," Nina answered, glancing at Tala.

"Muévete, Nina, let me see." Pepa squeezed in next to Nina and pulled up close to Jules. "Pienso que . . . hmm." She cocked her head from side to side like a dog hearing a squeaky noise. "I think you look . . . bueno, I guess he *does* look like el Chuck Norris!" she said, smiling. "Y la Luz, does she like it?"

"Yeah," he replied, his face blushing deeper.

"Then you should keep it." She patted him on the wrist.

Tala, Nina, and Jules ordered food. Pepa ordered another glass of wine.

"Oye, Pepa, sure you're not one of those secret stockholders in the Vino-Latino's winery?" Tala asked, gesturing toward Pepa's wineglass.

"Maybe I should be, que no?" she replied, raising her glass. "I could use some free wine." Everyone laughed. Benny brought over warm tortillas, beans, and chile colorado.

"All right," Pepa continued, laying her hands on the table. "We have to talk about what we're going to do now that it's been raining cats and dogs for three weeks." She looked around the room, checking for eavesdroppers. The rain pans added noise to the restaurant, each pinging with resonant tones as the water hit them.

"Well the mud's keeping the moving vans out, so the sellouts can't move yet. So that's good," replied Camilo.

"The mud's keeping everyone out, including the tourists," Tala added. "Word's gotten round that people think we've been jinxed with the evil eye." She looked over at Nina. "How 'bout giving us a report on Rolo, Sweetie?"

Nina cleared her throat, then took a sip of beer. "Well, Rolo's acting very strange these days. He's skinny as hell, dresses like a fisherman in a typhoon, and his eyes stick out now—kinda like a lemur. Then, the other day he declared me a slave and sent me out in the rain to get a latte. When I gave him the cup, it had a little water on it, but he acted like it had been coated with acid."

"What did he do?" asked Jules.

"Screamed like it was acid," said Nina. "I'm not kidding. Plus, these two guys from the planning commission were there who usually scurry around him like silverfish. This time, though, they stood up to him, which I've never, ever seen."

"Really!" Pepa said. Pleased, she shot a quick glance at Camilo. He nodded and smiled.

"Yup," Nina said.

Jules pulled out his notepad, and tapped his pen on the paper. "So for some reason he seems freaked out over the rain. What's he think of how it's affecting the city?"

"Well, he's sad because it's hurting business. He's been on TV telling everyone we're still alive, but the tourists aren't coming."

"What do you think he'll do if the rain keeps up?" Jules spooned chopped green chile onto a tortilla, rolled it up, and took a bite.

Nina shrugged, then grabbed a knife and sliced a bean on her plate.

"We sure could use someone who might be able to predict the future right now. Anyone here want to take a stab?" Tala stared directly at Pepa.

"Nooo," said Pepa, eyes flickering from the heat of Tala's accusation. There was no way she would tell her anything, not even her suspicions.

Jules took another bite of his tortilla. "Well, I can't predict the future, and I don't know what Rolo's going to do about the rain, but I checked the Santa Fe archives and we've never had this much water."

"And?" asked Pepa.

"And it's going to hurt us in all kinds of ways if it keeps up. We can't store any more water in our reservoirs and, with all the flooding, the sewer system's gonna tank. Even up at the lab they got more rain then they can handle. I heard they suspended several projects because they feared moisture contamination." Jules smiled gleefully. "Isn't that sad? Not to mention the big fire they had a few years back seems to be eroding the shit out of the soil. They keep getting rain, they might slip into bigger trouble." Jules looked truly joyous at the thought.

"Hmm, that's interesting. You'd think they'd be prepared for any kind of issue," Tala replied, looking steadily at Jules.

"You'd think, but they're not. The lab, or the people who run it, like all the other labs and nuclear plants across the country, are trained for typical accidents or events. I would say this rain is very atypical."

"Should we be worrying?" asked Nina.

Jules shook his head. "I don't think so."

"What I'm worried about is what will happen once the rain stops," said Tala.

"Sí, la gente que vive aquí está muy triste," added Pepa. "And it's making them sick."

"Speaking of ailments, I'm getting sick of Rolo." Nina dipped her spoon into the chokecherry jam and spread a big dollop on a sopapilla. She took a bite, chewed, and swallowed before continuing. "I mean, I've been there over three months now. And nothing new's been happening. I think I'm wasting my time."

"No, you can't quit yet," answered Pepa. "We still need you."

"Sorry, Nina," added Jules. "But I agree with Pepa. We get the behind-the-scenes information no one else has access to."

"It's not like the info I'm getting is world breaking news. And I'm so sick of dressing in drag, kissing his ass, talking like a ditz, and working with Dahlia, the ice-roach. But you know what I'm most sick of?" She looked around the table. "Plucking my eyebrows. Any of you pluck yours?" No one answered. "Well, I encourage you to try plucking a few hairs around your eyes so you can see what the torture's like."

"Why do you have to pluck them anyway?" asked Camilo.

"Because Ciel says femmes don't wear miniskirts and makeup with hairy caterpillars on their heads." She paused to think. "Except Frida Kahlo."

"Frida Kahlo was muy sexy, no?" added Pepa, examining Nina's eyebrows. She wished she could pull Nina in for several more limpias. The girl could use a few more calmatives, too.

"Yeah, but she didn't wear miniskirts," said Tala.

"She didn't have to," added Jules.

"Then why don't you be a Frida, and phase out the femmy drag?" asked Camilo. Everyone, including Nina, started laughing.

Pepa took a cigarette out and tapped it on the table. "Bueno, can you work there a little while longer?" She lit the cigarette and exhaled toward the ceiling.

"I guess so," Nina pouted. "But they should give me hazard pay. *You* know what it was like, Camilo."

"He *is* awful." Camilo said. "But isn't he just a little bit different now?"

Nina sighed. "I guess." She looked momentarily at the dripping ceiling. "I wonder what would happen if he got lots of rain on him?"

"What do you mean, *lots*?" asked Tala.

"I don't know. I just wonder what he'd do if a whole bunch of rain hit him without his wet suit."

"He'd probably melt," answered Pepa. Everyone laughed again. "Either that," she continued, "or go loco."

40

"THE LORD BE WITH YOU." Father Miguel lifted the chalice high above his head.

"And with your spirit," the congregation replied.

The priest lowered the chalice, giving his blessing to its contents and to those at the evening Mass. As he listened to the rain pounding the windows, rain that had now fallen for twenty-five straight days, he knew that if it continued, they'd reach the equivalent of what Noah had faced. With hands trembling ever so slightly, he wondered whether the rain was more than a strange quirk of nature. Surprisingly, none of his fellow priests had even mentioned it to each other. They'd probably think he was too old school if he spoke of the possibility that the rain was more than a simple weather aberration.

Finishing Mass, Father Miguel removed his priestly garb and journeyed back to his office. He used his umbrella but it failed to keep much of him dry. The rain rapped his window like pecks of an angry bird. His eyes moved from the window to the political posters adorning his walls, stopping briefly at the lone cross over his door, then back to the window. All this rain had to mean something.

The weather had even made the scientists from the National Oceanic Atmospheric Administration scratch their heads. The priest had called them on a whim, and they offered only plausible suppositions, global warming being their primary guess. "The severity of storm growth in the Gulf could possibly instigate residual wind drafts," they'd told him.

The padre knew it wasn't so. "No," he replied. "It would affect more of the state. It's a thirty-mile radius around Santa Fe we're talking about."

"Well, you're the priest," said one of the scientists. "Maybe you should tell *us* the answer." He paused, then continued. "Explain how such a storm could suddenly appear over the Santa Fe area and stay. It's as if the clouds over the city continually replenish themselves from some mysterious source."

Grabbing his raincoat again, and ignoring the umbrella, the priest walked over to the chapel. He knelt down, eyes resting on the statue of Jesus. He didn't pray much to the Madonna on the altar, particularly since she'd been brought over by Don Diego de Vargas after the reconquest of Santa Fe. It wasn't that he disliked Madonnas, he just liked other things better, like this statue of Jesus. Unlike many, this one had muscles, looking far more appealing than the wasted looking Jesuses in all the other churches he'd seen. And he looked strong. Muscles can do that. They give you hope. And right now that's what he desperately needed.

The padre did a quick sign of the cross and clasped his hands. "Dear Father," he whispered. "I've come to you for guidance, for this unending storm is troubling me. Why, dear Lord, are we being deluged with water? Are you giving us a warning of some kind? Have we done anything to anger you? Why do you make us suffer so?" He rubbed his hands together, eyes intent on the statue's face. "Everyone, Dear Lord, is scared, especially me. Could this rain be a sign of our failure—our inability to care for one another?" He glanced around the chapel, making sure no one was eavesdropping. "I know I have not always been a good carrier of your Word, but I am listening, Lord. For I believe this has to be a sign—one clearly of your displeasure. Offer me your guidance, dear Father, and know that I am truly listening."

Finished with his prayer, Father Miguel concentrated on the sound of the rain pummeling the window. The tree boughs next to the church whipped back and forth, brushing against the walls with clamoring scrape. Lightning sliced through the sky, momentarily illuminating the dimly lit chapel. The priest knew the sounds were only those of the storm, completely certain that not a single one of them was the answer he was seeking.

41

THE PUNCH OF AN EARLY phone call slammed Jules out of bed.

"Yeah?"

"Hey Jules, it's Flav." One of his old buddies from the lab.

"Flav?" Jules rubbed his eyes, trying to focus. "Flavio Flores?"

"The one and only."

"Hey, man, good to hear from you. It's been a while." Jules sat up, shifting the phone to his other ear. He recalled seeing the old chemist from time to time, the two complaining of the lab and its many secrets. Geeks with guilt, they called themselves, since they felt like hypocrites over the defense-driven research they were ordered to do. Their constant complaints jettisoned them from social outings with other employees, not to mention earning them crappy work assignments by supervisors who would fire them if they could.

"Yeah, if I hadn't been so damn close to thirty years I would've left with you. Hey, uh, I thought you might like to know, this rain's started a little problem over by F-Two. Mudslide, which we thought might happen after that big fire last year, knocked over an old storage building. Went to check on it and found a couple boxes outside the fence—at least technically. Maintenance says I'm the one who's got to find a new place for the stuff. They helped me load them in the truck since they were cardboard and worried about damage. Later on, I poked inside 'em and found something that might interest you."

"Like?"

"Well, looks like some old fallout patterns, radiation reports, all of it from testing done in forty-five."

"Trinity?"

"By the looks of it."

"That's very cool." Jules had to keep himself from getting too excited.

"I haven't gone through it, yet, but this stuff might give you a few extra data points—especially since there might be numbers here on a couple big bangs. Wanna see it?"

"Absolutely. Where can I find it?"

"Storage shed—one of those places you pay by the month."

"You're kidding me."

"I wouldn't count on it being there too long since I gotta bring it back, like right away."

"Understandable." Jules looked at his watch. "I'll be there in about an hour, give or take the weather."

"Meet me at the Rightway storage facility. Bring a camera."

"You got it." Jules heard him light a cigarette, inhale, then exhale. He wondered what Flavio had really done to wrangle the data.

"Hey, let me just say, since this shit is classified I'm not sure how you'll be able to use it—exactly."

"Well, maybe I can write about it as an exposé from my Deep Throat informant."

Flavio let out a long, cigarette-laced cackle. "Very funny. Look man, I'm doing this because I know I'll go to hell if I don't show it to someone. We lost too many from all this." Jules heard a hand placed over the mouthpiece followed by a loud cough. "Still got people dying."

Jules nodded, running a hand through his hair. "Then we owe 'em."

After he hung up, Jules told Luz what he was about to do, showered, and dressed. He grabbed the camera and truck keys and sprinted out the door. Realizing he'd forgotten to kiss his girl, he turned around and sprinted back.

"You be careful," she said, giving him a squeeze. "And don't do anything stupid."

"No worries," Jules replied and jetted out the door.

Flavio's truck sat parked at the entrance of the storage facility. Jules found him inside the main office cracking jokes with the old clerk who ran the place.

"There's my friend," he said, standing to retrieve a wet-looking hat from a hook next to the door. "I'll catch you later, Sal," he said, placing the hat on his head. The two men walked out in the rain over to Flavio's storage site. "I'm going to open it and leave you to your business. Close everything up when you're done. I'm taking it all back to the lab tomorrow."

"OK," said Jules, with a quick glance at the old man.

They got to the garage, opened it, and Flavio directed him to a small stack of cardboard boxes. The files were worn and tattered from years in storage. Jules couldn't believe they'd kept this information in plain old cardboard. They probably figured no one would be interested in the stuff. The boxes were sealed with yellowed packing tape, easy to undo. Jules started thumbing through the contents and realized they were indeed files filled with radiation details and old fallout patterns from Trinity.

"That what you're looking for?"

"Yep," Jules nodded with a smile. "It is." He pulled his camera out of a waterproof bag, and checked the settings. "I don't know how much of this stuff I'll be able to use, but thanks for letting me see it."

Flavio coughed, hocked up some phlegm, and stepped outside to spit. He returned with his truck keys in his hand, flipping them absently as he bent over Jules's shoulder, peering at the boxes' contents.

Taking a slew of photos on fallout patterns, Jules stopped and turned around. "Weren't you planning to go?"

"Yeah," said Flavio, holding his keys quiet. "I was just wondering . . . suppose you do use this stuff. How do you expect to do so without getting me in on it?"

"Infrastructure vulnerability."

"Meaning?"

"Meaning lab folks are trained for usual events. This one wasn't. The rain made it flood, which collapsed the fence, and damaged the building. Once you were notified, you acted in the normal OODA loop. You saw a bunch of old—I'd venture to say—*ancient* boxes, so you and the guys grabbed them and put them in your truck, figuring they were safe enough there until you found a dry place to store them. You went back to work, forgot about them—preoccupied with whatever project you were working on, and drove them home, exiting through the lab's amazingly lax security.

"The next day, you realized the damn boxes were still in the truck, so you checked on them and saw that you'd forgotten to lock everything, realizing to your horror that a couple of the boxes had been tampered with."

"It's a bit far-fetched."

"True, but totally plausible. You called it in, and drove the boxes back to the lab. You explain what happened and since the maintenance guys tipped you on the mess in the first place, they vouch having helped you put them in your truck. The rest is circumstance and human error."

Flavio shrugged. "Well, I guess it won't be the first time humans made a mistake."

Jules took another photo. "All this rain makes everything abnormal. Sound good?"

"I suppose. Yeah, I'd say this rain's thrown everything and everyone off. It's pretty God-awful spooky, more so here on account of it being a former holy site."

"Maybe it's punishment from the gods."

"Don't kid yourself. You never know . . . All right, I'll talk to you later. Let me know if you use this stuff, though."

"Will do. Thanks Flav."

Jules finished his task, and after studying the photos, gave Toni Pearlman from the *Washington Post* a call. Luz stood at the door listening. Jules smiled and gave her a thumbs up, as the reporter definitely sounded interested.

"You better not do that stuff I hear you planning," Luz said after Jules got off the phone. "I don't want you getting thrown in jail like they did that poor Chinese guy. You know they don't play when it comes to their secrets." She grabbed his hand.

He raised her hand to his lips and kissed it. "Sometimes jail is just a small price."

"The hell it is," she said, pushing him away. "I'm not putting up with that martyr crap. If you get caught I'll personally come over to your jail cell and kick your ass. I'll bring my mother along to finish you off."

Jules grabbed Luz and pulled her close. "I promise you I won't get caught."

Toni Pearlman thought she could use the new data in a follow-up piece to the "Dangerous Downwinds" article. She wrote a second story, agreeing to publish it without naming the source. It ran a week later. To Jules's surprise, it was met once again with little fanfare. As with the first article, no one, except a few antinulear folks or a victim or two, were interested. The whole issue was simply too old for anyone to care.

Jules called up Pepa, said he needed to talk, and would it be OK if he came over after she closed up the clinic that evening. To his relief, she said OK. On the way over, he stopped at the Saints and Sinners and picked up a bottle of Hennessey and a decent cabernet, splurging on something from California. He knew Pepa would appreciate the wine a bit more than the brandy, but *he* needed something with more punch to it—something that would stand up to such a soggy, disappointing week.

Pepa came to the door to greet him. Jules cut the engine and hustled to the shelter of her covered porch. He handed her the bag and stripped off his rain gear. Pepa beckoned him into her kitchen, searching his face for signs of trouble. It was warm inside, thanks to the wood stove.

The kitchen was empty and Jules wondered if Camilo had gone out for the evening. Pepa's dog lay on his bed, looking like he'd just awakened from a nap. He flapped his tail, not even bothering to get up. "Hey Joaquín, how you doing, boy?" Jules ruffled the dog's head then shuffled in his socks over to the kitchen table.

Pepa pulled the bottles from the bag and without bothering to ask filled Jules's glass with brandy. She poured a little wine for herself. "Qué pasó?" she asked, taking a sip. Seemingly satisfied, she filled the glass and pushed the brandy toward Jules. He lifted it, nodded, then slung it back.

"First, I want to thank you for allowing me to come over under such short notice."

"Bueno, you sounded like you needed to talk. Y también, I didn't have any plans tonight."

Jules offered a weak smile. "I uh, I brought you the wine as a small token of my appreciation—for your time."

Pepa laid her hand across his wrist. "No importa, hombre. I can talk to you without having wine."

"I know. I just thought you might like it." Pepa smiled and took another sip. He refilled his glass and delved into what had happened the past week—from Flavio's call to the reaction from the follow-up article. He hadn't told Pepa the details of his little trip to the lab, given the sensitivity of it all. But he knew he could trust her. Knowing Pepa, she had probably put two and two together anyway.

"Even though we finally got proof and the word out on the damage from the testing maneuvers across the state," he continued, "nothing, not a damn thing, made a difference. Not the data from the lab, interviews with the victims, desecrated land, or all the people who died. Nothing, *nothing*, for Christ's sake, made a difference. It just galls me!"

"I guess people figured they had to make sacrifices for the country," Pepa replied. "That's what they thought back then. Or pienso que people don't care about this stuff anymore." She shrugged. "People don't like to remember bad things. And for sure nothing bad they did. I've had patients I helped with problemas muy grandes. And half of them, unless they have to come back, don't even recognize me on the street!" She poured herself more wine, then lit a cigarette. "Everybody wants to go on with their lives." She exhaled smoke over her left shoulder. "And they do it the best way they can—even if it means living a lie." She took another sip of wine. "Wouldn't you?"

Jules finished off his glass. "I guess I can understand what the victims might think. But how do you deal with the regulatory committee being un-accountable for the damage done? Or even the watchdog agencies who just sit back and do nothing?"

Pepa got up and held her hand over the stove. "Bueno hombre, maybe there's a damn rule or law that keeps people from doing anything. You said it yourself—that all this work was probably never gonna amount to noth-ing." She retrieved a piece of wood from a bucket next to the stove, opened the lid, and threw it in. She sat down, took another drag from her cigarette and re-filled Jules's glass. "Pero, you have to remember there's lots of good people around us—people who want to make up for their mistakes. The ones who don't stay cabrones. And if they're guilty—hijo!" She drank more wine. "Pero, I have to say, I've seen some of the guilty ones go out and do good things. A few do stupid things. Some do nada." She paused to look out the window.

Jules wondered if she could see anything with the rain streaming down the panes. He rubbed his chin. "I hear what you're saying, and I understand the law of the land, but it doesn't make me any less disgusted by everything that *didn't* happen. Even the data on the radioactive counts and wind pat-terns I gave the reporter didn't make a difference. I mean, despite sovereign immunity and everything, I guess I still naively thought some part of this would have mattered. Can you tell me how hard it would be to give people a damn piece of paper with an apology?" He lowered his head and grabbed his temples, no longer able to contain his tears. "Pepa," he said, looking up to meet her gaze. "Do you have any idea how long I've worked to find that data in the first place, and then come to find out it was all a waste of time?"

"Bueno, hombre, look at it this way." Pepa patted his hand. "You still did the right thing. You got the secret out so everyone knows now. And that, at least in my book, is what counts."

Pepa's dog pulled himself out of bed, ambled over to Jules and leaned against him. Jules petted him, touched by his display of concern. "Thanks Pepa. I have to say you might be the only one who cares about this as much as me."

"I think that's probably true," Pepa said, tapping back her ash. "Pero, don't you think it's the same thing we're going through con esta pinche winery? We talk to anyone who'll give us the time of day. We get on TV, we're in the newspapers, we write Congress, sign petitions, pero nada. Then we get one of the best lawyers in town and even *she* can't help us." She drank more wine. "Now I want you to tell me how this country works where one guy can come in, throw down a pile of money, and make us leave our homes?"

"You got a point there," said Jules, drinking more booze. "I guess when you think about it, it *is* the same thing. People with money feel they can just step on whatever's in their way." He propped his head in his hand.

"They sure as hell do," Pepa said, pouring more wine into her glass. "Ricos think they can do whatever they want. Look at all the things they did to this country. Made people slaves, shot all the buffalos, cut down the trees, stole Indian land. Now they're fishing away the fish. And look what they're doing with the global warning."

"You mean global warming."

"That's what I said, global warning."

"No, it's *warming*."

"Qué warming or warning, it's the same, no?"

"Yeah, I suppose," said Jules, squinting one eye to focus.

"And they all get away with it. The government did it with the bomb and el Gilbert is doing it with his winery," she said, drinking more from her glass. "I love wine—maybe a little too much by the looks of it." She burped, pushed the glass away, then brought it back. "And I would love nothing better than to have a good winery close by. But what I can't figure out is, with so much land in this state—hell, in this country—why este Gilbert can't find someplace else to put it?"

Jules noticed Pepa's words seemed a little slurred. "You got me," he answered, wondering if he sounded the same. "I've been asking myself that very same question."

"And that phony-baloney president from Texas is doing the same thing all over again." She smashed her cigarette into the ashtray.

"What, grow grapes? I didn't know he wanted to do that."

"No, hombre!" Pepa let out a gut-ripping laugh. "Step on the people! He's already started it with his pinche executive—executive—cómo se dice?" She grabbed her forehead.

"Privilege?" Jules hiccupped.

"Sí, privilege so he can keep his secrets. I'm telling you right now as I'm sitting right here," Pepa said, pointing to the table. "It's gonna get worse."

"Unless we keep fighting."

That stopped Pepa in her tracks. "Pues, you're right, hombre! We might not be able to do anything con esta nuclear mierda. But we don't have to give up on the pinche winery, no?"

"That's right," echoed Jules, now sitting up straight. "Things might be tough, but we're not rolling over like a bunch of scared dogs." He looked down at Joaquín, still sitting at his side. "Not you, boy," he said, rubbing his head.

"Or chickens," said Pepa.

"Yeah, those, too," said Jules, watching Pepa wobble to the cupboard to retrieve a small glass.

"I'm switching to the brandy," she said pointing to the bottle.

Jules noticed his hand shook a bit as he filled their glasses.

"Pero, we'd better come up with a new plan. And its gotta be something that'll really raise hell." Pepa lit another cigarette, inhaling it like she was filling herself with a special power.

"Like what?" asked Jules.

"Bueno . . . no sé," she replied, blinking through the smoke. "Pienso que we'll have to think of something." She gazed at her glass. "Camilo has good ideas."

"He does." Jules looked around the room. "Where's he at tonight?"

"Out with his friend . . . Or maybe he's volunteering at the vet. I can't remember right now."

"That's OK." Jules cleared his throat. "So we need to toast." He raised his glass.

"To what?" said Pepa, refilling hers.

"To a new plan—whatever it is."

"Órale, then, to a new plan," said Pepa, holding her glass high. "And to faith and fat chances."

42

FRIDAY MORNING. Twenty-six days of steady rain. Rolo went to the bathroom, flushed the toilet and, to his dismay, the toilet's contents refused to go down.

"Shit!" he exclaimed, fishing under the bathroom cabinet for the plunger. He wasn't about to let his housekeeper try to pump down his own mierda. "This goddamn rain is screwing everything up!" Finding the plunger, he began several useless thrusts. "No matter what we try, or what we do, everything is still fucked." He gave the plunger a couple more thrusts. "And everyone's screaming bloody murder about the goddamn flood control. What flood control? We live in a damn desert!" He watched the toilet water color. "Throw down a pinche sandbag!" He pumped the plunger a couple more times. All it did was make it worse. "Sonavabitch! I pay all these people to solve this problem and the pendejos can't do anything except sit around with their thumbs up their asses." He tried flushing again, but this time the water overflowed the toilet, spilling across his shoes and the newly tiled floor.

Rolo shut the toilet lid and stomped out of the bathroom. He knew he'd been pushing his luck about the city's sewer system, but he kept putting off the repairs. Now they were all paying the price—spewing manhole covers, toilets in rebellion, and sewage backed into bathtubs. The problem had finally followed him home. Three of the four toilets in his house had clogged through the night. And this one, sputtering all morning, had finally given up the ghost. Scurrying down the steps, he heard his wife negotiating with a sewer repairman from Mr. Pipe Pleasers. He stumbled upon the man in the process of gathering his tools.

"Where the hell you going?" Rolo asked, spit close. "This work isn't finished. I got toilets out all over this house. It can't be that hard to ream these pipes!"

The worker paused to give him the once over, eyes lingering on his monogrammed cuffs. "It's got nothing to do with knowing or not knowing our jobs, Mayor Reyes." The repairman, all five and a half feet of him, puffed up big. "You and your wife can stand there and scream all you want, but I can't clean out your pipes because nothing's draining. The sewers are backed up—get it? Backed up! And ain't nothing gonna change that until the rain stops."

Rolo, outraged to be addressed in this manner, placed his hands on his dilapidated hips. "You mean to tell me I got four toilets filled with shit and you can't do anything about it?"

"Yeah, I guess that pretty much sums it up." The worker bent over to roll up his electric snake.

"Now hang on there. You're talking to the fucking mayor of this city, and you're saying you can't fix my toilet?"

The worker paused his snake rolling and stood, hands on his own hips. "That's correct."

Christina, who had been standing in the background, pushed past her husband. "What the hell are we supposed to do then?"

"Well, you can rent a Porta Potti, like everyone else. They can probably get one out here in a day or so. Maybe since he's the *mayor* and all," he jerked his chin toward Rolo, "they'll *expedite* it." He chuckled slightly. "I'd call them right away if I were you, though." He put on his jacket. "Seems we're having a rush on Porta Pottis." He raised his eyebrows and gave Christina a fake smile. "That's about all I can tell you. We'll send you the bill later for our services," he yelled over his shoulder as he exited.

Christina walked up to the door and slammed it. "Cabrón!" She turned toward Rolo. "And you! You haven't done a damn thing about the flooding or anything about the rain! Why haven't you sent out anyone to fix this, find out what's wrong, sprinkle something in the clouds, do something, for chrissakes!"

"'Stás sonsa? What do you mean sprinkle something in the clouds? That's for *making* rain, mujer. Besides, people can't stop the rain, just like people can't stop the sun. Don't you think I would have done something if I could?"

Crossing her arms, Christina walked slowly around her husband. "You're not telling me the truth, are you?"

"What?"

"That you're afraid. Afraid of the rain." Her words felt like a slap. "Which is why you haven't done anything about it."

Rolo refused to look at her.

"Well let me inform you," she paused, face raised in defiance. "That I'll be damned if *I* use a Porta Potti. If that's what you want to put your scrawny little ass on, go right ahead. But I sure as hell won't."

"Look, mujer, I've been trying to get those pendejos in sanitation to move on this." Rolo flicked his hand in the air.

"That's not my problem, Mayor Reyes. Oh wait," she said, placing a hand to her chin. "It actually *is* my problem—and until you fix it, I'm leaving. And taking the kids."

"What? You can't leave over a toilet!"

"Watch me," Christina replied, marching past him to the bedroom.

"Where will you go?" Rolo followed, realizing she was serious.

"I don't know. I'll send you a postcard when I get there." She pulled two suitcases out of the closet.

"What'll people think when they find out you've deserted me in this hour of need?"

"Hour? What hour are you talking about?" She slammed open the suitcases. "It's been raining for a goddamn month!" She moved back to the closet and pulled out several pants and blouses. "As for answering your precious public image question, why don't you tell them, hmmm, I don't know. Maybe that Rolo Reyes is really a weenie?" She grabbed clothes out of a drawer. "Or, I know, you can say Christina finally got fed up with her husband's ass-chasing. Wait," she opened her eyes wide. "Why don't you just keep it simple: Rolo Reyes, just like his house—is full of shit!" And with that, she slammed the suitcase shut and marched out of the room.

✺

Rolo removed his pith helmet, nodded hello to two janitors frantically sopping up a small pond near the door, and hopped into the elevator. Nothing happened. He pressed the third-floor button again. Then with a grind and two quick bumps, the elevator came to life and chugged upward. Halting, the doors paused, then opened onto a scene out of an Amazon nightmare. The myriad of plants and trees placed in intricate patterns by a green-loving interior designer drooped heavily to the floor encumbered by torrents of water falling from the ceiling. Hearing muffled shouts from various offices, Rolo shifted his gaze to the marble wall where water sluiced down in rivulets. The paver tiles across the landing, now covered with water, gleamed in the light like the inside of a fountain. Up above him and down the hall, rain literally fell from the ceiling. Shocked to see no one attending to the mess, he slammed his pith helmet back on, took a deep breath, and opened his office door.

Inside water blew, dripped, spritzed, and gushed from every crevice across the ceiling. Rolo stood motionless, absorbing the state of the room while Nina zipped around covering furniture. Clad in her raincoat, rain hat, and boots, she looked like a gnome on speed. Dahlia, hoisting an umbrella over a damp new hairdo, marched behind her, the two enmeshed in a fury to save the furniture from the pummeling water. Emptied trashcans and cookie tins stood like lost children under the larger leaks, doing little to hold off the deluge.

Rolo scanned the rest of the office, blinking back the assault of multi-colored tarps blanketing file cabinets and computers. Dahlia and Nina, so absorbed by the desperation of the moment, still hadn't noticed him. The combination of trashcans, cookie tins, gushing water, and tarps, all dripping together in paradoxical chaos, stunned him into a grip of growing panic. He felt dizzy, as if all the blood had been shunted from his body.

Nina, now on the phone, spotted Rolo standing at the door. His body wobbled as if repeatedly hit by waves. Both women had begun making calls, canceling appointments on phones that still miraculously worked, while also phoning in desperate pleas to the physical plant. Nina left a message on Tala's answering machine saying the roof seemed to be caving and that the office was ankle-deep in water.

"What the hell happened?" Rolo bellowed.

Setting the phone back in its cradle, Nina lifted her hands. "Not sure, boss, but it's pretty bad." She managed, somehow, to still retain her "M" voice.

"Clearly the roof couldn't take it anymore," added Dahlia, who placed her caller on hold. She hoisted her umbrella to give Rolo her full attention. "We did our best with the furniture and computers, but uh—well we didn't have as much luck with *your* office." Her eyes angled toward his closed door.

Nina watched Rolo set his jaw and march across the room. She parked the phone, and followed her boss toward his den of self-importance, a room he'd meticulously decorated with fine art, mementos, mahogany, and rugs. Earlier, when she and Dahlia surveyed the damage to his office, Dahlia had sadly closed the door, writing off everything as a lost cause. Rolo gripped the brass handle, took a deep breath, then burst inside. Even Nina couldn't believe the room's degradation since she'd set eyes on it a mere hour ago. Everything, every-last-bit-of-every-little-thing lay saturated, soaked, or ruined. The ceiling sprayed, or spurted hydrant force water like a torpedoed battleship. Rolo's handcrafted sofa, carted all the way from Morocco, now looked pulpy and plundered. A Turkish carpet he'd carefully hung across the wall lay on the floor in a soggy heap. Business baubles that once annointed his desk had either floated away, such as the colored paper clips in their teak container, or had sadly drowned, like his prized Mont Blancs, soaking bleakly in a bath. Photos of Rolo with movie stars and dignitaries, a signed R. C. Gorman painting, a gorgeous Navajo rug, and an antique New Mexican flag were either destroyed, or wrecked beyond recognition. Nina felt bad about the art, forgetting in her haste to protect it. Water spurted in so many directions it actually hit Rolo in the face—the only part of his body not covered in rain gear.

Nina shifted her gaze back to her boss, whose body was trembling and unsteady. "Sorry this is so bad, sir. Maybe we should leave?" She moved to guide him out of the office, but they had lingered too long. Rolo staggered, then stooped over a chair, hyperventilating, his arm raised in an attempt to ward off the water. As he tried stepping away, he tripped on a bronzed palomino, falling head first toward his coffee table into an overflowing Nambé bowl. Nina would have laughed if Rolo hadn't looked so pathetic. Dahlia, silently observing from the office door, dropped her umbrella and sprinted across the room to rescue him, pulling him out of the bowl by his shoulders. Close behind, Nina helped her ease him to the soggy sofa. Overwhelmed, he collapsed, eyes rolled white, lips a faded purple.

"Oh God, he's unconscious. Call an ambulance, Nina—hurry!" Dahlia climbed on to the sofa and pulled the mayor to her wet bosom.

Nina stepped over the debris to Rolo's desk and picked up the telephone. The line was dead. She went back out to the reception area and dialed 9-1-1. Hearing the operator, she spoke quickly. "Yes, for the mayor . . . Mayor Reyes . . . It looks like he's fainted." She stretched the phone cord, leaning in toward his door. "Or maybe something worse, possibly a heart attack. His lips are now violet—just a minute—" she placed her hand over the phone. "Dahlia, is he still breathing?"

"Yes!" she yelled back.

"Yes," Nina said, returning to the phone. "Ten minutes? Can't you get here sooner?—No, I don't know what's wrong with him, but it looks bad—*He* looks bad—OK—OK—Uh, just so you know . . . we're kind of flooded up here—Right—Kinda bad—Kinda *real* bad—OK—OK. OK, bye." Nina hung up, realizing in her haste she'd forgotten to use her "M" voice. She glanced around the dripping office. No use keeping it up now.

She returned to Rolo's office. The spurting water had increased, releasing a stifling roar. She found Dahlia still holding Rolo to her bosom. Nina felt a pang of pity for the woman, since it was probably the nightmare of her life. "It'll be here soon," she said, squatting next to the two, marveling how the combination of Dahlia's wet hair and puffy eyes made her look dead on like a potato bug.

"Maybe we should try to move him." Dahlia's face shifted from Rolo to the door. "He'd be a little drier in the other office."

"Uh, I don't think so," Nina said, remembering Dahlia's skinny arms. "I know he's lost weight, but I don't think me and you could lift him, especially not over all this crap. I'll get your umbrella. At least that'll keep him part-way dry."

Dahlia nodded. Nina retrieved the umbrella—clear plastic with fuchsia polka dots. Absolutely one of the most hideous pieces of anything she'd ever laid eyes on. Returning to the sofa, Nina sat on the coffee table and held it over Dahlia and Rolo. The umbrella distorted their faces, reminding her of the fun house visits she had as a kid. And even though it wasn't cool to do it, she couldn't help tilting the umbrella forward, transforming the two into shiny, skinny weasels. Moving it backward flattened them into slobbery looking sloths.

"Poor baby," Dahlia muttered, snapping Nina back to the moment. "Poor, poor, baby."

Nina examined the room. The spurting water had intensified. She didn't like the feel of it and wondered if the crack above her spouting salvos of water would hold. What was happening? The building, old and dilapidated, was always breaking down. "It's shabby, an insult to me as mayor of this city," Rolo had harped. Well, she thought, looking at the water jetting madly through the cracks, he certainly got *that* right.

"You're going to be fine, my love, I promise. Don't worry. Don't worry. Help is coming." Dahlia cradled Rolo tight, rocking back and forth, pressing her wet face alongside the rain-hexed mayor's. "Poor baby. Poor little Rolo Honey. Just hang in there, my sweet." Dahlia seemed to have forgotten Nina was with her.

Nina studied the ceiling, at least what was left of it, seeing that it sagged heavy in one corner like an overfilled bladder. "Where the hell's that ambulance?" she asked, feeling increasingly anxious about the roof's stability.

"Hey, Dahlia." Nina lifted the umbrella so the woman could see her. "Things are getting really bad." Dahlia only nodded, then carried on with her rocking. Nina's eyes darted back to the ceiling. She heard it give a high-pitched screech, like something important was bending. "Uh, I don't like this."

Shifting the umbrella to her other hand, she felt a hard jolt to the building, followed by a loud cracking sound. "Dahlia, we need to get the hell outta here now! Let's try dragging him out anyway. I don't think the roof's gonna hold."

Dahlia looked above her, eyes widening at the state of the ceiling. "All right," she replied.

The building jerked again, as if punched from an earthquake. But since Santa Fe didn't have earthquakes, Nina knew it had to be something worse. The break in the ceiling had widened across the middle. It didn't take an engineer to know the crappy building couldn't take the rain. The rain bladder in the corner widened further, then gave way, throwing a boatload of water over them. The movement must have upset the building structure, as water now gushed through the fissure over their heads, carrying plaster, wood, and tiles. The force of the water grew, tumbling inward from too much rain for too many days. Nina watched helplessly as the ceiling continued caving, suddenly collapsing in a water-bombed rush.

"Shit!" She screamed and dove under Rolo's desk. Thanks to his buffalo-sized ego, the sturdy desk saved her butt as the roof detritus began falling around her. Panicked, Dahlia shrieked, then covered her head as one beam tilted, teetered, then fell on top of her—Nina's cry of warning useless. She watched helpless as Rolo and Dahlia lay pinned under the wreckage. Nina shuddered over the state of her coworker, unconscious, blood trickling from the back of her head, body spasming from her injuries. Pinned across Rolo's chest, Dahlia resembled a specimen pressed between two plates of glass. Normally, this would be enough to scare the bejesus out of anyone. And sure enough, when Rolo awakened moments later to find the injured Dahlia on top of him, he screamed as if he really did have a giant bug smashed on top of him. Nina watched the trapped man trying to move, unable to twist himself away. Though she wanted to, she didn't dare venture out to help, not with all the mess falling from the ceiling. Instead, she stayed put, squatting under the desk, blinking back the roof's onslaught as it caved in around her. Rolo's efforts to pull himself out of the rubble proved useless since he was not only stuck under Dahlia, but the wreckage as well. Even worse, the office door had disappeared, the windows shattered into what was left of their frames. They were all, in the true sense of the word, horribly trapped.

Finally, the building stopped shaking. Nina managed to crawl from under the desk after kicking away a pile of wreckage.

Seeing Nina, Rolo tried to grab her, but couldn't budge in his Dahlia straight jacket.

"Nina, get her off me! Can you get her off me? Please!"

Water still poured over the three, spraying faces and bodies in a nonstop torrent.

"Yeah, I'll try. Hang in there. I'm gonna help you. Just let me see how Dahlia's doing first." Nina grabbed Dahlia's wrist looking for a pulse, but it was no use, since her own hands were shaking too much to stay steady. She removed some of the smaller pieces of wood and ceiling tile on top of the woman, then pulled in closer to see if she was breathing. "She's still alive." Relieved, she tried moving the ceiling beam. "I can't budge it. It's too heavy."

Rolo looked stricken. "Nina," he whined, "you've got to find a way. Please!"

She continued struggling, doing her best to pull off the wreckage, but it would take lots more than her stringy little muscles to free the mayor. Giving up, she crawled across the rubble closer to the trapped man. "I'm sorry, boss, but the stuff's too heavy. I called 9-1-1. Maybe they're here now. I'll go see if I can hear them. Maybe I can get through an opening somewhere." She studied the area where the door used to be. It would take a miracle to get through the mess. "Hang on. I'll be right back."

Lumbering over the wreckage, she found the general location of the door. It had become completely entangled with part of the wall and the collapsed roof. Even if she could remove some of the debris, she still wouldn't be able to get out. The water from the broken pipes and the rain pummeled her like an assault. She managed to pry away a few of the lighter pieces, but since so much of the wall, ceiling, and door had smashed together, it became totally impenetrable.

"Shit!" she exclaimed.

"Nina!" Rolo cried out. "Forget it! Let it go. Just let it go. I need you over here!"

Nina turned to face him. Striving with supreme effort, Rolo managed to free one of his arms. "Please!" he cried waving her back. "Come back."

Nina picked up a piece of wood and threw it against the wall. "Fucking hell," she mumbled to herself. She sighed, than began crawling over the rubble again till she returned to where Rolo and Dahlia lay.

"Nina," Rolo grabbed her by the hand. "I can't die alone here. Don't leave me, please!"

Nina studied the crazed man, realizing he seemed more scared than injured. She felt confused, her feelings alternating between pity and repulsion, her memory seared from all the people he'd catapulted from this very office, their own faces etched in fear. She looked away, then toward the general direction of where the door used to be. "Don't worry, I'm not going anywhere. We're all trapped." Rolo grimaced in pain, holding on to her tight. He closed his eyes, tears mixing with rain.

Clamped in Rolo's grip, Nina assessed his situation. She definitely agreed he was in a tough predicament. Anyone would hate to have a slightly crushed human, much less a slightly crushed Dahlia, on top of them, but hell, the guy needed to be strong. At least he was alive. Shit, she thought, looking around the room, accidents like this happen every day. With all the earthquakes and terrorists everywhere, trapped bodies were almost part of modern living. And humans were actually tougher now, like those people who lived through that earthquake in Mexico. Or those poor old grannies who survived days under concrete in Tehran. And what about that kid trapped in that crushed freeway in California? Shit, they had to cut his leg off, then cut through his own dead mother to get him out. Now *that* was a fucking nightmare. She glanced at Rolo. But, she had to admit, she was damn glad she wasn't him right now. She watched him writhe, his head the only thing visible, wondering whether the rain pummeling his face contributed to his craziness. She tossed a piece of tile across the room. OK, so he's crazy, now what do I do?

Nina forced herself to examine Dahlia, wishing she could move the beam off her back. The bleeding looked like it had slowed. She hoped the woman wouldn't die. As hateful as she was, she didn't deserve it. Nina found a piece of ceiling tile and erected a rain barrier over her face. All I can say is I hope she makes it through this mess, and with enough brains left so she doesn't do macramé all her life. But shit, Nina threw another tile across the room. If she hadn't sucked onto Rolo when he passed out, she'd still be running around barking out her roachified orders. Man, Nina thought, staring at Dahlia's bleeding head, what women do for love.

Nina tried moving to a more comfortable position. Rolo, hyperalert, suddenly opened his eyes, accosting Nina with both anger and pain. She couldn't stand it. "You know what, Rolo? You know what you look like?" He didn't answer. "A jelly doughnut," she said, chuckling. "Only smashed." She remembered how she used to go in the back room at the Donut Time and crush jelly doughnuts whenever she got mad at customers. Sometimes she'd scratch a facsimile of their face on it first before punching it. Tala told her she needed to grow up and learn to control her anger—but it had felt so good, she secretly persisted.

"Nina!" Rolo broke her reverie.

"Yeah, I'm here," she said, wishing she most definitely wasn't. Bits of ceiling tile flecked Rolo's face which, with the blood, made him look like a raspberry now. Nina began laughing. Rolo only watched her. "Hey, Mr. Ambulance Driver!" Nina yelled in the direction of the door. "You might want to bring the jaws of life! We got a trapped raspberry under a smashed jelly-roll." She laughed again, tears streaming from her eyes. "Jesus, now *I'm* going nuts." She took a deep breath, trying to regain her senses.

Rolo's lips puckered in and out like a bullfrog. Nina wondered if he might have a heart attack. Even though he was flaco now he could still have one.

Skinny people had them all the time—even marathon runners. "Rolo, quit doing that. You're gonna give yourself a heart attack. Settle down. There's nothing we can do till the rescue people come."

"I don't think I'm gonna make it," he sobbed. "I'm dying, Nina. I really feel I'm dying."

"You're not dying."

"But I am. Can't you see?"

Nina felt pretty sure Rolo wasn't dying, but he did sound pretty bad. She thought of Tala, then of Jules, wondering what they would do if they were in her shoes. Looking across what was left of the office, she figured she'd try a more logical approach to freeing Rolo. "Look, I got a new idea to move the beam off Dahlia. I'm gonna use physics. I think I can leverage something underneath it but you have to let go of my hand."

Rolo didn't respond.

"Boss, did you hear me?"

"Physics! No . . . No. No!"

Nina felt the building creak, then lurch downward with a heavy jolt. Another surge of panic slammed her chest. "Rolo, look. I just want to help you."

"You can help by not leaving. Don't you see I'm dying!"

"You're not dying, or should I say, *we're* not dying—at least not yet."

"But I am!"

Nina took a deep breath. All right. What harm did it do to agree? Maybe he actually has a smashed liver or something. "OK," she replied, giving up the beam-moving-with-physics idea. "I'll stay with you. I won't leave your side. But I need you to do something for me." She felt the building shift again. She didn't know if the damn thing would completely collapse, killing all three of them.

"For you? Anything. Anything, Name it, if I live, I'll do anything. Just don't leave me."

The rain pelted Rolo like a pulse-driven sprinkler. Nina had lost her rain hat in the wreckage and her wig had slid halfway down her face. She pulled it from her head and flung it across the room.

"Hey! Hey, Nina, do you think you can stop the water?" Rolo sniffed, still crying. "Stop it from hitting me? Think you can do that? Huh? Can you, Nina? Can you please?"

God, what a drama queen. She let out a long breath of air. "I can try," she replied, "but like I said, I need *you* to do something for me."

"OK . . . OK . . . OK," he said, still sobbing.

Nina looked around and saw what was left of the umbrella sticking out from under smashed particleboard. She spoke to Rolo like he was a child. "You have to let go of my hand for ten seconds so I can get the umbrella for you. I'm only gonna be gone ten seconds, OK?"

Rolo nodded, then immediately let go. Nina was able to pry the umbrella free and, upon opening it, realized half of it still worked.

"I'm going to stop the water from hitting you, but you need to promise you'll do something for me."

"What? Anything. Anything."

"The winery. You need to stop it."

"Winery? What are you talking about?" he replied, shaking his head.

"Gilbert's winery. The mess with Dogtown. I need you to stop it. Make Gilbert go someplace else."

"Gilbert? Gilbert Córdova?"

"Yeah, him." Nina brushed wet debris off the umbrella.

"OK. I'll work on it. I promise. Just stop the water, please! Please! I promise I'll do my best to make him move. Just stop the water, please."

"How do I know you'll really do it? You can promise anything now, but bail on me when we're rescued." The rain continued hitting Rolo with its tortuous drumbeat.

"I won't, if I live. I promise you. Please! Just stop the water. I give you my word."

Nina watched his eyes zigzag from her face to the umbrella. The poor guy was in a sorry state, more now with Dahlia's blood on him. Nina studied the injured woman. Her breathing appeared shallow, but steady. Though she and Rolo were a mess, their bodies at least kept one another warm. She turned back to Rolo.

"Shake on it," she persisted, bent on trying to squeeze something out of the pathetic situation they were in.

"I gave you my word."

Nina put the umbrella down and crossed her arms. Rolo squinted through the rain. "I said I gave you my word!"

"Sorry, no handshake, no umbrella." Nina looked him right in the eye, startled by her own desperation.

Rolo gulped a huge breath of air. "OK."

"OK?"

"OK." He stuck out his hand. Nina bent over to shake it. "I give you my word," he said, as he feebly shook her hand.

She paused briefly, noticing a flux of pain cross Rolo's face. Then, without hesitation, she picked up the umbrella and held it over his head. Though it only opened halfway, it was enough to keep the rain from hitting both him and Dahlia.

"Better?" she asked.

Rolo immediately relaxed. "Yes, thank God." He took a deep breath and opened his eyes all the way. Nina used her sleeve to wipe away the blood from his face. Dahlia shifted slightly on top of him, groaning with the movement. "Thank you. Thank you, Nina." He looked at her, his face softer. "Thank you so much."

"You remember your promise, right?" said Nina in the mad mom voice she used on Chucho when he peed on the rug.

He nodded, as much as anyone with all that weight on top of him could. "The winery. I need to try to stop Gilbert."

"Right. And you'll meet with him as soon as you get back to work."

"Right," he said, breathing calmly. His crazy jabbering had finally subsided.

Nina wedged the umbrella between two bricks so she didn't have to hold it then sat back to wait. The building shifted, throwing more roof debris, though, none of it big enough to crush any heads. The room slanting now at such an extreme degree made it feel pretty scary. Rolo hadn't let go of her hand, and Nina, for some reason, felt compelled to hang on. Even in the rain she felt sweaty. Too bad she didn't have a rainproof cigarette right now. Not that she smoked, but she would if she had one. She bit off a hangnail, glad Tala wasn't around to tell her to stop. Rolo hadn't moved in a while, his silence a welcome relief from his locofied ranting. Maybe he'd fallen asleep. Fat chance, she figured, not with Dahlia and all that goo on him.

The rain and spurting water continued with a pounding, driving force, some of which trickled down her wig-free back. "Stupid rain coat couldn't keep a fly dry." Nina squirmed with discomfort. Dahlia moaned and moved again. Nina felt sorry for her, wishing she could do more to help her. Leaning over, she checked on her bleeding. It had stopped.

"Nina," Rolo squinted his eyes open. "What happened to your hair?"

Nina ran a hand through her wet, wig-free locks. "I got tired of wearing it long."

"You talk different, too," he said, still squinting.

"Well. You'd better get used to it, 'cause this is the real me."

"Real is good," he replied, sighed, then closed his eyes again.

"Glad to hear it," said Nina.

She couldn't fathom what the hell was holding up the rescue people. The whole building must've gotten the shit kicked out of it. The room lurched again. "Hijo, I sure hope baby Jesus and his friends are looking out for us," she muttered, gaping at the water's continued onslaught. "We could use some of his help right now." Nina knew people often prayed in these situations, yet she hadn't prayed since second grade when she had her first Holy Communion, so starting now seemed a little foolish. Still, she figured it couldn't hurt to call up a few saints. "Santos were usually sinners first before they became saints. So they're a little more flexible," Pepa had once told her. Trouble was, Nina didn't know many.

"All right . . . can you come down here and give us some help, Mary?" she whispered, looking upward. "Let's see, who was her husband?" She paused to think. "Maybe you can give us a hand Saint uh . . . Joseph! Right. Saint Joseph. Can you see us in here? And how 'bout you, San—" She thought real hard, then remembered the saint on Pepa's altar, "Martín! We could really use some of those healing powers you got right now . . . Let's see, who's the guy with the animals?" She rubbed her forehead, trying to remember.

"Francis," Rolo responded.

Nina glanced at the mayor, one eye squinting in her direction. "Right, Saint Francis!"

She counted out the saints on her fingers. "Shit, no wonder they kicked me out of catechism." She paused, trying to remember others. "Hell, there's Mary Magdalene! How did I forget her? Mary," Nina continued in a low murmur, "if you can hear me, please help us. And please know I never believed all those jerks who said you were a prostitute. Those cabrones were just trying to make you look bad . . . OK, now let's see, what about," she tried to remember some of the things Tala had taught her. "Guadalupe." She nodded, proud of her recollection. "I know how the church used you. But despite it all, I still honor you." She sighed, trying to recollect others. "Well, there's always Saint Jude." She looked around the room. "And I would say we're in a bit of a lost cause situation here, so if you're hearing me, Jude . . . I guess you know what to do."

She paused, thinking of all the old TV movies she'd seen. "Wait, Joan of Arc! You were a saint! And even if you weren't—you should be after all the things they did to you." The building shifted down another notch, coupled with a long, low moan. "Uh, so if any of you guys heard me, Mary—Joseph—Martín—Francis—Mary M.—Lupe—Jude—and, Joanie," Nina counted each one on her fingers as she squinted through the hole in the ceiling, "could you get us the hell out of here?"

Startled by a muffled cry, Nina thought one had actually responded.

"Anyone in there?"

"Yes, yes! There's three of us!" Nina jumped up, yelling. She heard several shouts from people behind what was left of the door. Sighing with relief, she yelled an exhausted, "Hurry!"

"OK, hang tight. We're coming to get you!"

Nina gave Rolo's hand a squeeze. "Hey man, they're finally here!"

With one eye clenched in a squint, he remarked, "I guess one of your saints was listening."

Dahlia moved, groaning slightly. "Mmmm."

"Even she agrees." Rolo added.

Still hanging on to his hand, Nina examined the shattered room with the collapsed ceiling, crushed windows, and rubble piled around them. The rain continued its steady drumbeat, pelting hard against her body. Her neck throbbed, and her muscles had begun to stiffen from sitting in a crouched position for so long. She figured it'd be a while before the rescuers would actually get through the wreckage. But it didn't matter, not now at least. For Nina knew from this moment on, that someone, somewhere out there, had her back. And no matter what might happen she knew she'd always be safe. Pausing in gratitude, Nina bowed her head, grateful to be rescued, and hopeful for so much more.

43

PEPA HATED LATE-NIGHT CALLS, but on this particular Friday, she didn't mind. Round about two, she wobbled half asleep to the ringing phone in the kitchen, relieved at last to hear from Tala. With exhaustion tinging her voice, Tala reported she'd just returned from the hospital and that Nina had made it through the building collapse miraculously intact—a few cuts and bruises. The on-duty psychiatrist had decided to keep her a day for observation, though.

"Por qué?" Pepa asked, glancing at Camilo who had just joined her.

"I don't know. He wouldn't talk to me, of course, but told Nina's parents she'd been through a tough time and he wanted to keep an eye on her. Said he thought she'd be fine, which is a relief."

"Sí, creo que it must've been pretty rough." Pepa lit a cigarette, exhaling toward the ceiling. She cracked open a window to let out the smoke. The rain continued its patter against the glass, falling in the darkness in a steady stream of ticks. Watching the water slide down the pane, she wished for just one momentary bit of silence from the storm's constant throbbing.

"The doctor says she's exhausted but, despite it all, seems to be in great spirits, 'strangely happy,' he said."

"Parece que she's happy to be alive, que no?"

"Yeah, I suppose so. The doctor says she's just sitting in bed grinning."

Pepa scratched her head. "Bueno, can she talk?"

"Oh yeah. Anyway, they want her to rest, no visitors except family— makes you wonder what the hell I am. The mayor's fine, too, a few cracked ribs, cuts, and bruises. Even that repunosa Dahlia's going to be OK. I heard the doc say her brain stayed put, spinal cord didn't get damaged. Broke her collar bone, scapula—damn miracle, if you think about it—considering she also broke three discs, and some ribs."

"Pobrecita." Pepa shook her head with another look at Camilo. He shot a worried look back in her direction.

"I wish I knew more about what the hell happened to Nina," said Tala. "She's been my compañera for five years, and yet they don't tell me shit— damn dark ages we live in. I guess I got no choice but to wait till they release her. I'll call you when she gets out."

"Bueno," said Pepa. "Give her a big abrazo from me and take care of yourself, eh?"

"Will do."

Sunday morning, groggy and depressed, Pepa got up and dressed for her walk. She still hadn't heard from Tala. Sitting in the kitchen before setting out, she looked through the window at the falling rain, seriously considering playing hooky. The rain's assault had finally gotten to her. She had to admit she was damn tired of being wet, worn-out from trudging through muck, and shit-ass sick of never seeing the sun. But her dog, knowing the smell of her walking clothes, jumped around the room excited about his daily adventure. "Oye, Joaquín, you still want your walk no matter what, eh?" Pepa sighed as she rubbed his head. "Bueno, vamos." She grabbed his leash and stepped out the door. She stopped off at Irma's to pick up her dog, but the shades were down, so she decided against waking her. With rain sluicing down her back, she marched up the soggy street, passing muddy cars and houses tossing streamers of water from their roofs. Crows cawed their daily greeting as she hiked to the top of the mesa. The red dirt, puddling in the rain like blood, posed a stark contrast to the wild columbine in bloom, its vibrant purple poised upward like sudden exclamation points.

Pepa paused to examine the flowers. Their arrival sparked a strange inkling. She could almost feel movement in the air, a different smell in the wind.

When she returned home Camilo sat in the kitchen waiting for her.

"Y tú también?" Pepa removed her raincoat. She took a towel and dried off the dog, rubbing his head with affection.

"Sí," Camilo answered, looking serious.

"What is it?" she asked, suspending her dog duties to give Camilo her full attention.

"I don't know, pero I think we need to go to church today."

Pepa crinkled her eyes. "Church?"

He nodded.

"Del Padre Miguel?" She grabbed a coffee cup and set it on the counter.

"Sí, de él."

Pepa poured the coffee, adding milk and sugar. She sipped the liquid, relishing the surge of heat through her body. "Por qué? No me gusta, y también, el padre gets nervioso when we're around." She put bread in the toaster and lit a cigarette.

Camilo tapped his fingers on the table, looking like he was concentrating on something important. "I can't tell you why. We just need to go."

Pepa studied Camilo, then glanced at the clock. "Bueno, I guess we better do it."

❋

Despite Father Miguel's doubt about the existence of God, his Mass was still popular. Simple optimization he figured. People preferred the more humane hour of ten A.M., rather than the heavy-lidded seven o'clock Mass, or the waste-of-day noontime hour. The padre didn't realize a more simple truth, that his popularity remained solid since he spoke to people as equals. Many priests, especially now that the Church had resorted to using men from the bottom of the priest barrel, were pompous, patronizing, know-it-alls. Father Miguel didn't tell people what or how to believe. He only asked them to think—not just about God, but about how they lived their lives.

As he walked into the cathedral that morning, he saw Pepa and Camilo sitting in the front row. Surprised to see them again, he hoped they weren't planning to give him any more of their wacky herbs. He'd dealt with more than his share of their unpredictable potions. As he proceeded to the altar, he looked up to the statue of Jesus, illuminated like a star above him. Less hunky than the bigger guy in the chapel, this statue reigned over the congregation, arms stretched to their limit against the cross. Marching slowly under this smaller-sized Jesus, he nodded and said a silent prayer for guidance, for faith.

The church, crowded with the soggy, damp, and dripping, took longer than usual to settle in. Father Miguel stood, patiently waiting for them. Their unusually large number today concerned him. He wondered if they were there for any special reason. Yet nothing came to mind. It was just another Sunday—another blasted, rainy Sunday. He settled into his ritual, managing to keep an eye on the restless congregation. Outside, the storm continued its onslaught, twenty-eight days and still counting. The trees thrashing back and forth with the force of the wind reminded him of seaweed under water. The rain had worn everyone down. No one could stop talking about it. Even getting to church had become an ordeal. Houses were flooded, trees uprooted, and animals stood miserably in muck. Nothing was as it should be. And the number of confessions had risen—disturbing confessions from people asking if their sins were responsible for all this water. "Maybe it's accumulated sins," he replied since he felt compelled to respond. In truth, he wondered if the rain signified something profoundly deeper. This, he decided, tossing out his planned sermon, was what he'd talk about today.

"For the past twenty-eight days, our city has been battered by a storm defying logical explanation, with rain falling far beyond what all of us have ever seen. Many of you have asked if this rain is a sign from God, a punishment, or a warning." He paused to study the faces focused on his words. Even Domingo Salazar, looking somewhat haggard, gave him his full attention. "Initially I thought it was nothing more than a weird weather pattern, an aberration, a quirk in the clouds. But like you, I found it hard to explain how our little part of the world could be singled out for such a deluge day after day, week after week, especially after months of drought.

"In twelve more days, if the rain continues, we will experience, at least to some degree, what happened to Noah." He paused to scratch his head. "Now, I honestly have to admit I never believed the world flooded like they said it did. My reasoning was based on logic, that there was no way Noah would've been able to gather two of every kind of animal, not to mention insects and birds, in that short amount of time. And, even if Noah had been able to collect every species, how could he truly house them all and keep them from killing each other?"

He looked down and saw Pepa nodding to his words. He wondered if she, too, had thought of this.

"But, let's say Noah *did* have to deal with forty days and nights of rain. And we, just like Noah, have had more water than almost anyone anywhere would consider normal. Our sewer systems are clogged, streets flooded, roofs caved in. Even our adobe is melting. And with the tourists gone, many of you have been laid off from work.

"I'm a priest, so you're probably thinking I'm going to say there might be a connection between all this rain and God." He leaned hard into the podium. "But the fact that I'm a priest doesn't really matter. Because any man, woman, or child can clearly see this rain has to mean something. Indeed," he said, glancing toward the ceiling, "it could be such a sign." He gestured toward the mountains. "Or perhaps a warning from ancestral spirits . . . the spirits many of our Native-American brethren believe reside in these mountains. In either case, I believe this rain signifies a sign of our weakened souls. A sign of greed . . . lack of compassion . . . struggle for power . . . lack of faith." He studied his hands as they gripped the podium. "At the very minimum, it's a sign we need to think of others besides ourselves."

He stopped, took a deep breath, and examined the faces around him— all of them poised, alert to his words. "The simple fact is that rain is water, and water is life. The rain we've had for the past twenty-eight days has been frightening to many of us. But perhaps it's an attempt by God, or even," he said, glancing at Camilo, who was looking up at the statue of Jesus, "something very powerful, that wants us to listen.

"Let us each pray then, from the depths of our souls, for forgiveness and guidance. And maybe by doing so, we'll see the truth, and then light, and finally an end to this storm." He clasped his hands together. Looking upward, he was about to begin an impromptu prayer, when a cry shot across the church.

"Look!" someone shouted. It was Jaime García, pointing toward the statue of Jesus. Two hundred eyes moved from the man to the statue above them. Part of the first group who had elected to move out of Dogtown, Jaime stood with his mouth agape and body quivering. His wife Myrna, looking alarmed, followed his eyes toward the ceiling.

"What is it?" asked the priest, both perplexed and annoyed that his sermon had been interrupted.

"It's Jesus," Jaime exclaimed, still pointing. "The statue is crying. It's a miracle! Es un milagro! Oh my God, he's crying! It's a miracle!"

People rushed from their pews and gathered in a clot under the statue. Many held their hands out, hoping to catch the tears. Others made the sign of the cross, praying with reverence. Those farther away darted through the aisles, hoping to catch a closer glimpse. They gently and not so gently moved each other aside, wanting this most holiest of water to fall into their hands.

"Sonnava . . . whoa, Son of Christ!" cried Domingo Salazar, squinting at the statue. "I got a hell of a hangover, gente. But I ain't hallucinating this."

Father Miguel let out a long, long sigh. Never a believer in the so-called miracles of bleeding statues, or "sightings" of the various Virgin Marys and Jesuses on trees, tortillas, and sandwiches, he took a deep breath as he stepped off the altar. Why do people still believe in these things, he wondered, walking carefully down the steps. With hands clenched he marched toward the statue, knowing most certainly that it wouldn't be crying any more than any other statue in the church would be.

He made his way through the crowd until he was directly underneath Jesus's outstretched arms. He looked up, squinting in the dim light of the church.

"And where are these tears?" he asked.

"Right there!" said Jaime, still pointing. "Look at his eyes! Look at my hands!" He showed the padre the wetness on his palms.

Father Miguel glanced at Jaime's hands then stood very still as he studied the statue. Yes, water from the statue, a statue that happened to be close to the ceiling, a ceiling weak from rain, rain upon the statue, and the statue dripping water. There you go—perfectly, completely logical. He held out his hand and let a "tear" hit it. Bringing it to his nose he sniffed it like a detective. Nothing, no scent of mold, mildew, or decay. He rubbed the moisture with his fingers—it almost had the viscosity, the thickness of a tear. The congregation murmured softly around him. He arched his neck back up to the statue. Well, he thought. It did look like Jesus's eyes were dripping something. And based on the moisture on his hand, it seemed to be a water-like substance. But it was hard to see clearly since the statue was high above them. Perhaps it was simply condensation, albeit dripping strategically.

Then again, he wondered as he continued his scrutiny, it could be a combination of condensation and the lights reflecting off the windows. Certainly, there had to be a reasonable explanation, some kind of wayward leak.

"I need a ladder," Father Miguel said.

"What did you say?" asked Jaime.

"I said I need a ladder. I want to get closer." The deacon and two servers jumped at the request. "When they return, I'll climb it, and then we shall see." He folded his hands and looked around the church. Not a soul had left.

"Padre, why don't you tell the truth?" It was Cleo Córdova, Gilbert and Tala's mother. "You don't need a ladder to see it's a milagro! Jesus is crying. Crying for our souls, just like you said." She stood facing those around her. "The padre spoke the truth! The rain and these tears can only be a sign from God!"

Several people gathered around Mrs. Córdova murmuring in affirmation, bodies hunched with reverence and fear. The priest studied Mrs. Córdova. "Bueno, then we shall see."

A tall folding ladder appeared. It was the one used by the custodial staff to change the high-hanging light bulbs. The deacon set it up, and the servers stood beneath it, holding it steady. The priest glanced at the people gathered around the ladder, then he began his ascent. It wasn't exactly easy to climb in his priestly garb. He kept stepping on the chasuble, and had to kick out each foot in order to climb. When he reached the top, he was still a good ten feet from the statue. He leaned as far forward as possible. Even from this vantage point it was difficult to see.

"Bueno," the priest hollered from the top of the ladder. "I think," he said, looking upward, studying the wetness on the Christ statue's face, "that what we're witnessing . . . is . . . well it seems to be . . ."

"A miracle, no, Padre?" shouted a voice from the base of the ladder.

"A miracle? Well . . ." he answered. He didn't see any leaks coming from the ceiling.

"Sí, un milagro. A sign," the voice added. "Like the señora said."

"A sign?" Eyes still intent on the statue, he thought the voice below him sounded like Pepa.

"Sí, that what you said was true." She continued bellowing toward the priest. "That we need to come clean and stop being greedy."

Now he wished he'd asked for binoculars. "Well, we do need to stop being greedy," he replied, distracted by the water on the statue's face. Where the hell was it coming from?

"Bueno, then this proves it, no?"

"Well, it could." He looked below him and saw that, indeed, it was Pepa. "But I feel I did speak the truth." He looked back up at the statue. Maybe it was made of lime or alabaster, stones that attract water. Yet the dripping eyes looked like more than condensation.

"Well, rain or no rain, the statue is crying, Padre. You see it just like we do." Pepa tapped the bottom rung of the ladder.

Was this woman right? Could it really be a miracle?

"Come down, Padre," Pepa yelled, tapping the ladder again. "We're waiting for you."

The priest nodded, finally accepting the reality of unexplainable wetness on the statue's face. He stood transfixed, studying the statue another thirty seconds, then slowly descended. When he reached the bottom he felt so hot and light-headed, he had to hold the ladder to steady himself. "I've examined the statue." He took several rapid breaths, then opened one arm toward the people. "And I can find no visible explanation for the water on his face."

"In his eyes," corrected Pepa.

The priest glanced at the healer. "Sí," he said with a sigh, "in his eyes. So indeed if this is a sign, in reference to everything I spoke of," he said, turning toward the congregation, "may God, or the spirits among us, help our very souls."

The deacon whispered in the ear of the server, who returned shortly with a pocket camera. The boy zipped up the ladder and captured a shot of the statue's eyes. In less than an hour, they had dried completely.

44

Several days later, Nina reported for work, fully recovered. With the rain still nonstop in its onslaught, she walked into the new temporary City Hall—a slew of rented trailers housed on the parking lot. Dressed down in jeans, waterproof boots, make-up, and no wig, she knew she could never go back to her Barbie doll getup no matter how much Rolo liked it. Her hair, now more stylishly cut, looked better anyway than that old flap of hanging strings.

"Hey, Boss, how goes it?" Nina called out to the mayor as she walked into the trailer. She stepped into the doorway of Rolo's private office and waved.

Rolo, clad in a wrist brace, his face puffy, and eyes purple-yellow, barely looked up from his work. He replied with a gruff, "Glad you're back," and nothing more.

Nina shrugged, figuring he might be embarrassed after their roof crunch ordeal. It wasn't until lunch when he had to leave for a meeting that he limped over to her desk.

"Something's different about you," he stated, as if just awakening from a nap.

"Yeah, lots," Nina replied as she sipped root beer through a straw. "We gotta hire a temp replacement for Dahlia. She'll be out for a while. Oh, and did you send her flowers?"

"Yeah, on Monday."

"Good." Nina took another sip from her root beer.

"It's shorter. That's what it is." Rolo leaned toward Nina like he was observing a specimen at the zoo.

"Uh-huh, I cut it," she replied, realizing he'd apparently forgotten her wig's demise during the roof collapse. "I got tired of the wear-a-dress routine, too. It's a drag dealing with skirts and nylons every day, especially in this rain."

"You're even talking different," Rolo tilted his head as he continued studying Nina, now looking like he was expecting an alien to come plunging out of her chest.

"I, uh . . ." She paused, realizing she'd forgotten to use her M-voice. "I found my real self during the cave-in, something I feel is a truer sense of me." She smiled, satisfied with her answer.

Giving her a weak smile in return, he picked up his briefcase. "I guess I can relate."

"Good . . . so, uh, just so that you know, I'll have your notes prepared and appointments with city planning regarding your new plans for Dogtown by the end of the day." Nina folded her hands on her desk, giving Rolo her happy kitten face. "I'm glad you've decided to make the changes to help this impoverished community." She handed him a piece of paper. "Here's a brief outline indicating what your promises were, just in case you wanted to refresh your memory during lunch." She waited while he glanced at the list. "By the way, how's your appetite?"

Rolo opened his briefcase, then slid the paper inside. "Better," he replied, still eyeing Nina.

She could tell he still hadn't decided what he thought of her.

"Bueno, I'll see you after lunch." He walked over to the coat tree and put on his rain gear.

"Okey-dokey," Nina said, watching for any signs of his going back on their deal. "Oh, Mayor Reyes?"

"Yeah?" he said, as he opened the door, the hood from his slicker encapsulating his face.

"I'm glad you're a man of your word. Have a nice lunch."

※

A bit chagrined over what had occurred between him and Nina, Rolo considered firing her, since it could also get him out of his commitments. But glancing at the rain sliding down the window, water coursing through the streets, and the wreck of his former office building, he knew from the bottom of his heart that the day that roof collapsed, she had truly saved his life. And for that, he owed her. It was his credo.

Three days later, the mayor took a deep breath and called Gilbert himself. He didn't reveal much about the purpose of the meeting, only remarking that they needed to catch up on business. Gilbert appeared the next afternoon, adorned in a crisp white shirt, black waterproof boots, and Chimayo vest. Motioning him to join him at his new conference table, Rolo watched how Gilbert studied his new digs, now devoid of art or decoration, save the surviving Turkish rug and Nambé bowl. Nina, away at a doctor's appointment, had left for the day.

Rolo pulled out a chair and sat down. He retrieved a cigar out of a plain cardboard box, cut the end off, and lit it. Gilbert declined the mayor's offer of a cigar and sat, hands relaxed in his lap.

"Bueno," he said, puffing his cigar. "The reason I called you in today is that I want to talk to you about this winery of yours."

"I'd be happy to update you on our current business plans. We've revised a few items."

Rolo studied the man. He had that look of conscious entitlement. Either that, or it was simply balls-out drive. Rolo knew that look since he, too, possessed it. "Let me tell you, I'm still in support of this winery. But there's been a lot of bad publicity regarding it—publicity that, coupled with the rain, has had a negative impact on the city, and on me."

"Well that can be easily remedied," Gilbert answered, hands still relaxed. "Just get the city manager to run a positive media campaign. We could use a stronger counter-message from the mayor's office regarding the winery anyway. The stuff you first ran with when we got started was pretty good, but it seems to have," he said with a shrug, "lagged a bit."

Rolo hated it when people critiqued him, but he hated it even more when they told him how to do his job. "You of all people should know," he said, pointing with his cigar, "that the positive media blitz didn't work. These people got professional shit-disturbers working for them, shit-disturbers with law degrees. And no one likes to see poor people being given the shaft."

"Now hold on." Gilbert rocked to the edge of his chair. "I'm paying them fair market for the neighborhood. What you're stating is incorrect—"

Rolo held up his hand. "Would you just hear me out?"

Gilbert flexed his jaw and waited.

"I want to propose a change." The mayor took a moment to compose himself.

Gilbert softly drummed his fingers on the side of his leg.

"I've had a pretty good relationship with Brent and Mary Weaver of the Arroyo Blue Foundation, and they've always been great supporters of innovative causes."

Gilbert nodded, since everyone in town knew who they were.

"And—" Rolo tapped the side of his cigar on the ashtray. "I spoke to them recently about the possibility of leasing, or maybe even selling, part of their land to you over by the opera house. They sounded pretty positive—liking the winery idea and knowing New Mexico could do a lot better on its wine quality. They want to work with you, and they're proposing giving you the same acreage as Dogtown, but at below market value. All in exchange for a small share of the profit." Rolo eyed Gilbert through the smoke.

"You're kidding, right?" he asked.

"No, I'm not." Rolo held the cigar steady between his fingers.

Gilbert looked confused. "I'm not understanding this."

"I want you to give up Dogtown. The reason—now hang on—" He held his hand up again. "Is that it's now politically unfeasible for me to continue supporting the project—at least in its current location." He set the cigar in the ashtray. "I got key sources telling me to pull out of this completely. So consider this a favor."

Gilbert's face shifted from shock to anger. "But the work I've done, building plans, impact report, zoning laws, courts. I put a hell of a lot of time and money into this!"

"You did. But I finally had to admit," he said, realizing the human angle of it all, "that I was wrong to let you talk me into kicking these people out. I can't pay you for your time, but I'll grease your wheels as best I can for the move to the opera house land. I had a geologist check it out—owed me a favor. Said the land had good soil construction." He crossed his legs. "Anyway, you can probably set up something nice for the folks going to the opera, maybe make a few more dollars. I think this is even better than what you had before, don't you?" The mayor looked briefly through the window at the rain. Hell, the more he thought about it, the more he liked it. He even wondered why he hadn't thought previously of doing this.

"You know, you're something else." Gilbert's breathing labored; he could barely grit out the words. "I don't know what the hell happened to you in that accident. A week ago," he said, pointing his finger, "you would have never changed your mind. Now look at you . . . I don't even think *you* know who you are."

Odd, since Rolo hadn't felt this clearheaded in months. "Put your damn finger down! I'm closing the Dogtown deal as it currently stands, and I want you to accept the Arroyo Blue offer."

"I can't do that," Gilbert replied, lips pressed into a defiant white line.

"What'd you say?"

"I said I can't do it. I've already got everything planned, signed contracts with nearly half the residents, and I'll get the rest out on eviction. You can't stop this project. I've got city ordinances behind me." He smiled as he picked up his jacket.

Rolo stood. Despite his injuries, he still imparted an imposing presence. "Look," he said, slamming his hand on the table. "You got three days to think about it. After that, I'll can both deals. And if you don't believe me— watch me. This is a damn good offer I'm giving you, thanks, I might add, to Brent and Mary. You won't lose much, and we'll expedite the impact report. I'll even get the council to approve a lower tax ratio. That's a good patch of land. Don't turn this down out of pride."

Gilbert shook his head, amazed. "You really have lost it, haven't you? I'm sorry it's come to this, but I'll see you about it in court."

"You do that," Rolo replied, keenly aware how the cabrón was challenging him. "And then you'll see what happens. I've made nice with you over this pinche winery, and it's been nothing but a pain in the ass ever since you've proposed it. So I'm telling you now, accept this offer and move. I'm not giving you a choice."

Gilbert flung his jacket over his shoulder. "We'll see, Mister Mayor," he said, as he walked out of the room. "We most definitely shall see."

45

THAT SAME EVENING, eleven days after "El milagro del Cristo," which is what everyone had begun calling the crying Jesus event, Pepa got word that the Dogtown sellouts had called a town hall meeting at the El Rio Bar. She got a hold of Elena and asked her to come crash the meeting with her and Camilo. Elena obliged, and the three of them wormed their way into the rickety building with its large dance floor and painted skylight. Several rows of mismatched chairs were arranged across the floor. The skylight, a local artist's rendition of red roses in bloom, retained little of its original glory, due primarily to the heat from the previous drought and mold from the rain. The resulting pattern resembled little more than pink and green paint chips with squiggly black veins.

Pepa took off her raincoat and hung it on the rack in the back. The bar's interior smelled of stale beer, mildew, and faded cologne. The rain, now in its thirty-ninth day, pounded the skylight with a staccato dance. To stay in business, Angie Apodaca, manager and direct descendent of its previous gangster owner, rented it out on Tuesdays as a card parlor. That night's game had been shuffled to the dining room, drinks served by Angie's grumpy one-eyed cousin who wore a black eye patch like an old-time pirate. Other invitees to the meeting such as Father Miguel and Cleo Córdova were also there—witnesses to the milagro.

Balancing a glass of wine for herself, a juice for Camilo, and a Coke for Elena, Pepa nodded a greeting to Father Miguel, clad in black pants and his Padres baseball hat. She handed the drinks to Camilo and Elena, then sat with them in the back, anxious to see what the sellouts had to say. Jaime and

Myrna García appeared to be the organizers, the two running around like busy jaybirds. After waiting for latecomers, Myrna gave the signal and Jaime weaved through the people to the front of the room.

"All right, gente, listen up." Dressed in a clean white shirt and neatly pressed jeans, his eyes circled the people assembled. "We need to take a roll call of who's here before we get started, so raise your hands if you live in Dogtown." He counted hands. "Bueno, thank you. Also with us today is Bill Takash, the lawyer for Gilbert's winery who we asked to come to our meeting." He gave a nod toward Bill who tossed a quick wave to the crowd, his eyes resting momentarily on Elena. "Now, to get started, how many of you took the winery's offer?" Only a few hands went up. "Qué hombre? We know who you are. That's how you got invited. Now stick up your hands so we can count you right." He mouthed each number as he counted, double-checking his numbers with Myrna, who placed her results on a clipboard.

Pepa took a sip of wine, fidgeting absently with her glass. Elena seemed focused on the meeting, notepad and pen handy. Camilo had set his juice down, untouched. Pepa watched his eyes flit around the room. His energy seemed different, as if his body emitted an electric current.

"Is Dora Cabrillo here?" Jaime's eyes searched the seating area, then drifted toward the bar.

"I'm here," she replied, seated on a barstool holding her baby. Her other kids had already taken off, exploring the building.

"Were you a witness to the milagro?" Jaime asked.

"No, I wasn't," Dora sniffed, eyes rolling upward.

"Pinche cabrona," Pepa whispered, which Elena reacted to by shushing her with a finger across her lips.

"Bueno," said Jaime. "Anyone else not there that day?"

Seven more hands shot up.

"OK, we got eight people who didn't see the milagro. Otherwise, everyone here is a witness, que no?"

"Either that, or we just believe," said Mrs. Maestas, with a defiant flick of her chin toward Dora. Several people nodded in agreement.

"Bueno," continued Jaime. "I'm sure all of you heard by now that right after Father Miguel told us the rain might be a sign from God, the statue of Cristo started crying. Isn't this true, Padre?"

Hunched over his chair, Father Miguel nodded.

"Padre?"

The priest cleared his throat. "Well, I didn't exactly put it like that, but I guess you could say yes." He lifted his eyes, glancing briefly at Jaime.

"And the padre said that this rain could mean God wants us to clean our souls." He stopped for a moment to look at the priest. "And that we need to think of others, not just ourselves. Is this right, Father?" The priest nodded again. "Well I'm here to tell you those tears from that statue fell right into my own hands." Jaime opened his palms with a reverence signifying that they'd been touched by the divine. "Now, I don't know about you, but after—what's it, thirty-nine days of rain." He stopped to think for a second. "Right. After thirty-nine days, I think we need to start paying attention to what this priest is telling us. 'Cause if all this rain and a Christ statue crying isn't a sign of something, then I don't know what else is."

"What, you want us to join a convent?" Dora twirled her hair, then glanced at the priest.

Pepa snorted, cutting her eyes at the woman.

"Dora, if you want to join a convent, you go right ahead." Jaime bowed in her direction. Several people in the audience chuckled. "Pero, the reason we called you in here today is to talk about the milagro, the rain, and the selling of Dogtown. Me and my wife, Myrna here," he paused to look around the hall, "think that all the stuff that's happening, is God telling us what we're doing is wrong."

"Oh, please." Dora crossed her arms. Frank Tafoya, arms folded across his belly, caught Dora's eye and nodded.

Jaime glanced at the two, then looked around the room. "Anyone here think the same as us?"

"Yes," said Mrs. Maestas. Several others echoed her. Pepa added a soft "yes."

Jaime turned an empty chair around and leaned on it. "If you go back and look at what's happened these past few months, you'll see we had a drought, then we had a flood—which is what I'd basically call this rain. Then we got people backstabbing each other over money. Finally, we got the milagro. And it's this milagro del Cristo that I think was sent to us as a final sign." He swallowed a big gulp of air. "So I think, and my wife Myrna here agrees with me, that what we need to do to set things right, is to give up—what's that word again, Bill?"

"Rescind," said the lawyer, chewing slowly on a toothpick.

"Rescind our agreement to sell our homes to Gilbert."

Elena caught Pepa's eye, looking shocked. She grabbed Camilo, but immediately let go since he was too hot to touch. Several gasps, followed by a loud, murmuring rumble rolled through the crowd. Even the bartender stopped his pour, his one eye glinting toward the speakers.

Dora, her face matted in anger, leapt off her stool. "Did I just hear you say you want us to give up the money?"

"That's right," said Jaime. "It's what I think we have to do. This winery has brought nothing but trouble. We've been at each other's throats, calling each other names, shooting off guns, acting greedy, and thinking only of ourselves. And all it's done is made people sick! Ask Pepa, she's sitting there in the back. Oye Señora, how many people have come in to see you since all this stuff started?"

Setting her wine carefully beside her, Pepa stood. "Bueno. Almost half of Dogtown has been through my door. And some of them were sick with things I've never seen in my thirty years of doing this work."

"You've probably never seen it because you're not a medical doctor," said Frank Tafoya, giving Dora a sly smile.

Dora returned the look, eyes crinkled with mirth. She glanced again at Pepa, then began laughing, first with a low grunting sound, then with eyes darting madly towards the priest, into a rapturous, full-bellied laugh. When she finally finished, she blew her nose and wiped the tears streaming down her face. "You're all a bunch of lunk-headed, old-world idiots. That priest pulled a fast one on you. There ain't no such thing as crying statues. Hell," she said, swinging her head in the priest's direction, "that padre doesn't even believe in God, much less crying statues—just ask 'im."

Father Miguel examined his feet.

Dora switched her baby to the other arm. "Go on! Ask 'im if he believes in God. Then ask 'im about the statue. See if he believes it cried, too."

Pepa's eyes shifted from the priest to Camilo. Riveted by Dora's accusation, his face appeared almost translucent, as he gripped his thighs, hands flexed like talons.

Jaime cleared his throat. "I, uh—I don't think it's a polite thing to ask. I think he wouldn't be a priest if he didn't believe in God."

Pepa thought Jaime's voice gave away his true feelings.

Father Miguel kept his head down, lips pressed closed.

"Oh yeah?" Dora replied, with a scornful laugh. "Then, did anyone else climb up the ladder that day to see where the water was coming from? Anybody there wonder if there was a leak in the roof? You only got to spit on these old roofs to make 'em leak. Look what happened to the mayor."

The rain, as if agreeing, continued to pummel the skylight.

"Bueno, I saw the priest climb the ladder!" Cleo Córdova stood facing Dora, hands clenched in anger. "I could tell at first he didn't want to believe it. We've heard him talk. We know how he thinks. But the milagro spoke the truth, didn't it, Padre?" she asked, turning toward the priest. Still silent, Father Miguel glanced at the woman. "*I* saw the Cristo cry with my very own eyes," she said, tapping her chest. "And I wouldn't be here today if—if I didn't think something bad is happening. Even if it was a leak, I'm scared enough to know that thirty-nine days of rain has to mean something, some kind of warning from something bigger than me or you." She lowered her voice, eyes tearing. "My son never meant to hurt people. He just wanted this winery with all his heart. But I honestly believe that he has—that we have," she looked around the room, "to let it go." She paused, and let out a long breath. "We can't go on living like this."

Pepa fell back in her chair, shocked by Señora Córdova's remarks. She tried to get Camilo's attention. But his body, so intent on the señora, was immovable. Pepa studied her acolyte, the young man who seemed to have wandered into her life. She had always wondered what, specifically, he'd been sent to her to do. Now she was beginning to understand what that reason might actually be.

"Well—I—still—ain't—doing—it." Dora tilted her head back and forth with each word. "I already told everyone, in case you hadn't heard, that I need that money. I don't mean to be making a fuss, but I got this kid—" she held the baby up. "And four more to feed, and that money is going to help me get them squared away."

"I agree with her," said Frank Tafoya. "I'm not budging either."

"Then we should vote," said Jaime.

"You can all vote as much as you want, but I'm not rey-cinding nothing." Dora cocked her head in defiance.

"Ni yo," said Frank.

"Ni yo," said a young woman Pepa didn't know.

Jaime widened his eyes, as if slapped by their words. "Bueno then, anyone else want to say something?" Jaime asked, looking around.

"What happens," said Manny Padilla, one of the people who hadn't been in Mass that day. "If we go back on signing our contracts?" Heads turned to Gilbert's lawyer.

"Well," Bill Takash sighed. "My client could sue all the people who rescind, but chances are he won't. Reason is," he said, pausing to pull the toothpick out of his mouth, "that he doesn't have a majority of signers yet, even with the eviction proceedings. It's easier to get people to move if they're willing. Evictions are a pain to do. And all the non-signers can still fight *him* in court. Course I can't guarantee what he will or won't do, but if you rescind, I figure he'll probably just give up and go someplace else."

"Any more questions?" Jaime asked.

"So we just tear up the contract?" asked Gloria Vigil, who had been silent through the meeting.

Bill turned to face her, "No, but all you gotta do is let Gilbert know you're rescinding with a letter. I'm sure there'll be someone around who'll help you write it," he replied, staring at Elena.

"Others?" Jaime's eyes scanned the room.

"Nope, no, uh-uh," were the collective replies.

"Bueno, let's vote."

"I don't know if you all heard me," Dora said, voice raised. "But I said—"

"Wait, I'd like to say something." Father Miguel put his hand out, interrupting Dora. He stood up and took off his baseball cap. "This lady," he said, gesturing toward Dora, "has accused me of not being a believer. I—" he cleared his throat—"have always felt challenged throughout my life, about who to trust and what to believe. As a young boy, I always believed in God, mainly because I was *told* to. Regarding Dora's question about the statue, I don't know a priest anywhere," he paused, his voice trembling. "Who can honestly answer it with a definitive yes. That is, until he sees the truth himself. My truth had never really occurred—and I feel embarrassed confessing this—until I was up on that ladder that day. Mrs. Córdova is right," he paused, facing her. "I didn't want to believe that statue was crying. But when logic couldn't explain what I, or all the people in the church witnessed, or thirty-nine days of relentless rain, then I knew something else had to be responsible.

"I'm not going to stand here and tell you what to believe, since you all have to answer that question on your own. But I do want you to know my beliefs about God, and whoever else might be guiding us, go far beyond our immediate world or the puniness of my body. This," he said, looking at Dora, "is what I believe. And I stand by it with all my heart. You can call it what you want. And for that matter, you can call me what you want. But it will never change how I feel."

Except for the rain, the room remained silent. Pepa noticed Camilo seemed less agitated now, his body relaxed, almost peaceful.

Finally, Jaime García spoke. "Bueno, anyone else want to say anything?"

"I'd like to," Elena said, standing. "I'm the lawyer representing—rather, working on helping Dogtown stay . . . well, as Dogtown. My name is Elena Luján. And just so you know, I'd be happy to help you all write your letters to Gilbert." She started to sit, then caught herself. "For free."

"Bueno, gracias, Señora," said Jaime. "Anyone else?"

No one replied.

"Then all in favor of staying in Dogtown and rescinding our acceptance of Gilbert's offer, raise your hands."

Everyone, with the exception of Dora and Frank, held their hands high. The young woman Pepa didn't know who had spoken earlier looked down at her lap, then slowly raised her hand.

Myrna double-counted to make sure of the tally. Pepa watched Bill Takash chew his toothpick with quick round thrusts of his tongue. He flexed his fingers until his knuckles cracked, rounded his shoulders, and walked out of the room.

46

THE NEXT MORNING PEPA GOT UP, roused her dog, and readied herself for her walk. Stepping onto the porch with the rain still falling, she laced her muddy hiking boots. She stopped next door to pick up Irma's dog, noticing the clouds had shifted colors—from a constant smoky gray to a soft, billowy white. The wind had calmed. The rain now felt almost comforting as it fell upon her.

Pepa leashed the dogs and began her daily journey. As she walked past a grove of piñón trees, green again with life, she heard the familiar chirp of a blue grosbeak. She remembered the sound since it was the same bird she'd heard when Camilo came to help her. She smiled as she listened to its cheerful chee-ar-re-up, chee-ar-re-up. She hadn't heard this bird in almost a year and wondered if it might be migrating home.

Pepa crested the mesa, stopped, then faced the four directions. Despite the fall day, she felt warm currents of air envelop her. While the dogs sniffed and played, Pepa leaned against her favorite rock to rest, studying the violet-blue Sangre de Cristos in the early morning light. She noticed other birds had begun singing, the canyon towhee, dark-eyed junco, and mountain chickadee, each calling out their own particular song. Even her old crow friends raced each other across the hills, diving playfully through the trees.

Pepa called the dogs, gathered herself, and began the trek back home. As she gazed across the mesa, she spotted a hole in the clouds, with golden streaks of light pouring through. She stopped, taken away by this cloud break and the light, light she hadn't seen in forty maddening days. "Qué maravilloso!" She remained completely still, staring open-mouthed. The rain patted her shoulders as she stood transfixed. Finally, growing impatient, the dogs whimpered slightly, and Pepa resumed her journey back down the mesa.

Continuing her descent, eyes darting to the sky, she hoped the cloud break would last until she arrived home. Distracted by the sunlight, she slipped on a rock, lost her balance, and fell. Unhurt, yet amused by the state of her mud-splattered hands, she lifted her palms to let the rain caress them, sensing suddenly that the droplets had diminished in size. She wouldn't dare let herself smile. Instead, she picked herself up, brushed muddy hands on her pants, and continued down the trail. Half a mile later, as she approached her street, the sunrays still beckoned. *Now* she creaked open a grin, the rain tickling her face like confetti. She picked up her pace, anxious to tell her neighbors. Three more blocks, and the rain had miraculously transformed to nothing more than mist. "It's over!" she said. "It's over!" she said again. Leaping high in the air, she screamed shouts of joy. "The rain se acabó! It's over! It stopped!" Water flowed everywhere, running final crescendos down gutters, streets, and creeks. Even the mud glistened in the liquid light.

Pepa knocked on Irma's window. "Oye, amiga, come out! The rain's stopped!" She pointed toward the sky.

Irma rushed out, looked up at the sky, and let out a wild "Eee-haa!" The two jumped up and down, holding on to each other's shoulders in an ecstatic embrace. Pepa unleashed the dogs, then hurried off to spread the news.

"Gente, miren!" Pepa shouted, as she scampered down the street. "La lluvia se acabó. Come out! Vengan!" she hollered, like an exultant Paul Revere. "The rain's stopped!" Pepa marched down the street shouting the good news as people slowly emerged from their houses, palms open in wonder.

After making sure her entire street had heard, Pepa dashed home. Camilo stood on the porch grinning, looking like he'd timed her arrival. "Bueno, Pepa," he gestured toward the sky, "think you're still going to need me around here?"

Pepa ran up the steps and gave him a big hug. "Pienso que you'll have to tell me." The two turned to face their Dogtown neighbors, some of whom were dancing polkitas in the street.

Tala and Nina pulled up to Pepa's house, horn honking, truck bursting with animals, waving and shouting. "Que viva la victoria! Que viva Dogtown! Ahúa!!"

"I think," Camilo said, watching the two women join the festivities, "that me and you will always have plenty to do."

Pepa turned to face Camilo. "What about when I'm gone?"

"Then I hope you'll be somewhere close by, watching over me."

Then, as if on cue, a young man walked into Pepa's yard, took off his hat, and tucked it under his arm. She recognized the face of the good-looking hombre she'd treated several months ago for the bad ticker. Thinner now, he had on a new pair of jeans and a white shirt with a beautiful turquoise bolo. He still wore cowboy boots, but they were simple black leather, not the monstrosities he'd strutted around in the last time she saw him.

"Buenos días, Señora."

"Buenos días . . . Emilio, no?"

"Sí," he said, looking surprised. "You remember me."

"Well you were a little hard to forget," Pepa said, with a smile. She gestured toward Camilo. "This is my ayudante, ay, perdóname," her hand darted toward her heart. "This is my healing partner, el Señor Camilo." Pepa offered a fat grin as the two men shook hands. She pointed to the sky. "Oye, did you see? The sun's come out."

"The sun?" He seemed momentarily confused. "Oh, yeah. It's great having it back." He studied the receding clouds, then swiveled back to the people jumping and shouting around him. "Big celebration, no?"

"Pues sí," said Pepa. "Everyone's happy because they don't have to leave their homes. But I think I'm the happiest of all." She smiled again and gave Camilo a wink.

"Why's that?"

"Because she doesn't have to worry anymore," Camilo interjected.

"That's gotta make anyone feel pretty damn good," said the young man, eyes darting to the celebration, then returning to Pepa. He removed his hat from beneath his arm and started bouncing it back and forth between each hand.

Pepa nodded, watching Tala and Nina out of the corner of her eye. She hadn't seen the two look so happy in such a long time. Their animals ran barking, clucking, and crowing in and around the celebrants, adding to the ruckus.

Emilio's gaze shifted between Pepa, Camilo, and the merrymaking. "I don't think I've ever seen animals party before."

"Ni yo," added Pepa. "Creo que they're happy, too." She turned her full attention back to her patient. "Bueno, was there a reason you came in today?"

"Well, I've been thinking a lot about what you told me the last time we spoke. And even though I got trusted sources who say you always hit the bull's-eye when it comes to figuring out what's wrong, I gotta admit it was hard for me to give up my life's goal. Especially since all you did was run an egg over my heart." He scratched his forehead, "Pero, everyone I talked to said you spoke the truth, and that I'd been driving myself too hard. So I knew I needed to pay attention to what you told me."

"Bueno, that's good, no? You want to come inside?" Pepa took one last look at the festivities.

Emilio nodded and followed the healers past the empty waiting area into the treatment room. He spent a moment gazing at the new additions to Pepa's altar. "I like that picture of Shiprock."

"Me, too," said Pepa. A pot of chicos cooking in the kitchen perfumed the air with the fragrance of roasted corn. "Siéntate, Señor. What can we do for you?" She lit a cigarette, then with a quick glance at Camilo, put it out. Today, she figured, was a good day to change her own life. She took a deep breath and waited, listening to the soft din of the celebration.

"Well." He set his hat on his knee. "After I saw you I sold my business which, like I said, was hard to do. But something good happened . . . I started working at the continuation school."

"Oh, yeah?"

"Yeah, turns out I like working with kids, especially the ones who need another chance." He offered a weak smile. "But I'm here because—well," he glanced at Camilo. "I'm still not so sure I did the right thing."

"Because you're poorer?" Pepa inhaled the fragrant breeze coming through an open window.

"You got it, and it's pretty tough."

"But your family, are they happy?"

Emilio sat up in his seat. "Well, my wife laughs a lot more. And I'm helping the kids with their homework now more than ever."

"Bueno, it sounds like you're doing good things, que no?"

"Yeah, but I think I might need a little more help channeling that drive I put into making money into what I'm doing now." He cracked his knuckles then rubbed his hands together.

Pepa raised an eyebrow. "Let's have a look." Camilo stood up and gathered materials for the examination. Pepa checked Emilio's eyes, and instructed him to go to the bathroom and pee in a jar. When he returned, both healers studied the urine, after which Camilo poured it down the toilet. Next, Pepa took a bit of amalgam and rubbed it over Emilio's face, heart, and stomach. He stood rock still, a glint of wonder in his eyes. She melted the soft metal in a skillet and examined the resulting shape.

"A ver," she said blowing softly to cool it. "Here's your problem."

Emilio peered closely at the melted silver. Pepa knew it probably looked like a glob of liquid bottle caps to him.

"Remember when I told you before that you had a strong spirit?"

Emilio nodded.

"Bueno, that's good, because a strong spirit will always keep you going. Pero, you have anxiety, hombre, and it's not just a little. It's a lot. And this makes you always want to prove you're a big man making big money."

Emilio looked like he'd just eaten a moth. "Pero, how did I get this way? My parents were good people—not even alcoholics."

"No sé. Pero, éste es tu problema. Maybe someone was mean to you when you were a baby."

"It could have been anyone," added Camilo.

"We'll give you a limpia and see if you feel better."

Pepa watched him give her a curious tilt of his chin.

"Bueno, hombre, I know you might be thinking I'm full of mierda. So you can leave, and I'll only charge you half price. Pero, if you want to be cured, you have to believe in what we're doing, otherwise it won't work."

"Like magic?" he asked.

"No," said Pepa, frowning. "Not like magic . . . More like," she shot Camilo a quick smile. "Bueno, like faith. Shall we give it a try?" Pepa watched him consider her offer, knowing he probably had nothing to lose.

"Let's do it," he said with a definitive nod. "I didn't come here to waste time."

"Good," said Pepa, patting his knee. She got up, nodded to Camilo, and pulled out the pallet from under the altar. She instructed Emilio to remove his jewelry and open his shirt, then lie down on the pallet. She lit a purple candle and burned a bit of aceite de las siete potencias in a container over the flame to remove any bad luck or intentions wished upon their patient.

Emilio lay still, eyes wide as he inhaled the bitter smelling oil. His attention shifted when Camilo began sweeping branches of ruda and romero along each side of his body. Camilo kept contact with his left shoulder, continually chanting healing prayers, while Pepa massaged lemon oil into her hands and pressed them on his heart. She held them there for a full minute. She concluded with a gentle sweep of albaca across his stomach to give him comfort and strength. Camilo finished with his prayers and ended the limpia by rubbing agua preparada on Emilio's temples. Lastly, Pepa prepared a cup of tea mixed with chamomile and lavender to relieve anxiety.

"Levántate and come to the table so you can drink this." Pepa set the cup down and blew on it to cool it. She filled a small baggie with the dried tea. "Take this home. Steep it for five minutes and drink it every twelve hours for seven days."

Emilio sat at the table and took a sip of tea. He already looked relaxed, the nervous edge to him gone.

Pepa gave him a solution of frankincense and lavender oils, adding bits of camellia. "Recuerda this oil I gave you the first time I saw you?" She held up the little vial.

Emilio nodded, his face reddening. "The ceramic thing you gave me broke, and I never got to use it." The color in his face deepened.

"It's not a problem. I have plenty on hand. But this time I need you to use it because it'll help you"

"Sí, Señora."

"Now, tell me, how do you feel?" Pepa asked, studying him.

"I don't know what you did," Emilio answered, "but I feel—more relaxed." A smile slipped across his lips.

"That's good," Pepa replied, satisfied. "I'm glad you feel better. Pero, this work's hard, and we're gonna have to charge you full price—which is fifty bucks." She paused, then glanced at Camilo. His expression remained flat, save for a thin line across one eyebrow. "OK," Pepa said with a sigh. "I guess, on second thought," she continued, eyes still on Camilo. "We can probably work out a little deal."

ACKNOWLEDGMENTS

I am grateful and indebted to the following people and organizations who gave me encouragement, guidance, or a place to write. I will always remember your kindness and generosity.

Stéphanie Abou
Yvonne Yarbro Bejarano
Lily Castillo-Speed
Doretta Chavez
Margaret Cecchetti and Carla Javits
Sandra Cisneros
Paul Cohen (and our writing group)
Community of Writers at Squaw Valley
Manuel Cuellar
Curbstone Press/Northwestern University Press
Joan Drury
Katherine Forrest
Foundry Literary + Media
Teresa Heger
Caroline Kane and Mike Chamberlin
Amy Kastely
Art Larson
Leslie Larson
Lorraine López
Tiffany Ana López
Macondo Writers Workshop

Robert McCree
Gianna Francesca Mosser
Mujeres Activas en Letras y Cambio Social (MALCS)
Kristin Naca
Norcroft: A Women's Writing Retreat
Colette Patt and Zack Rogow
The PEN/Bellwether Prize Committee
Laura E. Pérez
Alexander "Sandy" Taylor and Judy Doyle
Helena María Viramontes